A Norman de Ratour Mystery

COUNTERFEIT
MURDER in the
MUSEUM OF MAN

ALFRED ALCORN

ZOLAND BOOKS
An Imprint of Steerforth Press
Hanover, New Hampshire

For information about permission to reproduce
selections from this book, write to:
Steerforth Press L.L.C., 45 Lyme Road, Suite 208,
Hanover, New Hampshire 03755

LIBRARY OF CONGRESS CATALOGING-IN-PUBLICATION DATA

Alcorn, Alfred.
 The counterfeit murder in the Museum of Man : a Norman de Ratour mystery /
Alfred Alcorn.
    p. cm.
 ISBN 978-1-58195-234-6 (alk. paper)
 1. Museum curators — Crimes against — Fiction. 2. Museums — Fiction.
 3. Murder — Investigation — Fiction. I. Title.
 PS3551.L29C68 2010
 813'.54—DC22

                          2010006856

FIRST EDITION

For Margaret and in memory of Bill

the COUNTERFEIT MURDER in the

MUSEUM OF MAN

1

It struck me as strange the way the car had been left there, not quite aligned on the rough road separating the museum's parking lot from that of the Center for Criminal Justice. It looked like it had come to a stop rather than having been stopped. And while I usually mind my own business in such matters, I went over with Decker, our black retriever, to investigate.

The closer I approached the vehicle, the more I sensed something amiss. It might have been Decker, straining at the leash and making those low whines that from a dog sound so articulate. The car itself, oddly familiar to me, didn't quite fit the scene. It was a sleek late-model maroon Jaguar, so polished that I could clearly see in its brilliant surface the reflection of my own tall figure and that of the straining dog. Indeed, as I drew closer, I could discern the features of my face, my thinning hair a bit mussed, my pale eyes quizzical above the rather too prominent nose, my mouth resigned to apologize for intruding on, say, some vehicular lovemaking.

I remember it all in vivid detail — the crunch of gravel underfoot, the midmorning, early-May air moist and bright, the breeze just strong enough to be chilling, the mottled forms of the scattered maples in the chartreuse effusion of their leafing sliding up the mirroring window as I moved closer. I remember especially my own audible gasp of incredulity as the glass of the car shifted from reflective to transparent and I looked in at the body of a middle-aged man slumped over the wheel, a patch of dried blood on his prominent temple where the bullet had gone in. From the swept-back iron-gray hair and from the strong jaw, I recognized the still-impressive form of Heinrich von Grümh.

Shading my eyes, I peered around the front seat area but noticed nothing out of the ordinary. I resisted an impulse to open the car door, to reach in and try to render assistance. Because I was sure he was beyond help from the utter stillness of his body, from the bemused stare of the opened eyes, and from that sense of how each dead person holds inviolate within the mystery of life.

I backed away, talking to Decker. "Come on, boy. We need to call Lieutenant Tracy."

And so, with a sharp sense of urgency, with a world-weary sigh, and with a quickening of the blood as the hunt begins, I opened the mental notebook I keep ready and began to take notes, to begin, however unofficially, an investigation into another apparent murder here at the Museum of Man.

To be frank, as director of the museum, one of my first concerns, ignoble as it may sound, was for the adverse publicity a murder on the premises would engender. Strictly speaking the murder of Heinrich "Heinie" von Grümh did not occur on museum property, but in an area between the two parking lots, a kind of access right-of-way that only nominally belongs to the MOM. More to the point, Heinie served as Honorary Curator of Numismatics in the museum's small but exquisite collection of Greco-Roman coins and had proved a generous contributor over the past few years. It didn't matter. As director of the MOM, I would be involved. There was to be no shirking this responsibility.

Though loath to leave the vehicle and its very still occupant unattended, I turned to go up to my office to call the police. Were I more of my time, I would have been carrying one of those pocket phones people are incessantly talking into in the most noisome way. But I have never been much of a "phone person," preferring in solitary moments to converse with myself rather than with others, that is, to think.

My office occupies a corner on the fifth floor of the magnificent old pile dating from the nineteenth century that houses the museum. As I walked toward its gentle, redbrick conflation of Gothic and Romanesque styles, I felt that once again it had become haunted by evil. Once again, somehow, somewhere, a murderer lurked among the ancient galleries and oaken cabinets full of priceless objects. Or in among the state-of-the-art, highly digitized premises of the Genetics Lab, which is part of the museum and the crucible of so much mischief.

I took the rattling elevator up to my office, put through a call to Lieutenant Tracy's private number, and left a message. I was scarcely back downstairs and heading across the deserted parking lot, it being relatively early on a Sunday morning, when the first cruiser came careering off Belmont Avenue like a blue flashing banshee and headed straight for the death car.

As I approached on foot, I was appalled to see the two uniformed officers charging around the vehicle in a way that would have compromised any clues left in the surrounding gravel. One of them, a brash-faced young man with a waxed crew cut, looked up as I drew near and said, "This is a crime scene. You can't hang around here."

I stopped well short of the car and replied, "I'm the one who called it in. And if I do say so, I think you should both stand back and wait until Lieutenant Tracy and the crime scene unit arrive."

They both huffed and puffed at me for a moment, but they knew I was right and withdrew rather gingerly to stand at a distance. One of them, rather portentously, told me I should wait as well, to give a statement if nothing else. I replied that it was exactly what I intended to do.

More sirens sounded presently, and it wasn't long before an unmarked sedan with one of those stick-on roof flashers pulled up and Lieutenant Tracy got out and came over to me. We shook hands and exchanged pleasantries. It was the first time I had ever seen him in casual clothes — chinos, sneakers, and a windbreaker over a turtleneck jersey. He then approached the Jaguar, but carefully, and peered inside. He conferred briefly with the two officers before returning to me.

Decker sniffed and wanted to lick him, but I kept the leash tight.

"Anyone you recognize, Norman?" he asked.

"The real estate developer Heinrich von Grümh," I said. "He's also one of our honorary curators."

The lieutenant looked at me and shook his head. "What is it about this place, anyway?"

His reference to a series of bizarre and unsavory murders at the museum gave me an inner wince. I managed a shrug. "It's the last thing we needed."

When the crime scene crew pulled up with their new van and began unloading technical gear, Lieutenant Tracy accompanied me into the museum. It being a Sunday, there were plenty of visitors in the galleries, but backstage it was deserted as we took the elevator. When we got to my office, the police officer, an old friend by now, took a moment to gaze westward toward the Hays Mountains and then to the north, to Shag Bay and the breeze-brittled water dotted with the taut sails of pleasure craft.

"A beautiful day," he said, sounding a rueful note as we got down to business.

He sat in front of the desk, and I pulled open the drawer where I keep files on all our curators, actual or honorary. I took out that of Heinrich von Grümh and slid it across to him.

"One of Seaboard's richest men, if not the richest," I said.

"Old or new money?" He was writing, taking down address and telephone numbers.

"Both. He inherited Groome Securities from his dad, Albrecht Groome. The old man anglicized the name when he came here in the midthirties, a Gentile refugee from Hitler. Heinie, Heinrich, was something of a snob. He Germanized the name back to its original and added the *von*. He claimed he found it while climbing around in the family tree. He never tired of telling people you pronounced it *fon*. People began to call him *Fonny*, which elided easily enough into *phony*. My own father . . ." I trailed off, not wanting to go into family history. "Anyway, Heinie, as he was usually called, sold the firm for a very good price and went into the real estate . . ."

"Next of kin?"

"That would be Merissa, Merissa Bonne. His wife. His third wife, actually. She's considerably younger. My wife Diantha and Merissa know each other. I think you could call them tennis friends."

"So you knew the victim himself?"

"Quite well. We served together on a Cold Stream Prep alumni fund-raising committee. I've been to his home several times socially. For parties mostly. And, of course, he was Honorary Curator of Greco-Roman Numismatics. He donated some very fine specimens of his own recently. Indeed, that's why he was named an honorary curator."

"I suppose his donations helped with his taxes?"

"To say the least. But he was not above the vanity of the thing." I began to add something and stopped.

As a matter of fact, my relations with Heinie were considerably more involved than the edited version I gave to the officer. Indeed, my last encounter with the man remained freshly and

vividly impressed on my mind, making unreal if not surreal the
very palpable fact of his violent death. But at the expense of
some scruple I decided not to disclose any of my other connections to the victim. They could hardly have been germane to the
case.

If the lieutenant caught my hesitation, he didn't let on. He
said, "I see . . ." He glanced at his watch. "Listen, Norman . . .
You wouldn't mind accompanying me over to see the widow. It
might make it easier on her." The wryness in his voice told me it
would also make it easier on him.

"Of course." I glanced at Decker.

The lieutenant smiled. "He can come, too."

So the three of us set out on that fine Sunday morning in May for
a drive that took us out to the bypass and then southward, along
the coast to Bayville, a gated community on Purdy's Neck, on
which Heinie had made a mighty bundle. It has, I'm told, a very
good golf course for those given to that kind of tedium. The new
marina, full of sleek white sailboats and cabin cruisers, pennants
snapping smartly in the breeze, looks like it belonged in Florida.
The old fishing village has been malled, to use a Diantha term,
with a lot of little boutiques specializing in authenticity.

As my good friend Father S.J. O'Gould, S.J., has remarked,
the human species has become something of a weed, ecologically
speaking; he likens us to an "invasive exotic." Which doesn't
sound like a man of God, though the God of this particular Jesuit
is not your run-of-the-mill deity. And, of course, in a hundred
years, when some new developer comes along and starts tearing
it all down to put in a jetport or whatever, sentimentalists like
me will be protesting the loss of the old, the familiar, and the
real.

To be fair, Heinie did leave some of the land in a conservation trust, and the gestures toward a bygone bucolia have been tastefully preserved. Perhaps a bit too tastefully.

We pulled up to "Raven's Croft," one of the pricier "units" in Kestrel Meadows, where there are no longer any kestrels or meadows. It was a big rambling affair hedged in by dutiful pines and fronted by an immaculately kept lawn with clipped, funereal shrubs, mostly rhododendrons and azaleas, snug against the foundation. I noticed a drive that went around to a garage large enough for a small airliner. It wasn't the first time I had been to Raven's Croft. The house oppressed me with its stonework, lattice, and Palladian touches. I once remarked to Diantha that it could serve nicely as a funeral home for the newly rich newly dead.

Nor did I look forward to the lugubrious office that had brought the lieutenant and me there. I confess to a certain unease should the widow, in her shock, disclose any of my own complicated relations with the deceased.

It took a while for Merissa, casually elegant in jeans and boatneck sweater, her painted toes elegant in heeled sandals, to answer the door. Her smile at my appearance turned quickly to puzzlement. Perhaps it was the lieutenant, right behind me as we entered and went through the usual pleasantries of greeting. "Norman! What a wonderful surprise," she exclaimed, ushering us into a wainscoted parlor with large windows giving out on the bay and brilliant parquet flooring under Turkey carpets.

The place reflected with Germanic punctilio the tastes of Heinie Grümh. The very smells seemed newly minted to go with the new house, new cars, new, expensive replications of antiques, and gorgeous new wife. Merissa Bonne is a striking woman of dark red hair, appraising gray-green eyes, a nose too perfect for nature, and a lush mouth given to frequent, ephemeral smiles, as though she found life to be a series of small jokes. I sometimes wondered if she considered me among them, in part because I've always had a weakness for her, for her beauty and her crassness.

"Whatever brings you here . . . ?" The smiles were gone as concern rearranged her pretty features.

I coughed. I sighed. I said, "Merissa, this is Lieutenant Tracy of the Seaboard Police Department. I'm afraid we have some dreadful news for you."

"Heinie . . . ?"

Lieutenant Tracy nodded. "Your husband was found dead about an hour and a half ago. In his car."

Her eyes grew large with horrified incredulity. "No!" she cried. "No."

"I'm afraid so . . ."

"How . . . ?"

"A preliminary investigation indicates murder."

Despite my own involvement in the emotion of the moment, I could not help but remark an odd note in her surprise, and in her ejaculation "He wouldn't!" before she covered her mouth with her hand. She appeared shocked not only by her husband's untimely and unseemly death, but by something half expected.

I took her by the arm and helped her to a sofa, an imitation antique love couch in the French style with the back sloping down halfway across to seat level to allow the comfortable arrangement of one's limbs for whatever contingencies arose. Lieutenant Tracy pulled up a chair and gently went through some preliminary questions.

"Mrs. . . . or is it Ms. Bonne?"

"Ms. Bonne. But call me Merissa." She took my handkerchief, which was clean if a little starchy, and wiped her eyes with it.

The lieutenant nodded. "When was the last time you saw your husband?"

"Yesterday afternoon."

"Do you know where he was going?"

She shook her head. "He said something about going into Seaboard to see someone and then working on the *Albatross* . . . that's his sailboat. He keeps it at the marina."

"I see. And you didn't find it strange that he didn't come home?"

Merissa sighed and shook her attractive head. "He calls it his bolt-hole. His boat. It's where he goes when he wants to duck out."

"And why would he want to duck out?"

She dabbed with the stiff hankie. "We had a little spat . . ."

"You argued?"

"Yes."

"About . . . ?"

"About personal things. Very personal things."

"I see." The lieutenant was taking it all down, flipping the pages of his reporter's notebook. "Ms. Bonne, do you know anyone who might want to murder your husband?"

She glanced at me, but not in any accusing way. She shook her head. "No. I mean he had enemies, Lieutenant, but no one . . ." Again she shuddered.

"Would you like me to get you coffee or something?" I asked. I wanted to feel useful.

"There's a pot just brewing," she said. "I'd ask the maid, but she has the day off . . ."

Assuring her I could find things, I went down the main hallway to their vast kitchen, a place with enough immaculate counter space and high-tech gadgets to pass for a working lab. It gave onto a semicircular conservatory, the French doors of which opened onto a sloping lawn and another sweeping view of the bay.

I do not like to snoop among other people's personal effects whatever my proclivities as a sleuth. Indeed, I usually would rather not know the titillating or embarrassing details of another's life, especially if that person wants them kept private. But in this case my investigative instincts had been stirred, and I poked around for the coffee things with my antennae positively bristling.

In finding a tray, a black-lacquered affair with a stenciled rose pattern, some modern Danish mugs, a set comprising a pewter creamer and sugar bowl, antique sterling spoons with a raised monogram I couldn't read, some Christmas cocktail napkins, and the lower half of the coffee contraption — I felt more like a butler than a detective. The place appeared utterly clueless, as, perhaps, it was.

But as I started out of the kitchen in the direction of the parlor, I noticed a wall phone with a hanging pencil and a pad of paper on the sloping shelf beneath it. The top leaf was clear but with an obvious and perhaps decipherable imprint on it. Putting the tray down, I quickly and delicately removed the square of paper and slid it into the side pocket of my jacket.

In walking back toward the parlor, I hesitated when I heard Lieutenant Tracy ask those awkward, necessary questions of one who is presumably grieving. "Can you tell me where you were yesterday evening, Ms. Bonne?"

"I was here."

"The whole night?"

"Not all of it."

"I see. And what time did you leave and return?"

"I left around seven thirty and returned . . . not long after midnight."

"About what time?"

"One. Perhaps one thirty."

"Was anyone else here with you?"

"No. Not when I came home."

"And were you with someone else during the time you were away?"

"Yes."

"Would you mind telling me who that was?"

Perhaps because I was not directly present, her hesitation seemed the more pronounced before she said, "Yes. Until I've spoken to him."

I took that opportunity to make my entrance. I came into the room and put the tray down on a faux antique Sheraton coffee table. As I did so, I noticed a Pissarro over the fireplace very much like his *Chaumières au Valhermeil,* which I had seen in a private collection. It's a stunning oil, with an impressionistic gauze muting the scene, a marvelous rendering of thatched cottage, curving road, stone wall, red-bonneted figure, and trees against a blighted sky. Indeed, I forgot the circumstances of our visit altogether in going up to it and examining it closely.

"When did you get this?" I asked, quite amazed.

"Oh, we just got it. It's what Heinie calls, called, a real fake." She got up and came around to stand beside me.

"A real fake?"

"Yes. I mean I guess somewhere along the way, a very good artisan copied the original. We have some dupes of Sargent watercolors done with permission back in the nineteen twenties. And upstairs we have a Monet done by an Italian just after World War Two that would fool an expert. They're valuable now."

Merissa sat back down and attended to the coffee things. She appeared to have composed herself quite well. Until, in continuing, as though her husband were still alive, she said "Heinie says . . ." and her face again constricted, but more, I thought, in horror than in sorrow.

Lieutenant Tracy brought us back to the grim business of murder investigation with a new line of questioning, delving gently into von Grümh's relations with his present and past business partners. He recalled for Merissa the dispute her husband's company had had with a local Indian group as to exactly who owned the land. There was speculation that the Native Americans in this case were fronting for a mob-based syndicate out of New Jersey that wanted to build a casino, a big gaudy thing called Pocahontas North.

Merissa prettily and tragically sipped her black coffee and shook her abundant chestnut hair. "Heinie never talked to me about his business dealings. He might have had enemies. Sometimes he complained about a Jeb Jordan he did a deal with down in the Caymans. But that was last year."

"What kind of a deal?" the Lieutenant asked.

"Real estate. A development of some kind . . ." She started to say something else and then hesitated. The lieutenant cocked his head, waiting.

"When he was doing the Neck . . . this place . . . he got a couple of really nasty calls from some eco-nuts."

"The Green Terror Brigade?" I put in.

She nodded. "That's what everyone thought at the time."

"Did your husband own a gun?" The detective picked up his coffee and took a sip.

"Several. He has a high-powered rifle with a scope for elk hunting."

"No pistols or revolvers?"

"No. Not that I know of."

We concluded not long afterward. Lieutenant Tracy asked her if it would be all right to bring in some technicians to go over the house. When she hesitated, he said it would be a matter of routine for him to get a warrant, but that, well, it would look better all around if she simply consented. At that she nodded numbly and again her face was touched with a kind of dread I found puzzling. But, of course, I've never had anyone close to me murdered.

"Do you want me to call Diantha and have her come over?" I asked.

She shook her head. "My brother Paul . . ."

We took our leave and drove back to the city proper. I mentioned my impression of Merissa's initial reaction.

The lieutenant nodded noncommittally and stared out at the beautiful day. He said, "She knows a lot more than she's telling us."

On the drive down to Merissa's, I had used Lieutenant Tracy's phone to call Diantha and leave a message to the effect that I would be late in returning from walking the dog as something had come up. Even so, she said, "You were gone a long time," as I came in the door with Decker. "I made soup for lunch, if you want some."

I nodded, gave her a kiss, and asked her if she wanted a drink. I told her I had something horrific to report. Just then Elsie, who is two and a half, tottered in, but showed more interest in the dog than in me, which is no doubt natural.

Di's evident excitement at the prospect of hearing bad news I took to be a measure of how dreary her life had become.

Anyway, I, with a gin and tonic English-style — no ice — and she, with a glass of chilled Chardonnay, went into the solarium that, because of the old hemlocks outside, seldom gets much sun, but has pleasant wicker furniture.

"Mommy has to talk to Daddy right now," Di signed to Elsie, trailing in after us. Elsie, who suffers from an inexplicable mutism, is named for Elsbeth, Diantha's mother and my late wife, who died more than three years ago.

"Decker wants cookie," Elsie said, her little hands amazingly articulate.

"Okay, darling."

Di, looking quite trim and fetching in jogging shorts and a leotard top (she has been following a rigorous regime of late), got up and brought in some dog biscuits, giving one to Elsie to hand gingerly, dropping it and laughing, to Decker.

In the midst of this tender scene, I said, "Heinie has been murdered."

It was as though I were speaking to her from a distance because the words seemed to register a measurable time after I had uttered them.

"No . . . *No!*" She put both hands to her throat, as though to protect herself, and her lips went thin as her face knotted with pain. "Poor Heinie. Oh, my God. Merissa . . ."

I got up and sat beside her on the small sofa. I put my arms around her. Di's grief, I knew, was something more than vicarious. Because, you see, what I was reluctant to tell Lieutenant Tracy is that, about a year after Elsie was born, Diantha had had an affair with Heinrich von Grümh.

It wasn't a protracted, passionate thing. Or so Di tells me. Indeed, she refuses to call it an affair. It came and went during a weekend when she went down to Bayside for an overnight cruise on the *Albatross*. She went with Elsie and Bella, Elsie's nanny. I didn't go because, frankly, I found Heinie to be, over long stretches, something of a bore if not a boor. I went out to the cottage instead and did some gardening. It happened that Heinie and Merissa were going through a bad patch at the time — and well, all the ingredients were there.

"When?" she said, lifting tearful eyes to mine.

"Sometime last night or early this morning. They'll have to wait for the coroner's report for a precise time."

"How?"

"Gunshot. In the temple at close range. With what looked like a medium-caliber pistol." My voice sounded mechanical.

"A revolver?"

I frowned at the question for some reason. "Or an automatic."

"Oh, God, God . . ."

"I'm very sorry."

She composed herself. "I'll have to call Merissa." Then: "How did you find out?"

I sighed, knowing that my story would take its toll on her just as it was taking its toll on me.

"I was the one who found the body."

She gasped audibly. "Where?"

"On the roadway between the parking lots behind the museum. He was in his red car."

"The Jaguar?"

"Yes." I've noticed before that details take on an exaggerated importance in circumstances like these.

"Oh, Norman. I'm so sorry. It must have been . . ."

"It's okay." I was touched by her concern. "I drove out with Lieutenant Tracy to inform Merissa. I told her you would call her later." I found I was drinking my gin and tonic without tasting it.

"How did she . . . ?"

I thought I detected more curiosity than concern in her eyes and voice.

"Shocked, of course. And surprised."

"Why wouldn't she be?"

"Of course it was just . . ." I let it dangle.

"I'm going to call her. Will you watch Elsie for a minute."

I nodded that I would and sat there, trying to amuse the little one, who has a finely honed instinct for knowing when her mother wants to be alone. I tried my foolproof ploy. I signed a familiar sentence. "Let's take Decker for a walk." Which worked. It meant getting his leash and snapping it on his collar. Then, with great ceremony, we went out into the garden, where I had begun to prepare the flower beds.

Despite her affair or whatever it was with Heinie, Diantha and I are doing well enough. That had happened during a spell when Di had grown restless. She talked of wanting to move to New York City. We had the kitchen renovated. We bought a new car for her of truck-like dimensions and sturdy enough to survive a direct hit from a howitzer.

Our tastes differ in some important things. She is indifferent, with a couple of exceptions, to objects and antiques, while I, more and more, cherish them. On evenings at home, she will watch a police drama on television while I read. Like her mother, she cannot abide Brahms, whose music for me grows more sublime as I grow older. She is fond of Broadway musicals while I remain all but clinically allergic to the things, a few caterwauling bars of which send me into something approaching anaphylactic shock. But then, I suppose there are inherent difficulties in any marriage where the age differences are as pronounced as ours.

Diantha has her moods. It's been obvious for a long time that motherhood is no longer enough for most women of her station. Nor, it seems, is her profession. She has what she calls an idiot-savant facility for solving intricate computer programming problems for which companies large and small pay her generous sums of money. At the same time, she yearns for a larger world without quite knowing what.

Out at the lake she likes to lounge on the new deck we've put up, while I work in the garden, which I have enlarged considerably with hedges of highbush blueberries, a long lattice of climbing roses, and some dwarf apples espaliered against a south-facing wall. I had to put in a pergola of rough-hewn hickory poles for the wild Concords that grow like great clinging weeds all over the property. Di likes to potter about as well, but with nothing like my newfound enthusiasm. She all but accused me of "crucifying" the apple trees as I gently pruned or eased back their limbs and tied them to the tautly strung wire.

For all that, and despite our ages, we enjoy remarkable stretches of happiness together. Given Elsie's condition, we are both growing fluent in signing, indeed resorting to it between ourselves from time to time. So that not only our little girl, but her condition, draws us close and keeps us together.

I can hear Diantha now, walking around with the cell phone to her ear. It scarcely sounds like she is consoling a grieving friend. More like a regular chat, more like a good laugh together.

2

Heinie von Grümh's murder could not have happened at a worse time for the museum. (I suppose for him, as well, but who can tell?) The fact is, we have reached a critical and delicate juncture in our endeavor to be free once and for all from any claims by Wainscott University. And whatever the legal basis of our cause, public perceptions do count, particularly regarding the competence of an institution like the MOM to govern itself.

Alas, the effects of crime splatter like blood, besmirching the innocent as well as the guilty. The headline from the *Bugle* proves my point: "Murdered Curator Found on Museum Grounds." Then the tagline: "Killing raises concerns for safety at Museum of Man." In vain did I point out to Amanda Feeney, who wrote the story, that von Grümh (he insisted on the umlaut, by the way) was an honorary curator and that, technically speaking, the road between the parking lots of the museum and Center for Criminal Justice belongs to no one. But then, the *Bugle* takes every opportunity to disparage me and the museum.

In short, I and the MOM are left vulnerable to the campaign by Wainscott to "reinforce the historic ties," to employ the current euphemism for their efforts to take us over.

It doesn't help that we have not been doing as well financially as we had hoped. The Food and Drug Administration has yet to approve the aphrodisiacs Lubricitin and Priaptin, the development of which here in the Genetics Lab led to so much mischief, though I've heard there's a booming market in generic knock-offs. (A firm in China is apparently marketing the latter under the trade name *hu gao wan,* which translates roughly as "tiger testicles.") Nor has ReLease, the hangover pill, sold as well as expected. Attendance is up, it's true; but running a museum, even one as well endowed as the MOM, is an expensive undertaking.

Malachy Morin has proved to be a far more wily and tenacious adversary than might be gauged from his hale-fellow half-drunk demeanor, not to mention his huge and growing bulk, his red face and bulging eyes. A Falstaff on the outside and a Cassius on the inside, he has been using the law like long-range artillery. Wainscott's suit to claim the museum as part and parcel of itself has dragged on now for several years with a battery of lawyers — certainly on their part — filing and counterfiling before a sleepy, incompetent judge who has been heard to mutter that he regards the whole matter as "academic."

Mr. Morin, who is University Vice President for Affiliated Institutions, not only snipes at us through articles his wife Amanda Feeney writes for the *Bugle,* but also has provocateurs here in the museum ready to betray us when the time comes.

Nor is our case in the courts a foregone conclusion whatever its merits. The legal tangle of thorns has been complicated by the bequests that have come in from benefactors over the decades who appear to assume that the university and the museum are parts of a single entity. The phalanx of attorneys from a private firm, hired by the university at great expense, contend that these generous individuals, many of them prominent and prosperous members of the community, would not have endowed the museum had they not considered it integral to Wainscott, their *alma mater* in many cases.

Felix Skinnerman, our general counsel, has argued persuasively that the confusion in the minds of these worthy people, many of them long dead, does not alter the documentary evidence of the founding charters.

I do not wish to go into the antecedents of the Museum of Man, which can be found profusely documented in my own well-received *The Past Redeemed*. Nor do I wish to repeat in any detail here why I oppose our submergence in the corporate monolith into which Wainscott University has evolved. Suffice it to say that the Museum of Man would suffer an irreparable decline were it to become a subsidiary or operating unit of Wainscott, Inc. All one has to do is look at the university's Frock Museum. Once considered a first-rate if small institution, it has of late both grown and stagnated. It has launched an ambitious fund-raising effort for a new building. For additional exhibition space? No. For more curatorial work space? No. It wants something on the order of twenty million dollars for a new addition for administrative offices for the panoply of staff, which has grown in direct proportion to the means available to support it.

Blindfolded Justice remains blind to these apprehensions on our part, as perhaps she should. But due notice should be given by the courts to the university's conduct as litigation proceeds. It is no exaggeration to say that the Wainscott apparatchik, in the gross person and character of Mr. Morin, has waged an unscrupulous and unrelenting campaign to undermine my management of the museum. I am reluctant to rake over the still-smoldering coals of that man's ignoble history, which includes, at the very least, a case of manslaughter, a veritable *sale histoire*. Suffice it to say that the Museum of Man once more stands endangered as a vital, independent institution and a living link to our common past.

Having said this, I would like to affirm, yet again, that I want the living links between the museum and the university to remain strong and meaningful. Wainscott faculty work with our curators and with the collections to great mutual benefit. The research staff at the Ponce Institute include a good number of university professors and postdocs. Yet as long as I am in charge, the Museum of Man will remain a separate entity as in law and reality it always has been.

Which is why I roll my eyes, inwardly at least, when people, upon hearing what I do, begin to wax exclamatory about what an interesting job I must have. All of those beautiful and fascinating things. All of those interesting people. And even when their reactions are accompanied by a dismissive smile, I detect a note of envy, summed up on one occasion by an aging, oblivious socialite who volunteered, "What a plum you have, Norman."

Ah, if they only knew. Quite aside from answering media calls regarding the murder of Heinie Grümh, three other headaches landed on my desk this morning. In my mail there was one of those large, ominous-looking envelopes from Limpkin, Limpkin, and Leech, Seaboard's preeminent law firm. I knifed it open to find a friendly note scrawled by Elgin Warwick on notepaper with an embossed letterhead. Elgin is the scion of an old and wealthy family, a member of the Board of Governors, a generous supporter of the MOM, and a true eccentric if not barking mad.

I could feel my hair whitening as I read the legalese on the attached document. It stated that Mr. Warwick, upon his demise, wished to have his remains mummified "in the manner of the ancient Egyptians" and placed in the collections of the museum in perpetuity, there to be displayed periodically in a sarcophagus that he had chosen from his collection of Egyptiania.

In exchange, he would bequeath an amount of no less than ten million dollars to the museum. An additional five million would be left to the MOM should it create a room in the museum to be called Temple Warwick, which would house not only his mummy but his collection of ancient Egyptian art and artifacts as well.

What, one might ask, are the objections? After due consideration, I saw many. First, it is not in line with the "mission" of the museum. (*Mission* is one of those buzzwords like *transformative* that I heartily detest, but it serves here well enough.) Whatever our mission, it is not to provide mortuaries for the privileged.

Second, were we to accede to Mr. Warwick's request, surely others would importune us to allow them to park their mortal remains here. We would become a laughingstock in the museum world. Or maybe not. Others might envy our endowment as it fattened on bequests from the well-heeled waiting to get into our upscale necropolis.

Of course, we could count on the local media to criticize us in no uncertain terms. Especially when the heirs to Mr. Warwick's fortune challenged the matter in court, as they most surely would.

But, as I thought it over, equivocation began. Egypt is of unparalleled importance in human history. Yet all we have are a few small items in a case next to the Greco-Roman display. Temple Warwick could be done tastefully, a few toned-down inscribed columns in the style of Karnak, but nothing too pharaonic. As well, Elgin is of old Seaboard money and lots of it, mostly in vast tracts of woodland north of here. Old money does come with a patina of respectability when you think about it. And think about it I must. I've been up the coast to his mansion by the sea where he has his Egyptian collection on display. The sarcophagi alone stir my museum director's highly refined and, I like to think, justifiable cupidity. But there is much more there. Statuary from the Second Dynasty; tomb furnishings including a small painted throne, probably for a child; mummified ibises; scrolls; an obelisk of polished red granite.

Some of it could be fakes, of course. Except that Elgin is a sly old fox. He is a large, genial, courtly man whose eccentricities, according to people who have done business with him, are part of an elaborate pose.

So I will do what I usually do in these circumstances. I will stall. I will have Doreen work up a letter stating that I am studying his very generous and interesting proposal in consultation with our general counsel.

I was in the midst of ruminating on this matter when Dr. Harvey Deharo, director of the Ponce Institute, under which auspices the Genetics Lab now operates, called to arrange a meeting with me and Thad Pilty. It seems that, according to the latest research, the skin tones of the mannequins in the Diorama of Paleolithic Life in Neanderthal Hall are not quite accurate.

For those not familiar with this award-winning and very popular attraction at the museum, some years ago, after considerable controversy, we created a lifelike tableau of daily life among what are called Stone Age people. Our models, which move and interact, however minimally, with the visitors, are based on the Gerasimov reconstructions. Not knowing what their pigmentation was at the time, we settled on a dusty hue, more gray than brown, that we hoped would not offend anyone.

Harvey, who was hired to take over the lab nearly two years ago after a lengthy search, told me that researchers have turned up DNA evidence that the Neanderthals were pale-skinned and perhaps red-haired. He chuckled in that soft Caribbean accent of his. "Don't worry, Norman. This, too, will pass." But how, I wonder, how? Because there's no alternative but to confront and resolve the matter. Without at least the attempt at authenticity, we would be providing little more than a circus sideshow filled with fakes.

And, finally, I opened my e-mails to find a missive from

Constance Brattle, the hard-bottomed chair of the University Oversight Committee. She wants to convene a special meeting regarding "disturbing events at the museum." She mentioned the murder, of course, but also the chimpanzee Alphus, a remarkable beast by any standards. He has been back in the news as a porn star. It seems that the university's recently established Victim Studies Department and some local animal rights advocates have been complaining to the committee about the matter.

Indeed, the *Bugle* recently ran a long article rehashing an unfortunate incident in Alphus's past. No doubt because it involved the museum, the paper took the liberty to malign the poor beast with half-truths and out-and-out distortions of what happened. To begin with, Alphus is not a "wild" animal, though try telling that to the troglodytes of the *Bugle*. (Come to think of it, the epithet in this case should be considered a slur against members of that species.)

Anyway, the incident occurred last spring, at just about this time. Alphus, who is a thirty-two-year-old chimpanzee from the remaining population we keep in the Pavilion, feigned a medical emergency and, while en route to the animal hospital at the Middling County Zoo in an ambulance, overpowered his attendants and escaped into the leafy refuge of Thornton Arboretum. There he eluded several attempts to capture him in a humane way. At one point the Seaboard Police Department's SWAT team apparently had him cornered in a large tree. But even their best sharpshooter, encumbered, it's true, by a lot of high-tech protective gear, couldn't bring him down with one of those dart guns.

The animal rights groups took up his cause. They filed for a cease-and-desist order in Middling County District Court, which a judge promptly issued. Alphus's supporters, a well-intended group of young idealists, brought him food and water and generally stood watch to make sure no harm befell him. They were, however, under the mistaken impression that *Pan troglodytes* is an herbivore when, in fact, like us, chimps will eat just about anything. And who's to say that what happened wouldn't have happened even had they brought him steak tartare on a regular basis?

Because early one warm summer evening, Royale Toite, one of those wealthy, adamantine club women with a sense of entitlement bordering on the pathological, decided to walk her querulous toy poodle through that part of the arboretum where Alphus led his largely arboreal existence. As they passed under a tree where Alphus sat minding his own business, the dog began yapping at him. Alphus swung down, grabbed the noisy dog, and climbed back up to a stout limb well out of reach. Had the poodle been secured with one of those leashes that play out, it's possible that Ms. Toite might have been able to yank it back to safety. But that appears not to have been the case.

A tourist who had been looking for Alphus happened to be there. He videotaped the whole sorry scene from beginning to end: the barking dog, the swooping grab, and the owner, mad with anger and grief, shrieking at Alphus as he calmly strangled her wriggling dog before peeling back its hide with marvelous strength and eating a good deal of the exposed bloody flesh.

The video made it onto the national news, and an awful ruckus ensued. A militia group from a remote part of the state set up camp in the parking lot of the arboretum and, labeling Alphus "a demented, dog-eating pervert," vowed "to protect the neighborhood and if necessary take out the killer ape." Animal rights groups again came to Alphus's defense, mounting a watch around the area where he nested. One of the more pongiphilic opined that Alphus may have been provoked by the poodle, which the video shows barking insultingly at him. I and the museum, of course, were caught right in the middle and came in for most of the blame for allegedly having created the situation in the first place.

Litigation ensued. According to her attorneys, Ms. Toite, whose name, incidentally, is pronounced in the English fashion, remains in the throes of traumatic shock disorder and wants several million dollars for the pain and suffering of watching her pet get killed and eaten by "a rogue chimpanzee."

Through my connections with the SPD, I know I could have had Alphus destroyed one way or the other. But I desisted because I could not bring myself to order the killing of a chimpanzee, a species very much like us, after all. I and the museum got pelted from both the dog and ape sympathizers.

At that point something wonderfully adventitious occurred. A group of hearing-and-speech-challenged individuals, deaf-mutes in the old parlance, living communally in a place called, appropriately enough, Sign House, announced that they would become Alphus's caretakers, or caregivers as they say nowadays. Because of Elsie's condition, Diantha and I have been there several times and have become friendly with some of the residents.

One of the inhabitants of the house, which is an old Victorian in an area of genteel shabbiness that borders the Arboretum, had been among those bringing Alphus his food and had gotten to know him. Overnight, with no fanfare and no fuss, Alphus left his trees and went to live in the rambling old place with people who, for all intents and purposes, were as unvoiced as he. The militia types packed up their sad little camp, grumbling about do-gooders and no doubt disappointed not to be able to take on the ape *mano-a-mano* with their automatic weapons.

I have since learned that one of the residents of the house, an attractive young woman of sympathy and grace with the euphonious name Millicent Mulally, had struck up a friendship with Alphus while he was still living in the trees. The other occupants of the house apparently had no objections to his coming to live among them, even helping her construct a "nest" for him in the attic.

Because the animal still belonged to and remained the responsibility of the museum, I had Felix Skinnerman draw up papers to the effect that Alphus was "on loan" to the young woman, who agreed to accept all liability for his behavior. (Adoption was not a legal possibility, and to sell Alphus seemed unseemly.) I arranged as well to have a stipend sent to her for his upkeep. Our veterinarian also makes regular visits.

Now it appears that someone has been videotaping the "conjugal" visits of Alphus to the MOM's Primate Pavilion, which we now refer to simply as "the Pavilion." A large male in his prime, Alphus made it clear through some graphic signing (he apparently has learned a considerable vocabulary in that silent language) that he wanted to consort with females of his own kind from time to time. Thus, whenever one of our females came into estrus, Dr. Angela Simone, the Ruddy and Phyllis Stein Keeper of Great Apes, called Sign House and a visit was arranged.

As a matter of routine, for security and for a research project a graduate student was conducting on the sex lives of captive chimpanzees, the sessions were video-recorded. It was perhaps only a matter of time before some unscrupulous individual made copies of the recordings and uploaded them onto a pornographic site on the Internet.

It means that we will have to take steps to secure any further video recordings. Of course, were we not to monitor the animals in our care and something happened to them, the same groups would castigate us for negligence.

It raises the larger issue of what to do with the remaining chimps. Over the years, we have been trying to deacquisition them, to put things in museum jargon. But that is easier said than done.

As it stands, I will go before the Oversight Committee, of which I remain an honorary (some say ornery) member for the sake of good relations with the university, and not only answer for the exploitation of our chimps as porn stars, but also fend off insinuations regarding security at the museum.

I do wish Felix, our very competent general counsel, were here to handle the matter. But he's in Brazil for another week or so on honeymoon with his latest bride. He sent me a postcard from one of the beaches of Rio de Janeiro, describing himself as "a pale northern peeper among flocks of great-breasted thong birds," a pleasantry even I get.

All of which pales, of course, next to the murder of Heinie von Grümh. Even in the privacy of this account, I am reluctant to reveal the source of qualms that have plagued me since the moment I discovered the man's body. The fact is, I was not as frank with Lieutenant Tracy as I should have been. Had I been so, I would rightly be considered a prime suspect in the case.

For one thing, I did not tell the lieutenant that I had been in the museum around the time the murder was committed. Let me explain. That evening, after a very early dinner, I had gone to my office to finish some paperwork dealing with the expatriation of specimens from the Skull Collection. A tribe in Arian Jaya have petitioned us to return about a dozen skulls collected there at the turn of the last century. The fact that most of the skulls are of European origin apparently has no bearing. They make up, we are told, "an integral part of the tribe's cultural heritage." The fact that they have no adequate facilities for preserving this heritage also has no bearing on the case.

Second, I did not inform Lieutenant Tracy that my wife had had an affair with the victim. Indeed, my animus toward the man has remained sporadically murderous despite something Diantha told me in the wake of their affair. During one of our tender moments of reconciliation, the keener for being edged with the savor of jealousy and curiosity, I had asked her how Heinie had been in bed. She paused in her ministrations and a sly smile lit her face. "He was classy enough. But as Marilyn Monroe said about Frank Sinatra — he was no Joe DiMaggio." Implying, I assumed, that I'm a real slugger in this regard.

Still, I conceived a visceral hatred of Heinrich von Grümh. In the guise of worldliness, he deigned to patronize me, making what he probably thought were subtle allusions to having slept with my wife. But then, Heinie was a force of nature in the way of a big wind. He had to win or, rather, beat everyone else in the smallest things. At the same time, I pitied him. He was the echoing shell of a man who had everything and nothing. The more wealth and expensive toys he acquired and displayed, the less there seemed of him. *Is this all there is?* his expression seemed to say. As though all would never be enough. In the end, he had become the ultimate impostor, that is, someone posing as himself.

Why then, one might ask, did I accept coins from him for the MOM's collection? The fact is, a responsible museum director does not turn down objects worth hundreds of thousands, if not millions, of dollars, however many strings come attached. In fact, a conservative estimate of Heinie's donation of coins to the museum amounts to well over two million dollars. It's not a matter I would allow personal feelings to interfere with.

The final reason I might be considered a suspect in the case is that I have a license to not only own but also to carry concealed the Smith & Wesson .38-caliber revolver I inherited from my father. Oiled but not loaded, it is locked in a chest in my study. Ballistics would easily prove that my gun had not been used as the murder weapon.

Then why not tell Lieutenant Tracy? I submit that my motivation is nothing less than exemplary. As a suspect, I doubt my friend would consent to my help on the case, however distant and unofficial my involvement. It would be false modesty to deny that I played a key role in bringing to justice those responsible for past murders in the Museum of Man. At the same time, I relish the role of investigator, of participating in a direct way in what is nothing less than a manhunt.

But I must also be candid. I confess that I did not want it known, especially by Lieutenant Tracy, that my wife had not only been unfaithful to me, but had been so with a man of Heinie von Grümh's ilk.

3

Merissa Bonne does make a most fetching widow. She dropped by early last evening for a drink and to ask for a favor. I couldn't tell whether she wore the black satin choker with its circle of small diamonds in celebration or in mourning. "I just hope he didn't suffer," she sniffled, wiping away a nonexistent tear and holding out her glass for a refill of the house Merlot, a sturdy red we buy by the case.

We were comfortably ensconced in the tree-shadowed conservatory with Di up and down getting drinks and things and taking care of Elsie. Merissa sat close enough to me on the small wicker sofa for the effects of her perfume, redolent of spring flowers, to sharpen the effect of the wine on me. So much for the trappings of woe, I thought, though in fact the favor she finally got around to asking involved the arrangement of obsequies for her late husband. She wanted me to petition the Reverend Alfie Lopes to have a memorial service for Heinie in Swift Chapel.

"Heinie was absolutely devoted to the museum and to Wainscott," she said. "He went to all the graduations although he didn't graduate himself."

I doubted Heinie's devotion to anything but himself, but did not feel it my place to demur. Grief, even feigned grief, must be served. Still, I nodded only vaguely, hesitant to make such a request on her behalf, although it would be, I suppose, the Christian thing to do. I did not want to help dignify the memory of this man, regardless of his apparent generosity to the museum.

I say *apparent* as he got a thwacking great tax break in giving us those coins.

It is more complicated than that. At the risk of sounding petty, indeed, of being petty, I am all too aware that Swift Chapel is part of Wainscott, and the museum's relations with the university are at a delicate juncture. To have a memorial service for an honorary curator of the MOM at Swift Chapel could be construed as an admission on our part that we are more closely a part of Wainscott than we want to concede.

Merissa sensed my reluctance and backed off immediately. "It doesn't really matter. It was something he wanted me to do. In case . . ."

"Really?" I said, my investigative instincts piqued. "In case of what?"

She shrugged and let it drop. With more wine we passed on to other topics — how she had already moved out of the big house and into an apartment in town. How the first and second wives were at each other's throats and leaving her alone. How she wanted to get her own lawyer because Heinie's lawyer was nothing more than a well-dressed thief.

Out of nowhere, or so it seemed, she put her hand on my knee and said, "Frankly, Norman, I'm glad he's dead. Oh, I know it's an awful thing to say." She lifted her mildly mad, beautiful eyes to mine. "But he had become a regular dispenser of misery. He went around handing it out. Especially to himself. I know we're not supposed to speak ill of the dead, but in Heinie's case, being dead is a definite improvement."

After she had left, not altogether steadily, I mentioned to Diantha that Merissa's demeanor had not been that of a bereft widow. Indeed, she seemed quite jolly toward the end of her visit, a result perhaps of the wine.

Diantha came and sat next to me on the sofa, putting her hand on my knee as though to reclaim me. "Norman, darling, I think there's something you should know, but you have to promise me not to tell anyone else."

I nodded, but noncommittally.

"You promise?"

"Does it have to do with Heinie's murder?"

"It might."

"You know I can't promise that. I'm already part of this investigation." I winced inwardly, given how much I was already holding back, even from my wife.

"I'm going to tell you anyway."

I waited, watching her troubled expression, which gave depth to her pretty features, showing character as well as beauty.

"Well, you know about the affair she's been having with Max Shofar?"

"Yes."

"Well, it's been hot and long and it's still going on."

"Enough to give Max . . . ?"

"And Merissa . . ."

"A motive?"

"Maybe."

"Why didn't she just divorce him?"

"They had a prenup. She would have only gotten a pittance."

"And if he died?"

"She stands to get a hefty chunk of his estate."

I nodded slowly, thinking back to that trip down to Raven's Croft to tell her what had happened. The way she said, "He wouldn't!"

Diantha's disclosure was very much on my mind the next morning when I found a message on my voice mail to the effect that

Lieutenant Tracy wanted to drop by. I left word that I would be in, all the while worrying even though I knew what it was he wanted to talk about.

I was restive, anyway, the result in part of an e-mail from Worried regarding the coins Heinrich von Grümh donated to the museum. Worried, some may remember, is the anonymous tipster who works in the Genetics Lab and who has proved helpful if not instrumental in resolving some decidedly tangled mysteries in the museum. He wrote:

> Dear Mr. de Ratour:
> I see you're back in the news with this Grum [sic] guy murder. And I don't know if what I've got to tell you has anything to do with the case. But the scuttlebutt going around the Labs is that the coins he gave the museum are fakes. The way I heard it is that the guy with the long name in charge of the Greek stuff brought some samples down to Robin Sylphan who runs the electron microscope which gets you in as close as you can get. It's all very hush hush for some reason. You might want to check with Robin. I mean she's a dike but she's nice. I thought you'd want to know this because maybe it had something to do with the murder. It probably don't mean squat, but you never know.
>
> Worried

Professionally, of course, I am concerned by even the remote possibility that the coins are forgeries. There are so many good fakes out there that it has become the bane of the collector's profession. And that, ultimately is what people in my position do: We collect rare and beautiful things; we study and classify them; we curate and exhibit them. Quite aside from the aesthetic bliss such objects afford, their beauty, utility, and timelessness give meaning to our past, indeed, to our very existence. At another level, any forgery undermines the appreciation of what is genuine and unique, of things that, in their essence, cannot be duplicated. Which is not an insignificant consideration as the world lapses ever deeper into a coma of virtuality.

Truth be told, I don't entirely trust Feidhlimidh de Buitliér, Curator of the Greco-Roman Collection. A few months back he proposed that I appoint him assistant director of the museum, intimating that he could be useful in that position in our ongoing efforts to remain independent of the university. When I asked him how he might be useful, he evinced an evasiveness that had an undercurrent of insolence. It wouldn't surprise me to find him in league with the ever-looming Mr. Morin.

But then, possible forgeries seemed the least of my concerns as the lieutenant took his accustomed seat in front of my desk. Though we remained cordial enough in our greetings, I remarked an edge of wary reserve as he told me he wanted to bring me up to date on the murder and that he had questions about Heinie von Grümh's relations with the museum. Doreen, who is very happily married to and now hugely pregnant by the divinity student who came by as a grief counselor in the wake of the Ossmann-Woodley murders, brought us coffee and closed the door.

I took some solace from the thought that the officer's attitude toward me undoubtedly sprang from a weariness with investigating murders at the museum. He began with a sardonic jest, wondering if we shouldn't call it the Museum of Murder. I countered that we could certainly consider starting a collection or perhaps mounting a special exhibition that would draw from other museums and from the grisly detritus of homicide kept in police departments all over the world. Certainly, I said, warming to my rejoinder, murder and man, both as a gender designation and in the larger sense of *Homo sapiens sapiens,* go together like cakes and ale. But I did wonder to myself why the MOM attracts these acts of ultimate violence.

I reminded the lieutenant, who wore a suit of dark summer-weight wool, an impeccably turned shirt, and a jazzy tie with a design that look like linked handcuffs, that, technically speaking, the murder did not occur on museum property. I might, unconsciously, have been trying to exculpate myself. Because, for the whole time, I teetered on the edge of disclosing my own qualifications as a suspect.

"Close enough," he said ruefully. Then, abruptly, "Who on the staff here or at the university might have had a motive for murdering von Grümh?"

Though I expected the question, I feigned musement, something, I think, the lieutenant noted. *"Qui bono?"* I said. "Well, let's see, I suppose we could start with Feidhlimidh de Buitliér."

"Felonious the what?" he half joked.

"Not quite. More like *felimi.*"

"Could you spell that?"

"Not off the top of my head." My laugh sounded nervous, even to me. I rootled through a file and came up with a document with the man's official name. "Feidhlimidh o Súilleabháin de Buitliér," I said, spelling it out. "It's Irish Gaelic. Or, as he informed me, a Gaelicized Norman name, at least the Butler part of it. I don't how real it is. Someone told me his original name was Philip Buttles or Bottles and that he has Sullivans somewhere in his family. We call him Phil for short."

"What does he do?"

"He's Curator of the Greco-Roman Collection."

"And why would he want to murder von Grümh?"

"Well, Lieutenant, I'm not saying he wanted to murder him. In fact, I doubt very much he could have."

"Why do you say that?"

"I doubt very much he has the . . ."

"Testicular fortitude?"

"Exactly. What I'm saying is that the two of them never got along. Heinie always managed to treat Phil as a lackey. And Phil had difficulty accepting Heinie's appointment as Honorary Curator of the Numismatic Collection. Heinie kept telling Phil how to do his job. Phil insinuated on several occasions that Heinie's coins were fakes . . ."

"Is that a possibility?"

I paused for a moment, wondering if I should disclose the e-mail from Worried. "When it comes to anything in a museum, forgery is always a possibility. It is an art form in and of itself." I paused. "As a matter of fact, here's an e-mail sent anonymously to me this morning." I handed him a printout of Worried's communication and waited as he read it.

"Have you asked the curator about it?"

"Not yet. But I plan to."

He nodded. "Let me know if you turn up anything."

"Of course."

"So your curator and von Grümh didn't get along?"

"There was a chronic, low-grade aggravation between them, but nothing, as far as I can see, that would lead to murder."

"Anyone else?"

"I suppose Colin Saunders wouldn't mind seeing Heinie among the dead."

"Who's Colin Saunders?"

"Col Saunders is the Groome Professor of Ancient Greek Civilization and Curator of Classical Antiquities in the Frock. You know, Wainscott's . . ."

"I do. Groome with an *e*?"

"Right. Heinie's late father. He funded the chair in a bequest, and Heinie was on the search committee that helped select Saunders. Only he campaigned against his appointment."

"Why?"

"Who knows. Heinie was like that. A gadfly in the ointment, as Izzy Landes called him."

"So Saunders might carry a grudge?"

"Indeed, but it goes deeper than that."

He waited and, I must say, his skeptical gaze put me on edge.

"Well, as you know, we are having some battles royal where the university has been concerned. We have conceded that, though independent, we are historically affiliated with the university and want to remain so. But there is an element in the Wainscott administration that will settle for nothing less than unconditional surrender. For them the revenues from the Genetics Lab . . ."

"Saunders and von Grümh," he said, cutting off what might have become a familiar recitation.

"I'm getting to it," I said, worried now about his acerbity, wondering what it might signify. "The sticking point has been our Greco-Roman Collection. Saunders has been claiming that it belongs in the Frock because, in truth, the various bequests to the MOM that resulted in our very modest but excellent Greco-Roman inventory contain ambiguous language in which it would appear that the donors considered the university and the museum as part of the same entity."

"So?"

"So Saunders, perhaps in league with this cabal in the university's administration, has been insisting that the museum accede to the transfer of the items in that collection to the Frock."

"How might this tie in with von Grümh's murder?"

"Well, Heinie has been a significant contributor to the museum, and he's been more than vociferous in his opposition to combining the two collections." I paused. I lowered my voice. "Strictly off the record, Lieutenant, I should tell you that for ethical and professional reasons I am willing, with proper legal safeguards, to consider joint title to any item with ambiguous provenance. But not everything. We are, after all, the Museum of Man in His Many Manifestations."

"Did von Grümh know this?"

I hesitated. "I don't think so." But what if Diantha, in their pillow talk, had mentioned it to him? I'm afraid I colored just a little. "I mean these things have a way of circulating."

The lieutenant gave me a keen, hard look. But he didn't press me. He said, "What can you tell me about Merissa Bonne?"

I shrugged, a little too theatrically perhaps. "Not a whole lot. She was Heinie's third wife. A trophy wife, as they say."

"Did they get along?"

"I wasn't that privy to their relations . . ." I hesitated, letting my small truth cover a large omission as I recalled the evening before and what Diantha told me about Merissa and Max Shofar. The substance of which I should have disclosed to the lieutenant. But I was reluctant to venture into the entanglements in which I found myself snared. I told myself it wasn't that important. I told myself I would tell him later if it became necessary.

Keeping my expression neutral, I asked, "Was there any evidence of powder burns on von Grümh's hands?"

The lieutenant thought for a moment. "No. None whatsoever. The GSR was negative."

"GSR?"

"Gunshot residue. Why do you ask?"

"To rule out suicide."

"Was he suicidal?"

"He should have been," I said with a queasy laugh.

"Why do you say that?" The lieutenant did not laugh.

I sighed. "He was a very unhappy man. In my opinion."

"What made him unhappy? In your opinion."

I glanced sharply at the lieutenant to let him know I didn't like his tone. I said drily, "He was one of those people who suffer the tragedy of getting everything they think they want."

"Anything else?" he asked, grim with suspicion.

I shook my head outwardly and inwardly at myself. There was in fact much else to tell him about myself and Heinie and the night of his murder. About Merissa and Max and the motive they could have shared. I had even neglected to tell him about Col Saunders and the Dresden stater, one of the world's most valuable coins. So I feigned thoughtfulness and lied. I said, "Not that I can think of."

He briskly folded up his notebook. He stood up. He said, "And you, Norman, what did you have against Heinrich von Grümh?"

Again resorting to small truths, I said, "Oh, I thought the man a bore. But I'm sure I'd have been murdered myself long ago if that were a possible motive."

At the door he granted me one of his wry smiles. "Don't leave town, Norman."

Which, though presumably meant as a jest, rattled me. I again cursed myself for not being candid with him. His questioning and especially his manner left me in a rare state of anxiety. How much did he already know? How much did he suspect? It is bad enough to sense when a friend begins to dislike you; it is worse when he ceases to trust you.

The best response to anxiety being action, I determined to walk down to Phil's office to ask him about the coins when Doreen came in with the mail. I leafed through it listlessly. It included a letter from Millicent Mulally of Sign House that contained some remarkable information and the promise of another headache for me.

Dear Mr. de Ratour:

I am writing to inform you that I am engaged to be married on July 10, and that, well before that date, I will no longer be in a position to care for Alphus and to act as his guardian. My future husband and I will be moving to New York, where he works, to an apartment scarcely big enough for the two of us.

I will miss Alphus very much and hope to be able to visit him regardless of what his future living arrangements are. In this regard, you should know that it would be inhumane in the extreme to return Alphus to the cages in the museum. He is not like other chimpanzees in the least. It would be like condemning a man to prison for no reason whatsoever. It would be unjust.

Right now I am doing everything in my power to find Alphus another situation. I would suggest that he be left in the care of Boyd Ridley, who is a devoted friend. But Boyd has difficulties of his own and, to be candid, is not always stable. Unfortunately, at this time, I am not in a position to underwrite any suitable living arrangement for Alphus. I am hopeful that you, with all of the museum's resources at your disposal, will be able to find him a real home.

You should also know that Alphus is not just an animal or even a pet. He is a highly intelligent and very sensitive individual. In fact, Alphus has learned to sign at an advanced level and has started to teach himself how to write using the computer. It seems he was familiar with the keyboard and already knew quite a few words. He told me he once participated in a writing program at the museum a few years ago.

I know I can trust you to help me find Alphus a place to stay other than those horrible cages. It might help if you could come up here and meet him socially. We have tea about four every day. Please do come.

Sincerely yours,
Millicent

I must confess I find myself incredulous at the idea that the animal can "sign" other than, perhaps, a few rudimentary gestures. As everyone knows, the so-called literary output generated under the aegis of Damon Drex turned out to be a hoax of stupendous proportions. I thought about possible places for Alphus to stay as I made my way down the two flights to Phil's office.

To my relief, he was out, apparently on holidays. I made a note of when he would return and considered taking the rest of the day off. Because, for all my complaints, I have found that living with Diantha has again become a marvel of happiness. It's as though von Grümh's murder has lifted an enormous weight from our life together even as my detestation of the man remains a troubling source of possibilities.

Elsie grows more communicative by the day. My own fluency in signing barely keeps pace. Sometimes I think the world would be better off if we all just shut up and used sign language. I know, I know, the beauty of the human voice and all that. Perhaps vocalizations could be limited to singing — by those who know how. Because signing, a dance of the hands, the arms, the whole upper torso, has a grace and eloquence all of its own.

It took me a while to reconcile to Elsie's condition. When a child is handicapped in some way — yes, I know, that's not the word, but being mute is a handicap whatever word or phrase you use for it. The reality remains: My child cannot or will not speak. Even as the tests go on and the reassurances grow thinner (at least her giggle is normal, one expert reassured us), a complex reaction begins. At first you think that what you cherish most in life has turned out to be damaged goods. Someone you love is less than whole, less than what they could have been. It's difficult to resist the inevitable assessment and the kind of inner discounting that ensues. Which in turn provokes a fierce love and pride alloyed with tragedy. And, out of pity and guilt (*What did I do wrong?*), you find yourself in the grip of a deep, protective love. My dear silent little girl is ever more precious to me.

And then, gradually and without exercising what I would call deliberate virtue, the notion of deficiency abates and the state of being mute becomes just another kind of normality.

Speaking of which, Felix has returned to Seaboard to my great relief. But he can be a strange bird. Rio, he told me, "is tush city, derrière central, butt capital of the world. Talk about neck pain. What I mean, Norman, is don't ever go there for a honeymoon."

4

That I had yet to tell my friend and colleague Lieutenant Tracy all that transpired on the night of Heinie's murder provoked in me an unease that shadowed and sharpened everything I did. In all honesty, I felt like an impostor. Even as I met with Dr. Harvey Deharo and Professor Thad Pilty to discuss the Neanderthal problem, I kept recalling what had happened on that fateful evening. And what I had not told the police.

I managed to be plausibly attentive when I sat down with these two eminent scientists along with Emmanuel Quinn, the representative from Humanation Syntectics, the firm that designed and manufactured the animated mannequins we use in the Diorama of Paleolithic Life.

As I have mentioned, in an attempt to render the models in "postracial" hues, we had tinted them a light grayish brown, a complexion that may be the future of the human race but apparently wasn't that of our Neanderthal antecedents.

I let Thad, who personifies gravitas with his Amish-like beard and stolid squareness of stature, delineate the problem. He pointed out that the issue had also arisen several years before while planning the diorama. He admitted he felt troubled then about resorting to a kind of non-tone for the skin color of the models. All the same, he emphasized that the real purpose of the diorama — informing the public about life among these extinct humans — had been very successful. He conceded that perhaps it was time to review the whole thing.

Mr. Quinn, one of those salesmen who believe in what they sell, took the opportunity to tell us about a new line of models with up-to-date robotics that looked and acted so real, they scared people.

"That would be quite an investment," I put in.

"Big bucks," said Mr. Quinn. "But worth it. I mean from a revenue point of view."

Harvey Deharo nodded thoughtfully. He is a Harvard-trained specialist in genetic anthropology. Of Caribbean origins, he claims Spanish, African, Converso, Irish, and French antecedents. A regular salad, he called himself at a dinner party where the host had been pouring drinks with a generous hand. His pale eyes, set in a long, strongly sculpted face, remain in one's mind a good while after one meets him. He is tall, graceful of movement, and articulate in at least three languages. The man could get by on looks and charm alone, but he combines his worldliness with competence in his field and with an offhand managerial flair I marvel at. We've had Harvey and his delightful wife, Felice, over for dinner and have been to their farmhouse, which is located some miles out of town. He is gracious and subtle toward me in his gratitude while I, mellow with his good wine on one occasion, told him, "It is you, sir, that makes me and the museum look good."

Now he cleared his throat. "Perhaps, if the investment was not too great, we could consider updating the whole exhibit." In that easy island accent of his, he pointed out the cost would also have to include revenues lost during the time the diorama was closed to the public.

I ventured the possibility that we could, given the latest research, gradually phase in lighter-skinned and more fair-haired models into the diorama.

The others, including Mr. Quinn, looked dubious. He noted

the expense. "These are top-of-the-line units. You can't just paint them a different shade until you get what you want."

"It's going to be expensive anyway," Professor Pilty put in.

I said, "We could just leave things the way they are. At least for the time being. As for the pigmentation issue, we could put a placard explaining . . ."

Harvey Deharo shook his head. "No. The exhibition has to represent the best and current research. If Neanderthals looked like Irish from Roscommon, then so be it." He paused. "Let's not temporize on this. To duck this issue for the sake of political correctness would be unworthy of the museum and what it stands for."

Thad Pilty agreed with him. "What we can't lose sight of is the issue of historical accuracy."

I found my own backbone stiffening. We concluded that Mr. Quinn would get back to me with several alternatives and their costs, including how much time it would take to install the new mannequins and how long the diorama would have to be shut down.

The whole thing took less than half an hour. If only meetings of the Oversight Committee were as brisk and efficacious. Sadly, those exercises in patience and credulity are usually a waste of time and spirit. And while I have often mentally composed a letter of resignation, I remain on the committee in an *ex officio* capacity mostly to keep an eye on things. Because it does like to meddle. Certainly the next meeting, held mostly in my honor, if I can be droll for a moment, lived up to my low expectations.

All the usual suspects and a few new ones showed up to discuss "a range of concerns involving the Museum of Man." Since the agenda directly involved the museum and since there are facilities available in the Twitchell Room, I agreed to hold it there. My good friend Professor Izzy Landes, ageless in his aging, his nimbus of white hair more ethereal than ever, his bright eyes full of secret amusement, his bow tie like a Nabokovian butterfly, took me aside quietly before the meeting to ask how things were going with the investigation.

"Marvelous," I said. "It's starting to look like something out of a book."

He laughed. "Someone should do a book on that."

"On what?"

"On the entertainment value of murder. Where would we be without it?"

Tall and clerical in an offhand way, Father S.J. O'Gould, S.J., whose *Paragon of Animals* continues to create a stir, asked when we would have another meeting of The Group. Along with the Reverend Alfie Lopes, Izzy, Professor Thad Pilty, Corny Chard, and one or two others, we hold a dinner about once a month to go over issues of some weight.

Corny Chard sported a new leg he claims is better than the original. He also has a prosthetic arm and hand he manipulates most wonderfully. Corny, of course, made news a couple of years ago when he survived partial dismemberment at the hands of cannibals whose rituals he had gone to observe in a remote part of the Amazon basin.

He remains as cocky as ever with a grizzled short beard beneath his red face and balding, close-cropped skull. His best-selling account, *A Leg to Stand On,* has formed the basis of a two-hour television documentary, the public opening of which Diantha and I have been invited to here in Seaboard.

Ariel Dearth, the Leona von Beaut Professor of Situational Ethics and Litigation Development, sat there like a man with better things to do. He has been so successful in being universally despised, I sometimes wonder if I should pretend to like him, if only to disconcert him.

He was flanked by Professor Randall Athol of the Divinity School, a staunch ally of Professor Brattle in whatever foolishness she indulges in. He is of the same stripe as Professor J.J. McNull, who, with no books or original research to his name, has made a very successful career out of committee work.

One pleasant surprise at the meeting was the transformation of Bertha Schanke. Now civilly united to the woman she had been living with for some time, she is no longer an active member of BITCH, a coalition of complainers, as someone put it, and is obviously pregnant. She has also lost weight and has let her rich brown hair grow out. She greeted me warmly as "Norman," and said it was good to see me after such a long absence on my part.

Professor Constance Brattle, the well-known expert on blame and chair of the committee, introduced Professor Laluna Jackson, chair of Wainscott's recently established Victim Studies Department, as a new member of the committee.

Professor Jackson stood for a moment and said she was honored to be joining the committee, "whose work I have found both stimulating and necessary in an age when so many vulnerable groups continue to suffer the agonies of victimization."

I was very taken with her voice. Its locutions were those commonly associated with people of African American descent. And, despite a decided if strangely dark tinge to her complexion and her hair done in what are called cornrows, she could have passed for Caucasian quite easily. Not that these things matter much anymore.

Chair Brattle shuffled some papers in front of her, furrowed her brow in an accusatory frown, and said, "It seems that the sad spectacle of murder has once again turned the spotlight of sensationalism on the Museum of Man. I realize that, until the murderer is brought to justice, no specific blame can be assigned for this criminal act.

"But the community in general and the museum in particular cannot escape the aura of what is called diffuse blame. What we need to question about the museum is its *genius loci*. What, in short, makes it such a place of murder? What is it that makes it so conducive to such crime? More to the point, what are our responsibilities as those in leadership roles in creating a venue amenable to more normative behavior?"

"Are you saying that Heinie Grümh's murder was the fault of the museum?" Izzy Landes asked.

Despite the scattering of smiles, the oblivious chair took his question seriously. "No. I wouldn't go that far. But I am saying that what has happened at the Museum of Man is of overweening concern to this committee, enough so that I am going to move that we appoint a subcommittee to examine in depth the situation at the museum and to come up with a series of recommendations including specific initiatives and active modes of implementation."

Professor Jackson raised her hand off the table. "I would like to second the chair's motion. Because . . . while actual murder is the ultimate victimization of an individual, there are other, more subtle kinds of murder that, together, we must all struggle against."

Again, she evinced a deliberate, not to mention portentous, articulation.

Thad Pilty said, "I think we should go slowly on any such idea at this time. I move we table the motion."

Izzy Landes snorted. "I move we wastebasket the motion."

To my astonishment, Bertha Schanke led the murmur of ayes with a smile in my direction.

Flustered, Professor Brattle rapped the table as though calling for order when in fact no disorder existed. She moved quickly on to other business on the printed agenda, which involved the committee's role in choosing Wainscott's next president. It seems that George Twill, the current incumbent, will be stepping down at the end of the next academic year.

Listening between the lines of the chair's remarks, I surmised that the recently formed search committee had decided to limit any oversight functions on the part of the committee to little more than "suggestions from individual members," that is, the same privilege accorded everyone in the greater university community.

A deal of time and words were spent on the issue before Professor Brattle succeeded in appointing a subcommittee chaired by Laluna Jackson to "investigate ways and means by which the responsibilities of the Oversight Committee can be brought to bear on the matter in an effective manner."

After a couple of other items, we came to what the chair called "the issues surrounding complaints about the sexual abuse of fellow primates."

There followed some preliminary fussing with electronic gear. The lights in the room dimmed and a rough, grainy image appeared on a large television screen attached to the wall. It showed the inside of a commodious cage and two chimpanzees. The male, Alphus, squatted in one corner, his member pinkly erect, while a female, her hindquarters inflamed, moved about as though uninterested.

A few moments passed before the female, Madon (don't ask me where these names come from), approached Alphus and with no preliminaries proceeded to squat on his lap. From their grimaces, I assumed there were vocalizations. It was over in a matter of seconds before the couple went back to the boring life of being caged chimps.

The lights came back on. The chair, speaking from a prepared statement, said, "This and similar scenes appeared both on a Web site called Different Strokes and on the university's site. So we have before the committee not merely the issue of invasion of privacy and that of animal rights in general, but the spectacle of animal pornography appearing on Wainscott's window to the world, cybernetically speaking."

Corny Chard started in with little ceremony. "If people are getting their jollies watching that kind of stuff, they must be pretty desperate. But I don't think it's a big deal."

"I disagree with you," said Professor Athol flatly. "It is not the kind of thing you want broadcast, not when the public is starting to take a critical look at universities and their culture."

"Not to mention their expense," Professor Pilty added.

"Why are cameras there in the first place?" Attorney Dearth asked me in a hostile tone.

"Security," I answered. I avoided looking at him because to look at him is never a pleasant experience. "In the wake of the Bert and Betti incident we equipped each cage with monitors. But, also, a graduate student was conducting research on the sex life of chimpanzees in captivity."

"And any number of people have access to these visual records?"

"I presume so."

"But you don't know for sure?"

"I don't know for certain."

It was an answer that appeared to puzzle the learned counsel. In the lapse, Izzy Landes said, "I think the university has to be aware of its reputation. I mean if the best Wainscott can do for pornography is a couple of copulating apes, we are sure to get a bad name."

"That remark smacks of speciesism," the chair sniffed with a significant glance around the table.

"What exactly are you suggesting?" Professor Athol asked of Izzy.

Professor Landes beetled his brows in feigned seriousness. "I think we could ask the students and the junior faculty to come up with something better. Something arousing and yet tasteful. Perhaps we could get the Visual Arts Department involved."

"The real question," said Corny Chard, who is always ready for silliness, "is whether the students would get course credits."

Keeping my voice deadpan, I kept up the badinage with, "You mean give courses?"

"Yes. Something like *An Introduction to the Theory and Practice of Pornography*."

Izzy demurred. "No, no. Let's keep it dignified. More like, *The Theory and Practice of the Erotic Arts*. Then, *Advanced Erotic Technique in Film. The History of Erotica. The Erotic Imagination: A Survey Course*."

"But not a degree?"

"Not at first. More like a specialty in graphic arts."

"Lots of workshops . . ."

"With hands-on instruction?"

"Absolutely."

"A graded course or just pass–fail."

"Lots of passes."

Chair Brattle bit heavily into the facetiousness. "I don't think it would be appropriate for either the student body or the junior faculty to get involved in production of pornography."

Corny shrugged. "It would prepare them for the real world."

Professor Jackson shook her head. "I take very strong exception to this kind of attitude. Pornography in any form constitutes victimization."

"Of whom?" Bertha Schanke asked.

"Of those participating in it. Of those who watch and encourage it. Of everyone."

"Even if they're consenting adults?"

"I think we should agree that we need to question the whole concept of consent. Consent is a fiction used by the power elites to maintain their control over all of us."

Professor Athol said, "Well, these two chimpanzees certainly did not consent to have their . . . intimacy broadcast to the world."

"They didn't complain."

"Do they even know?"

Professor Jackson held up both of her hands. "We don't know if they knew. Nor do we know what it might have done to their self-esteem. It is always safe to assume suffering."

I felt like a stiff drink by the time I sat down in the sanctuary of my office, the more so to find Lieutenant Tracy there waiting for me.

"We'll have to fetch our coffee," I said, prematurely cheery, you might say. "Doreen won't be in until later."

The officer, in a light, well-pressed chino suit and plaid tie, nodded noncommitally. "Let's go down and get some." He added, in a tone that took me aback, "We need to talk, Norman."

I do not shrug very easily, but tried to indicate the moral equivalent thereof. In fact, his demeanor made me quite nervous, and I grew talkative as we wended our way down through the exhibits.

"As you can see, our Greco-Roman Collection is really quite

small," I pointed out. We were on the fifth floor, not far from my office and just under the delicately ribbed, domed skylight that crowns the atrium around which the collections are arranged both on the overhanging balconies and in the adjoining rooms. Most of the time I am soothed and reassured by the precious and beautiful objects on display from far and near, from recent and ancient times. And I remain proud of how we transformed Neanderthal Hall, the ground floor, into the Diorama of Neanderthal Life.

None of which availed me as we went down the marble, open stairway at a businesslike pace. I feared the worst — that he would confront me with what I had not been frank about.

The somewhat stark cafeteria, which is open to staffers and the public, was nearly empty and thus provided us with a privacy for which, under the circumstances, I was grateful.

For hardly had we sat down with our coffees, when the lieutenant launched right into it, saying, "Norman, we have it on good authority that you were in a bar with von Grümh not long before he was murdered." He let that register. "We received an anonymous tip, which we followed up on. Both the bartender and the waiter who served you recognized photographs we have of you and the victim."

I nodded and avoided his eyes. "Yes. I should have told you."

"Why don't you start at the beginning."

I sighed deeply. I said, "Around seven fifteen on that evening, I met by arrangement with Heinie, Mr. von Grümh, at the Pink Shamrock. It's the gay pub down on Belmont Avenue. That venue signifies nothing. It was handy to the office and I was working late when he called."

"What were you meeting about?"

I hesitated, embarrassed. When I spoke, I felt like I was making an official statement. "About a year and a half ago, Heinie . . .

von Grümh had an affair with Diantha, my wife. Di called it a fling, a weekend thing. In any event, it didn't last long and in the meanwhile we have patched things back together." I was gratified to see he was not taking notes but just listening very intently and with what might have been sympathy.

"But lately Heinie had taken to calling Diantha. At first it was just friendly calls, looking for advice and sympathy."

"Regarding what?"

"I don't know all the details. I think his wife, Merissa, Merissa Bonne, was having an affair. In fact I know Merissa was having an affair, and it was driving Heinie mad."

"Do you know who the person was? The one she was having an affair with?"

I hesitated a moment. Then I said, "Max Shofar."

The detective took out his notebook. "Anything to old Abe Shofar?"

"His son. He's a coin dealer. In fact, he was von Grümh's principal locator."

"He found coins for him?"

"Yes."

"Including the collection von Grümh gave to the museum?"

"Some of them. Most of them, I think."

"So von Grümh started to call your wife?"

"He did. It turned compulsive. He kept asking her to meet him for coffee. It became a kind of stalking."

"So you arranged to meet with him instead?"

"Yes. We were supposed to have a cup of coffee, but he wanted a drink. So we went to the Shamrock."

"Had you been there together before?"

I resented the possible insinuation in his question. I said, flatly, "No. We went there because it was handy. I had a glass of ale. He had whiskey and soda. Several in fact."

"And you talked?"

"It was quite civilized actually. I told him he could not continue to call Diantha, that she was not interested in him or in resuming her liaison with him."

"How did he take that?"

"Surprisingly well. He apologized profusely. You know, one of those apologies that become embarrassing. It was all I could do to resist apologizing for making him apologize. And then . . ."

The detective waited patiently.

"Well, it was then that he began to complain to me about Merissa's affair with Max Shofar, and I could tell that he was shifting the burden he had imposed on Diantha onto me."

"What did he tell you about Max Shofar and his wife?"

"Oh, the usual things. He couldn't see what she saw in him. He said he was little more than a petty playboy, a shallow character who would go broke if it weren't for the help and business that he, Heinie, threw his way."

"Is any of that true?"

"The playboy part, maybe. But Max actually does a large mail-order business."

"Anything else?"

"Not really. He repeated himself *ad nauseam,* variations on the same theme. He said he was at his wits' end. That life had lost its meaning for him."

The lieutenant waited, his patience apparent as I paused to catch my inner breath. I went on. "He also said that it shouldn't have bothered him as he didn't care about Merissa anymore. That he had decided to divorce her."

"But he was still strung out about it?"

"It seemed that way."

"At what time did you leave the pub?"

"Not long after eight. Ten past maybe."

"And did you part company then?"

"No. He drove me back to the museum."

"Where he dropped you off?"

"Yes."

"And what did you do then?"

"I took a walk. To clear my head."

"For how long?"

"I'm not sure. Ten, fifteen minutes."

"Where did you walk?"

"Over to the Arboretum. There's a well-lit path along the edge."

"Then what did you do?"

"I returned to my office."

"Do you have any proof of that?"

I thought for a moment. I had checked my e-mails but I had not answered any. Then I remembered our new security system. "I had to swipe my museum card to get in after hours . . ."

"Is there any way we can verify that time?"

"Indeed there is. The mechanism at the door is wired to a computer that records the card and time of any employee coming in or going out after hours."

The lieutenant noticed my reaction. "That will help, Norman, but the time of death could have been before that." He sighed. "I wish you had told me this earlier."

I nodded an apology. "But you see, Lieutenant, when one is innocent, and I am innocent, these kinds of coincidences seem irrelevant."

It took me a while to recover from this interview. If not a suspect, I had become a "person of interest" in the case. Had that been all, I might have been able to shake off the queasy feeling of having been less than frank with a trusted colleague. Sometimes a walk around the exhibits helps. Or a call to Diantha for a chat or to arrange lunch. Not this time. What a tangled web we weave and all that.

What I did do finally was make my way over to the Genetics Lab and the facility that houses the electron microscope. It has a verification capacity that the curators use from time to time for objects in the collections to ascertain their authenticity. The facility is impressive in its own way, with clean-room equipment and what seemed like, to me at any rate, an array of futuristic-looking devices. Of course, people of my generation tend to forget that what used to be the future has already arrived and in some cases gone hurtling by.

Perhaps I should have called first, but right then, in the wake of the lieutenant's visit, I needed to do something, to act.

Robin Sylphan was not in, I was told by her assistant, a young woman with close-cropped hair and hostile, suspicious eyes.

"When do you expect her back?" I asked.

"Tomorrow. She's taking a personal day."

I was about to quip that I thought all days were personal days, but thought better of it. Instead, I said, "My name is Norman de Ratour. I'm the museum's director . . ."

"Yes, I know."

"I'm here about the work Ms. . . ."

"Doctor . . ."

"Doctor Sylphan is doing on coins from our collections."

"You'll have to speak to her directly about that."

I did not have the moral stamina to persist. People think being director gives one power. But institutions like the Museum of Man comprise little fiefdoms defended in depth by thickets of procedures, precedents, and prerogatives. So I glanced around, gritted my teeth, and kept myself from speculating aloud about just how essential to the museum was this particular facility.

At the same time, I knew myself well enough to know that I was desperate to find any scrap of evidence, however tangential to the case, that I could give to Lieutenant Tracy. If only to appease him.

5

All things considered, I was not unreasonably happy when, in pajamas and slippers, steaming cup of coffee in hand, I went out into our bird-loud front garden to pick up the plastic-sheathed *Bugle*. It looked to be another jewel of a late-spring day. Not only that, but warmth, rain, and no doubt high levels of carbon dioxide in the atmosphere had conspired to produce a plush of green vegetation seldom seen before.

Diantha and I had just returned from two marvelous days together in Boston, where we had gone to visit some friends, attend a concert, and take in an exhibition at the Museum of Fine Arts, a sterling place. We stayed at one of those small, boutique hotels where we took the honeymoon suite and indulged ourselves to sybaritic excess. Not that we both weren't anxious to get back to Elsie, whom we left in the care of Millicent Mulally from Sign House and Bella, her nanny.

My not unreasonable happiness dissolved into a nasty chagrin when, in the silent kitchen, I unfolded the paper to read the headline, "Museum Collection of Rare Coins Found to Be Fakes."

My heart did not skip a beat so much as suffer a few extra ones, real thudders, as I read, "The investigation into the murder of real estate tycoon Heinrich von Grümh took a new twist yesterday when the *Bugle* learned that the large and presumably very valuable coin collection he donated to the Museum of Man has proven to be mostly if not all counterfeits.

"Norman de Ratour, director of the museum, was not available for comment and did not return telephone calls as the story broke."

Of course I wasn't available, I stormed silently at Amanda Feeney, who had written the article. I was in Boston. And I don't wear a cell phone. Even so, had she really wanted to, she could have gotten in touch.

"Feidhlimidh de Buitliér, curator of the museum's Greco-Roman Collection, confirmed earlier background reports that the coins, originally valued at more than two million dollars, were 'extremely good copies.' He added that they had been fabricated with a process that he had not encountered before.

"De Buitliér told the *Bugle* that he had suspected the authenticity of the coins from the very start, but was discouraged from having them tested. An expert numismatist, the scholarly de Buitliér stated that 'the coins all had the same feel. They were all too perfectly imperfect.' A spokesperson for Authentech, an independent lab, said a sample of the coins were subject to EDXRF, energy dispersive X-ray fluorescence. The results showed that while the alloys in individual coins differed in their compositions, their constituent base metals were isotopically identical.

"Von Grümh, the son of the late Albrecht Groome and owner of Natural Realty, was found murdered in his car on museum property on May 11. A spokesperson for the Seaboard Police Department, which is investigating the murder, said the discovery of the faked coins may or may not have a bearing on the case.

"Malachy Morin, Vice President for Affiliated Institutions at Wainscott University, stated, 'My office will shortly be conducting a thorough-going investigation into the museum's acceptance of the forgeries. We will examine procedures involving acquisition, verification, provenance, and matters relating to a possible cover-up.'

"An informed source, who did not want to be identified, said the university would also be investigating 'rampant corruption and cronyism on the part of the museum's management.'"

I paused for a moment to let a flush of anger recede. Interesting, I thought. It sounded more like a prepared statement than something Mr. Morin, a verbal slob among other things, might be able to summon off the cuff.

It also made me believe the rumors that he is now the real power behind President Twill, who, upon announcing his resignation, has become something of a figurehead.

What the article failed to report is that the coins came to us with certificates of authenticity from, among others, the IBSCC, the International Bureau for the Suppression of Counterfeit Coins. Of course, the certificates themselves could have been faked.

The *Bugle* piece went on, rehashing other murders at the MOM and taking indirect, gratuitous potshots at me. Gratuitous in the sense that the news of the forged coins was itself damaging enough. To learn by whatever means that some presumably priceless object or collection in one's domain is a fake remains a museum director's worst nightmare. A disputed provenance is bad enough. To have bought at several removes a Klimt or a Mondrian looted by the Nazis six decades ago suggests venality at worst. But fakes make us look incompetent and cast a long shadow of doubt on everything else we love, care for, and display.

I cringed inwardly remembering how fulsomely we had wined and dined and feted and patted Heinie when he began to hint that he would donate his collection to the museum. How extravagant had been the unveiling ceremony just a couple of weeks before. How craven I had been to get my hands on those solid emblems of quotidian antiquity. Because there is something palpable, precise, ordinary, and romantic about old money. Countless Romans, Greeks, Hebrews, Persians, and others had handled these tokens of value. With them they had bought bread, wine, shelter, love, power, and betrayal. With images of gods, emperors, and Athenian owls stamped on them, old coins constitute nothing less than the hard currency of history. Who wouldn't want to hoard them?

I restrained myself from anything like an outburst until I arrived at the office. I restrained myself even when Doreen told me that "Mr. Butler," as she referred to him, had already called and wanted to see me.

"I'm sure he does," I said. And I would have let him dangle awhile longer had not reporters begun to call.

Feidhlimidh de Buitliér is a smallish, ill-favored man, his hair tonsured like a monk's above a hirsute if well-trimmed face of a piece with the coarse tweeds he wears regardless of the season. Now he sat in front of me behind a frown of puzzled apology and explaining how he had scarcely begun to write a report to me about the counterfeit coins when unknown parties leaked its contents to the press.

"Why didn't you inform me earlier that you were testing the collection?"

"Sure, I had no real proof," he replied with what seemed to me feigned and overplayed incredulity. Or perhaps it was the effect of his brogue, which thickens and thins according to context. I have on occasion heard him in unguarded moments sound like someone from the Lower Midwest.

"That's not the issue," I said coldly.

"I have it all here," he said, placing a folder on the desk between us and ignoring my remark.

"Last week I sent you no less than three e-mails and left a telephone message," I persisted.

"I was out of the office. All week. Sick leave." His yellowish brown eyes met mine with a glint of challenge before turning away. He reminded me that he had gone on record, in writing, as opposed to acceptance of the collection until at least a few of the coins could be tested for authenticity.

"You should have been careful about confidentiality," I said, opening the folder.

"We're part of the academy," he said with a significance I didn't gather right then. "People don't believe there should be secrets."

I caught again the insolence of his eyes. I said, "I don't care what people believe. I want all press inquiries directed here. I want no show-and-tell with you on camera."

When he began to protest, I put up my hand. "Mr. Butler . . ."

"De Buitliér . . ."

"Yes. De Buitliér." I smiled pleasantly to put him off guard. Then I said, "Was Mr. von Grümh aware that you were testing samples from his collection for authenticity?"

He simulated puzzlement with a convincing frown, but with the hesitation of someone dissembling. "I don't think so. I don't know. To what is it relevant?"

"His murder."

"I don't see . . ."

"I don't expect you to."

He again gave me a challenging glance.

I returned it and said, "I should tell you that I have grown very ambivalent about our Greco-Roman Collection. I am of half a mind to give the whole damn thing to the Frock."

"Really?"

"Yes, really. But I'm sure you would find working under Col Saunders to your liking, if he would have you. I think that's how they arrange things there."

He subsided back into his beard and tweediness, his eyes revealing nothing.

"That's all for now," I said presently without looking up from his report, from language such as ". . . despite my objections as to the authenticity of the specimens in the collection and as to their provenance . . ."

I don't trust the man in the least. It wasn't just that he had challenged me, which he had done in his muffled, occluded way. No, it was recalling how, as he entered my office, he had cast an appraising eye around, as though sizing up what he hoped soon to occupy.

I read through the report and then again. It was competent enough, indeed, quite thorough. Worried had been right about the use of the electron microscope and its ancillary equipment.

Between press calls, I contacted young Edwards, who is in charge of exhibitions, and told him to remove the von Grümh collection from display and secure it.

The media asked me the same questions in the same way. What was going through your head when . . . ? When did you first find out that . . . ? They got tough. Why didn't you verify at least a sampling from the collection before taking it? How is it possible with all of today's hard science to be fooled by fakes?

And then the most provocative question of all: Does the fact that the late Heinrich von Grümh gave the museum a collection of fakes have anything to do with his murder?

I pondered this question with considerable mental effort off and on as the morning progressed. My suspicions revolved around Max Shofar, particularly in light of what Diantha had

told me about him and Merissa. Working with expert counter-
feiters, had he duped Heinie and perhaps others out of millions
of dollars? How else could he live the way he did?

Perhaps Heinie found out about the forgeries. It might have
upset him more than Max's playing around with Merissa. He
confronts Max and threatens to expose him, ruining him and the
profitable mail-order business he conducts. Max, facing disaster,
either has a gun or gets one, no difficult task for someone in his
position. He gets close enough to Heinie and shoots him.

I was in the midst of these conjurations when Felix sidled
into my office with mischief showing in his acne-scarred and
yet attractive face. He was also in a state of rare excitement, his
eyes as big as his grin. He sat down and plunked the Warwick
file on my desk. "Norm, this is fantastic."

"What," I said, "a fake mummy to go with the fake coins."

"What coins?"

"The von Grümh collection."

He shrugged. "The guy was a three-dollar bill all the way. But
this is real. This is the beginning of something big."

"I'm not going to allow it. I don't care how much he gives us."

"No, no, no, Norman. This is a no-brainer. This is win, win,
win all the way to the bank. Old Warwick is only the start. He's
a genius . . ."

"Please, Felix . . ."

"Look, most people with dough embalm their names on
buildings and benches and you name it. A couple of years later
nobody knows or cares who they were. The name turns into
nothing but a name. Sometimes it doesn't take a couple of years.
Look at the Prunce Parkway. Who was Prunce . . . ?"

"Harold Prunce developed . . ."

"Yeah, yeah, you know, but nobody else does. But there, in
the Warwick Wing, in the Temple Warwick, will be Warwick

himself, all bandaged up in an open sarcophagus. A real live mummy. We take this idea and run with it. Big time. We could set up . . ."

"In the first place, we don't have the space."

"You've got to be kidding. We'll take back the Pavilion. I've been wanting an excuse to do that anyway. Look, Norm, Mr. de Ratour, Lord Museum, the Wainscott lease of the Pavilion space is up next year. We won't renew it. That's proof that we are an independent entity. It'll underscore the fact that Wainscott agreed to rent it on other than an intra-university basis. We'll make it into the Mortuary Wing."

"But . . ."

"But nothing. We not only set up the Warwick Room, but we leave space for others, lots of others. We'll have a big churchy kind of place, tastefully done, one that we call . . . the Hall of the Permanent Collection. There, for a goodly sum, you can have your cremated remains put into a space a cubic foot in size. Each niche will have its own marble door with your name and dates on it forever and ever and ever."

"You're being absurd."

"Norman, think. Even a dinky ten-by-ten-by-ten space has a thousand cubic feet. Of course we'd only use the walls. And maybe a stack or two. Like a library. We could also have an urn room, open shelves. If someone wanted to upgrade, well, there could be family vaults, little separate temples or templets . . ."

"Felix, we are a museum."

"Yeah. Full of dead things. A few more won't hurt." He bent forward, his scarred face brilliant with intensity. "And that would only be the beginning . . ."

"That's what I'm afraid of."

"But think about it. Nothing happens here at night. We could hold . . . mortuary receptions. Funeral parties. Catered wakes.

Even services. People will line up for this stuff. We'd have a waiting list . . ."

"You are describing a nightmare."

"And that crematorium you used for the monkeys . . ."

"Felix . . ."

"It still works. We could have it fixed up better than new with scrubbers, state of the art . . . Okay, okay. That's pushing it."

"The whole thing is pushing it."

He calmed down. He said quietly. "Okay. But I think you're making a big mistake. And remember, old Warwick is on the Board of Governors. And we need everyone on our side if we're going to keep Wainscott from taking us over and, not incidentally, save your institutional neck."

He was right about Warwick and the board. I agreed readily enough to that and stretched my imagination to consider his take on Warwick's proposal. I couldn't do it. Even if we charged outrageous prices to keep it a dignified arrangement, it would become a circus.

"So fake coins, huh?"

"You've seen what the *Bugle* did with this?"

"Nobody takes the *Bugle* seriously. Nobody serious, anyway." He stood up to go. "Beat them to it. Set up an exhibition using real fakes."

"Instead of what, counterfeit fakes?"

"Hey, don't think they don't exist. Those Lipanov replicas get knocked off all the time."

It wasn't a bad idea, but one I had little appetite for right then. I merely looked at him and silently shook my head.

"Cheer up," he said at the door. "Tonight's your big night. I'll see you there."

· · ·

It had completely slipped my mind that there was to be a private screening, a premiere so to speak, of the documentary based on Corny Chard's account of his amputational adventures in South America. The invitation, which had arrived some weeks before, was for drinks, large hors d'oeuvres, and *A Leg to Stand On* at the Seaboard Players' Little Theater. It's located in a refurbished waterfront warehouse of some vintage judging from its small size and the eight-by-eight posts and beams they've left in place.

Diantha had not forgotten, and it lifted my spirits to find her wearing a fetching summer dress and keeping on ice a perfect martini, which she knew I would need. After a quick shower, I put on my off-white linen suit, faintly striped shirt, and silk tie of muted paisley pattern. What, after all, does one wear to a film about cannibalism?

Rather than finish my drink, I sat on the living room floor with Elsie and Decker to teach one of her dolls, the one with life-like hands, a few new words. I swear that my toddler already has a larger signing vocabulary than I do. In the midst of all this I realized that, whatever happened to the museum, I was a profoundly lucky man.

Diantha drove us over in her powerful motor car. We arrived at a gala scene, a party of more than a hundred clustered around tables on the side deck of the building lit by paper lanterns. I was greeted like the star of the show by the star of the show, Corny himself, who led me through a scattering of applause to the bar.

Ah, to have friends. Korky Kummerbund, looking a bit haggard, arrived just behind us with a new friend named Merwin. Korky, who was very close to my late wife, has gone national with his upscale food pantry called Best Leftovers, and I think the strain is starting to tell.

Izzy and Lotte were there for a handshake and kiss. He suggested a wine he described as "a quite good if complacent little Bordeaux." Father O'Gould or "S.J.," as he likes to be called when wearing mufti, came with his aging mother. Aging, but in no way decrepit, Theresa O'Gould ordered bourbon, a double shot, from the busy bartender.

Soon, Harvey and Felice Deharo were adding to the buzz of conversation along with Corny's wife, Jocelyn, who, I suspected, had been looking forward to widowhood when it seemed her husband wasn't going to make it back from the Rio Sangre. Felix introduced me to his new wife, Flora, a sloe-eyed beauty of Filipino descent. (Asked once about his taste in wives, Felix replied he was taking a swim in the gene pool.)

I was surprised when Merissa Bonne showed up with Max Shofar in tow. I expected her to make at least a pretense of mourning in public. But then I am inclined toward the old decencies even at the expense of hypocrisy.

I was more surprised and quite delighted when Lieutenant Tracy arrived with his wife, Katlin. She is a quiet, observant, and very pretty woman in her thirties.

The hors d'oeuvres were large indeed. There was grilled shrimp, a warm pesto salad with rigatoni, a green salad with oil and lemon, baguettes so good they should be a controlled substance, and the usual plethora of cheeses and little hot pastries with stuffing.

The Reverend Lopes came alone. Though he plays for the other side, as he likes to say, he keeps his private life very private. He joined in the sympathy I received regarding the coins. We waxed philosophical about the difference between a good fake and a bad original. He recalled how a Dutchman, Han van Meergeren, forged Vermeers so well that he sold a fake of *The Woman Taken in Adultery* to Herman Goering.

Someone tapped a glass. A black woman of regal bearing from the managerial ranks of the Boston PBS station responsible for the film thanked us all for coming. She said her station had been honored to work with Professor Chard, the university, and the Museum of Man. She mentioned the production staff and thanked the Seaboard Players for letting us use their wonderful facilities.

We settled down eventually in the theater itself, which felt like a large living room. Music reminiscent of Villa-Lobos started just as the enormous screen on the stage filled with an expansive aerial view of the Amazon rain forest. Credits rolled, the music faded, the camera closed in on rising ground in the distance, and the authoritative if somewhat unctuous voice of a well-known actor began.

"Professor Cornelius Chard is a modern-day Indiana Jones. The world's preeminent expert on human cannibalism, he is also an indefatigable explorer who has traveled the world in search of those people who eat people. Not long ago, his search led him to the headwaters of the Rio Sangre, a tributary of the Amazon, and the homeland of the fierce Yomamas, a tribe that has successfully resisted the predations of loggers, miners, and other outsiders by killing and eating them."

Corny appears on screen laboring up a dense jungle trail following loincloth-clad porters. The cut is taken from the video that Corny sent to me through an intermediary. Breathless from his exertions and reminiscent of that famous British naturalist, Corny stops to describe where he is and where he is going.

The scene changes abruptly to a dizzying flyover view of Seaboard before coming down to street level and driving, as it were, up to the massive front doors of the museum. The voice-over intones, "Meanwhile, back in the quiet coastal city of Seaboard, a drama quite different but related to that of Professor Chard's was unfolding in the Museum of Man. There, two academics, sane, sober people, appeared to have killed themselves with sex."

As I watched the documentary with interest, I let my gaze wander around the assembled group, gauging their reaction. They appeared riveted. All except Merissa Bonne, who was on display in a diaphanous number that in certain backlit situations left little need for figural inference. I noticed that she fidgeted, distracted. A bit brazen, I thought, showing up with Max like that. Perhaps too brazen. Too much like a gesture calculated to show that they had nothing to hide. Which didn't necessarily mean they had something to hide. But they, more than anyone, had a strong motive to murder Heinie von Grümh. Not only that, but Lieutenant Tracy told me that they were each other's alibi for the time when the murder occurred. A flimsy one at that, something about a drive up the coast.

Merissa caught me looking at her and, judging from her private smile, not altogether mistakenly thought I was thinking of something other than the film.

The documentary moved briskly on, dramatizing with deft strokes the intertwining strands of bizarre murder, drug dealing, Corny's gruesome adventure, and the all-important videotape. I spend some time myself in front of the camera explicating the development in the Genetics Lab of a powerful aphrodisiac and the attempt by the mobster Freddie Bain, aka Manfred Bannerovich, among other aliases, to get control of it. I mention the tape and how it came into my hands.

Returning to the rain forest, the documentary built skillfully to the horrific climax at the village of the Yomamas. The gasps were audible as the chain saw did its bloody work. Cut to dark, green jungle, bird sounds, moving water.

Music over and a distant shot of Swift Chapel along with close-ups of obituaries and snippets of local news coverage documenting the belief that Corny has been killed and eaten. Another drive to the museum and an actor somewhat resembling me reenacts my foolhardy journey out to the monster's lair in the Hays Mountains, where I rescue Diantha and kill the miscreant Freddie Bain with my father's revolver.

Then Corny's apparent resurrection and return to Seaboard in a blaze of media glory. Articles and interviews galore, one pundit calling him "The risen Christ of anthropology," who had "suffered for the sins of anthropologists."

The interview with Barbara Waters or someone of that name is the most egregious. In the course of it, she flutters her eyes and lowers her voice, intimating that a really difficult question is about to be asked but one that she, we all know, has the courage to ask.

"Professor Chard, what was going through your mind when you smelled your own flesh roasting?"

"My mind? Well, you might say I didn't have much of a mind at that point."

"And, after they cut you down, it's reported that you asked for some . . . of yourself. Just to try it."

"Well, I was offered some actually. The Yomamas are very hospitable in their own way."

"What part was it?"

"A piece of the lower thigh, if I'm not mistaken."

"And what was going through your mind when you actually bit into a piece of yourself? How did you taste?"

"A little like lamb. Or, rather, mutton. A bit chewy, actually. Like shank when it's not quite done enough."

"It's not the first time that you've tasted human flesh?"

"Right."

"There was the young man on Loa Hoa . . ."

"Right."

"How did you compare?"

"In taste?"

"Yes."

"Well, I was cooked differently to begin with. He was baked in a hole in the ground using heated stones. I was flame-broiled."

"It's not an experience you'll want to repeat?"

"Well, I don't have that many limbs left."

"Professor Chard. Thank you very much."

The scene then changed back to the village where, with some trepidation, a camera crew returned with Corny. He was carried up the steep path by well-paid porters to a ceremony where he was welcomed with great acclaim.

As Corny recounted in the book and as the narrator retold it in the film — his voice over the welcoming rituals — just after the amputations, a harpy eagle soared above the village with a huge snake in its talons. This was taken for a sign from the gods, and Corny was medicated as best they could and asked to join the feast. It was seen as significant that the old chain saw wouldn't start, either.

"I think they should make a real movie out of it," Merissa said to Harvey Deharo after the film ended and we were standing around with coffee. "I think Dennis Hopper should play Professor Chard."

Harvey laughed. "I think it would be difficult to get any more real than what we've just seen."

"Yes, but don't you think a really good movie . . . ?"

Alfie Lopes of all people chimed in, "Wouldn't Anthony Hopkins be a better choice? It would serve him right to get eaten this time."

"But who would play Norman?" Diantha asked. "I mean, he has a big part."

I tried to hide my pleasure. "Oh, come on, they'd probably write my part out of the script."

"Oh, don't believe it," put in Lotte Landes, taking hold of my elbow. "I still find it hard to believe, Norman, that you actually shot someone dead."

"But sure it's extraordinary what we're capable of," said S.J. — Father O'Gould — with a philosophic sigh.

To one side, I glimpsed Lieutenant Tracy watching and listening as he so often does.

6

Mere anarchy has been loosed upon my world. My humiliation is complete. I scarcely know where to begin this account of a debacle so sudden and total that I have hesitated these several days to commit what happened to words. But words are all that I have left. However ephemeral, self-damning, and difficult, words are the only lifeline I have in this sea of troubles.

The very success of the documentary screening revived and exacerbated my problems. That is, I remained very much in a damage-control mode, on the phone mostly with reporters, patrons, and members of the governing board both about the coin forgery and my own legal predicament. I began to envy George Twill his impending retirement as president of Wainscott.

In the midst of this, two members of the Seaboard Police Department, both of whom I know very well, showed up unannounced at my office door. The lieutenant sat down wearily. He had Sergeant Lemure with him, never a good sign. The sergeant closed the door. An even worse sign. No coffee, thank you. The worst possible sign.

"We've got a real problem, Norman," Lieutenant Tracy began.

The sergeant fixed me with his tough-cop stare. "Actually, Professor, you've got a real problem."

I looked from one to the other and kept silent.

The lieutenant leaned toward me. "The ballistics on the bullet removed from von Grümh's brain match the ballistics on the bullets that killed Freddie Bain."

"You mean . . . ?"

"I mean they came from your Smith and Wesson."

I shook my head, reassured. "That's impossible. My gun's at home locked in a trunk. It hasn't been fired in more than a year. When I took it out to the cottage. You know, to keep it functioning."

"We'll need to take a look at it," Lieutenant Tracy said equably.

With something akin to alacrity, I drove with the two officers to my house, which is a rather quaint Federalist affair with Greek Revival touches and a Victorian turret toward the back. I called ahead to let Diantha know we were coming, but she wasn't at home. It mattered little. There's a fudge factor in ballistics as in any technical procedure calling for human judgment.

Decker growled when we came through the front door, but only at Sergeant Lemure, who looked ready to draw and use his gun. After quieting the dog and putting him in the kitchen, I led the police officers to the attic, where I have my study. I took the key from the hiding place in the top drawer of the antique desk that had once been my father's and used it to open the lid of the sturdy oak chest where, among other things, I keep the Smith & Wesson, its holster, and extra ammunition.

My misgivings began as I worked the old lock, twisting the key the way it should go, but locking the chest rather than unlocking it. Puzzled, I reversed the key to counterclockwise and felt the mechanism, which did need oiling, switch again, this time to open. Still, I confidently expected to find the weapon and its accoutrements in a lacquered box that fit snugly into one end of the chest.

Alas, the box was empty except for some bullets. With frantic incredulity, I rummaged through the rest of the chest's contents, mostly family memorabilia, Bibles, documents, framed photographs, several batches of letters, and an old passport I had been looking for.

"I think we need to go downtown," the sergeant said ominously. He meant police headquarters, even though they had been moved out to the bypass several years ago.

We came back down the two flights of stairs and I was overwhelmed by an impending sense of disaster, which rendered me weak in the knees and in my heart, which felt as though it had stopped beating.

At that moment, Diantha and Elsie came through the door, the former carrying a bag of groceries, the latter running toward me, signing ecstatically something about Momma getting frozen pops. Behind the kitchen door Decker barked.

I picked the little one up and held her close to me, as though it were she and not I who was in jeopardy.

"Diantha," I said, before greetings or explanations were offered, "do you know what happened to my revolver?"

Had she dropped the bag of groceries, it would have been utterly congruent with the expression of surprise, guilt, and an ineffectual attempt to dissemble both that brought color to her face. But she tried, convincingly enough for the two detectives.

"Your gun?" she said, her actor's training coming to the fore.

"My revolver. I kept it in the trunk."

"Norman, I don't . . ." But my dear wife did not have the capacity to be blatantly dishonest. She turned to the policemen. "I want to talk to my husband . . . alone."

The sergeant looked doubtful. Lieutenant Tracy said, "Of course."

We took Elsie and went into the sun-struck kitchen, its new fixtures gleaming now with a kind of mockery. Diantha took out a Popsicle to placate Elsie and a cookie for the dog. She looked me in the eye and said, "I loaned your revolver to Heinie."

"Good Jesus," I said, and sat down. "When? Why?"

"He was here . . . back in April."

"When? What date?"

"Early, mid-April. It was still chilly. He told me he needed a handgun for his boat. He said it had valuables on board and that he was thinking of sailing to the Bahamas."

"I didn't realize you were seeing him again."

"I wasn't. He came over here. I couldn't get him to leave . . ."

"Diantha . . ."

"Norman, I gave it to him to get rid of him more than anything else. I know I should have told you."

"No," I said coldly. "You should have asked me."

"Why is it so important?"

"The bullet that killed Heinie came from my gun."

"Oh, Norman, I am so sorry."

We rejoined the police in the living room. I cleared my throat. "Diantha tells me, and I believe her, that she loaned my revolver to Mr. von Grümh when he was here last."

"When was that?"

"Sometime in early to mid-April," I answered for her.

Almost gently, Lieutenant Tracy asked Diantha, "What did Mr. von Grümh tell you he needed the gun for?"

"Heinie said he wanted to keep it on his boat. He said he had valuables on board and that he would be sailing near the Bahamas."

Lemure made one of those facial gestures. "Sounds to me like something you both just cooked up."

"Why didn't he just get one of his own?" the lieutenant pressed.

Diantha said, "He told me he had had a scrape with the law. He had a wild time between his first and second marriages. He got involved with some druggie types. Anyway, he got a police record out of it."

Elsie dropped her Popsicle and Decker started licking it. She sniffled and tears started down her face.

"Just a minute, honey, I'll get you another one," Diantha soothed her. She excused herself to rustle in the grocery bag.

"Did anyone else know you gave the gun to Mr. von Grümh?" the lieutenant asked.

"No."

"Nothing like a receipt maybe? An acknowledgment? Correspondence?"

Diantha said, "I had e-mails from him. But I erased them. I don't think there was any mention of the gun in them. But maybe."

"So nothing?" The sergeant shook his head.

To one side, Elsie slurped on her pop. She held it up for me to see and with her other hand signed "orange."

The lieutenant gave a most human sigh. "I'm sorry, Norman, we're going to have to take you in."

The sergeant read me my rights with an edge of malice. Amazing how accusatory they sound. The right to remain silent.

I listened respectfully and then turned to Diantha. "Would you call Felix for me and tell him what's happened."

She nodded numbly and then erupted in tears and put her arms around me. "Oh, Norman. I'm so sorry. It's all my fault."

The sergeant took out a pair of handcuffs.

"They won't be necessary."

"I know. Just kidding." He turned to me, "But don't try anything stupid."

So I was not handcuffed except perhaps morally as they led me out to their unmarked car and ushered me into the backseat, Sergeant Lemure putting his hand on the top of my head to keep me from bumping it, a gesture I have seen in crime movies when the culprit is taken away.

Even good writers resort to the expression of "going into a daze." And that's exactly how it felt. Nothing seemed quite real, as though what was happening was happening to this other person, this other Norman Abbott de Ratour, who was to be charged with murder in the first degree.

The suspect docilely rolled his fingers in ink. He emptied the contents of his pockets — wallet, spare change, pen, small notebook, handkerchief — into a sealable plastic bag. He added his belt and shoes. He held up his trousers as he stood next to the vertical ruler marked in inches to have front and side shots of his sad, fazed face. He waited for a while in a holding cell with other suspects, a pathetic collection of defeated souls. He was finally shown into an individual cell, which had a fold-down bunk and a toilet and sink in the corner.

He paced around the enclosure like the trapped animal he was. There was no high, barred window through which he could glimpse the sky or natural light of any kind. No books or magazines, which, however dated and irrelevant, one finds while waiting for the doctor or the dentist. His plight closed around him. He sat on the hard cot and covered his face with his hands.

To be imprisoned is to experience a humiliation like no other. The bars and solid walls enclosing you are symbol and substance of your existence at that moment. You are caged. A chain around your neck welded to an eyebolt embedded in a cement wall could not be more definitive. You have no freedom. You are on display like a live exhibit. You are presumed dangerous. But, unlike you, the animals in a zoo are considered innocent, even those that might kill and devour a saint.

Not long afterward, Lieutenant Tracy dropped by and asked if I would be willing to answer some questions. He said I could wait for an attorney to be present. I demurred and we walked to an interrogation room smelling of futility and guilt and Sergeant

Lemure. I sat down in the chair indicated. They asked if I wanted coffee. I nodded, thinking an honest cup of bad coffee might help. It was brought in. They started.

"Do you want to tell us what really happened on the night of Heinie Grümh's death?"

I sighed. My shoulders slumped and my bones felt weak. A kind of hopelessness had begun to settle in.

"You're right, Lieutenant, I did leave out something. It's true that we left the pub on good terms, though I must say he was still in an agitated state. He mentioned at least twice that he had to meet someone. He kept looking at his watch."

They both waited impassively.

"When he offered me a lift back to the museum, I accepted."

"What time was that?" the sergeant asked.

"As I told you, just after eight, ten, fifteen past."

"Did you go to the museum's parking lot?" the lieutenant asked.

"No. He pulled into the drive that swings in front of the main doors. There's a basement entrance to one side."

"On Belmont?"

"Yes."

Again they waited, the lieutenant's eyes neutral, the sergeant's heavy face hostile with triumph.

"So what happened then?"

"He said he wanted to talk, and I told him I had to go. I could tell from his face that he was huffy, but I had had enough. I went for my walk in the arboretum."

"So how long did you walk in the arboretum?" the sergeant asked.

"Ten, fifteen minutes."

"And then?"

"When I came back, I started for my car in the parking lot. I hadn't gone very far when it occurred to me that I needed to close up the office. It was then that I noticed Heinie's car. I didn't recognize it and wouldn't have given it much thought, but the interior light went on and I saw who it was. I would have avoided him except that he saw me and called for me to come over to him."

"That must have been what, eight thirty?" the lieutenant said.

"I would think so."

"What happened at that point?"

"He opened the door for me to get in and began apologizing for burdening me with his problems. Which he continued to do, going on and on about Merissa Bonne and her affair with Max Shofar. But then he did say something that didn't make sense until later on."

"We're listening."

"He said that de Buitliér, you know, the curator of our Greco-Roman Collection, had been messing with him."

"Messing with him? What did he mean by that?"

"I don't know. I asked him, but he wouldn't tell me."

"Go on."

"When I began to open the door, he said he had something to show me. I watched as he reached over to the glove compartment. I was naturally alarmed to see that he had a revolver in his hand and was pointing it at my heart. 'I could shoot you, Norman,' he said. 'I could make it look like a suicide. No one would know.'

"I was amazed and scared, of course. 'Whatever for?' I asked. 'What have I ever done to you?' His face had a wild expression. He cocked the gun and said, 'You're out to ruin me. You and all the rest of them.' I was afraid he really would shoot me. I said to him, 'Heinie, I don't have any idea what you're talking about.' Then he brought up de Buitliér again. 'Sure you do. You and de Buitliér are in on this together.' I shook my head. 'Heinie,' I said, 'don't do anything foolish.' Or words to that effect. 'Don't destroy everything you have.'" I paused then in my narrative, trying to recall anything else that happened.

"So he obviously didn't shoot you," the sergeant remarked as though it were some kind of quip.

I ignored him and kept my eyes on the lieutenant. "Right then he just laughed. He said, 'You don't know, do you?' And I said, 'Don't know what?' But he just laughed again. I think I know now what he was referring to."

"What's that?"

"The fact he had my gun."

"You didn't recognize it?"

"No. One revolver of that type looks pretty much like every other." I paused. "Or, he could have been referring to the coins, the fact that they were forgeries."

"Yeah," the sergeant said dismissively. "Then what happened?"

I took a sip of coffee. "He grew even more . . . deranged. He told me he wanted to murder someone. When I asked him whom he wanted to murder, he interrupted me and said he wanted someone to murder him. He pushed the cocked weapon right into my ribs and, really, I thought that was it. I wouldn't even hear the shot."

"But obviously he didn't?" The sergeant again sounded snide.

I gave him as dismissive a glance as I could muster and said to the lieutenant, "He then turned the gun on himself, first at his heart and then at the side of his head. He said, 'Please help me do this.'"

"But you didn't?"

My face froze in a frown of confusion. Of course I didn't. But a venomous vapor of self-doubt clouded my mind. I couldn't tell them the truth: I had wanted, in my fear and loathing of the man — he had just threatened my life, after all — to hold the revolver to his head and fire it. "I couldn't have," I said weakly.

"But you're not sure?"

"You shot him because he was doing your wife," the sergeant snarled.

I looked beseechingly at the lieutenant. He shrugged. "What did you do then?"

"I told him to go home and get some help. I pushed open the door and turned my back on him. At least if he shot me then, I thought, he couldn't make it look like suicide."

"And that was the last time you saw him alive?"

"Yes."

"Then you went back to your office?"

"Yes."

"How long were you there?"

"Perhaps an hour."

"You know what I think happened?" the sergeant started in, leaning toward me until I could clearly see the pores on his thick nose. "I think you arranged to meet von Grümh in the parking lot. Maybe you only wanted to scare him off because you thought he would start up something again with your wife. Maybe you knew already about the fake coins. Whatever. You took your revolver along. You took it out and pointed it at him. Maybe he laughed at you. Maybe he said, Sure, go ahead, you can make it look like suicide. And you got mad because he was taunting you, making you feel like a wimp. So you put the gun up against his temple and pulled the trigger."

"No. No! I couldn't have."

"But you could have."

I took a moment. I collected myself. I said, "So why didn't I try to make it look like suicide?"

"But you couldn't have." The sergeant smirked at me. "It's your gun. You would have to explain how he got it."

"My wife will testify . . ."

"That's not good enough, Norman." The lieutenant spoke with a heavy sadness in his voice. "We have enough to take this to the DA and talk to him about a plea bargain."

"Richard, I swear, I didn't do it. I had no reason . . . Diantha was finished with him."

"How do you know?" the sergeant asked.

"I just know, that's all. I just know."

"Think it over, Norman. About the DA. This doesn't look good for you."

"Can I ask a question?"

The lieutenant nodded.

"Are you sure, absolutely sure, there were no powder burns on von Grümh's hands?"

With evident satisfaction, the sergeant shook his head slowly. "No way. I double-checked it. The GSR came up negative. Not a trace."

The lieutenant looked puzzled. "Why do you ask?"

"Because he was suicidal."

"I think you've got suicide on the brain," the sergeant said with a sneer. "It was murder, pure and simple."

Later I spoke on a phone through a barrier of reinforced glass to an attorney, a colleague of Felix Skinnerman. She was a brisk young woman in a business suit with an air of impersonality who told me she had arranged for a bail hearing that afternoon.

I was not interested in the lunch of chicken salad, potato salad, green salad, and ice cream. I was not interested in anything really, until, in a void deep enough to make me scream, I asked for paper and pencil, the original word processor, and wrote the following.

I feel in the wake of these admissions that I owe my readers an apology. In the relative privacy of this journal, I should have been completely candid. I really have no defense. I scarcely have an explanation. I did fear, I have to admit, that, were this document ever to be subpoenaed and placed in evidence, it and anything else I wrote could be used against me in court.

The truth will make you free. I understand and believe in that dictum. But the truth is not always self-evident. As it involves me in this matter, I am not entirely sure what the truth is. The fact is, I had fantasized more than once about murdering Heinie von Grümh. I had enacted on the stage of my mind precisely what happened to him in that car. I held my revolver to the side of his head, and, while he begged for his life, I taunted him.

Of course I would rouse myself from these dark dreams with an acute self-shame and a determination not to indulge them henceforth. But, once you've killed a man, as I have, it's not difficult to conceive of doing it again, to feel in your hand the heft of the weapon, to trigger the jolt of deadly power, to watch someone disappear into death.

Thus does imagination conflate with and confuse memory. In the syntax of what may or may not have happened, I cannot parse what I did from what I dreamed of doing. But, I tell myself, I did not kill my wife's lover. I'm sure of it. Until doubt, as right now, begins to seep in like a cold, deadly fog. Because, like Hamlet, I could accuse myself of such things it were better my mother had not borne me.

In brief, as I had the motive, the occasion, and the capacity to murder Heinie von Grümh, I must consider myself a suspect in this case until the murderer is found.

It pains me to realize that I have completely vitiated, through my lack of frankness, my friendship with Lieutenant Tracy. I fear I will also forfeit the trust the board has had in me as director. And while Diantha will no doubt continue to voice her support of me, I don't blame her if she is having second thoughts.

As, no doubt, are you, my reader and, next to God, who probably doesn't care, my final judge. Am I a reliable narrator? I am certainly not an omniscient one. Mostly, I fear that I have given you little basis to believe what I write in this account or, anywhere else, for that matter. To paraphrase a wordsmith far superior to me, if you don't believe me, I won't exist.

I would fain entreat you to consider me, at the very least, a naive narrator, one, that is, who doesn't have all the facts or know what to do with the ones he has. But in my own defense, would it not have been a more egregious naïveté to reveal in this journal everything I knew about the circumstances of Heinie's murder?

And was it really naive that I didn't know that my young wife, in the confused aftermath of her liaison with this man, would be so foolish as to lend him my revolver? (And I'll leave to those thus inclined to ponder the symbolistic implications therein.)

Even if the police believe Diantha's story, and I'm not sure they will, it's still my gun that killed the man. There is nothing I or any sort of defense witness can do to alter that fact. I am, to lapse into the argot, not so much an unreliable narrator as a screwed one. I am the naive, the unreliable, the shortsighted, the cuckolded, the venal, even the pompous narrator. But I swear on everything I hold holy that I am not an evil narrator.

Unless, of course, I did murder Heinie von Grümh.

(Felix, playing with my name, once pointed out that the lower-case French preposition it contains, if transformed, as it was in the case of Scotland's Robert the Bruce, into the English definite article, I become The N.A. Ratour. Which, under the circumstances, gives me little comfort.)

I have not been entirely honest, it's true. But I really did not recognize the death car on that morning when I discovered Heinie's body. I have a blind spot when it comes to cars and the vast, tedious subject of how people convey themselves from one place to another.

Yet I was truly more shocked than surprised to look through the rolled-up window to see the still form of the honorary curator. He had been most careless with my weapon the night before. I could at several points have taken it away from him. And there is a detail, a maddening, pertinent detail to this whole affair that I cannot for the life of me recall.

I scarcely know what I would have done without Felix. He showed up as the day began to wane along with hope of freedom before nightfall. He and his colleague had pushed for and gotten a bail hearing.

Jason Duff, the district attorney, a surprisingly young man

with gelled hair and a complexion of steroid pink, shuffled papers at the table to the right of Judge Arlen McHenry, who glared out from his perch with the jaundiced look of one who has spent a long life weighing human foibles.

The proceedings began so abruptly, I scarcely realized that Mr. Duff was claiming he had enough evidence to have me charged with first-degree murder and held without bail.

Counsel for the defendant demurred. "Your Honor, I can prove that my client, a longtime and respected person of this community, was not present at the time that Heinrich von Grümh died from a gunshot wound."

"Proceed, Mr. Skinnerman."

"Your Honor, the electronic records of the Museum of Man show that Mr. de Ratour entered the building at precisely eight fifty-four on the evening in question. They show that he did not leave the building until close to ten past ten PM."

"Your Honor . . ."

"Mr. Duff, you will have a chance to respond. Continue, Mr. Skinnerman."

"I would like to place those records in evidence, Your Honor, along with a copy of the preliminary report from the office of the coroner. According to Doctor Cutler, this report, based on body temperature, lividity, and the incipient state of rigor mortis, puts the time of death with 'high probability' at between nine fifteen and ten o'clock on the night in question."

District Attorney Duff's pinkness deepened. "Your Honor, the museum records are of negligible value. As director of the museum, the defendant could easily have rigged the system to show what he wanted it to show."

But Felix had another trick in his cards. "Your Honor, that is very unlikely. The alarm system at the museum is up to date and, according to the company that installed and maintains it, virtually tamper-proof. I would like to place in evidence a copy of the guarantee that Securart, the company in question, gave the museum upon installation of the new system."

"Your Honor, the defendant was in the vicinity at the time of the murder. He had a motive. And it was his revolver that fired the fatal bullet. And he has admitted that he has already killed one man with the weapon in question, a man, Your Honor, who, like the murder victim, had been carrying on with the woman he professed to love."

"Your Honor, the man my learned colleague is referring to was none other than Manfred Bannerovich, aka Freddie Bain. A criminal mastermind. And at the time, Your Honor, Mr. de Ratour was defending himself and the woman who was to become his wife."

The judge looked skeptical.

The district attorney shrugged. "Your Honor, a killing is a killing."

"Please approach the bench," the judge said, indicating both attorneys.

I waited with bated breath as they went back and forth with emphatic if lowered voices. Felix returned smiling. "Deal," he said. "We got it reduced to accessory to murder and a bail of fifty thousand dollars, which I'll take care of."

It wasn't until I stepped outside into a still-bright summer evening to face a knot of feisty reporters that I realized my troubles were only beginning. There should be a new case added to our description of English grammar — the accusative interrogative. Did I murder Heinie von Grümh? Was it a crime of passion? Was I going to resign now as director of the museum? Where was the missing murder weapon?

Such was my befuddlement at the moment, I nearly answered, *You know, I'm not sure I didn't murder him.*

7

It is a gorgeously warm, bright June day. The local *Cardinalis cardinalis* is in full throat along with other members of his class. The roses are primping for their triumphant, blushing glory. Honeysuckle scents the air. And I am living in hell.

Alone.

Out on bail, I returned home from police custody. Felix drove me through familiar and now estranged streets to what I thought would be the refuge of my home and family. I envisioned the scene. Diantha would be tearfully, fulsomely apologetic. I would hold her in my arms. I would comfort her. I would tell her that we would get through this together.

Life, alas, should never be rehearsed.

The remnant media included one of those television vans and a ten-year-old girl from her school newspaper. A police cruiser parked in front of the next house. I imagined the neighbors peering furtively through curtain slits at me as I profusely thanked Felix one more time and made my way through the unabashed reporters.

Diantha met me at the door not with a kiss but with finger to lips. "Elsie's asleep," she whispered and shut the door on the Third Estate. Still no kiss. No hug. I followed her into the kitchen where she was working at her computer.

"Just let me finish this one item," she said and focused on the screen.

The bell and then the phone rang.

"Oh, Norman, is there nothing we can do about those people outside?"

I said nothing. *Perhaps,* I thought, *she thinks a shared annoyance will bring us together. Or does she even care about that? Is this her way of diminishing the enormity of her betrayal?* Which enormity ballooned in my closing heart as I turned in stony silence and walked from the room.

I went up to my study. The chest where my weapon had been locked remained open, its contents askew. The sight revived the scene of my humiliation in front of Lieutenant Tracy, who had been my friend and colleague.

The telephone rang again. I ignored it. It rang again and again. I picked it up finally. A crank caller who said, "You're finished."

When it rang again, I went downstairs to a master switch that shuts off all incoming communications on a fat cable that serves telephones, television, and, I forgot, computers.

Diantha came storming at me. "Norman, what are you doing! I just lost several hours of work."

"You've lost more than that," I hissed at her.

Thus began a long bout of acrimony, accusation, bad feelings, and feeble attempts at reconciliation.

Over the next few days, I became a bear to live with. Not always outwardly. I could be agreeable, even cordial at times. But I could no longer bring myself to talk directly to Diantha, to engage her face and eyes. I took to sleeping in my study where an ample couch serves as a comfortable bed. I found excuses for avoiding regular meals, preferring to snack. I hid my worst thoughts under a thick layer of inner frost.

To explain it, I suppose I must take the blame. I cannot bring myself to forgive her for lending my revolver to Heinie von

Grümh without asking me or telling me. The offense is primal: You don't give a man's weapon to his rival, certainly not if you are the man's wife.

Her folly revived in the worst way her sexual betrayal with the man. I am not in the least inclined toward Freudian explanations, but I could not separate finally her granting him her womanhood and giving him, in a sense, my manhood. It had nothing to do with reality. I am not a man who fondles weapons to bolster his confidence. But in fact, did I not win Diantha with that gun by killing another man?

Fortunately, Elsie was napping when we had our knock-down drag-out. We've found that she hears perfectly well and understands a lot of what we say. She's also very sensitive to any conflict between us, however much we dissemble our disagreements.

I cannot recall the trifle that sparked the conflagration. We were in the kitchen, tiptoeing around each other, when I made some casual, wounding remark. Diantha erupted. "What do you want me to do, Norman? Bleed? I've apologized, haven't I? I know it was stupid to lend Heinie the gun, but, really, is it that big a deal?"

"Of course it's a big deal," I retorted, anger cracking through my mantle of ice. "Because of your . . . stupidity and your . . . lack of respect, I have been charged with a serious crime. My whole career is in jeopardy. My life's work . . ."

I felt reduced to pompous fatuities. At one point, I proclaimed, "Your love was your own to give, Di, even if it was pledged to me. Vows get broken. We've gone through that. But my revolver was not yours to dispose of."

Our verbal punches grew repetitive. Finally, with true pathos, Diantha said, "Norman, what do you want?"

And I could not tell her.

"Listen," she said, sounding a conciliatory note, "Felix told me the DA doesn't have the beginning of a case against you."

"When were you talking to Felix?" I could not conceal that twitch of alarm that precedes jealousy. Felix, newly married and all, was attracted to and attractive to good-looking women. And Diantha was certainly one of those.

She rolled her eyes. "He called last night looking for you. I told him you were out."

"The point being that it is immaterial what the merits of the case are. I have been charged, and in my position that is all that matters. You've seen the articles in the *Bugle,* on the radio, on the television. If the board doesn't support me, I will be finished, the museum will wither to nothing in the clutches of Wainscott, my whole life . . ."

"Jesus, Norman . . ."

"Yes, Jesus, Norman," I threw back in her face, turned and walked away.

I found that returning to work — the actual going there — took a certain amount of courage. I half expected to find my office barred to me, the locks changed, yellow police tape draped around the place.

Doreen, God bless her, welcomed me back with as big a hug as her very pregnant belly would allow. I swear she is going to have a litter. She had also brought in a small bouquet of flowers and put them on my desk. I had to hide my tearing eyes.

Outwardly, things seemed normal. I was not exactly shunned except in a couple of deplorable instances. Rather, people were just a little too nice, their smiles like sweetened grimaces. I came to expect the limp handshake, the averted face, the hurry to be away. They kept their distance, as though news had gotten around that I had contracted a disreputable and contagious disease.

But my real friends did not fail me. Izzy Landes called that first day back. He invited me to join him and Lotte at Albert's, an old-fashioned sort of place with an excellent cellar. I should have accepted considering what happened later. But I was in no mood for company, for either the avoidance of the topic or, more likely as the wine flowed, explanatory excess.

The Reverend Alfie Lopes came by unannounced and sat with me for nearly an hour, just chatting. He is a charming and, in his own way, a profound man. Not once did he allude to my difficulties. He simply sat and talked, drinking café au lait of a shade that matched his complexion. It was as though he were administering the balm of normality.

I've also gotten a note of support from Father S.J. O'Gould, S.J. After commiserating, he stated I could call on him at anytime for support, references, and any useful advice he might render.

I was surprised and not a little reassured to receive an e-mail expressing support from Harvey Deharo who, as Director of the Ponce, is a member of the Board of Governors. "Dear Norman," he wrote. "A quick note to let you know I am behind you one hundred percent. I think the savaging you have gotten from the *Bugle* has been nothing less than scandalous, and I have written to the editor saying as much. Call me anytime and let me know anything else I can do to help you. Yours fondly, Harvey."

Support of that kind is more than academic. I spoke to Robert Remick, Chairman of the Board and an old family friend. He has been unfailingly polite and sympathetic, but I can tell he is worried. Old Wainscott alumni have been calling him with all kinds of questions.

"I have polled the other members of the board and convinced them that you are innocent until proven guilty, Norman," he said. "But one more embarrassing incident and we will have to consider placing you on administrative leave and appointing an acting director."

Which would be the end. The jury of public opinion would see to it.

That same afternoon I received a squirrelly little note from the Wainscott President's office saying that my participation in this year's commencement exercises would not be welcome. Each year, for decades now, I have donned my particular plumage to join in the self-congratulatory mardi gras of the academy — what are honorary degrees, after all?

Strange how academics and their administrative keepers, for all their rhetoric about freedom and for all their freedom — the whole point of tenure, after all — can be so pusillanimous when it comes to respectability. But then so many of the faculty these days are the new Babbitts, such unapologetic careerists as to make corporate executives blush.

Of course, I see the machinations of Malachy Morin in all this. His problem will be how to get this news into the media without making Wainscott look as petty as it has become.

I stayed late at work. I took a stroll around the galleries after closing time. The unfailing aesthetic bliss rendered by these timeless objects is like oxygen to one's soul. I stopped and meditated for a while in front of the seagoing canoe of Polynesian origin. Here, in one object, is distilled the spirit, courage, and intelligence of a remarkable people. In such contemplation, my horizons widened and time stretched so that I and my problems shrank to liberating insignificance.

I would have gone home, but I could not face the queasy peace of an improvised reconciliation. Instead, I decided to go to the Club, which has been my refuge through so many troubles.

Quelle difference! The headwaiter, a man with pomaded hair and a waxed mustache, a man with whom I have been generous in the past, studiously ignored me as I stood waiting for a table. When I finally protested, he showed me to a place in a corner near the kitchen entrance that felt like it had been reserved for pariahs. As he led me there, people I knew casually — faculty, staff, administrators — people who acknowledged my presence in the past with friendly enough hellos, pretended not to notice me.

Once seated, though the place was hardly busy, I was again ignored. I glanced around, trying to catch the eye of a waiter. But to no avail. I sat and fumed. I wrote letters in my head to the management, withdrawing the museum's institutional membership and the hefty support that went with it. I scowled. I wanted to tip my table over with a crash and storm out of the place.

I suppressed an impulse to go to the headwaiter and tell him that he was a jerk of the first order and walk out with dignity. But I managed to calm down. I began to understand in some small measure what Jews, blacks, and other historically despised groups had suffered over the years. Not that it helped a whole lot to place my hands on the table before me, bow my head, and submit to this exercise in public shame.

It wasn't humility that finally made me hold my head up and wait; it was pride. I knew who and what I was, and that was all that mattered. When I had had enough, I rose and, with as much dignity as I could muster, quietly walked out of the place.

In the wake of this small debacle, things at home came to a head. We had a cruel exchange in which I drew tears if not blood. Diantha asked me, as it were a matter of idle curiosity, if I had murdered Heinie.

Again that question caught me off balance. My automatic "Of

course not" sounded hollow, and fear of possible guilt seized my heart along with a recollection of the awful wrath that could have made me murderous. I chafed that wound, nearly wanting the pain of it as I snarled, "Did you talk to him about using it on me?"

For a moment something akin to shock registered in her swollen eyes. She said, "Never." Then she gave me a look of sincere loathing. "For Christ's sake, Norman, I've tried to explain. It was a fling. It wasn't even that. I was bored. I drank too much. I smoked some dope. I couldn't wait to get away from him. The second time . . . He begged. He turned pathetic. It was a . . . mercy f*ck."

"I wish I could believe you, Diantha," I said quietly. "I wish . . ."

"What do you wish?"

Her tone of bored annoyance maddened me. I couldn't resist saying what I had said before. "You told me, you swore that you had stopped seeing that ridiculous man."

"So that's what it comes down to. I screw a guy a couple of times and you can't get over it."

"You swore to me you wouldn't see him again unless I was there."

"Look, I wasn't seeing him like that. I never 'saw' him after that stupid weekend on the boat. He kept calling. What could I do, close the door in his face? So I gave him a drink and listened to him complain yet again about Max and Rissa. He knew you had a gun. He said he needed it to protect himself because he thought they were plotting to have him murdered . . ." She broke off as though having said something she meant not to.

She quickly resumed. "Anyway, It was getting late in the afternoon and I didn't want you to come home and find him here. So I said screw it and gave him the gun just to get rid of him. How was I to know someone would get it from him and shoot him with it."

I might have missed her lapse had not my penchant for sleuthing twitched into operation. I took a moment to calm myself. "Diantha," I said with as much quiet authority as I could muster, "please tell me everything you know about Max and Merissa and what Heinie said about them."

It only exacerbated things. "God, Norman, please don't play detective with me."

"Diantha, I am not playing anything with you. You told me before that he needed the gun to protect things on his boat. Now you say he wanted it because he felt threatened by Max and Merissa."

"I thought I told you that before."

"No, you didn't. But isn't Max well off if not wealthy?"

"Yeah, maybe. But Heinie told me he had found out through friends that Max had lost a bundle on some sort of Franklin Mint coin deal. You know, a replica of an old gold dollar. He didn't lock it in when the price of gold was a lot lower than it is now. It kept rising, making the thing too expensive for most collectors. The ones that watch television ads. Anyway, he lost his investment."

It all fit neatly. Max loses a bundle. He takes up with Merissa, and then murders Heinie for his money. It fit too neatly. "I'm not sure it signifies," I said. "Still, I wish you had told me."

"I suppose I should have." Her tone, like mine, had grown conciliatory. Then she said, "Norman, I think I'm going to take Elsie and spend some time at the cottage."

I nodded, not wanting her to say what she said anyway.

"I really can't stand being around you when you're like this."

"Like what?"

She shrugged again. "I don't know. You don't trust me anymore. You don't look at me anymore. You don't touch me or smile. I feel like a . . . leper. In my own house."

I wanted to protest, but I knew she was right. Better than I, she understood that this latest betrayal revived the other one. Although our life together had resumed quickly and facilely after her affair, the wound had yet to heal completely. Now it opened again, magnified into something allied with the tangible consequences I faced.

I understood what she meant because I could barely stand being around myself. I felt like the road of my life had turned into a dead end after all. Worse, an ambush. I stood and took her by the hands. "Let's not lose each other," I said. "Go, but don't go."

She collapsed against me tearfully. "I'll go and not go," she repeated. "Just for a while. If you need me, I'll be there. I'll wait for you." She turned away, wiping away tears, and I already missed her.

We began the sad task of splitting up, however temporarily, sorting through stuff for her and Elsie to take with them for an extended stay at the cottage. I helped Diantha load her big vehicle. It tore at my heart and almost made me relent, to watch her and Elsie drive away.

So I'm alone in this great shack of a house, licking my wounds like some trapped and dying beast. I did make a large and powerful martini to assist me in my self-pity. But I only took a sip before placing it in the freezing compartment of the refrigerator. Because . . .

Because I have found self-delusion is preferable to self-pity — if only because the former can lead to action whereas the latter leads to more of itself. Thus, for a few heady moments, I saw myself as the character who, falsely accused, must venture forth to prove his own innocence. I made a mental note to drop by the Coin Corner and have a chat with Max Shofar.

At least for now the reporters have gone. It appears there's been a suicide that the police are investigating. According to the *Bugle,* the body of Martin Sterl, who recently sold his high-tech firm for a tidy bundle, was found slumped over the wheel of his Mercedes by his young wife of some six months. "Although an apparent suicide, police are treating it as a suspicious death."

That may be a sop to the man's children by his first wife. In a tearful appearance at a press conference I happened to watch on television, the man's grown daughter vehemently denied that her father had committed suicide. "I talked to Dad the day before. I'd never seen him happier. Except for that . . . woman . . ."

As for *that woman,* the news clip showed a petite, pixie-haired gamine in black averting her eyes from the camera. How well I know that response. At the same time, I realized that I had seen her before. The name Stella Fox did not ring a bell. And I had met but did not know her late husband, who had been much older than she. But where had I seen her? The recollection tantalized. I racked my memory. I cut her picture out of the *Bugle.* I went online and copied the news footage of her in dense shades as she hurried away from the blaze of lights. I studied them. Of course it may be just that my detecting instincts had been triggered. Not, I told myself, that I didn't have a far more pertinent mystery to solve.

8

Alphus has come to stay with me for the time being. Despite our best efforts, no suitable place has been found to lodge the animal, a word I use with inner quotation marks. I went over to Sign House with every intention of telling Millicent Mulally that Alphus would have to go back to the Pavilion with the other chimps. I was going to tell her that she and other members of Sign House could have visiting rights, could even come and take him out for afternoon forays. But I now understand exactly what she means: It would be like sending an innocent man back to jail.

It's not simply that he and Millicent exchange signals at a rapid and decisive pace; he responds appropriately whenever I say anything vocally to him. I did some signing, but I couldn't follow all of his deft answers, a problem I have when practicing my awkward French on native speakers.

In person, the first impression Alphus gives is of a hairy, good-natured individual. His clear, amber eyes are deep-set beneath thick supraorbital ridges. His brow slopes back to thick, coarse hair, which he parts in the middle and which might be reminiscent of an old-fashioned style except that he combs it over his ears to minimize their marked protuberance. He has freckled skin that ranges from tawny to dark, an insignificant nose with small nostrils, and a prominent upper lip that bows out over a wide mouth set in what appears to be a permanent smile. A bristly beard, flecked with gray, frames his face and covers his slightly receding chin. The habit he has of resting an index finger against his cheekbone makes him appear thoughtful.

Which I found him to be. Indeed, Dr. Simone had told me not to be surprised at his intelligence. It turns out he had been involved in a risky procedure conducted by the demented Dr. Gottling when he was trying to genetically engineer a new human prototype. The operation, something called peripheral vascular angioplasty, killed two of Alphus's fellow chimps but apparently worked for him. It is a procedure in which a catheter is inserted into the main artery leading to the head. A balloon is then introduced into the catheter and inflated in successive stages along the artery, enlarging it and concomitantly increasing the flow of blood to the brain.

One of his Pavilion mates went utterly mad and had to be euthanized in the recovery room. One died of a brain hemorrhage, and Alphus, already a very bright animal, underwent what one researcher called an increase in intelligence of several magnitudes. Once he had recovered from the procedure, it became obvious to everyone involved that he had become not merely smart but smart by human standards. Indeed, it was this enhanced IQ that allowed him to escape.

We were sitting in the small parlor of Sign House each with a cup of tea when I told them what my original intentions were. They both listened gravely. Then, when I said I had changed my mind, they gave each other that raised slapping handshake you see athletes using.

We discussed practical details. Alphus understands that if he leaves the house unattended he will be apprehended, forcibly if necessary, by the authorities. Millicent told me in simple signage that Alphus had friends at Sign House who would be willing to come over from time to time, especially during the day, to keep him company and take him for walks.

She then quickly wrote a message on what looks like a pocket computer and showed it to me. It read, "A. has a very close friend named Ridley living here. He is a very nice young man, but he is still not quite mature enough to have him be responsible for A."

She showed the communication to Alphus. He nodded.

At that point we went around the house, meeting some of the residents, including Boyd Ridley. A stocky young man with blondish hair, a handsome broad face, and blue eyes touched with glints of manic mischief, Ridley, as he likes to be called, hails from a prominent and quite wealthy family in Tennessee. He is also mathematically gifted, according to Millicent.

We packed Alphus's belongings — a lot of CDs, books, and clothes, including some shirts, two ties, and a suit jacket. When I noticed him carefully wrapping a bottle of expensive single-malt Scotch, I looked quizzically at Millicent. But she just shrugged.

I won't deny I found it unsettling to have a chimpanzee sitting next to me in my ancient Renault with his seat belt buckled on. But then, even with people gawking and pointing at us, it quickly grew to seem normal. Especially when, indicating the radio and signing "okay?" he tuned in the local classical station and we listened to a Brahms clarinet trio.

"Nice place," he signed as we entered my empty house.

I had planned to let him have what had been, in my parents' day, the maid's small room. Located toward the back of the house, it has its own minimal bathroom and a narrow stairway leading into the kitchen.

Alphus looked at me dubiously. He shook his head. He pointed to the door leading up to the attic. "Can I look?" he signed.

I said why not and led him up. I didn't want to give up my own eyrie. But he wasn't interested in that. He went directly across a jumbled storage area to a door that opened into a small round room, the upper part of the turret that had been stuck on the house in Victorian times. "Okay?" he asked.

I said fine. An hour later, we had the room, also full of odds and ends, cleared and even cleaned using the vacuum and a damp rag. There was an electrical outlet and a table, but not much else.

I took out a notebook and wrote, "We can get you a mattress for the floor, if that's okay?"

He shook his head. From a duffel I hadn't noticed, he took a hammock and two strong screw-in hooks. With admirable skill and real strength, he twisted the hooks into the sloping rafters of chestnut high above the floor. On these he slung the hammock, which was made of closely netted cord. On this he spread a down comforter with a leaf-green cover. He turned to me and signed "leopards." When I didn't get that, he signed "big," hands together then pulled apart; "cat," hand pulling at figurative mustache; and "spots," closed fist held next to face, then pointing with index finger. When I didn't quite get that, he spelled it out for me, letter by letter.

I explained to him that there were no leopards loose in Seaboard. And that, even if there were, they wouldn't be able to get into the house at night as all the doors and windows are secured.

He wagged his finger at me and shook his head. The tedium of having to explain the obvious came across in his signing, which had slowed down and become exaggerated. Patiently, he told me that there were leopards everywhere, we just don't see them. Not only that, but there was virtually no place they couldn't get into. He told me he remembered how they were even in cities, right in people's houses.

I nodded as though I understood.

Now all I had to do was explain to Diantha that we had a

fellow primate living with us. Despite our tearful departure, our telephonic relations had not gone as well as I had hoped. Long-distance reconciliation between a loving couple lacks the opportunities for those more convincing expressions of body language.

After stalling around, checking e-mails and other stuff, I finally called the cottage. No one answered to my great relief, as the possibility of a cold response made me timid. The relief proved short-lived.

"Norman!" she exclaimed in calling me back. "I was just thinking about you. We miss you. Elsie told me this morning she wants to go home however much she loves the lake. And Decker's been asking about you."

"Of course, darling," I said. "But I'd like to come out there. For a weekend."

"But that's three whole days away."

I hemmed and hawed. I played detective. Casually, as though it had just occurred to me, I said, "I don't want to bring up a sore subject, but could you tell me exactly what Heinie said when he asked to borrow the revolver?"

Into her silence, I quickly added. "I think it's important because, as you know, the coins in the collection he gave the museum have turned out to be fakes."

"Well, let's see. He did mention that he was using the boat to store some valuable things. I mean as well as sailing into dangerous waters. He said he couldn't get a license for a gun. But you know that."

"But he didn't say what the valuables were?"

"No. Why?"

"I was just thinking. Perhaps that's where the originals are."

"What would it prove?"

"I don't know. I'm trying to figure this thing out myself. I'm wondering how it might tie in with a motive."

When she fell silent again, I went on, "By the way, you saw the news about the apparent suicide of Martin Sterl?"

"I did."

"Did you recognize his widow at all? Have we seen her anywhere?"

"No. Why do you ask?" Her voice had cooled. She knew me well enough to know I was delaying telling her about something important or unpleasant.

"Because I've seen her before and I can't remember where."

"You see lots of people, Norman. Hundreds, perhaps thousands of people come into the museum every week."

A tiny, muffled bell rang in my mind, but then I was distracted as Diantha sighed audibly and said, "Oh, Norman, are we going to be all right?"

"I hope so."

"We want to come home. We miss you."

It was my turn to sigh. I said, "I know. But there's been another development here that you should know about."

"I don't care . . ."

"Well, it's Alphus."

"Alphus?"

"He's the chimp that has been living at Sign House. You know, the one who got loose about year ago."

"The one that killed and ate what's-her-name's dog?"

"Right. Well, it seems that the young woman, the deaf one, the one that took care of him, is getting married. And he really is a remarkable animal. I mean, there's no way, really, we can put him back in the Pavilion . . ."

"What are you trying to say."

"I'm saying that he may have to spend some time here."

"In our house?"

"Yes."

"For God's sake . . ."

"Diantha, listen, he's not . . ."

"You're going to have that ape living in our house . . . ?"

"It's not . . ."

"Norman, did you see what he did to that little dog . . ."

"Yes, but . . ."

"You want to subject Elsie and me to that . . . that animal?"

"Diantha, I'm looking for an alternative situation. It will only be for a short time . . ."

"God, Norman, sometimes I think you're just weird." And hung up. Or punched off. Or whatever people do these days to disconnect.

That's it, I thought. I made my way up the stairs. I was going to let the poor creature know that he couldn't stay. But there he was in his little room, sitting at the table on a chair I had provided for him, bent over his laptop and slowly, painfully, with one finger, tapping out a message to someone.

Over the next few days, I found living with Alphus to be both more challenging and more rewarding than I could have envisioned. To start with basics, I would like to report that he keeps himself very well groomed. He likes to shower and I'm sure the electric bill will reflect the amount of time he spends using the blow-dryer. He goes through a lot of shampoo and other toiletries. Not long after his arrival here, I found that a bottle of expensive cologne that I keep in the bathroom, a gift from Diantha, had been nearly depleted. Small wonder he has been shuffling around the house smelling like a royal pimp.

At meals he sits at the table and dines with a knife and fork. He likes his steak rare, but is perfectly happy with pasta and the house tomato sauce with lots of cheese on top. He is capable of making himself a respectable sandwich, which he eats carefully, dabbing at his mouth with a napkin. But it will be awhile before I let him use the stove unattended.

Alphus is a voracious and eclectic reader, and he often has the television on with the sound off while dipping in and out of a book. Yesterday I came home to find him watching something called the Jerry Springer show while perusing Nietzsche's *The Birth of Tragedy*. He was quite taken by the antics of Mr. Springer's guests, two obese white women fighting over an equally obese black man. "Look, look!" he gesticulated. "They're worse than chimpanzees!"

He spends a lot of time listening to classical music when he doesn't have the television on. He is particularly taken with Schubert, especially his chamber music. The String Quartet in D can move him to tears, or his equivalent thereof. He has one of those pod devices barely larger than a deck of cards into which he has packed hours of music, which he plays through a set of small but powerful speakers. At the same time it is unnerving to see him bend over and lope along on all fours.

He certainly has a mind of his own. For one thing, he is not nearly as tolerant as one might expect. He has a low opinion of dogs — "fawning curs" he spelled out for me on his laptop. And he is downright bigoted about gorillas. "They have no class. They are the primate equivalent of bovids. What have they ever contributed to the world? All they do is sit around eating vegetation and shitting. Koko gets all that attention, but she's nothing special."

When I gently suggested that people might say the same thing about chimpanzees, he grew visibly indignant. "You must be joking. Chimps played a leading role in the American space program. Not only that, but we have made our mark in Hollywood and in other forms of entertainment. The advance of modern medicine is impossible to imagine without our participation. After elephants, we are the most visited exhibit in many great zoos. No less an authority than Jared Diamond has suggested that chimps and humans be classed in the same genus. We didn't just come down out of the trees. And what have gorillas contributed? King Kong?"

Contributed to what? I wondered but did not ask.

Like all of us, Alphus is tormented from time to time by the larger questions of existence. Why are we here? Where are we going? One evening, over snifters of single-malt for him and a decent brandy for me, he asked me, "What exactly is the soul?"

I held my cognac up to the light and stared into its pale depths. "The soul," I said, trying for a *bon mot,* "is something we may or may not have but can definitely lose."

"That doesn't make sense."

"Okay, call it our inner essence, our moral core. Christians, a lot of Christians, believe it survives death and lives forever."

"Forever?"

"Forever."

"Sounds hellish."

So that, by degrees, we got onto the subject of religion. "I don't know about God or any of that," he said without preamble, "but I do sense wonder all around me. I remember feeling that all life is sacred even before the procedure that opened my mind to real thoughts."

I nodded in agreement. "I've often thought in agreement with Father O'Gould, whom you should meet, that there are degrees of divinity in everything, even inert matter."

Alphus nodded dubiously. "I've been reading up on the 'great' religions," he signed with a world-weary tone to his movements. It was then that he stated why Islam didn't interest him. For that declaration he had to teach me the signing for "Islam."

"Why not?" I asked.

"It's too total. Too intense. And I'm not interested in virgins."

I didn't respond as I could tell he was on the point of another observation. Instead, he asked me, "Why are you a Christian?"

"I was brought up to be one," I said, knowing that wouldn't satisfy him. "Why? Have you thought of it yourself?"

He sipped his malt and put it down. He nodded. "I have thought a lot about it. Christianity has many marvelous things about it. The music alone . . ." He spelled out Bach, Handel, Rutter.

"Rutter?" I questioned.

"He's contemporary. Someone played his Christmas music at Sign House. Then there's the art and the architecture. I would love very much to see Hagia Sophia. To think it was built in the sixth century." He paused and looked at me with that face of his.

"But," I provided.

"But I'm not particularly reassured by a creed one of the central metaphors of which is that of a shepherd and his flock."

"Really?"

"Not when you consider what happens to most sheep."

"Hmmm," I hummed, unable to think of a telling rebuttal. "It certainly puts Bach's *Sheep May Safely Graze* in a new perspective." I sipped from my own drink and came up with the predictable, "Have you considered Buddhism?"

"Very seriously. *Mudras*—" He stopped to spell it out for me. "—are, after all a form of nonverbal communication." He got off the sofa where he had been sitting and sat on the carpet with his legs folded in front of him, his posture erect, his right hand turned up on his lap, fingers together, and his left hand palm up with the fingers extended. "This is called the *Varada Mudra*. It symbolizes charity, compassion, and boon granting."

I was impressed. "Then why not become a Buddhist?" I said

as he resumed his seat on the sofa and picked up his drink.

After a moment he freed his hands. "To be honest, I don't like the kind of people Buddhism attracts. Mostly the kind of white people, that is."

"Hinduism?"

"Too many deities."

"Okay, then what about Judaism?" I asked, more or less to complete the catalog of major faiths.

He shook his head. "Jews worship themselves. And I am not a Jew."

The tone of his gestures made me glance at him sharply. Did I have an anti-Semitic ape on my hands?

"You mean that they are devoted to their history, their traditions, their prophets, their laws . . ."

"No. I mean they worship themselves. But in that they are merely exemplary of humankind as a whole, humankind with its deep, unquestioned, and doting self-love."

Food for thought does not always taste good, however nourishing it may prove. I chewed over Alphus's observations, thinking I could come up with a different recipe (to work this trope into the ground), but found myself stymied. How to explain religion to a member of another species without sounding absurd or disingenuous?

"But," I started.

He waved me aside. "Do you actually believe in any of this stuff?"

I am generally reluctant to talk about my personal beliefs in final things, mostly because I find it difficult to separate the eschatological from a species of the scatological, as used in a figurative sense. But in this case I thought it incumbent upon me to defend the Judeo-Christian legacy of which I consider myself a beneficiary.

Speaking slowly and deliberately, I said, "Unlike many of my contemporaries, Alphus, I do not have any difficulty in believing in God. Rather, I fear that God does not believe in us. If we are indeed made in the image and likeness of the Almighty, as the Good Book tells us, we may well be something of a disappointment. I wonder at times if we and the world, in the grand scheme of things, may be little more than a petri dish gone bad."

Alphus nodded. "Certainly for the rest of life on the planet." Then, "Yet still you pray?"

His incredulity, as expressed in the emphatic way he moved his hands, daunted me. I nodded as though admitting to some embarrassing personal habit.

"What do you pray for?"

I took a moment to cast back to the last time I had been in church. I had been half sitting, half kneeling toward the back of St. Cecilia's on that Sunday. I go there for solace and to dwell on the larger imponderables of life and because I take pleasure in the restrained, High Church grandeur of the stained-glass windows that surmount and light the altar beneath the vaulting web of age-darkened beams.

On that occasion I'd had much to pray for. I asked the Lord to keep Diantha and Elsie safe, healthy, and happy. *Dear God,* I had prayed, *grant me the grace to forgive Heinie von Grümh whom I continue to despise, even in death. I know I should hate the sin and not the sinner, but I'm afraid I've gotten it backward. Please let me know with moral certainty that I did not murder that wretch, that poor excuse for . . . Forgive me. And help me forgive all who may have trespassed against me.*

I said to Alphus, "I prayed for the power of forgiveness."

"Forgiveness," he signed and shook his head. "That is too human for me."

9

Little has changed at work, except for Feidhlimidh de Buitliér, who has begun to act like he's about to take over. The man, always tireless in his committee work, especially on the Council of Curators, has just been elected the Executive Moderator of that body for a second term. I will admit he has the courage of his small ambitions. No peak is too insignificant for him to climb.

It's an evolving situation. I exist in a fog of rumors, most of them about me, about the Board of Governors, about moves Wainscott might make. It's true I'm still the boss. But you can tell, in a dozen subtle ways, who is for you and who against.

It was certainly that way at the meeting of the Oversight Committee, which I felt compelled to attend, if only to defend myself. Indeed there seemed to be surprise that I should deign to show up at all in my fallen state.

Chair Brattle lost little time in making her own view known regarding my legal status. She had scarcely gaveled the meeting to order when she said, "I mean this in no way personally, Mr. de Ratour, but I wonder, under the circumstances, just how appropriate your presence here is at this time."

I asked, "Are you suggesting I leave?"

"I think that may be best for all concerned."

Izzy Landes, the dear man, stood up, his face flushed with anger. "If Norman is made to leave, I will leave as well. And I won't come back. Indeed, I will start a committee to investigate this committee. And put it out of business."

Father O'Gould also rose to signify his agreement. Then the Reverend Lopes and Corny Chard. Then Bertha Schanke, who said in an aside, "Let's face it, half of Wainscott's big benefactors are under indictment. Or should be."

The chair withdrew her suggestion.

But I was utterly unprepared for an attack from an entirely different quarter. The new member, Laluna Jackson, chair of the Victim Studies Department, presented a report, as she called it, about the Museum of Man. Her voice emphatic in the style of African Americans, her cornrows tied with things that clacked as she gestured with her head, she read, "Not long ago, I conducted a lengthy examination of the Museum of Man and its exhibits with one of our visiting professors. And I must say that the scales fell from my eyes.

"As my colleague pointed out to me, that institution could just as well be called the Museum of White Male Victimization. Everywhere you look you see the detritus of the white male scourge that has made the planet such a living hell for all other peoples. That museum is a catalog of victimization. Everywhere you look there is nothing but the loot of imperialism. In the most brazen manner, it unapologetically documents how the world peoples had their cultures stolen from them lock, stock, and barrel."

In listening to this poisonous nonsense, it occurred to me that I remain a member of the committee to remind myself, if reminders were necessary, why I do not want the museum to become an integral part of the university.

I let the woman spew on in this vein until she appeared to have exhausted her venom. Into an uncomfortable silence, I said, "I'm assuming that, even though a white male, I might be allowed to respond."

Amazingly, Chair Brattle appeared to consider my request

as though on its merits. Until, coming to her senses, she said, "Of course. You're still a member of the committee in good standing."

"*Ex officio,* to be exact," I said. "As you have all heard me say before, this is a Wainscott body and I attend its meetings in order to continue the mutually enriching relations that exist between the two institutions. Among other reasons."

I turned directly to the dean. "Tell me, Professor Jackson, how long have you been at Wainscott?"

She feigned puzzlement at the question. "Nearly seven years in one capacity or another. What relevance has this?"

"And was this the first time you visited the Museum of Man?"

"Well, yes. What does this . . . ?"

"Let us say that I find your lack of curiosity of a piece with your narrow, ignorant, and mean-spirited view of my museum . . ."

"Mr. Ratour . . . ," she began.

"Please. Allow me to respond to the pile of rubbish you have dumped on the table."

"Here, here," said the Reverend Lopes, voicing what I hoped to be the general sentiment of the committee members.

I took a breath and calmed down. "I won't try to rebut the statements of Professor Jackson as they are too absurd to be taken seriously. But I would like to say, as I have on other occasions, that the Museum of Man has and will continue to show the public that human beings everywhere and at all times, through their art and artifacts, are not mere creatures, but creators and as such partake of the godliness that is our common legacy. The exhibits you label as trophies are nothing less than solid testimony that beauty is innate to our species whatever level of formal technology or material culture we happen to occupy."

"Amen," said Izzy Landes. "I couldn't have put it better myself, Norman."

The chair rapped her gavel. "We need to move on to some pressing matters . . ."

I subsided into my seat, but continued to fume inwardly. This was what civilized discourse had descended to — cultural correctness gone amok and certified fools elevated to positions of authority. Of course there's been victimization. The Romans overran the Gauls who became French, who helped overrun the Chinese who stayed Chinese and overran the Tibetans who, given half a chance . . . Man hands on misery to man . . .

At the same time, her remarks struck a nerve. Conquest always involves inventory, be it appreciative or dismissive. Papuans do not collect Rembrandts, not yet, anyway. We judge and select because we are, for the nonce, more powerful whether we want to admit it or not.

I slowly calmed down and retreated into my own thoughts as the committee pondered with gravity one absurdity or another. I had much to think about. Mostly, I realized, I was anxious to help the investigation into the murder of von Grümh. To this end, sitting there, feigning attendance, I let my mind run through a maze of conjectures with all of their dead ends. I am desperate to find who killed the man in large part to eliminate the possibility that I am the one who did it.

On the notepad of my mind, I wrote: All of the suspects had motives. All of us had the opportunity. And Heinie, it would seem, had provided them with the means. What I couldn't shake was the notion that someone had shot him with his consent. And that could have been any number of people. Merissa. Col Saunders. Max Shofar. Myself. Even a bad Samaritan in the guise of a passing pedestrian. Because murder is, after all, murder.

Someone on the committee was about to make a motion. I

glanced at my watch, stood up, and said, "I'm afraid I have a prior engagement. With my PO."

There were puzzled glances. "His probation officer," Bertha said, and laughed to let the frowning ones in on the joke.

Back in my office I put in a call to Lieutenant Tracy and left a message regarding my suspicions about von Grümh's boat and the possible location of the real collection. No response. I suppose I should accept it. I have been charged with accessory to murder, after all. I am out on bail. I could go to prison. I am not someone the lieutenant can relate to except as a suspect.

I was at a very low point when I came home to find a message from Diantha asking me to call her at the cottage. Her voice sounded friendly and enticing, which surprised and elated me as we hadn't spoken since I told her that Alphus was staying at the house.

"How are you, Norman," she asked when I returned the call. "Elsie misses you."

"I miss her very much." We both knew that we were using Elsie as a kind of proxy for our own feelings, our love for her being unconditional.

"What I want to tell you, Norman, has to do with Heinie's murder and may be of some help."

"Okay."

"But I don't want to talk on the telephone."

"I see."

"Can we meet?"

"We can. Do you have a sitter?"

"Bella's here."

As Ridley was already at the house to keep an eye on Alphus, though, frankly, I'm not sure who keeps an eye on whom with those two, I said yes and mentioned a roadhouse with dinky little cabins about halfway between the cottage on the lake and Seaboard. We agreed to have dinner there together.

I showered and shaved my already smooth face. I fussed with what to wear, making myself sporty in a short-sleeved button-down oxford, a pair of Levi's she had given me, a chino safari jacket with shoulder tabs, and loafers with no socks. I wanted to look the part.

Diantha was there when I arrived, sitting at the bar with a glass of pale wine. She wore one of those thin summery dresses that cling just a little, along with a light green sweater that she draped on her shoulders like a cape.

Our greeting kiss lingered. She put a hand on my thigh as I sat on the barstool next to hers and ordered a Jack Daniel's and soda, no ice, and easy on the soda. Though a decent if ramshackle kind of restaurant, I didn't trust them to make an acceptable martini.

So we cooed *tête-à-tête* over our drinks until a waitress with a knowing eye, *real lovers these two,* led us to a table off by ourselves. We ordered a bottle of *vin* not entirely *ordinaire* and two of the steaks being grilled on the barbecue outside.

Diantha leaned toward me and turned serious. "Okay, here's what Merissa told me a couple of nights ago. She drove out to the cottage and we had a few drinks. And when Merissa has a few drinks, well, she likes to talk."

Diantha hesitated. I reached across the table and took her hand, as though that might steady and encourage her. She took in a breath. "Merissa told me that Max talked about getting rid of Heinie. I mean she didn't actually use the word *murder,* but that's what she meant. With Heinie gone, she would not only be free, but very wealthy."

"When did she say all this?"

"A couple of weeks before he was found dead."

"Are you sure it was Max who initiated the idea?"

She lifted the glass of wine to her lips and paused. "That's a good question. It could have been her. She was the one who brought it up in our conversation. At first, I thought she was joking, but now I'm not sure."

I remembered the strange look of excitement and surprise, the double take, when the lieutenant and I had driven out to tell her about Heinie's murder. How she had said, "He wouldn't."

"How was it supposed to happen?"

"Oh, they had several scenarios . . ."

"They?"

"Oh, yes, Merissa was in on it, too."

"Go on."

"Anyway, Heinie drank a lot, and they thought they could doctor a bottle of whiskey on his boat so that he would pass out and fall overboard when he was out sailing. Merissa said they talked about how she would sneak Max on board and how after she got Heinie drunk, they would dump him overboard and say it was an accident."

"And what other way?"

"She was going to get him drunk and drugged at home and Max would have someone burn the house down."

"Nice. Real nice."

"But, you see, she treated this whole thing as though it were a joke."

"What about using a gun?"

"Oh, that was their favorite. They thought of having Max shoot him . . . Max has lots of guns. Or he knows how to get them. His father used to own that pawnshop. And making it look like a suicide. Or self-defense."

"Self-defense?"

Diantha, I could tell, had already told me more than she meant to.

"Well, okay. It seems that Heinie got all worked up one morning after Merissa had been out with Max. He took your gun and went to Max's office."

"To shoot him?"

"No. Just to scare him off. Merissa and Max were going at it hot and heavy at the time."

"Did it work?"

"I guess not. Heinie came back lower than ever."

"Why didn't you tell me this before?" I asked.

"Merissa swore me to secrecy and then said she was joking, that it was only a fantasy. And even after they found Heinie murdered, I still couldn't believe she had anything to do with it."

She paused, pondering, and I could sense there was more. "Okay, but you've got to promise me that you won't tell a soul. Especially not the police."

"I can't promise, Di, you know that. But you can trust me to be discreet."

"Okay." But she hesitated. "Okay. On the night Heinie was murdered, he had set up a meeting with Max."

My nose actually twitched. I experienced that atavistic, very nearly spinal response of a hunter sensing his quarry. "Do you know at what time?"

"The meeting? She didn't say, but I think it was late."

"Did they meet?"

"Merissa didn't tell me that. She said she didn't really know."

"You asked her?"

"Of course."

I refrained from telling her how smart she was. Compliments like that flatter the giver more than the recipient. Instead I thanked her. "I know Merissa is your friend."

She shrugged her pretty shoulders. "Yeah, she's also kind of a ditz. I mean she wouldn't know which side of a book to open."

We drank our wine and ate our steaks, which were quite delicious. We looked into each other's eyes. It was she who said, "Want to take a cabin for a while?"

It was very simple. To the buxom lady behind the cash register, I asked if there was a cabin available.

"You want it for a couple of hours or for the night."

"Half an hour will do," Diantha giggled beside me.

The woman rolled her eyes. "It's seventy-five dollars until ten thirty."

Passion, alas, can neither be feigned nor premeditated. Perhaps it was our surroundings, a sagging bed in a mean little room quaintly and disagreeably redolent of postcoital cigarette smoke. Or perhaps our expectations got ahead of us, or ahead of me, at least. Simply put, I could not rise to the occasion. With the bases loaded, I struck out. I didn't even swing.

Diantha's sympathy shriveled me inwardly edged as it was with the kind of concern one expresses for a medical condition. "Norman, it's all right," she said, patting my knee. "You've been through a lot lately."

It was then that I confessed, though it might have sounded like bragging, my worst fear. We were sitting on the sad bed next to each other. I held her hand. I said, "Diantha, you once asked me in anger if I murdered Heinie . . ."

"And?"

"I think I may have."

Shock touched with excited admiration showed in her pretty eyes. "Really!"

I nodded.

"But you're not sure?"

"I'm not sure. I either shot him or I fantasized about doing it with such vivid intensity that it seems in retrospect like the same thing."

"Because of me?"

I should have lied or at least fudged the truth. It would have been a declaration of love, however twisted, one that I might have believed in enough to inspire what the dear woman has called my better part. I shrugged instead and told the miserable truth. "Mostly it was the way he treated me after you and he had been . . . together. He acted as though we shared an unspoken, obscene joke. And I could never figure out if it was at your expense or mine."

The words, bad enough, were made worse by a resurgent anger I could not keep out of my voice. We were back to square one. Or completely off the board. Quietly and modestly, she got off the bed and began to dress.

I should have gone to Lieutenant Tracy with what Di told me about Max and Merissa. But there wasn't really much to go on. And the lieutenant had not returned either of the two calls I made to him. Besides, I could not resist taking a crack at Max Shofar myself.

I called ahead to the Coin Corner, the downtown shop where Max runs his business. Max was in, and I took the twenty-minute walk into old Seaboard, which has undergone something of a revival of late. The Coin Corner is just across the street from Waugh's Drugstore, where you can still get breakfast over the lunch counter as you could when I was a boy.

Though not impressive from the outside, the Coin Corner turned out to be more than its name implied. A long counter of polished walnut with locked glass cabinets below ran nearly the length of the room, with more glass-fronted cabinets behind it.

There, as below the counter, beautifully mounted and displayed, were coins from all over the ancient world along with early American money, both of paper and metal.

The displays made me feel at home. Though no numismatist — my father did leave me a small collection with some exquisite pieces — I recognized the breadth and quality of what Max had on display.

The place was also uncannily familiar, including a stairway toward the rear with carpeted treads ascending to a balcony on the wall opposite the counter. Here were more displays, interrupted by a substantial doorway with an old-fashioned transom above it. I stopped in my tracks as time pulled a U-turn and I was a teenager again, checking the boy's section of Sternman's Books for an overlooked adventure by Zane Grey.

"Mr. Shofar," I said to the person behind the counter, a young woman with frizzy hair and small diamond studs wired to various parts of her cranial orifices. "He's expecting me."

She gave a gesture toward the stairs and made a fleeting adjustment of her face that could be taken for a smile and went back to reading her magazine. I went up the stairs and knocked on the door. A woman of late middle age with a severe gray bun, an old-fashioned gray suit, and blocky shoes admitted me. She did not waste time on pleasantries, either, and showed me into the main office, where Max Shofar sat behind an antique desk in front of a large half-moon window. More coins, presented like pictures, adorned the otherwise plain walls. Another desk with computer gear, hedged in by utilitarian files, reminded the visitor that this was a business, not a hobbyist's retreat.

"Come in, Norman, come in," he said, the enthusiasm just a bit forced. A man of medium height and build, with dark hair that looked cultivated, a noble nose, intense blue eyes, and a ruddy complexion, Max Shofar seemed out of place in this office, in this business. Perhaps it was the impeccably cut and pressed suit of silk and linen, silvery white, and the flash of cuff links, two ancient coins, the hand-painted tie, the expensive Swiss watch a bit too obvious. Coin-collector types tend to wear cardigans, be tolerant of dandruff, and have poor eyesight from years of squinting at the objects of their passion. He struck me as the kind who had followed a passing childhood obsession into a dead end.

His "Norman" didn't take me by surprise. We had met several times at occasions given by Heinie and Merissa.

"Max," I said, shaking his bejeweled hand and sitting down in a comfortable chair opposite.

He tented his glittering fingers and let the white gleam of his smile fade to an expression of spurious concern. "I was sorry to hear about the . . . situation you find yourself in." His voice went with the eyes, hard, but with the promise of charm. Again, he struck me as too big for this station in life, even if the ample half-moon window, stretching nearly to the floor, gave out on the riverside park where the New Humber wended its way through the city to the harbor.

"Well, that's why I'm here, Max," I said, regarding him steadily.

"Really?" His eyes looked away and came back. "How can I help you?" The promise of charm grew more pronounced even as his mouth took on a tentative twist.

"As you know, I've been charged as an accessory in the murder of Heinie. Which, in my position, could prove ruinous."

"I follow you."

"So I'm trying to find out as best I can what happened the night Heinie was murdered."

"Okay. But I'm not sure I can help you."

I looked out the window for a moment at a woman walking

a Great Dane along the embankment. I could feel my jaw tightening as my personality morphed into that of the blunt-talking private investigator. In this persona, my diction grows more clipped and my gaze becomes relentless. It is a version of myself that I don't particularly admire, but which I know is necessary if people are going to take me seriously.

I said, "When did you learn that de Buitliér was investigating the collection Heinie gave to the museum?"

"When I read it in the paper. Same as most everyone. How is it relevant?"

"I'm going to be frank, Max . . ."

"Of course. All cards on the table." But he gave me a poker smile.

"I'm interested in motive. Who might want Heinie dead?"

"Okay. And you think I gave Heinie a collection of fakes. He found out about them and threatened to expose me. To keep him quiet, I shot him."

"Something like that."

He laughed and shook his head. His voice had just a hint of condescension in it when he said, "Norman . . . I run an international mail-order coin business serving some of the top collectors in this country, in Asia, the Middle East, and Europe. The world is full of suckers, but the people I deal with are not among them."

"Except, perhaps, for Heinie?"

"Especially not Heinie. He may have been a fool in other ways, but not when it came to coins. He had what I would call 'the touch.' He turned down what I considered high quality at times, and upon further examination he almost always proved right. Indeed, when anything I thought dubious came over the counter and I needed a second opinion, I held my nose and turned to Heinie."

"How do you explain the wholesale duplication then of the collection he gave us?"

"I suspect he had his cake and got to eat it. He gave you coins, got a huge tax break, and got to keep the originals."

"Who might have made the forgeries for him?"

Max shrugged in a way that told me he wouldn't tell even if he knew. "The best forgeries used to come out of Italy. Then Bulgaria. The Lipanov stuff. Now it's gone high-tech."

"What about around here?"

"Oh, I'm sure there are people doing it. Some of them as a hobby. There are fake coin collectors, you know. Or, rather, collectors of fake coins."

I nodded, satisfied. Then I said, "You and Merissa were and are having an affair."

"So? What, motive again?"

I leaned into him. "Max, I have it on good authority that Heinie came right into this office not long ago, took out a revolver, and threatened to kill you if you ever saw Merissa again."

Max's attempt at a derisive laugh shriveled to a *huh, huh* sound. He shook his head most unconvincingly.

"He insulted you, didn't he, Max? He called you a conniving Jew, didn't he?"

"Look, Norman . . ."

"Is that what made you want to murder him?"

"I didn't murder him."

"But you had a motive. You needed money because of that failed Franklin Mint deal."

He said nothing.

I pressed on. "You and Merissa talked several times about getting rid of him. You discussed drugging his whiskey, getting him disabled and throwing him overboard while sailing on the *Albatross*."

He still didn't respond except to look at me with his eyes like pieces of polished turquoise.

"Merissa never could keep a secret, could she?"

"Listen . . . :

"You talked about shooting Heinie with the very revolver he waved in your face, shooting him and making it look like a suicide."

He sat there pale, the swell gone out of his shoulders. I had touched a nerve and for a moment I thought I had my man. Until he smiled and shook his head. "Merissa has a habit of voicing her fantasies aloud and then attributing them to the person she is talking to. Not only that, but she has a rich imagination. I'm surprised she didn't tell Diantha about 'our' scheme to find Heinie's hidden gold, which she tells me he buried somewhere under his lawn, and escape on his boat and spend the rest of our lives sailing around the world."

I had to smile. "Do you sail?"

"Yeah. My idea of sailing is the *Queen Mary*. The one that's docked."

I believed him if only for the implicit self-disgust he betrayed about his weakness for the crass, lovely, scatterbrained Merissa. And perhaps because he had, if only by silence, indulged her fantasies.

But I still had a trump card and played it. "You met with Heinie just around the time he was murdered."

"I told you, Merissa makes up things . . ."

"True. She told Di that. But I also met with Heinie the night he was murdered, and he told me he was on his way to see you." I spoke with enough vehemence to cover my lie. I could tell I had struck home.

"You don't have any proof."

"I'm not saying you murdered him, Max. But if I'm going to

clear myself, I need to know everything that happened that night between the time I saw him and the time he was shot."

He turned his head and glanced away, a tic a lot of contemporary actors use. But I could tell he was thinking about what to tell me. He said, "If you tell the police what I'm about to tell you, I'll deny it."

"Fair enough."

"I did see Heinie that night."

"At what time?"

"Ten. A little after."

"But he was . . ."

"Yeah, he was dead. The fact is, we were supposed to meet at the Café Club for a drink. But I blew him off. I knew it would be more of the same, and I was tired of his bullshit, his whining, his threats. I went to the club and had a drink. The waitress can verify this much. About ten minutes before he was to show, I left. I had a . . . date. I was taking a shortcut through the parking lot of the Center for Criminal Justice when I heard what sounded like a loud bang."

He paused as though having second thoughts about telling me any of this.

"Anyway, I'm no hero. I kept out of sight for . . . I don't know, five minutes. Then I got curious. I stayed in the shadows. I made my way over. I recognized Heinie's Jag. I also noticed someone, a man of medium to small size, walking away from the car in a hurry."

"You couldn't tell who it was?"

"Not a chance. The lighting gives out at the edge of the lot, and it was a dark night."

"So what did you do?"

"I went over to the car. I carry one of those little pinch lights. I looked through the window. I could tell he was dead. But I reached in anyway and took his pulse. Nothing. I wiped any prints I might have left, and walked away from it."

"Why didn't you tell this to the police?"

"What? And become a suspect? Police question coin dealer in murder of coin collector. No thanks."

I had no choice but to believe him. Or pretend to. I stood up to go. "I'll keep this to myself, Max. At least for now."

"I'd appreciate that." He shook my hand. "You know, Norman, you wouldn't make a bad cop."

10

Upon waking this morning, I felt that my whole being had become a hyperdelicate organism in which even thinking had to be done slowly and tentatively. Recovery did not seem possible as I lay alone on my marital bed, my imagination vulnerable to waking nightmares inspired by imperfect memory.

Recollections of what led to this state thumped into my consciousness like barbed arrows of shame. My outward winces and muffled groans as I lay there merely signified deeper, more nebulous hurts. I could see that my life with its claims to probity, high-mindedness, community spirit, and general *gravitas* had begun to unravel. The moral high ground to which I aspired had turned into a slippery slope.

It began the night before with the arrival of Ridley in a celebratory mood and a bottle of single-malt of the kind Alphus particularly likes. What we were celebrating was never made clear, not that it mattered. We began, slowly, even decorously. One doesn't "do shots" with Lagavulin; one sips it slowly, appreciatively. Even I, no lover of Scotch, could appreciate this distillation of barley to its essence of pale gold. Besides, signing means that your hands are not free. And my friends were in a talkative mood.

Alphus put his glass down after a long, deliberative sip to explain how Lagavulin is an island malt made with the local grain, peat, and water. How it was then aged in old wine casks permeable to the sea air that wafts into the storage sheds, lending the final liquor its subtle tincture of iodine. He was required to spell out this last word as I certainly had no idea what he was signing.

Indeed, our evening began as a quite civilized little party in the living room, which is the grandest space in the house with several elegant antiques, a Turkish rug, and a chandelier fashioned of Lalique glass early in the last century.

Alphus had dressed for the occasion in his longest trousers, which came just below the knees, a long-sleeved pin-striped shirt, and his special sandals.

I should mention that neither Alphus nor Ridley handles alcohol very well. Not that I should talk. I soon switched to martinis, a drink Alphus dismisses as tasting like "distilled piss." It wasn't long before their sips of malt turned into shots with far less signage about complexity and finishes.

Ridley, slurring his gestured words, recited the Porter's speech from *MacBeth* about the effects of drink. It took me a line or two to catch on. Then I chimed in to make it a duet of signs and voice, ". . . Therefore much drink may be said to be an equivocator with lechery: it makes him, and it mars him; it sets him on, and it takes him off; it persuades him, and disheartens him; makes him stand to and not stand to; in conclusion, equivocates him to a sleep, and giving him the lie, leaves him."

Which we all applauded and raised our glasses.

Alphus, who grows bossy under the sway of drink, insisted on playing over and over his favorite piece of music, which is Ravel's *Bolero*. Again and again and again until, still echoing in my hurting head like an aural nightmare, I hear the repetition within the repetition within the repetition.

But I think I understood his fixation when he explained how it came about. He told us that after the procedure that allowed more blood flow to his brain, *Bolero* was the first piece of classical music that he experienced. "I thought my head would explode. I thought my heart would collapse. My whole being resonated as it had never done before. It was the sound that led me out of my chimphood and into whatever it is I am now."

The arrival of large amounts of Chinese food that I had ordered by phone while still relatively sober did little to slow our collective derangement. I had gotten Alphus his own paper boxes of the stuff as he has the annoying habit of fishing out the choice bits with his long hairy fingers and then dosing the rest with so much soy sauce as to render it inedible. I made a large pot of scented tea to go with the food, not that it did much to dent the momentum of our inebriation. I was still tasting that collation in sour eructations a day later.

Outwardly calm and even serene most of the time, Alphus, under the sway of alcohol, grows agitated with what might be called existential angst. For not the first time he apologized for killing and eating the poodle in the park. "You have to realize that to me, a small live dog is a delicacy. The flesh has a slight, musky edge to it and is surprisingly tender, especially if it has been a pampered pet. And, other than an occasional squirrel, and there's not much flesh on those things, I hadn't tasted meat in days." He hesitated. "Okay, there was one or two cats."

His hands, semaphores of articulation, moved gracefully, even enthusiastically, but I could tell he was starting into one of his philosophical funks.

"I sometimes wonder, Norman, if we drink, like Oscar Wilde said, to make other people more interesting."

"Is that why you drink?" I managed, putting my own drink down.

"Not around you, certainly. But I do drink too much." He gave his version of a laugh. "I wonder if there's an AA group around that would have me?"

"Check at Sign House. Just because you can't verbalize vocally doesn't mean you're not susceptible to alcohol. Perhaps even more so. I mean alcoholism is another kind of . . ." I searched for a word and came up with "otherness."

Alphus turned to Ridley with a scoffing look they share. "Otherness. I've been reading about otherness lately. Everybody claims it these days. But you know, they don't know what otherness is. I mean real otherness. It isn't just that people look down on me as an ape, an animal. But I am profoundly different. I am a different bloody species. Try that for otherness."

Ridley, who had begun to slur his signing, said, "But you are one of us."

I groped for some word that might bridge the gap. I realized it is one thing to be an ape and quite another to know it. I leaned forward. "Yes, Alphus, but your essential . . . beingness is as authentic as that of anyone else. We are all God's creatures."

He shook his head. "We are all winners or losers in the great lottery called evolution."

"Yes, but Father O'Gould thinks it is through evolution that all beings share in the spark of divinity."

"Easy for him to say. He's not a five-foot hairy ape with bow legs and arms that reach to the floor."

"Your arms don't reach to the floor."

"Just about. All I have to do is lean forward a little. Let's face it, Norman, most people see me as little more than a big monkey. I'm not a real person. I'm a freak, a hairy, ridiculous freak."

I sipped some of my drink and met his eyes. "Don't ever, ever think that. Whatever you are, you are real."

"A real freak."

"Only in the sense that you are amazingly remarkable. Otherwise, I see you as a regular guy."

That brought him up short and his expression began slowly to change. He spelled out *guy* with letters.

I nodded.

"Guy," he signed to Ridley. "I am a guy. One of the guys."

"One of the good guys."

"You don't have to be human to be a guy, do you?"

"Not in the least."

"You know, Norman, you're a good guy, too."

The evening wore on, the snare drum booming faintly and then louder and louder, and then again. I was well into the pitcher of martinis I had mixed. The bottle of malt had suffered grievously at their hands. At which point, as I think I remember, I stood up and toasted Alphus and his remarkable life. Which I tried to sign, not quite achieving the word *remarkable,* which I spoke aloud. I added, "In fact, your life is so remarkable, you should write your memoirs."

Ridley got up and danced a little jig. He put down his glass and signed, "To Alphus and his memoirs," then picked up his glass and drank.

Alphus drank, but remained skeptical, at least from his expression. Finally, he signed, "No one wants to hear about the miserable life of an ape."

Ridley, his gestures vehement, disagreed. "The world loves to hear about misery. Especially interesting misery. And your misery has been uniquely interesting."

"I can't type," Alphus signed. "Only slowly."

"You can dictate to me," Ridley signed back. And turned to me for affirmation.

I nodded. "You just have to be sure to, well, you know, be honest."

Alphus looked insulted. Ridley signed, "Alphus doesn't lie."

I shrugged. "Everyone lies from time to time. It's only human."

Alphus mimed a laugh.

Ridley, who is scarcely ever serious, grew emphatic in his signing. "Alphus doesn't lie, and he has an infallible knack for knowing when others are lying. He can beat any lie detector cold."

We all drank from our drinks. I proposed a little test. I would make a series of statements and he would indicate with his thumb whether they were true or false.

"My mother loved chocolates," I began.

Thumb down. Indeed my mother was allergic to chocolate.

"I like to listen to Broadway musicals."

Thumb down again.

"My favorite color combination is black and orange."

Thumb up. Something about the colors of Lord Baltimore touch me deeply.

"I don't miss my wife and daughter."

Thumb down. A bit of a softball, that one.

Ridley signed to me covertly. "Tell him you don't want him to leave."

I shook my head. "That's not true. But it's not false, either."

"Try him."

I did. Alphus pondered for a long moment. His thumb went up, went down, and then went sideways.

"Amazing," I muttered to myself, half thinking that Alphus could be a very effective investigative tool.

The remainder of the evening is something of a blur. I vaguely remember the three of us holding hands in a circle and careering around the open parts of the room in a silly, sick-making dance. To that music. I like Ravel very much, but I will never be able to listen to *Bolero* without getting the equivalent of an auditory hangover.

I'm afraid the damage included a vase Diantha valued (it had belonged to her mother), a lamp of some antiquity, and stains on the carpet that look to be permanent.

I ended up drinking directly from the gin bottle while my

companions shared a fifth or two of what Alphus called "industrial whiskey." I remember him urinating into the fireless fireplace. I remember Ridley telling us — his mask of gaiety momentarily askew — of a young woman who had left him for a burly guy with no brains and a deep voice. I remember finally the bliss of silence as my friends fell asleep, or lost consciousness. Ridley lay down on the sofa and Alphus curled in an armchair while I managed, just, to climb the stairs holding on to the banister and, fully clothed, fall into bed.

So I woke up with the mother of all hangovers. I moved slowly. I took off my clothes and dumped them on a chair. In robe and slippers, I made it to the bathroom where, after prodigious urination, I showered in warm and then, slowly, cold water, placating the Calvinist within. And feeling marginally the better for it.

Indeed, I remembered waking up in the middle of the night in the middle of my self-induced coma knowing where I had seen Stella Fox before she made the news. But now I couldn't recall it. I could only hope that, like a piece of paper missing in the jumble of my desk, it would turn up.

Neither Ridley nor Alphus was where I had left them the night before. Ridley, I assumed, had gone home and Alphus up to his leopard-proof hammock. Still slowly, still hurting, I made coffee. I make enough for two of us as Alphus likes several cups, which he takes with milk and sugar, to start off his day. He also goes through a lot of bananas, which I bring home in large bunches.

Presently, I heard him upstairs in the same bathroom I use, as the more luxurious one doesn't have a shower. Other than enough hair to clog the drains and a heady mist of deodorant, he leaves few traces of himself behind.

We also have a morning routine of sorts. None the worse for drink, he came downstairs, signed "hello" a bit sheepishly, and made a face that is his equivalent of a smile. Per usual, he turned on National Public Radio, though, like myself, he prefers BBC when he can get it. He poured and doctored his own coffee, peeled a banana, unsheathed the *Bugle,* and checked the headlines.

With some excitement, he turned to show me the front page. There, above the fold, next to a not very flattering picture of myself, was the headline: "Museum Ponders Plans to Make Neanderthals White."

The story read, "The Museum of Man is moving ahead with plans to make the models in its Diorama of Paleolithic Life light-skinned, sources within the museum told the *Bugle.* Currently a neutral hue, neither dark nor light, the figures represent an early form of mankind and are visited by people from all over the world.

"Despite criticism from experts on the need for diversity in role modeling, officials at the museum, according to the *Bugle*'s investigation, will be spending several hundred thousand dollars to replace the current models with what one source called 'white-skinned, red-haired Caucasians.'

"The *Bugle* has also learned that Norman de Ratour, who is white, is proceeding with the changeover based on what some experts call 'narrow, unsubstantiated, and preliminary research.'

"Repeated efforts last night to reach de Ratour, who has been charged with accessory in the murder of Heinrich von Grümh, a curator at the museum, were unsuccessful. Some reports indicate that de Ratour has gone into hiding as the management situation at the museum, never very stable, has deteriorated alarmingly in recent weeks, according to an informed source."

In fact the phone had rung several times the night before. I vaguely remembered Amanda Feeney's flat voice squawking at me on the speaker as she left a message for me to call her immediately.

Right then, still in pain, I wanted to throw in the towel. That is, type up and send in a letter of resignation, leave this house to Alphus, Ridley, and chaos, and retreat to the country, to the bosom of my little family. And I might have done just that had I not, with sudden clarity, perhaps jolted by the story in the *Bugle*, recalled what it was I remembered in the middle of the night.

I had been in the Neanderthal diorama with Edwards experimenting with the lighting to see if we could do anything to make the skin tones of the models appear lighter than they were. I noticed Stella Fox not only because she is a striking woman in that small brunette way, but because she seemed out of place. The style of her couture, including black shiny high heels along with an extravagant choker of pearls, belonged more in Las Vegas than the Museum of Man. Not only that, but she paid scant attention to the elaborate display through which she walked. Because . . . because she was talking with a man who also looked like he had just flown in from Las Vegas. They were leaning in to each other talking quietly but emphatically. And I saw them there more than once. When my memory works, it really works.

I quickly went over Alphus's schedule for the day to see who would be coming to visit. Any excursions that might be planned. I usually hang around until someone shows up, even if it's Dolores, who comes in to clean up and tend to things in Di's absence.

But this morning, still nursing my head, just barely able to hold coffee, I drove to the museum. I was anxious to get to the office. I called ahead and left a message with Mort in Security to have one of the surveillance technicians on hand when I arrived.

By ten o'clock, I was sitting in front of a screen looking at digitized footage from a camera that covers a particularly well-lighted tableau called "Early Kitchen." It shows a group using primitive knives and scrapers to carve up the leg of a bison. Strange how even adults act when confronted with our distant ancestors. A lot of them laugh, but nervously.

I watched and watched and grew bored and annoyed. How fat, dull, and stupid our population appears to have grown. Whole families of fatties. Most of them scarcely glance at the informational placards or put on the available earphones to hear the recorded message. The kids fidget and whine. They waddle on. This is what has become of us. But then, I was still suffering from the night before.

I was about to arrange to have the feed transferred to the laptop on my desk when it occurred to me someone else could look for the sequence I was seeking. I asked the technician, a pleasant young man named Hank, if he knew of anyone on the staff willing to put in some overtime. He said he would do it himself. I explained what I was about and let him have the news photo and the news clip.

In my office, an imperious voice mail from Professor Brattle regarding the story in the *Bugle* about the Neanderthals awaited me along with a note from Felix that he would be dropping by. Chair Brattle informed me she was convening a special meeting of the Oversight Committee to discuss "this highly sensitive issue" and take "appropriate measures." I let that one hang.

I couldn't let Felix hang. He came by with the Elgin Warwick folder, which I noticed had thickened since the last time I saw it. Tanned, tall and energetic, Felix was positively beamish, his face at such a wattage I found it necessary in my recovering state to avert my eyes from time to time.

"Not now, Felix," I begged as he sat down and looked at me intently.

"You don't look happy."

"I have committed a dietary indiscretion."

"With a bottle?"

"With several bottles."

"You should take a personal day."

"I think a personal month would be more like it. Did you see the *Bugle*?"

"No big deal. It's become a regular rag since Don Patcher left. No one takes it seriously anymore. No one that counts. It's a newspaper that talks to itself."

"I need to get a statement up about the Neanderthals."

"Why? It's none of their business."

"They've made it their business."

"So tell them the issue is under consideration given the weight of scientific research, et cetera, et cetera. Swamp them with facts."

"I suppose. But I am very vulnerable right now. I need all the . . . non-enemies I can get."

Felix smiled. "That's why I'm here." He patted the file. "And good old Warwick."

"Felix, not now."

"Norman, this guy is on the Governing Board. You don't want to alienate him. You want him on your side. You want him in your pocket. You should be helping him to pick out the right *byssus* for his eternal wrapping."

"*Byssus?*"

"The fine linen used by the ancient Egyptians to bandage their departed. I've been doing my homework."

"There are principles involved."

"How about the principle of survival?"

"I am not going to stand by and watch the Museum of Man be turned into a mortuary for the rich."

"Of course not. Your active involvement would be very much appreciated."

"No, Felix, no. People will start calling it the Mausoleum of Man."

"That's not bad. That's a great tag. Instant brand recognition. This is so big, I can't believe it." He removed several sheets from the folder. "I've come up with a plan. We wouldn't just be storing the remains of people. No. For a modest fee, they could have their history kept in perpetuity on a special Web site sponsored by the museum. For a little more, no, a lot more, they could also have their DNA preserved in the Genetics Lab. With the promise, of course, that when the technology is available, we bring them back alive. We'll be taking over from God. And we'll do a better job. If we get proactive, it won't look like we're buckling under to a powerful and wealthy supporter. No, it will look like we are staking out the ultimate future. I'd sign up in a heartbeat. And talk about outreach . . . I've come up with some suggestions." He pointed to the folder.

"Such as?"

"We could hold an annual Halloween party there. Everyone comes in costume. All ghouls night. Charge a mint."

"No."

"Come on, Norman. . . ." He gave me his winning smile. "Why not?"

"Because . . . in all honesty, Felix, I do not want to be reduced to running a high-end funeral parlor."

"It's an honorable calling."

"Felix . . . I can't think about this right now."

"I'll think for you." He turned lawyerly. "Let's back up. According to the last communiqué you received from Robert Remick, the board will convene on July twenty-fourth for a special meeting to decide, and I quote, 'action to be taken regarding the directorship of the museum,' unquote."

"I know."

"He also said, you told me, that you are to serve on a probationary basis in close consultation with the museum's counsel. Which happens to be one Felix Skinnerman."

"Is this a *coup d'état*?"

"No, just a regular coup. Norman, let me remind you of the clause in the Rules of Governance."

"I know it by heart."

"'. . . the Director will serve at the pleasure of the Board of Governors. The Director may be removed for "dereliction of duty, obvious incapacity to perform his functions as Director, public censure, criminal activity, or moral turpitude."'"

"Yes, good old moral turpitude. What are you saying?"

"I'm saying you need Warwick on your side."

"Maybe it is time to resign."

"And let Malachy Morin have it?"

"He might be more amenable to this scheme of yours."

He leaned back with that look on his face. "Hmmm . . . Hadn't thought about that. Maybe you're right." Then, "Look, don't fight this thing. It's inevitable. It makes great sense."

"It would be a museum of the dead, the locally dead, anyway." I spoke morosely.

"But it's already that, Norman. You have that vast Skull Collection. You have thousands of pieces of human remains from all over the globe."

"So how would we proceed? What do we say to Warwick?"

"We agree to a meeting. We discuss setting up a mortuary wing based on his proposal. We talk up the visionary thing."

"The cemeteries might object."

"Nah, they're already overcrowded. Standing room only."

"I will consider it." I spoke without enthusiasm, still wondering why I could find only thorns on the flowering branch Felix held out to me.

11

I find myself in a dither over an incident that in fact I handled very well. I was clattering down the stairs that lead from floor to floor around the central atrium on my way to get coffee as Doreen's condition makes it difficult for her, even using the elevator. As I neared the ground floor, I noticed three men in shirts and ties, one with an expensive-looking camera-like device, one with a clipboard, and one with a tape measure.

I paused, trying to remember if any kind of restoration or refurbishment had begun. There's always something going on like that in a museum. But I could think of nothing. I felt a jolt of adrenaline as my territorial instincts took over. Still, I affected a calm exterior as I approached the three men, who were going about their work in a professional manner.

"Excuse me," I said to the one with the clipboard as he appeared to be in charge, "could you tell me what you're doing here?"

He pointed to the man who had set the camera on a tripod and was scanning up and down and around. "That's the boss."

I went over and stood by him until he glanced up. He was a pleasant-looking, clean-shaven sort of man who exuded competence. "Can I help you?" he said, noticing me waiting.

"You can. You can tell me what's going on here." I extended my hand. "I'm Norman de Ratour. I'm the director of the museum."

He freed his right hand and shook mine. "Marv Gorman. They mentioned you might show up."

"Indeed. So what is going on?"

"Sure. We're from Facilities Planning. We're doing a preliminary survey. It's the first step in any renovations. The architects need to know with some precision what's in place before they go changing it around."

"I see. And with whose authority are you conducting this preliminary survey?"

He turned to the man with the clipboard. "Pete, you got the req there?"

"Right here."

Marv took the paper from Pete and handed to me. He pointed to the signature. "Jack Marchand. He's in charge of Facilities Planning."

I read it over. I noticed with an extra pulse of blood pressure the name Professor Laluna Jackson under the heading "Requested By."

I had the presence of mind to ask in an offhand way, "Do you mind if I make a copy of this?"

Marv shrugged.

"I'll be right back," I said. I went into the financial office, which is nearby, and had a copy made.

I returned and handed back the original. I said, "Well, gentlemen, I don't regret to inform you that this is not university property. Mr. Marchand's signature has no effect here."

"I was told . . ."

"You were misinformed. I have a court order to that effect while the question of proprietorship is being litigated. So I will respectfully ask you to leave." I smiled. "Of course, you are all welcome to return as visitors."

They conferred momentarily. Then they all shook my hand and left.

But I was in a royal snit about the incident as I tried to sort through the coming year's curatorial budgets. Why does everyone always want more? More staff. More stuff. More space. More gadgets. More discretionary spending. Why do people think that the idea of an expanding universe applies to us? Not to mention the philistine notion that more is better.

All of which is piffling next to the documentary proof that L. Jackson has designs — in both senses of the word — on the Museum of Man. It's monstrous. Or do I detect the meaty hands of Malachy Morin, playing one of his games? He's not above that. Probing. Testing. Disrupting. Not that he doesn't have to be careful. Izzy informs me he's on the short list to replace George Twill as president of Wainscott, as incredible as that sounds.

Well, two can play this game. I'll have copies made of this req form to go along with an account of the incident to show the Board of Governors. And I'll give a copy to Felix and let him sleuth out the particulars.

On top of all this, I have marital woes. Diantha is scarcely speaking to me. It seems Max Shofar is angry with Merissa for telling Di about what their plans may or may not have been regarding Heinie. So Merissa is on the outs with Di and Di is miffed at me.

Nor has Diantha been amenable to any explanations I have proffered. She doesn't grasp that I have been charged with a serious crime and that I am out on bail, which means I can be sent back to jail on the flimsiest pretext. Moreover, if I cannot clear my name, everything I have worked for will be for naught. Instead, she talks about "my friend" Merissa and how I betrayed her trust. How a woman can go from devastating disparagement of someone one minute to being her soul mate the next is something I will never understand.

Of course having an ape living in the house has not helped. And when I told her, in a moment of unwise candor, about the broken vase, she hit the ceiling. But what can I do in all honor? If she knew Alphus as Alphus, if she had a chance to sit down and sign with him over a cup of coffee, she would realize that he is a sapient, feeling, trustworthy being who would not knowingly hurt a soul.

But distance makes anything like reconciliation very difficult. And during times of stress, the disparity in our ages starts to show. Even when she's here she lives in another cultural zone. When I glance at the covers of *People* magazine and other such publications left hanging around, I swear I do not have a clue as to who any of those celebrities are. Nor have I the least interest in their mismarriages or dining disorders.

I am also bored witless by the television crime dramas Di likes to watch. You would think that a real-life detective, as I consider myself, would enjoy such things. Not in the least. All I see are actors doing a lot of meaningful staring at one another as they talk half cryptically in the latest police jargon. How any reasonably intelligent person — and Di is far more than reasonably intelligent — can watch that stuff for more than a minute or two staggers my credulity. How, these days, can one not be a snob?

But I digress. Which is what I'm prone to when I'm in a quandary. I have in hand a letter that came in a sealed envelope to the mailroom with nothing more than my name on it. Inside, neatly typed (with printers, everything these days is neatly typed), I found the following letter. I will let it speak for itself.

> Mr. Ratour:
> I am writing to you in regards to the murder of H. v. Grumh. I'm afraid I must do so anonymously as what I

have to say may have liability.

I know that you know that Professor Colin Saunders had a long and bad relationship with v. Grumh. Their antagonism began with Pr. Saunders being appointed to the Groome Chair. Recent events have made their relationship worse. Of course I am talking about the Dresden stater. Pr. Saunders had wanted to acquire the coin for Wainscott University's Frock Museum. He is a wealthy man. He started the campaign "To Bring the Dresden to Wainscott." He is said to be very angry upon learning that H. v. Grumh had beaten him to it.

You may already know that Pr. Saunders lives very close to the scene of the crime. Number 417 Museum Place is only a couple of minutes' walk from the spot where the body of v. Grumh was found. Also, the pr. walks his dog around the parking lot of the museum around the time that the murder took place.

I would send all this information to the police, but I think it should come from you.

Sincerely,
X

Some background about the stater might be useful at this point. Experts have called it the most rare and valuable coin still on the open market. Unlike many ancient coins, it appears newly minted, so much so that, until modern times and advances in dating and metallurgic analysis, it was rumored to be a forgery. Referred to in the numismatic literature as a Thasos Satyr and Nymph stater, it depicts the former, bearded and long-haired and in an exaggerated ithyphallic state, about to ravish the latter whom, gesticulating, he holds on his lap. It dates from Thasos, Thrace, circa 490 BC.

The coin has a provenance worthy of a Hollywood film. Napoleon himself is said to have owned it. Then someone in Himmler's entourage. That person apparently obtained it from one Maurice Debas, a Parisian coin dealer, later shot as a collaborator. He had obtained it, no doubt very cheaply, from a refugee fleeing Hitler.

About a year ago, rumors started in the numismatic world that the Dresden, as it is generally called, would be coming up for auction in London. Max Shofar, through his connections, learned who was negotiating with Sotheby's. He convinced von Grümh to fly to London with him and go directly to the source. That turned out to be a London dealer by the name of Sidney Grabbe. Grabbe had it on consignment from a Kuwaiti sheik impoverished by a lavish lifestyle who was in desperate need of ready cash. They paid the necessary amount and walked off with the prize.

I went out to Doreen's little office and made several copies of the letter. My heuristic proclivities roused, I wanted to go over the style for clues as to who might have written it. Of course, its belabored style might have resulted from an effort on the part of the writer to conceal his identity. The bit about the Frock wanting the coin is true enough but not generally known. That institution has a truly superb collection of ancient money. I say *money* because they have some superb examples of ninth-century Chinese paper currency as well as a veritable hoard of old coins left by August Frock himself.

The question I asked myself was, Who would want to implicate Col Saunders? Max Shofar? But why? De Buitliér? I retrieved some of the memoranda the curator had sent me. There were affinities, but nothing definite. He and Saunders might be rivals if the worst happens, that is, should the board decide to force me out, leaving Wainscott to take us over. I wondered if it might not be Saunders himself? Some people, through a streak of perverse vanity, would not object to being considered capable of murder.

But I couldn't really concentrate. I was pondering when and under what circumstances to send the letter to Lieutenant Tracy. Or, rather, in what manner to present it to him. For instance, with the benefit of my opinions after I had perused it more thoroughly? With a curt FYI on a Post-it? With nothing but itself?

The more I pondered the question, the more my anger grew. We had worked closely together. We had esteemed each other in an unspoken friendship. I had helped him solve a number of unfortunate deaths here at the museum. To put it in Di's parlance, he owed me.

At the risk of being charged with withholding evidence, I decided to hang on to the missive until I had interviewed Saunders. What was it evidence of? That there had been a wrangle for a rare coin? That the man didn't like the murder victim? That he might have been walking his dog in the area when the murder occurred? Besides, the anonymity of its author vitiated an already weak circumstantiality.

I decided that, when I did forward it, I would send it to the office of the district attorney. Indeed, I determined that, should anything turn up regarding Stella Fox and the suspicious suicide, I would send that along to the DA as well. More than that, I would release any incriminating taped evidence to the local television stations at the same time. Two can play at this game.

Hank has yet to get back to me with anything regarding my sighting of Ms. Fox in the Neanderthal exhibition. I'm beginning to wonder if I simply imagined it in an advanced state of wishful thinking.

I put in a call to Col Saunders. His secretary told me he was in the Far East, but would be home by Saturday. I told her I was calling in reference to the von Grümh murder and that he should call me at the office at his earliest convenience.

I find it bracing to be around a man like Harvey Deharo. He very publicly walked me to our table in the Creole Lounge, a Caribbean restaurant with colorful decor and pungent odors popular with the movers and shakers of Seaboard, such as they are.

Diantha likes to come here, especially in winter, when the decor and the menu remind her of sandy beaches, swaying palm trees, and warm sunshine. I enjoy it, though when they have live music, very often young black men playing on what look like steel barrels, I find it intrusive.

I seldom drink at lunch, but could not resist joining Harvey in ordering a piña colada upon our being seated. While we perused the offerings and waited for the drinks to arrive, he leaned across the table, his memorable eyes holding mine for an instant. He has the knack of being relaxed and intense at the same time. Perhaps it's the softness of his accent.

"You're probably wondering, Norman, why I've asked you to lunch. I mean other than the pleasure of your company." He smiled, and I was struck by a note of uncertainty.

"It occurred to me," I said, looking up from the temptations of the menu, which included a seafood gumbo I had ordered before.

He leaned back as the drinks arrived and as we ordered. He asked about the stone-baked pork and settled for something "less damaging," as he put it. I settled for the gumbo with a green salad. We sipped our drinks.

"Anyway," he resumed, still awkward for some reason, "I

have a regular agenda." He smiled and relaxed. "Okay, first, I wanted to talk about some projects at the lab. You've asked me in the past for informal updates instead of the biannual reports that can be a nuisance for me to write and for you to read."

So we chatted about the lab for a while. Harvey has begun several green initiatives in an effort to reorient the focus of the work there. We are both of the opinion that research on genes, especially for applied genetics, is not as popular as it used to be, and for good reasons.

He mentioned a project to genetically modify a strain of bacteria to make it more efficient in the breakdown of cellulose. The object would be to create and capture methane gas that could be used directly in the production of energy. "It's cleaner than oxidizing, that is, burning the cellulose, and would allow us to fuel power plants from garbage, grass, leaves, waste lumber."

"Instead of it going into landfills," I offered. I was basking in a sense of well-being that Harvey has the knack of bestowing on the people he likes.

"Exactly. Where methane results anyway and has a far worse greenhouse effect than CO_2."

He spoke of efforts to produce a lawn cover "with minimal genetic tinkering"—something that didn't need mowing, fertilizing, or watering.

"A new kind of grass?" I volunteered.

"No, no. No one should be messing genetically with grass. The family Gramineae is too important to humankind. Think, Norman, of what would happen if we inadvertently unleashed a broad-spectrum pathogen that affected wheat, barley, oats, corn, rice, millet, sugarcane. A lot of people would starve."

"That might save the environment," I couldn't keep myself from saying.

He laughed his rich laugh and wagged a finger at me. Then,

serious again, he lowered his voice. "I also need to tell you in strictest confidentiality that we may be close to a breakthrough in an effective anti-aging therapy."

"In what form?"

"A pharmaceutical."

I felt a chill of wonder and surprise, not all of it pleasant. Death, for all its disadvantages, has been a reliable constant in human life. The richest and the poorest must both come to dust.

"What's the process?"

"That's the crux of the matter. We change basic cellular behavior."

I didn't have the wherewithal right then to explore my first reactions, including the possibilities of terminating the research as too radical and disruptive if successful. He told me, as though reading my mind, that he wanted me on a committee to consider the whole matter from an ethical point of view.

I nodded, but must have looked dubious as he waxed persuasive. "It's far too early to think about technology transfer and all that. But, Norman, if it's half as effective as I think it will be, the museum's financial worries will be over."

"Who's doing the research?"

"Doctor Carmina Gnocchi is heading the team. Along with me. She's in molecular biology at Wainscott. A real pistol. And not half-cocked, either."

"Yes. I believe I've met her."

"You still seem . . . doubtful."

What could I say? That there are already so many ageless old people, corporeal ghosts peering out from reconstructed faces like souls trapped in life. But other than a sharp yet formless unease about the whole issue, I really had no opinion. I said, "I'll have to think about it."

When the food arrived, we took a break to eat and to talk

about our families. I didn't mention that I had a chimpan-zee living at home and that Diantha and Elsie were out at the cottage. That we were, for all intents and purposes, separated.

I did mention that I would like his help in preparing for an Oversight Committee meeting that would bring up the whole Neanderthal business. I said, "Professor Laluna Jackson, you know, of the Victim Studies Department, will be on hand. And she already takes a dim view of the museum and its director."

He rolled his eyes. "You know, I doubt the woman has any African heritage at all. I mean she may have a touch of the old tarbrush, which I'm allowed to say, but I doubt even that. She frizzes her hair and applies skin darkener. Her black-speak accent is utterly bogus, and the chopping motion of her hands is so farci-cal as to make me cringe. What people like Laluna Jackson do is make an inadvertent and damning parody of black culture."

I had no reply to that and said nothing.

He continued. "You know something else . . . I have a feeling she started out as a he."

"I don't follow you."

"I'd bet that if you did a background check on Ms. Jackson you'd find she began life as a little boy."

"You mean she had herself rearranged?"

He laughed. "That's one way of putting it."

"Why do you think so?"

"I have a nose for these things. She's not all there. I don't understand why people can't just be what they are . . ."

"Not everyone is as blessed as you, Harvey."

"You're too kind, Norman, too kind. But don't worry. I'll come to that meeting with you. Let me do the heavy lifting on that one."

I smiled. "I look forward to it."

We ate well. We had a second drink. We got mellow. Harvey,

his handsome face glistening, leaned toward me and lowered his voice. "I'm about to burden you with something, Norman. And I hope you don't mind."

"Not in the least. I hope."

He hesitated. Then, "Okay, do you remember our first interview? You had my CV. You leafed through it, referring to notes you had made. Your questions were smack-on. And do you know why I like you, Norman? Do you know why I admire and trust you?"

I made a gesture of modest disavowal.

"Because, Norman, in the nearly two years I've known you, not once have you alluded, even indirectly, to the color of my skin."

I shrugged. "There has been no reason why I should."

He shook his head. "I don't think you understand. So many well-meaning and well-off white liberals I've met over the years feel constrained to signal in one way or another that they are not prejudiced, that they approve of me, and that they want me to approve of them. And I don't care how subtly it's done or how well intended, I find it maddening. Demeaning."

"As would I. But then, I don't consider myself a liberal. Except, perhaps in the old-fashioned sense."

He lowered his voice even more. "Do you know what liberals have done to people of color?"

"I would have thought they have tried to help . . . in one way or another."

"Oh, indeed they have. And in doing so they have made us their moral pets."

I sipped at my drink. I could taste the power of the rum. "I don't doubt you, Harvey, but I'm not sure I follow you."

He looked around. He kept his voice low. "To start with, white liberals would never dream of holding black Americans or black islanders or black Africans to anything approaching their own standards. To insist on that is to be called racist when exactly the reverse applies. Allowances are made for our behavior however egregious. Because, you see, we are moral pets."

"But . . ."

He held up a hand. "It's not only that, it's the way we have come to figure large in the identity of affluent whites who can afford to patronize us. It's mostly a class thing. As champions of us poor black people, white liberals can distinguish themselves from the benighted blue-collar workers, from Joe Sixpack. Your wealthy white liberal not only drinks better wine and eats better cheese, but he lays claim to being a better person. And people of color are part and parcel of that moral status. It matters not that most of them live comfortably and securely in white or upper-middle-class enclaves where any stray African Americans tend to be educated and middle-class as well."

He stopped and took a good slug of his piña colada. "I'm sorry, Norman, but this is one of my pet peeves."

"One of your moral pet peeves," I rejoined. Then I pushed back just a bit. "But surely, Harvey, there are many whites who have worked for civil rights out of honorable motives . . ."

"Of course, of course." But his acknowledgment bordered on the cursory as he went off again. Glancing around, he said, "It's deeper and more pernicious than that. I've watched white liberals getting a moral thrill of vicarious indignation by rehashing past injustices against people of color. They pick that particular scab with great relish. It is one of the ways that they establish their moral credentials. It doesn't occur to them that people who are encouraged to see themselves as victims remain victims."

"But, surely, we cannot ignore history."

"No, but there is no human group in the world that has not, at some point in their history, been enslaved in one way or another.

To make slavery such a large part of black history is to reinforce the worst kinds of stereotypes. And to keep opening a wound is to stay wounded."

He leaned back, his eyes askance. After a moment they came back to mine. "You don't watch much television, do you Norman?"

"Not when I can help it."

"Okay, let me tell you what you see these days constantly on the ads. They create a situation with a white person and a black person in it. Invariably, the white person is shown as far less intelligent than the character of color. Do you know why?"

"I haven't given it a lot of thought."

"Because white people are secure in their intelligence, they can afford to be portrayed as stupid. But because there are real doubts about the intelligence of black people on the part of the white, well-meaning ad producers, they must be portrayed as smart."

"Really?"

But Harvey scarcely paused. "There's another thing that nettles me no end." Again he leaned into me and lowered his voice. "Nice white people love to sniff out and expose the least particle of racism in what they regard as lesser whites. Because, you see, to label someone else a racist is to imply that you are not racist, that you are not one of them, regardless of any objective criteria."

"Such as . . . ?"

"Oh, where they work, where they live, where they weekend, where they can send their kids to school . . ."

He finished his drink. Then, smiling at himself, he said, "Oh, God, here I am, another black man complaining to a white friend about how we are treated. So I'll shut up. But let me say one last thing, Norman." He paused. "Do you know what the real advantage of being a white male is?"

"There seems to be fewer of them."

He shook his head. "The real advantage is that white males have no one else to blame when they screw up. No handy scapegoats, no excuses, no point in whining. That, my friend, is real empowerment."

12

It was a fine, summery afternoon, the Fourth of July weekend, and I was in a foul mood. Diantha was furious at me yet again. I told her I had to stay in town with Alphus as all my careful plans to have him taken care of had collapsed. "Norman," she hissed at one point, "I am a young, normal, healthy woman. I need a man."

Getting a "keeper" for Alphus has proven to be a tricky business. Ape-sitting is not the same as dog-sitting or even babysitting. I suppose I could just let him be by himself. He knows that if he leaves the house unattended, he could be captured and possibly killed. Worst of all, he might end up in the Middling County Zoo, where there are real leopards. But Alphus likes to have someone around he can converse with, that is, someone who can sign. There's always Ridley, but the young man, as Millicent attested, is not reliable. That means I not only have to get him someone like a graduate student from the university, but also allow him to have visitors from Sign House.

When I intimated very gently to Diantha the possibility of bringing Alphus out to the cottage with me, she could scarcely speak such was her anger. "I watched that beast killing and eating that little dog. God, Norman, you want to subject your child to that! You must be losing it."

I did not tell her that I suggested bringing Alphus with me because he had broached the subject earlier. In vain I tried to explain to him that my wife did not feel comfortable around chimpanzees. "Or around monkeys for that matter," I added, to make general any possible offense.

"I am not a monkey," he signed with emphatic indignation.

Later, in trying to make amends, I said, "there are mountain lions in the area." As I believe there are.

"Mountain lions?" he questioned, making up the compound with the sign for mountain and the one for lion.

I nodded. "They are big yellow cats that feed on deer and . . . well, whatever they can catch. They have also been known to attack and kill people."

"As big as leopards?"

"About the same size. Perhaps a little smaller."

That mollified him, but did little for my peace of mind. I decided to bring him with me into the office to get some work done. To wax parenthetical for a moment, I am always amused by those detective narratives in which the principals do little but drive around and meet each other and talk about the crime to be solved. Rather like a Henry James novel in which the characters appear to subsist on little but their refined sensibilities. Nor do fictional private eyes ever get sick or go to the dentist to undergo the indignities of a root canal. At worst, they suffer a kind of tidy angst well suited to Hollywood. But I digress.

Among other things, I had to prepare for a meeting of the Council of Curators on Monday. And while that may not seem like much, I can see that once again Mr. de Buitliér is persisting in efforts to build a bureaucracy where none is needed. The second item on the agenda he sent around reads, "Report of the committee on the motion to form a committee to consider the feasibility of establishing a department of curatorial services within the museum." It went on from there, mentioning necessary curatorial services, staffing requirements, departmental coordination, synergistic opportunities, and, the red flag, budgetary necessities.

The committee to study the formation of a committee to consider founding a department had been my ploy to stall the whole dismal process of bureaucracy building. Use the system to clog the system, I say. The question is how much longer can I resist, given my compromised position and the necessity for some kind of administrative apparatus for our growing collections, new methodologies, community outreach, public relations, and all that.

I was working away and Alphus had immersed himself in a book on batiks when the phone rang. I was hoping it was Diantha, but was surprised to find Professor Col Saunders on the line. He spoke somewhat gruffly. "You called," he said.

We had met several times so I didn't have to introduce myself. I asked him if he had a few minutes to spare, that I would like to drop by and talk to him if he were in his office.

"To what purpose?" He let his voice show impatience. I could tell that, like so many others, I had become something of a nonperson where he was concerned.

"I have received a communication regarding the von Grümh murder. You are mentioned prominently. I thought you might like to see a copy of it."

"Oh . . . I see." His tone changed decidedly. "Well, I'm pretty much free right now. Say in half an hour? I could come there."

"Very good," I said. This, I thought, would be an opportune time to test Alphus's lie-detecting skills. I turned to my hairy friend and explained who was coming over and what I wanted him to do.

"No problem," he signed with a sudden alertness I took for enthusiasm.

I then did something undoubtedly unethical and shrewd and, under the circumstances, justified: I rigged up a digital voice recorder I happened to have in my desk.

Col Saunders showed up twenty minutes later. A small hand-some man, he was dressed just short of dandyism in a beige summer suit, pink shirt, and blue patterned tie. When I'd once pondered aloud to Di about his youthful looks, she told me he had obviously had a face-lift along with a hair transplant that looked a tad too reddish. His wide, lifted face, now tanned, and his eyes, which matched his tie, smiled at me as though we were close colleagues.

"Norman, good to see you," he said with false heartiness, his voice still redolent of time spent at Cambridge. He shook my hand and did a double take upon seeing Alphus over to one side with an open book on his lap.

"This is Alphus," I said. "Alphus, this is Professor Saunders." They nodded at each other. Then Saunders took a chair in front of the desk. We exchanged the smallest of small talk before he said, with feigned disinterest, "So what's this about a letter?"

I took a copy I had made for him and slid it across the desk.

He read it rapidly, frowning and then consciously, I thought, making his face blank. He read parts of it twice. He looked up at me. "Have you given the original to the police?"

"I haven't yet."

"Do you intend to?"

"I'm not sure," I lied. "It will depend . . ." I paused. "On what you tell me."

He harrumphed. "I don't really have much to tell."

"Then you have no objection to my sending the original along to the authorities?"

"Obviously, I don't want to get involved in this mess."

"Nor do I want to have obstruction of justice, tampering with evidence, and lawyers only know what else added to the charges against me."

He nodded but without any empathy. He said, "The man couldn't even die without screwing it up."

"What do you mean?"

"Nothing."

"Professor Saunders," I said, my voice confiding and portentous at the same time, "why not just tell me what happened. Later on, if you need me to substantiate your . . . statement, I would be only too willing to."

He considered my offer for a moment. He glanced uneasily at Alphus who was watching him with seemingly neutral curiosity. He then looked around at objects in my office that I had borrowed from the collections. Abruptly, but still with an air of *arrière pensé,* he said, "In fact I did encounter Heinie that night."

"Do you remember at what time?"

"Just about eight twenty-five."

"How can you be so certain?"

"I recall it because I had a call coming in from a colleague in Bangkok at nine fifteen on my landline. I kept checking my watch."

When a pause on his part turned into a hesitation, I prompted, "So how did you happen to see Heinie?"

"Well, just a few minutes earlier I left my town house to walk Spencer, he's my Irish setter, which, as the letter indicates, I do around that time in the evening if I'm home. And I take a plastic bag along for you know . . . There's a Dumpster near the work they're doing on the Center for Criminal Justice. After Spencer had answered the call of nature, I took the results and tossed it into the Dumpster. Just then, I noticed a car on the gravel right-of-way between the parking lots. It seemed out of place somehow. Maybe it was the way it was parked and the way it had its motor and high beams on. I was heading home when it reversed and backed in my direction. The window rolled down, and Heinie called to me."

"How did he seem to you?" Again, Alphus's attention appeared to make him uneasy.

"I could tell he had been drinking. I mean his face was flushed and he sounded very agitated about something."

"What did he say?"

"He called to me. He said, 'Col, you're just the man I need to talk to.'"

I waited as he decided what to tell me next.

"So I walked over to the passenger side and said hello. 'Get in' he said, opening the door. Spencer, a friendly dog, jumped in before I could stop him and went right over the seat into the back. As I was apologizing and trying to pull him out, Heinie said, 'Don't worry about it. I'm used to dogs. Get in.'"

"So you got in?"

"I didn't want to, but I did."

"Why didn't you want to?"

He glanced at me suspiciously. "Well, everyone knows that Heinie and I have a history. The letter spells that out."

"Did he have a gun?"

He hesitated just long enough for me to think he was lying. He said, "No. I didn't see one. I mean it could have been there. On the floor or between the seats."

"So you were parked near the Dumpster? The one you mentioned."

He glanced at me warily. "Not that close. What are you getting at?"

It was my turn to lie. "Nothing. Really. I'm trying to nail down a detail." In fact I was thinking that the Dumpster would be a good place for the murderer to drop the gun. With an inner wince I dissembled with a frown, I wondered if that was where I had put it after I had used it on Heinie.

"Go on," I said.

"Well, he started right in apologizing. He said he had nothing personal against me, that the 'misunderstanding' about the chair was really between himself and his father."

"Did you believe him?"

"Not really. I was more embarrassed than anything else. He got profuse, repeating himself. Then he started abusing you."

"Really? About what?"

"He said you were trying to destroy him professionally by having the authenticity of the collection he gave the MOM tested. He said he had made a mistake giving it to you, that all the MOM had was a lot of native junk."

I nodded. "That does sound like Heinie when he gets going."

"Oh, there's more. He apologized for grabbing the Dresden stater before I, I mean the Frock, had a chance to bid on it."

"What did you say to that?"

"Nothing really. Something like what's done is done. Then he shook his head. His voice was quaking. He said, 'Listen, if you want the Dresden, it's yours. I'm not going to give it to that son of a bitch Ratour!'"

I could not suppress a smile. This part of his story rang true.

"Then he began rummaging in the back of his car. Spencer tried to lick his face. He pulled out a small briefcase from which he took a sheaf of writing paper. He used a regular ink pen, a gold Montblanc, I believe. His hand wasn't all that steady when he wrote something like, 'To whom it may concern, I Heinrich von Grümh, being of sound mind and body, do bequeath to Professor Colin Saunders and the Frock Museum of Wainscott

University on my decease a coin in my lawful possession known as the Dresden stater.' Then he signed and dated it before he showed it to me."

"Do you have that document?"

He took an envelope out of his jacket pocket and handed it to me. Inside was a photocopy of the words above in very shaky handwriting on monogrammed paper. I read it over carefully several times. When I made to keep it, he held out his hand.

I handed it back and said, "Have you asked his estate about the whereabouts of the coin?"

Again he glanced at Alphus. "Why is he staring at me?"

"It's how he is. He's totally harmless."

He nodded with uncertainty. "What were we talking about? Oh, yes, the estate. I did make inquiries. His widow's lawyer wrote that an inventory was being conducted of all of the man's collections. I was told that they would get back to us."

"Did that end your meeting with Heinie?"

"Pretty much. I thanked him. I told him I would let bygones be bygones. I have to tell you, it was a relief to get my dog and get out of there."

"Did he drive off then?"

"No. I glanced back a couple of times and he was still there."

"Why didn't you go to the police with all this?"

"As I said, I didn't want to get involved. One little taint in our cozy little world and doors start to close."

I nodded. "Too true."

"Will you be handing that letter to the police?"

"I don't know," I lied again. "I'll have to think it over."

He stood up. "You understand that the fact that it's anonymous makes it all but useless?"

"I do."

He shook my hand. "You know, Norman, it doesn't contain anything really damning." He nodded to Alphus and with some of his old strut intact, then turned and left.

I took out and carefully placed the original letter from X back in its envelope. I sealed this inside a larger envelope that I addressed to Jason Duff, the district attorney who had wanted me held without bail on a charge of first-degree murder. I decided I would take it over to the Middling County courthouse myself and hand it in.

"What do you think?" I asked Alphus.

He shrugged. "He was lying about the gun. The rest is more or less true."

"I'm a damn fool," I said. "I should have asked him outright if he had murdered Heinie."

That afternoon, as Alphus and I sat in the garden each with an iced tea, which we had begun to drink as a way of stalling the start of any happy hours, I related to him my doubts about the Museum of Man. I told him about Laluna Jackson's description and dismissal of the museum as little more than a trophy house of white male victimization.

I told him I could not dismiss her views as easily as I dismissed her — as a self-righteous, self-indulgent member of the moral class who was building a career on the misery of others. Her accusations had stirred grave doubts. Is the MOM, I asked rhetorically, are most museums, little more than repositories of historic plunder, the victors' spoils? For all my professions of high-minded dedication to these things of beauty, am I little more than an agent of cultural avarice?

He listened patiently as I went on. No, I answered my own question, absolutely not. She's wrong. But I wondered aloud if, in the postmodern morass where nothing means anything, her view and my view of the collections and the whole ethos behind them are merely two constructs, one as legitimate, if such a normative term is plausible anymore in these matters, as the other.

At this point he frowned, perhaps because the laboring loco- motive of my ratiocination had entered a long, dark tunnel with no hint of light at the end of it. I told him I had read that insti- tutions such as ours merely serve to aestheticize if not fetishize (hideous words) objects torn from their living contexts and mummified in cabinets and categories. It is but a short step from there to exculpating if not valorizing (another hideous word) imperial plunder. In short, all the things I cherish — art, appre- ciation, research, beauty — are themselves but words, are but the dimming, receding lights ahead of us in the tunnel.

He considered what I had said for a few moments. He sipped from his tall glass and put it down. I could tell from the way he looked at me and then away that I had touched a raw nerve.

"Neither you nor that woman can escape the profound and blind self-absorption of the human species," he signed. "It is not the white man's pride or greed that is the problem; it is human pride and blindness. You, all of you, destroy wilderness and countryside to build malls for the endless junk that doesn't make you any happier. You think nothing of taking a pristine meadow full of living things and bulldozing it flat and covering it with concrete or big tacky houses surrounded by sterile, chemically doused lawns."

He paused and spelled out some of the words I hadn't under- stood. "Think about it. You hunt your nearest living relative for bush meat. Bush meat! We're not even a delicacy."

"But . . ."

He swept aside my protest and went on, signing with great

emphasis. "The stink of human beings is everywhere now. The world has become one big latrine for your particular excrement, that is to say, for your chemicals, your by-products, your endless garbage, your smoke and fumes, much of which is not biodegradable.

"Think for a moment how alien and dangerous your cities are to other species. Listen to your environmentalists. They plead with humanity to save the wild places for what? To benefit humanity. To find more useful compounds. You want to clean the air and the water and the very soil from the mounting pile of civilization's filth for the sake of what? For the sake of people . . ."

"But . . ."

"No buts. You cannot see it because you are part of it. Your museum and its collections merely add to the cacophony of human self-applause that is loud, everywhere, and unceasing. Look at your religions, your touching faith in a god. You actually believe that some omnipotent force created the whole universe just for you. Small wonder you think humans are the only living things that matter. You assume you are the only ones with the capacity to suffer. You have no regard for the other creatures that must live in your effluence. The biosphere is sick and getting sicker. It has a cancer called people."

He paused in his emphatic signing long enough for me to say, "That's pretty dire. You see no hope at all?"

He gave me a wicked grimace. "Your internecine conflicts were once hopeful signs for the rest of the planet. But for all their death and damage, wars have scarcely impacted the scourge of more and more people. The best hope for the real world, and by that I mean the natural world, is a sustained, recurring pandemic that will get rid of all if not most people."

He sipped without relish his iced tea. He signed, "Present company excepted, of course."

"Of course."

He went on, "The great fear is that human beings will have turned the world into one big cesspool before some virus arises to wipe them out."

I didn't know what to say. Thank you for putting my doubts about the museum into a much larger and damning perspective? Push back? We are trying. Human life does have intrinsic value. We can and are doing something about the mess we have created.

But I would not have argued with much conviction. My own footprint — two homes, two vehicles, jet travel, decent wine, and plenty of meat — is sootier than most whatever gestures I make with new lightbulbs and recycled bits of paper and plastic.

"Alphus," I said at length, "you should include these views in your memoir. The human world needs another voice, one like yours, to join the discussion."

"I might mention them, but I'm already thinking about a separate book."

"Really?"

"I'll be honest with you. I'm writing my memoirs to make money. Bags of money, as the Irish say."

"What will you do with it?"

"I will buy my freedom. I know I'll always need a keeper although the word *companion* would be nicer. I want my own house. A really comfortable tree house. I want a decent car of my own. One of the older BMWs. They had class. I want a really good stereo. I want . . ."

"Be careful. People sometimes define themselves by what they have. And it's never very satisfying. Besides, isn't that the consumerist trap the rest of us have fallen into and which is polluting the planet?"

He thought for a moment. "You know, you're probably right. I should do a book on the environment. From the inside."

"You could be the voice of outraged nature," I volunteered.

He nodded thoughtfully. He picked up and looked at his empty glass.

"More?" I offered.

He shook his head. "Time for a real drink."

We opened a bottle of chilled white and returned to the garden. Without preamble, he signaled, "I may not be a human being but I am someone."

Once again we were discussing the question that gnaws at him more than any other: Who and what exactly is he? He has tried to joke about it. What are chimps that we are so mindful of them? The proper study of chimps is chimpkind.

When I tried, not for the first time, to explain that a lot of people ponder the same question, he shook his head. "I am a freak. I am no longer a real chimpanzee. I would rather be fed to the leopards than live among members of my fellow species. They are stupid and loathsome beyond measure. But I am not one of you, either. And never will be."

"That makes you unique."

"I don't want to be unique."

What could I say? He is a living, breathing lie detector, and he instantly reads my halfhearted affirmations and denials, dismissing them with a snort.

But he can't help picking at this running sore. He mulls over all the attributes of people — their freedom, their things, their work, their happiness, and, above all, their vistas for the future.

Later that afternoon, Ridley came by to work with Alphus on his memoirs. I happened by and watched the latter dictating with rapid gestures as Ridley typed in the words with extraordinary speed. I noticed that when they had done a couple of pages, Alphus would read it over on the screen of his laptop, making small edits with his hunt-and-peck method. He has promised to let me read a section "when it's ready."

I kept resisting a temptation to call Diantha. And say what? You must suffer because of my better nature? Or my weakness? Not that I didn't suffer. As the day waned, I realized that, instead of a lakeside cookout with Diantha and Elsie and some local friends, I would more than likely go with Alphus and Ridley to some fast-food outlet. Alphus has been asking me lately to take him to a restaurant, one of those places you see in old movies where there are chandeliers, where the ladies are coiffed and gowned and the gentlemen spruced in their tuxes, where the waiters bring you the wine to taste, where life looks like a dream of grace.

I have told him that it's impossible, that he is still classed as an animal, and that health codes are such that he would have trouble getting served a hot dog by a street vendor.

The best I can do is to take him to one of those eateries that litter the malls like structural confetti. (Not that the malls aren't themselves a kind of litter.) There, parked outside, Alphus consumes the wretched fare I bring to him. He is partial to cheeseburgers, which he eats with french fries dosed with liberal amounts of ketchup. He also likes a mammoth paper cup full of cola, which he slurps through a straw.

So there we were with Ridley in the backseat, going through the drive-by place, picking up our food, and parking where we could see the whole brightly lit interior. Sitting on his haunches so that he could observe everything that was happening, Alphus ate his meal looking longingly at the people inside.

Nothing of note happened on this holiday evening until a

blind man with a white stick and a Seeing Eye dog came in and, like the other customers, stood in line to order. Alphus stopped sucking on his Coke and sat straight up. He nudged me and signed, "What's that about?"

"A blind man," I signed back, improvising a gesture for *blind* by running a finger across my eyes.

He corrected me as he often does with the proper gesture, two fingers to the eyes then pulled away. He remained motionless as the dog led the man over to a table. Presently a young waitress brought them over a basket of fried chicken parts along with a drink and french fries.

Alphus remained calm in an agitated way until the unsighted man, who was tall and gaunt, began feeding bits of his meal to the dog, a German shepherd, which lay placidly at his feet. Alphus began signing so vehemently, I could scarcely keep up with him. "It's not fair. That animal gets to eat in there and I can't."

Ridley from the backseat egged him on.

"It's a Seeing Eye dog," I said aloud.

Alphus put his food down so he could keep signing. "I don't care. Dogs are nowhere as high on the evolutionary ladder as we are. We share ninety-eight percent of the DNA of people. How much do dogs share? Only they know how to fawn and wag their tails and pretend to be happy. They get to go into restaurants and get fed."

"It's a Seeing Eye dog," I repeated. "They're used to help . . ."

"I know that. But they let it in the restaurant."

"Of course. Public access and all that."

He turned and signed something to Ridley in the back that I didn't get. Then he slid down into his seat and put on his seat belt. I could tell that he was, to use his expression, "biting mad."

13

Hank from Security stood in the doorway to my office with an expression that looked like good news.

"I think I found it, Chief," he said coming in. But I noticed he carried nothing in his hands. Of course not. He came around the desk to lean over my laptop. With a few strokes, the familiar scene from the Diorama of Paleolithic Life appeared.

Then there she is, the alluring Stella Fox in clear, full focus walking toward the camera. She appears deep in conversation with a young man of cropped hair and brutal good looks, a villain right out of Central Casting.

The couple pause. The man gesticulates, his lips moving emphatically. After about a minute they walk out of that camera's range. Another, more distant camera picks them up. But again, there are clear shots of both of their faces.

I thought, watching with increasing excitement, that a forensic lip-reader should be able to decipher what they were saying.

Then, in what seems a cameo appearance, my own tall figure appears. I am in full stride and preoccupied, but not so much as to resist the temptation to give Ms. Fox an appreciative once-over.

Another camera picks them up as they leave the area, but it is a back view.

"Are the date and time . . . reliable?" I asked Hank.

"Stand up in court. It's hard to disprove when you've got all the stuff before and after. You could also testify that you walked through the area at that time and saw her. I mean you've got proof of that."

"Great work, Hank. Excellent. Could you make a couple of copies on disks?"

"Sure." He took several blanks from Doreen and made duplicates of the sequence for me.

As he worked, I said, "Remember, this has to stay strictly confidential."

He nodded. "I understand." He pointed to my screen and a little red icon. "It's right here, on your desktop. It's under the same name on the disks, but you can call them anything you want."

I noticed his bloodshot eyes. "How much time did you put in on this?"

He laughed. "Lots. I accessed it from home. My wife thought I was nuts. I don't want to look at television for a while."

I stood up and gestured him to follow me out to Doreen's desk. "Doreen, would you kindly get a requisition slip for five hundred dollars made out to Hank? On second thought, it's not a museum expense." I went back to my desk, wrote out and gave him a personal check for a thousand dollars, and thanked him again.

I sat down to contemplate what to do with what I had. Send it on to Jason Duff? Send a copy as well to Channel Five? Would that be tampering with evidence? But I had found it. It was my evidence.

I was pondering all this when Doreen announced that Lieutenant Tracy had arrived, was on the line.

"Yes?" I said.

"I'm downstairs. I need to talk to you."

"About what?"

"The von Grümh case."

"All right."

He came in alone, not quite hat in hand, but with a little less of his usual self-possession.

I remained seated behind my desk. I did not offer to shake hands. I said, "What can I do for you?"

He took the chair to the left and produced a copy of the letter regarding Colin Saunders that I had forwarded to the district attorney's office. "Duff turned this over to us."

I regarded him steadily. "Okay?"

"I would like to get some background on Saunders."

"I see. I'm sure they would be able to help you over at the university news office. He works at Wainscott."

"Norman . . ."

"I'm sorry, Lieutenant, but I do not like having my communications ignored. I am already enough of a nonperson around here."

He nodded. "Until the chief got this letter from the DA, I was under strict orders not to have any contact with you."

"The courtesy of a note to that effect would have sufficed."

"I realize that now. But I also don't like to blame others for what I have to do."

"Did you agree with Chief Murphy?"

"Under the circumstances, yes. But I was wrong. And I apologize. If you want to work with someone else on this, I'll understand."

When a man like Lieutenant Tracy apologizes, you know he means it. I felt the steam of the indignation I had been stoking slowly deflate. I shook my head. "No. I accept your apology."

"Thank you."

I waited a moment. "You already know pretty much what I know about Saunders. But when this letter arrived, I took it upon myself to question him." I picked up the several pages of printout and held them by both hands. "This is an account of that interview. I was about to make a copy and send it over to Mr. Duff."

The lieutenant nodded. A gleam of eagerness had come into his eyes.

"You should also know that I may have some evidence pertaining to the Sterl case."

"Go ahead."

I allowed myself a small smile. "I will turn over to you this and evidence I have just received pertaining to the Sterl case on two conditions."

"I'm listening."

"First, you and Chief Murphy are to do everything in your powers to have the charges against me dropped. My lawyer tells me they are completely spurious. I wouldn't be so anxious, but I have a meeting of the Board of Governors on July twenty-fourth. If I am still out on bail, I will be forced to resign."

"I'll do everything I can."

"Second, I want credit for what I've done in any statements to the media by the Seaboard Police Department."

"Agreed."

I hesitated.

"You've got my word."

I pondered awhile longer. I called Doreen and asked her to make a copy of my interview with Saunders for the lieutenant.

Then I positioned my laptop so that we could both see the screen. He leaned forward. I clicked the icon for the Stella Fox sequence. He watched with a keen concentration. Then he turned to me, shaking his head. "Amazing. This could help us considerably."

"You'll need a forensic lip-reader," I ventured.

"More like a Serbo-Croatian forensic lip-reader."

"Really?"

"She's from Croatia originally. A place called Split. I think he might be as well. Could you play it again?"

I clicked the icon.

"That's you, isn't it? Checking her out."

"That's me."

"Can I get a copy . . . ?"

I handed him one of the disks in a cover. Doreen came in just then with copies of my interview with Saunders. I gave him one.

He stood up smiling, took my hand and shook it warmly. "This will get the chief on your side. Duff listens to him. And I'll make sure you get full credit if this breaks the case."

Finally, I thought, after he left, things were starting to go my way. The tide had turned. If the DA's office dropped the charge, the board could not fire me. But I knew I was still vulnerable.

So that, even armed with an edge of self-confidence and with Harvey Deharo in tow, I faced the Oversight Committee meeting with the "Neanderthal Issue" at the top of its agenda in a state of some foreboding. I wanted to ignore them, but I remained vulnerable.

Not that it didn't feel like cheating, showing up with Harvey as an expert witness, so to speak.

All the usual suspects were there when Chair Constance Brattle began by thanking me for agreeing to attend the meeting to discuss what she called "this very important issue." Adjusting her bifocals, she went on, "I know you hold that this committee has no sway in matters involving the Museum of Man. Suffice it to say that the Chair and many members of the committee disagree with that assumption. And it may not be long before that misconception is cleared up."

I did not rise to the bait, but sat impassively, more relieved than ever to have Harvey there.

The Chair then read from the *Bugle*'s account. "'Despite criticism from experts on the need for diversity in role modeling, officials at the museum . . . will be spending several hundred thousand dollars to replace the current models with what one source called 'white skinned, red-haired Caucasians.'"

She cleared her throat and knit her hands together. "I will reserve any comments on the matter for later. I have moved it to first on the agenda to accommodate Mr. de Ratour's special guest, Harvey Deharo, who, as most of you know, is Director of the Ponce Foundation and runs the Genetics Lab."

"He also teaches a course in genomic archaeology," I put in.

Harvey bowed and nodded to those he knew.

Professor Laluna Jackson raised her palm. "I would like very much to start off," she said. And, with assent from the Chair, she began reading a prepared statement, one hand open, fingers together jabbing the air in front of her as though to conduct her emphatic speech, the jangle of her brightly colored plastic hairties adding a kind of timpani.

I regarded her closely. Harvey could be right about her origins, the he-to-she transformation. It might have been her jaw and the way she moved her shoulders. Or her slim waist and not much behind. I might have been fascinated in some perverse way by that possibility and from her manner of speaking were it not for what she said.

"First, I want to say, that the plans of the current management to eliminate the multicultural aspects of the Stone Age diorama strikes me as more in line with the museum's unstated purpose, which many of us view as a showplace of white male triumphalism."

She glanced around as though for applause and continued.

"Speaking professionally, I can assert with confidence that we will be victimizing all peoples of color by filling an exhibition devoted to our ancestors with white-skinned, fair-haired people."

She paused again, then lowered her voice to signal that she was about to say something profound. "It is not just the vulnerable groups alive today that I am concerned about. No, it is the Neanderthals themselves. To depict them as pale-skinned and fair-haired would be to victimize them all over again."

My friend Harvey raised a finger. "Could you tell us how they were victimized in the first place?" He wore a quizzical expression bordering on facetiousness.

"Well," said Professor Jackson, her elocution a touch uncertain, "it's not my field of expertise, but my research shows that the Neanderthals comprised a peaceful hunter-gatherer society living in harmony with nature when they were exterminated by white Europeans."

"I see. Could you tell us what research you're referring to?"

"Research?"

"Yes. Any references, sources, citations?"

"Well, nothing that specific. As I said, it's not my field of expertise. But it's common knowledge that the Neanderthals were exterminated. In fact, they comprise a group we call 'proto victims.'"

"Proto victims . . . Common knowledge, hmmmm." Harvey had just an edge of British archness in his voice. "It might interest you to know, Professor Jackson, that it is generally agreed among Neanderthal specialists, or, rather, specialists in Neanderthal studies, that the Neanderthals were vanquished by dark-skinned invaders from the east who originated not long before in Africa."

He had everyone's rapt attention.

"However, there is considerable debate as to whether the

Neanderthals interbred with the invading AMHs, that is, anatomically modern humans, or were driven extinct by them. It's entirely possible the AMH invaders used the Neanderthals as a food source . . ."

"You mean—?" someone asked.

"Yes. They probably ate them."

Harvey handed around copies of a paper he had brought with him. "What I've given you is the abstract of a research article regarding pigmentation among Neanderthals. As you can see, a melanocortin one receptor allele with reduced function is associated with pale skin color and reddish hair among people of European descent. I can send anyone interested the entire paper."

Professor Brattle said, "Where did the specimens originate, the ones they took the DNA from?"

"Italy and Spain."

Professor Jackson rolled her eyes. "That is precisely the problem. Why does everything have to be so Eurocentric in this country?"

"Maybe because most of us are of European descent," Father O'Gould suggested mildly.

"Europe is where most of the fossils and remnants of Neanderthal material culture have been found," Harvey said.

"Then all the evidence is not in?" Professor Jackson persisted.

Harvey looked amused. "You're right. All of the evidence is not in. If we waited for all the evidence to be in, nothing would happen. The world would turn into one big faculty meeting."

"Is there definitive proof that there were no black- or brown-skinned Neanderthals?" Professor Randall Athol of the Divinity School asked.

Izzy Landes said, "There's no definitive proof that whales can't do higher mathematics. How do you prove a negative?

Father O'Gould cleared his throat. "Most of the extant research on Neanderthals has been done in Europe and the Middle East . . ."

Chair Brattle rapped her figurative gavel. "We're not getting anywhere with this."

Professor McNull frowned.

"Why does that not surprise me?" the Reverend Lopes said. But with a smile.

Harvey glanced at his watch. "I'm afraid I must have my say and leave." He smiled. "Let me put this in terms on which Professor Jackson and like-minded members of the committee might be able to agree." He waited a moment.

"To begin with, there's the science, which, as far as Neanderthal skin pigmentation goes, looks pretty good. Mind you, there's lots more we need to know and won't know until a complete genomic sequencing is carried out. At this point, we can only guess as to how much body hair either sex had. There is much debate about Neanderthal speech. For instance, they may not have separated singing from talking."

"Life as an Italian opera you mean?" Izzy asked brightly.

"Well, certainly more than *parlando*. Perhaps like a Broadway musical."

"They were the original lowbrows," I said.

Harvey resumed, "We know that they had large noses, negligible chins, heavy brows, and tool development little beyond that of *Homo erectus*. But, whatever their development, in the popular mind, Neanderthals were, well, Neanderthals. Their lives were, if not solitary, then poor, nasty, brutish, and short. It could be argued that to assume these primitive humans were people of color would be to reinforce entrenched racial stereotypes."

He gathered his papers. "And on that note, I will take my

leave. But first, let me say that one might have expected resistance from the white community, such as it is, should we plan to show these primitive humans who were fated to go extinct as fair-haired and pale-skinned."

Having tossed that little bomb, he rose, gathered his papers, bowed toward the chair, and on the way out slipped me a folded piece of paper.

Izzy, at his facetious best, said, "So, is it not a slur against white people to have these early forms of humanity depicted as fair-skinned and red-haired? Should we not keep in mind the sensibilities of the Irish, for instance?"

"As prognathically challenged?" someone asked.

Father O'Gould cleared his throat. "I think if the physiognomies of the models were made hirsute and chinless, there shouldn't be any cause for concern on the part of Irish sensibilities."

Izzy, in all apparent seriousness, asked, "Are you suggesting, S.J., that the Irish are sufficiently well chinned to be secure in their chinliness?"

Thad Pilty, of all people, bit. He said, "I doubt very much there's any hard data on Irish chins."

"Then let's do the research," Izzy said with mock enthusiasm. "Norman, you could check the museum's Skull Collection. You must have any number of Irish specimens down there."

"I could find out easily enough."

Chair Brattle asked, "What would be the criteria?"

"Oh," said Izzy, pretending to be incredulous at her ignorance. "You could see how they measure on the ICI."

"The ICI?"

"The International Chin Index. It's an anthropometric term."

"I've never heard of it."

"That doesn't surprise me."

"This is all very well and good," Corny Chard put in. "But what about the chinless Hapsburgs? We could create an international incident."

"What's the point of all this?" someone asked.

"Ah," said Izzy. "If we can prove that the Irish are known to be well chinned, perhaps exceptionally well chinned, then we wouldn't have to worry about portraying the Neanderthals as fair-skinned and red-haired, especially if we emphasized their relative chinlessness for the sake of accuracy."

Then he laughed, thoroughly enjoying himself. It was Izzy, after all, who once said, *Of course I suffer fools gladly. They are a source of great amusement.*

As this frolic proceeded, I surreptitiously opened the piece of paper Harvey had handed me. It was a printout from a Web-based background checking service calling itself WhoWasWho .com. He had been right on. Laluna Jackson, PhD, sociology, Peachtree University, had graduated from Farland High School in Millerstown, Massachusetts, as John J. Johnson. The graduation picture showed a slight young man with dark blond hair and a resentful, uncertain smile.

I refolded the paper and looked up to hear the Reverend Lopes say, "Seriously, there is the issue of white pride."

"White pride is nothing but a euphemism for the worst kind of racism," Professor Jackson retorted.

"What about black pride?"

"Black pride is the response of a people who have suffered systematic victimization."

I was tempted to interrupt this collegial discourse and pass the printout around. But to what purpose? I have no stomach for embarrassing people in public, or in private for that matter. Besides, in this day and age, Ms. Jackson could well be commended for having the courage to be what she wanted to be, to have found and created her true persona at the cost of considerable trauma and expense. And who, anymore, is to say that she's not right?

I slipped the paper into a folder and turned to Bertha Schanke who was asking, "Why not just leave the diorama the way it is? No one's objecting."

I cleared my throat. "That's true, Bertha. But the Museum of Man is a serious institution. We deal in the truth as far as we can ascertain it." I glanced at Professor Jackson and allowed myself to add, "Besides, there's already enough counterfeiting going on."

14

At first I thought it was just a joke in questionable taste, an attempt by Alphus and Ridley to get a rise out of me. It wouldn't have been the first time. Little did I suspect it would end in nightmare. The fact is, I am lucky to be walking around like a free man.

Let me start with this afternoon. Actually with yesterday afternoon, as I am writing in the small hours, unable to sleep. I had tried several times during the day to reach Diantha out at the cottage. But she refused to pick up or click on, which always leaves me with an unraveled feeling.

A general staff meeting in the Twitchell Room had gone badly, in part through my own inattention. Ah, the problems. Everything from moldering skulls to accounting decisions to weakening attendance figures. My authority, never that of a tight-ship captain, has begun to slip. There was an absence in the room that turned out to be me. Several times I glanced through the tall windows at the deep blue sky that is endless and timeless and wondered what I was doing there. The thought of a large, powerful martini when I arrived home kept me going. Not for the first time I feared I might be slipping into alcoholism.

Because the construction of said drink began shortly after I came through the door of my abode. I am partial to Cork Dry Gin (not that it matters after the first one) and a touch of ordinary vermouth rinsed in ice and poured over an unstoned olive.

Though Alphus had been alone for several hours, which usually renders him morose, I found him in a strangely agitated state. He was dressed in a sports jacket, a kelly-green summer-weight thing, along with a shirt and tie and pressed Bermudas. He avoided my eyes and pretended an interest in the small kitchen television, which showed forest fires blazing in the remote West. He is not adept at dissembling, but when I asked him, putting some force into my voice, what was going on, he merely shrugged.

I was nursing my martini and feeling the better for it when Ridley showed up wearing very dark glasses. He, too, acted nervous in the manner of someone trying to appear casual.

"Okay," I demanded of both of them, "what's up?"

Alphus gestured that they were going to a restaurant.

"Really?" I did not take them seriously. I was confident no restaurant would serve them. "Sure, gentlemen. And I have a window seat on the next shuttle to the space station."

Alphus shook his head and repeated more emphatically what he had said before.

"And how do you plan to arrange that?"

Ridley signed in his slow, southern way, "Alphus is my Seeing Eye assistant." He took out what looked like a baton and tele-scoped it into the kind of white cane used by the blind.

It began to dawn on me that they might be serious, that they might try to carry it off. "Where do you plan to go?" I asked.

"The Edge," Alphus said, a note of defiance in his movements.

I shook my head. "I can't allow it."

"You can't stop us." Alphus managed to make his signing seem like a growl.

"I can call the police."

They both looked at me as though they had caught me cheat-ing at some elaborate game we played. More to the point, I was helpless. Call the police? And tell them what? That I am respon-sible in a semi-legal way for a chimpanzee who is pretending to be a Seeing Eye ape in service to someone who is not blind, both of whom are heading for an upscale restaurant on the Seaboard waterfront?

"All right. But how are you going to get there?"

Ridley took out his raspberry or whatever those things are called. "Text," he signaled. "Taxi."

I tried to divert them. I told them we could order in anything they wanted. I told them we could cook up a feast together. Invite people over. Have it catered so that it would be like a restaurant. But to no avail. They not only insisted on doing it, but pleaded for me to accompany them. I refused, of course. I told them I would not be party to such a farce. I told them it wouldn't work. I told them they might be breaking the law. Besides, they forgot that I was out on bail as an accessory to murder. Any trouble with the police, and I could end up in jail.

Alphus signed, "All they can do is not let us in."

"We need you," said Ridley and smiled. "We want your company." He had his berry in hand and was tapping something into it.

I remonstrated with them, repeating myself. It was no use. I could tell from the way Alphus buckled on a collar and leash and led Ridley tap-tapping after him that they had been practicing, the villainous pair!

Not long after that a taxi pulled up and sounded its horn. It was one, apparently, that they had used before, judging from the way the cabbie greeted Ridley and nodded to Alphus. I stood on the sidewalk, drink still in hand, still entreating them.

"Come on," they signed. "What have you got to lose?"

What indeed? Out of concern for their welfare, out of weakness, I capitulated. I went inside, put on a jacket, and squeezed in next to them in the back of the cab.

It being a Wednesday and relatively early, I assumed there

wouldn't be many people at The Edge. It is an upscale faux casual sort of place owned and run by Simon and David, two gay men of a certain age. It's right on the harbor. In fact, it's the same building where the Green Sherpa used to be. It's been changed radically, with a dark, atmospheric bar where the gift shop had been. In summer the dining area extends to a large deck built on piers over the water.

My heart went out to the official greeter, whose face froze in a pained smile as we came through the door, a leashed Alphus leading a tapping Ridley, with me in a cringe bringing up the rear.

"Can I help you?" said the unfortunate man from behind the reception desk. He might have been either David or Simon, judging from his aspect. He clearly struggled with his up-to-date conscience. How far does the desirability of diversity go? And if Seeing Eye dogs, why not Seeing Eye apes? But what about the other customers?

"Yes," I said. "We called. A table for three. The name's Ridley."

"Of course," said Simon David, recovering some of his aplomb. "We have a text message. I'll see what's available."

We stood around in front of the desk drawing stares. The hall from the main door had thick carpeting, sconces for light on dark, paneled walls, and doors opening into restrooms on one side and the bar on the other. I was wrong about Wednesday. The place was buzzing with people. We waited. Time began to drag. Other parties came in and stood behind us. Two couples, well oiled to judge from their demeanor, came out of the bar and began to make remarks. "Do you always make fun of the handi-capped?" I asked the chief offender, a young, crew-cut man with a head like a red pumpkin.

"I'm sorry," he confessed, and burst out laughing. One of the women had the self-possession to pull him away. I glanced around nervously with all the acute discomfiture of one in a false position.

Simon David finally returned. "We don't have any private rooms available," he said in a voice meant to sound accommodating but final. I'm sure he didn't have any to begin with, but that didn't matter.

"That's perfectly all right," I said, meaning we would leave.

Ridley poked me with his stick and shook his head.

"I'll be right with you folks," Simon David said to the people in line behind us.

Well, we finally got seated. As unobtrusively as was possible under the circumstances, Simon — as he turned out to be — led us to a table more or less in the shadows next to the railing above the shimmering water. In a *sotto voce* aside to me, he said, "It . . . he is . . . housebroken?"

"He'll be fine," I assured him, and resisted an impulse to slip him a twenty.

"We will need three settings," I said to the waiter, a gangly college youth with acne and an expression of earnest bemusement who had begun to remove two of the four place settings. I kept my voice as normal as I could. One couple had already gotten up and left. Simon watched nervously from the doorway. I was relieved when the moon slid behind a cloud, obscuring us momentarily.

"Are you expecting a third party?"

"We are a party of three," I said, indicating Alphus, who had taken a seat with his back to the other customers. In for a penny and all that.

"I see. Or rather, I guess, I don't see."

"Mr. Alphus, our Seeing Eye . . . assistant, is also joining us."

"Will he need a setting?"

"He will be joining us for dinner."

"I see. I'm afraid it's against health department regulations . . . to serve animals in the restaurant."

"He is completely table-trained."

"I see. Still . . ."

I closed my eyes as though that might dispel what I found to be a waking bad dream. I glanced in the direction of the distant, hovering Simon. "Could you ask Simon to step over here."

As the other patrons watched more or less surreptitiously, the waiter went over and conferred with the co-owner. The co-owner was joined by the other co-owner, judging from appearances. I would guess they were having a tiff. David finally stalked off and Simon went after him.

The waiter returned alone, his demeanor struggling to achieve an air of decisiveness.

"I'm afraid it's a no-go, sir. We aren't even allowed to have cats in the kitchen. Your Seeing Eye . . . companion is welcome, but we won't be able to serve it . . . him . . . food."

"We watched the other night when a sight-impaired person fed his Seeing Eye dog inside a McDonald's," I said.

He shrugged. "Yeah, McDonald's . . ." Then his demeanor changed markedly. I followed where he had glanced before shifting his attentions back to me. Ridley, pretending to fumble, had produced a hundred-dollar bill from his wallet.

"McDonald's. Yes . . ."

The money changed hands with admirable covert deftness, and Alphus was presently inspecting a fine cloth napkin and the cutlery that came with it.

The other customers did gawk. And I felt a keen embarrassment, in part because of the ruse and also because of the way we were taking advantage of people's better natures. Another couple at an adjoining table did get up abruptly and make their way toward the reception area. But all the others were soon back to their food and talk.

Our table, close to the railing along the water, was also up against a partition of varnished lattice that separated the deck into two sections. I was able to glance through and see that the couple who had left were being reseated a good distance away.

One well-meaning matron came over to bestow smiles and ask if she might pet Alphus. I said he allowed, but didn't appreciate it. Of course, she said, she understood. A distant relative had a Seeing Eye dog who could practically talk.

Alphus gave her his version of a smile.

The pretense we all agreed upon — the waiter, whose name was Marlen, the other patrons, and ourselves most of all — was that there was nothing extraordinary about an ape, a well-dressed, well-behaved ape, but an ape nonetheless, sitting like an upright Christian at table in an upscale restaurant. I could sense the amused amazement around us when Alphus took the menu from me and perused it with what, for a chimp, was a thoughtful expression. "Cute," I heard someone remark. "Well trained," said someone else.

Marlen came back for a recital of the specials. "We have a pan-seared tilapia in a hand-washed mint sauce on a bed of braided, whole wheat capellini cooked in wood-heated water. The chef recommends our second special of the evening. It's pulled loin of pork cooked *au feu nu* with a sweet potato rémoulade and wine-soused sautéed chard. But I'm afraid we're all out of the third special. I'll give you a few minutes. Would you like to see a wine list?"

"Please," I said.

Needless to say, I was on tenterhooks the whole time. Several times I had to tell Ridley not to sign. "Remember, you're blind."

Frankly, I was afraid that someone I knew would see me in this ridiculous situation. Or that someone would come in and make a scene.

The covert glances from the other customers continued, especially when Simon showed up with the wine list and I read off the choices to the other two. I suggested an Argentinean Malbec, which I had heard mentioned favorably at a meeting of the Club's wine committee. Alphus took the embossed folder and, after studying it, pointed instead to a recent Nuits-St-Georges *premier cru*.

"Very pricey," I said.

Ridley nodded okay. Then, on a scrap of paper he scrawled, "My treat. Go for it."

"Three glasses?" asked Simon, an eyebrow going up. But he shrugged when I said yes.

There were more stares as Alphus took a look at the menu and pointed out to me that he wanted the *filet mignon au poivre* rare with extra salad. For an appetizer, he picked a double order of *pâté de ferme* with honey-pickled gherkins.

I read the choices off to Ridley, who nodded twice at the lemon-poached scrod served in a froth of *bisque de homard* and, for a starter, *une tranche de foie gras* from un-force-fed geese. I ordered the pork.

Marlen brought the wine. He poured about an inch into my glass. I handed it to Alphus, who held it up to what light was available, nosed it, and then sipped. I could feel the incredulous amazement all around us. He nodded and the wine was poured. We raised our glasses. *Salut.*

The appetizers arrived not long after and we ate leisurely, sipping wine, breaking off pieces of bread, and carrying on a complicated three-way conversation in which Alphus would sign and I would pretend to interpret it vocally for Ridley, who would covertly sign back.

Our waiter deftly cleared away the plates in preparation for the main course and refilled our glasses before I had a chance to stop him. I did not want to add inebriation to the situation. Ridley indicated he wanted to go to the men's room. Alphus understood and rose to play his part, dutifully leading the convincingly tap-tapping Ridley toward the reception desk and the men's room.

I should have gotten up and accompanied them. But I felt that the apparent assistance being rendered to Ridley by Alphus served to justify the presence of the latter among us, especially to the diners who had stayed in our area. The performance made Alphus's claim seem entirely plausible: If a Seeing Eye dog, then why not a Seeing Eye chimpanzee? And if the chimp had table manners, then . . .

I dawdled there, thinking that we were going to pull this off. I knew there would be more requests in the future. I would simply put my foot down and say no. I buttered and ate some of the excellent bread. I sipped wine. I thought several thoughts. Restaurant time has an odd dynamic: You sit and wait until, of a sudden, it occurs to you that it's been longer than you think. I wondered where my companions had gone. And what they were doing. I began to grow worried.

Finally, I got up and, as casually as I could manage, went in search of them. They were not in the men's room, where I availed myself of the facilities, rinsing my hands and looking into the face in the mirror. *Fool*, I said to it.

From the reception area, I checked to see if they were at our table. I glanced into the bar. It was dark so that at first I didn't see them. They were there, at the far end of the polished counter with two quite good-looking women. The champagne glasses in evidence indicated that Ripley had been speaking again with his wallet.

"Are these your friends?" one of the women asked me as I approached. She and her companion were expensively and provocatively dressed, one in a short skirt with buckled boots to just below her knees, the other in black, skintight toreador pants.

"Indeed," I replied. "And dinner is waiting." I signed as much to Alphus and Ridley, who gave no indication of moving.

"They're so cute," said the woman in tight trousers, who, with broad blond features, could have been Ridley's older sister. "Hi, my name's Roxanne." She took my hand and shook it.

"Norman," I mumbled.

"And that's Kareena. We've never been picked up before by a blind deaf mute."

"Have you been picked up?" I asked, too distracted to keep the bartender from pouring me a glass of bubbly.

She giggled. "I think so. We're going to a party . . . Wanna come?"

"How was this communication effected?" I asked, collusive now in taking the glass of champagne and drinking from it.

"He texted me."

"Did he, indeed? By the way, his name's Ridley and he's not deaf."

"His friend's not so bad, either," said Kareena in the short dress. She had on a thin jersey that showed considerable cleavage beneath a heavy gold cross. "Not that, you know, it's my thing. I like his jacket." She gave me a once-over as though I might be her thing.

Ridley signed to me on the side. "Hookers," he spelled out. Then something about fishermen.

For a moment I thought he meant they worked on the trawlers that dock at the wharves not far from The Edge.

Ridley frowned at my obtuseness and made the hand sign for the letter *X*, tapping his upper cheek and then lower cheek, meaning "sex," which I got. Still, he made a circle with the thumb and index finger of one hand and gestured vigorously into it with the finger of his other hand.

Roxanne caught it and laughed. "Right on."

It should not have surprised me that Seaboard has ladies of the night plying their ancient profession. But it did.

Of course it was stupid of me not to have settled up the bill right then and left. And go to a party, go anywhere, anyplace, to hell, if necessary. Because it would have been a way of getting out of a situation that was to be the stuff of bad dreams for years to come. But I am a stick in the mud. I am of the old school. I am a fool. Simply because the restaurant had prepared a meal for us, I felt obliged not only to pay for it, but also to eat it. So I stood my ground and, to the evident disappointment of Alphus and Ridley, insisted that they say good-bye to their new friends and return to their waiting dinners.

"We'll be right there," Ridley signed, a bit brusque in his movements.

I went back to our table where, indeed, an anxious Marlen hovered with our main courses.

How I wish we had paid the bill in the obscurity of the bar, left a hefty tip, and disappeared into the night with the two ladies thereof. Because what happened next had all the simultaneity of a freak accident. I had scarcely sat down and sipped some of the *premier cru* when I heard the distinctive, New England honk of Elgin Warwick. Aghast, incredulous, I peered through one of the small, diamond-shaped openings in the lattice and saw the tall, courtly figure of the same sitting down not far away with no less than three members of the museum's Board of Governors. There was Carmilla Golden, a woman of fifty who is active in Seaboard affairs; Maryanne Rossini, the university representative and a tool of Malachy Morin; and the ancient but still somewhat alert Dexter Farquar.

Not seconds later, I glanced toward the reception area where Alphus, unleashed, and with all the aplomb of a worldly *roué*, was leading the still-tapping Ridley and the two ladies of the bar into the dining area, Kareena carrying the half-filled champagne bottle by the neck. People frowned. Marlen stood looking on like an idiot, his mouth agape.

"They're joining us for dinner," Alphus signed to me as he neared.

"I don't think so," I said as firmly as I dared. I did not want any kind of scene. I wanted to pay whatever bill there was and leave. Quietly.

"Will you need two more settings?" asked Marlen, mesmerized again by Ridley, who had his wallet out.

"No," I insisted. "We need a check. We have to leave. Immediately. It's imperative."

"What's imperative?" the blond Roxanne inquired, meaning, I think, the word.

"The food here is yummy," said Kareena, whose toreador pants made abundantly obvious her callipygian charms.

"We'll take it with us," I said, desperate now. Other diners, napkins in hand, were staring at us.

"You want doggie bags?" asked Marlen quite loudly.

"Doggie bags will be fine," I said.

"Could I have the peppered steak to go?" Roxanne asked.

"Make that two," chimed in Kareena.

"No, we are leaving. Right now." I had raised my voice.

"What about your doggie bags, sir?"

"Bring them to reception. Ridley, give the man enough money to cover this." I wasn't being cheap. I didn't want to wait around while people fussed with my credit card. As I spoke, I was calculating that to get to the reception area, it was necessary to cross a ten-foot space where people on the other side of the lattice would have a clear view of us. If we could make it past there and out to the main entrance, we would be in the clear.

But my augmented party were reluctant to go. Alphus sat down with that look on his face.

"Alphus," I said, bending down to him, "if we don't leave right now and if there's any kind of trouble, the museum will insist you return to the Pavilion and there will be nothing I can do about it."

"Why?" he signed.

"I'll explain later. Trust me."

Alphus glanced at Ridley. He signed, "Okay, let's go."

Ridley placed several of his hundred-dollar bills on the table as I lined up the two girls to walk to the right of Alphus, shielding him from sight as best they could. My face averted and my body hunched, I herded my group to the reception desk without incident. People, I could tell, were as glad to see us go as I was to leave.

We had just reached the desk, inches away from what I considered sanctuary, when I heard, with a sudden, heart-thudding thump, the shrill, reaching voice of Royale Toite. Coifed, expensively, pantsuited, with the eyes of a mad raptor, she came looming as though out of the wall, but was in fact leading a gaggle of her women's-club friends from the cloakroom to one side of the desk. She looked straight at me with a face glowering with indignation.

"What is *this* all about?" She turned her fury to an obviously distressed Simon, who was hurrying over. "How dare you subject us to this . . . outrage!" She approached within hissing distance. "Norman de Ratour, have you no shame? A beast just like that one killed and ate my dog, my little Miffy . . ."

I faced her feeling like I had woken from a bad dream into a living nightmare. I didn't care in the least what this wretched woman thought, but I wanted to avoid an encounter that would bring members of the Governing Board out to see what the ruckus was about.

"Royale," I said, my tone invoking a certain class allegiance as I pronounced her name *Roy Al,* the way she liked it, "there's no reason to . . ."

"No reason . . . !" She was all but screaming. "That's the very ape . . . !" She turned to Simon. "Unless you get rid of that thing immediately, I am never bringing the club here again. No, no. Never mind. I am going to call the police myself and put an end to this unspeakable . . . abomination right now."

With alarm, I noticed one of her coterie keying her phone and then speaking into it.

"Madame, please," Simon said in an aggrieved voice, "we are required to allow all Seeing Eye dogs on the premises."

"That thing is not a dog."

"Under the circumstances he has the legal standing of a Seeing Eye dog," I lied, thinking, *If she only knew.*

Alphus made some minimal movements with his hands and fingers, the signing equivalent of whispering. "Let's just go through the bar."

Royale threw me a venomous look. To no one in particular but loud enough for all to hear, she said, "What else do you expect from someone who would marry his own daughter."

"My late wife's daughter," I corrected her, making it sound worse somehow.

"What are you doing out of jail, anyway? Haven't you been charged with murdering poor Heinie?"

"As a matter of fact, I haven't."

An audience, including some blinking denizens of the bar, diners with napkins in hand, even staff from the kitchen, had begun to gather.

Royale, voice piping over the murmuring spectators, declared, "Simon, we are not dining in the same place as that . . . criminal animal, that despicable beast."

Simon bowed. "Madame, they are leaving."

We might have made good our escape, as the locution has it, but the words *despicable beast* stuck in my craw. To hell with Elgin Warwick, I thought, as I turned and walked several paces back to the woman. Through clenched teeth, I told her, "He is anything but a despicable beast. He is a gentleman of the first order. He is a considerate, rational, moral being. And that, lady, is more than I can say for you." I just barely kept myself from adding that she was an overprivileged rich bitch whose family wealth came from a whiskey-running grandfather who had been little more than a mobster.

"I'm very sorry, Mr. Ratour," said Simon, who had a little trimmed mustache, "but it would help matters if you and your party were to leave."

"We're just on our way," I said. "You've been most patient."

Alphus was tugging at me, signing. "It's okay, Norman. Let's just leave. Now."

But we had left leaving too late. The police sirens I had heard a moment before had stopped abruptly. Indeed, we were scarcely at the main door when it opened and two uniformed officers came in with guns drawn.

Keeping my voice steady — there is nothing more intimidating than the black muzzle hole of a gun pointed at you — I said, "We were just leaving, Officer. Your guns won't be necessary."

I felt a push from behind as Royale rushed past me in full screech. "That's the one, officer! That's the one that ate my dog!"

"In here?" asked the younger officer, whose gun now pointed directly at Alphus.

"No, no, no, in the Arboretum."

Marlen appeared holding several white containers. "Your doggie bags, sir."

I took them and said "Thank you." I turned and handed them to Roxanne.

When Marlen lingered as though for a tip, I nearly erupted again.

"The Arboretum?" asked the older officer, who was holstering his gun.

"Matt, we ought to call the animal squad," said the younger one, his gun still at the ready.

More diners and patrons from the bar had begun to gather and watch the show.

The older police officer, bushy browed and sardonic of face, said, "Christ, I thought I had seen everything."

Just then Alphus turned to me and signed, "Tell them they don't need their guns."

Officer Matt caught it and said, "What did he just say?"

"Officer," screeched Ms. Toite.

He waved her off.

"He just told me you don't need your guns," I said.

"Jesus Christ, I have seen everything." He turned to his younger colleague. "Vince, holster your weapon."

At which point, I succeeded in handing Lieutenant Tracy's card with his private cell number to Officer Matt. "Please call him before you proceed . . ."

"Vince, hang on." He turned away and I heard him muttering into the mike attached to the front of his uniform.

He seemed to talk for an eternity. Any minute I expected old Warwick and his party to join the onlookers.

Which in fact is what happened. He joined the scene accompanied by Ms. Rossini. "Norman . . . what is going on here?"

I tried to smile. "Very little, Elgin, I can assure you."

"Elgin, can you believe it, he brought that beast in here," Royale cried at him.

Elgin, God bless him, laughed. "Oh, Royale, and why not?" He turned back to me. "And these ladies . . . Are they in your party as well?"

"Yeah," said Kareena, checking him out. "We were in the bar."

Elgin laughed again. "Norman, you old dog . . ." Then nodded, as though to signal I owed him one as he took Royale and led her away.

Officer Matt finally came back to us. "All right, you guys, it would be best if you got out of here."

With great relief and with a thank-you all around over my shoulder, we exited. Not far off, I could see one of those television vans lurching into view. "This way," I signed to my companions, who, I suddenly realized, were either in a fairly inebriated state or too far into their blind act to relinquish it.

We headed for the busy part of the waterfront and a place where I could find a cab. At one point we had to duck into an alleyway to get out of sight from a second television van. We nearly tripped over a homeless man drowsing on a cot of cardboard.

"Please, no," he said at the sight of Alphus. "Please, God, no."

We finally hailed a taxi. When the cabbie, a hulking, T-shirted man with a shaved skull and a ring in his ear, saw Alphus, he got out of the driver's seat and came around to the curb. "Sorry, dudes, but that thing ain't getting into my cab."

"He's quite harmless," I said with as much dignity as I could muster under the circumstances. "He's a Seeing Eye chimpanzee."

"I don't care if he plays quarterback for the Patriots, he ain't getting in my cab."

The driver of another cab we managed to hail proved a bit more reasonable. "It's an extra ten for the monkey," he said. "And if he shits, you're cleaning it up."

I turned to the girls. "Keep the doggie bags. And here . . ." I handed them some bills. As they protested, I got into the back-seat and closed the door. "Drive," I said.

Alphus nudged me. He signed, "I'm still hungry."

"Where to?" the cabby asked.

"The nearest McDonald's," I said, trembling with relief.

15

It seems I have dodged any adverse publicity following our escapade at The Edge. The *Bugle* ran a small, confused item on page three mostly lifted from the police log. It referred to a disturbance involving a large animal at a Clipper Wharf restaurant. Needless to say I was relieved that nobody used one of those ubiquitous little phone cameras to take a picture that would have ended up plastered everywhere.

I put in a call to Lieutenant Tracy to thank him for his help in extricating me from what could have been a veritable debacle. Being out on bail, I am vulnerable to more than embarrassment. He told me he was in the neighborhood and wanted to drop by. I said of course.

He had scarcely sat down after warmly shaking my hand when, brushing aside my repeated appreciation of his intervention, insisted that it was he who was indebted to me for helping him on the Sterl case. "The chief is very pleased. He's been on the line to the DA daily to get the charge against you dropped. But Jason Duff doesn't like to let go once he gets his teeth into a case."

Pausing to change conversational gears, he said, "I'm still wondering if those fake coins have anything to do with the von Grümh case."

I nodded, but not in agreement. "You mean in terms of a motive."

"Exactly. Von Grümh could have known something. He could have been murdered to keep him quiet."

"I suppose that's possible. But who?"

"I'd like to know how Max Shofar fits into von Grümh's coin collecting."

I shrugged with my hands. "Everything. Heinie got a lot of his coins through Max."

"Maybe von Grümh found out that Shofar was passing him counterfeits. Von Grümh confronts him, threatens to expose him. Shofar, in a panic, shoots him."

His scenario made me realize how much more I knew about the case than he did. I said, "In fact I've already asked Max about that."

"And what did he say?"

"He told me, and I believe him, that the last thing he could afford is even a hint that he deals in fakes."

"When did you talk to him?"

"Not long after I was arrested."

"You should have told me."

"You left me out of the loop, remember?"

He smiled ruefully. "I did. It won't happen again."

"So we're back to square one," I said equably. "It's possible, isn't it, that the counterfeiting doesn't figure in the murder?"

The lieutenant looked at me doubtfully as though sensing I wasn't telling him everything I knew. "Anything's possible. But it doesn't ring . . . right to me."

"There is one way we might clear up the matter."

"How?"

"Diantha tells me that Heinie . . . von Grümh was very emphatic about needing the gun to protect something he had on his boat. Let's say that that something is the original collection of coins, the real ones."

"We've already gone over the boat."

"How thoroughly?"

He turned thoughtful. "We should have been able to find that many coins."

"But you weren't looking for them at the time."

"True, but what would it signify if we did find them?"

"It would at least clear Max. Of that motive, anyway."

He nodded slowly. "You're right. Eliminating suspects is as important as finding them."

We chatted for a while longer. Then, almost casually, he said, "You've got me thinking. We have a guy, an expert on conceal-ment, that we sometimes use on cases like this. If he's available, we could drive down to the boat this afternoon and go over it one more time."

"I see," I said doubtfully. I had planned to leave early for a weekend at the cottage with Diantha and Elsie. And the pros-pect of rummaging through the scene of my wife's infidelity did not appeal to me, to say the least.

He gave me a sharp look of entreaty. "I thought you might be able to help us. You've been on board before."

"Okay," I said. "But I don't want to make a career out of it."

"Short and sweet," he smiled. "I promise you."

So, packed for the weekend, I arrived a bit early at the dock and waited for the lieutenant, who showed up not long afterward with the expert, a small, dapper middle-aged man introduced to me as Mr. Randall. The manager of the marina, an old-salt type with whiskers and belly, made some protesting noises as a matter of form. He glanced over the search warrant and dug out the keys we needed. He seemed accustomed to having boats searched, perhaps because of the drug trade.

As we boarded the vessel over an aluminum gangway, I began to fully understand my reluctance to be there. It wasn't just that this vessel was the venue of Diantha's infidelity. On the deck of tightly joined hardwood, the nightmare of my possible guilt rose around me like a dark miasma. Because there are moments when I am not only glad that Heinrich von Grümh has been murdered, but would've liked to have done it myself. And perhaps did. Upon entering the master stateroom with its gleaming metal and waxed maple banality and taking in the very place where he and Diantha had been naked and lascivious in one another's arms and legs, I knew for a certainty I could have held a gun to the man's head, tormented him with words, and pulled the trigger.

Or could I have? Gradually, as I stood there amid the decor of what amounted to an upscale recreational vehicle, the significance of their encounter dissipated to what it had been. Sex without passion or love is about as meaningful as a rectal exam when you think about it. I realized anew that if I had murdered the man it was because of his subtle, patronizing taunts.

I collected my wits and got to work. It is extraordinary how many nooks and crannies there are inside the finite space of a sixty-foot sloop. With Mr. Randall's help, we found drawers within drawers, spaces within spaces. There was a series of brass-fitted compartments with covers that hinged up or down or slid smoothly sideways. We made some interesting discoveries, including a cache of exotic erotica, judging from the foreign-language titles on the videos.

I took a moment to thumb the folder of woodblock prints done in the Shunga style by Utamaro. They were mostly of extravagantly clothed couples in various positions with their salient parts exposed and their expressions impassive. Strange to me that the Japanese do not appear to associate the erotic with the nude. No Greek ideal of the human figure. The prints were valuable, I guessed, unless they, too, were fakes.

One well-recessed cabinet contained a regular pharmacopoeia.

We also found the holster to my gun along with extra ammunition in a trick drawer of a bedside table in the guest stateroom. The lieutenant photographed the items *in situ* before putting on a pair of latex gloves and placing the items in plastic evidence bags, which he sealed.

"That may very well be exculpatory," he explained when we were by ourselves in the lounge. "It's at least circumstantial evidence that von Grümh had the weapon in his possession."

We were on the point of resorting to the cordless drill to start unscrewing bulkheads and decking when I checked again the pictures in the master stateroom. They were a series of eighteenth-century prints depicting warships under full sail. They had been affixed to the walls by an ingenious-looking device to keep them from slipping or falling during rough seas.

After a moment of fiddling with the device, I struck upon the right combination of flicking and pushing. The picture tilted forward in such a way that I could take it down. When I lifted it off the wall, I noticed a small lever, not part of the mechanism, that protruded slightly from the wall in the middle of it.

"Lieutenant," I called. "I think I've found something."

He came in with the expert. They watched as I gently moved the lever from a down position to an up position. Nothing seemed to happen. But Mr. Randall, poking about, noticed that the sill under one of the two rectangular portholes that flanked either side of the bed, had lifted ever so slightly.

Donning a pair of latex gloves himself, he lifted the solid piece of hardwood, which hinged back against the inner glass of the porthole. As I watched with a giddy sense of expectation, he pulled out two zippered canvas bags of rugged construction, each approximately eighteen by twelve by six inches in size. He placed the bags on the bed next to the picture I had removed and shone his flashlight into the cavity. "That's all," he said.

"Let's hope it's not booby-trapped," the lieutenant said as he helped unzip the bags and spread apart the openings. I watched intently as they extracted several of what looked like those heavy leather stationery folders you find in the rooms of expensive hotels. He gave one to me, and carefully, on the bed, I undid the clasp that held it shut and opened it.

It didn't surprise me for some reason that it contained no coins in the variously shaped circles cut into the matting in the interior of the covers. It hadn't been heavy enough. The rest of them, ten in all, were empty as well. At the same time, something nagged at me. *Something* was heavy enough. And with that excitement that comes with discovery, I lifted up the print of the USS *Boston* under full sail. It was too heavy, considering that it was a reasonably simple if strong assemblage of wood, glass, and paper.

I handed it to the expert. "What do you think?"

"Yeah," he said, and produced one of those knives with a retractable razor. With precision and care, he sliced the brown paper glued in place over the back of the frame. Beneath that was a fitted piece of thin cardboard. Using the edge of the blade, he gently pried this up. And there, in their custom-cut holes under a thin piece of transparent plastic, were at least two dozen ancient coins.

"I think those are they," I said. "In fact, I recognize several of them. That one is a Mesembria War Helmet hemidrachm. And that is a Julian the Second bronze."

We dismantled a few more prints, of which there were a goodly number. When the Dresden stater turned up in a smaller print all of its own, I said, "I'm sure this is the collection."

"But you're not positive?"

"Not a hundred percent, but nearly . . ." I remembered going over it with Heinie at Raven's Croft, his eager hunger for approval.

"Who is?"

"Our curator."

"Phil?"

"Exactly, but I don't want him to know about this, if that's possible."

The lieutenant started to say something and stopped. "Okay. That shouldn't be a problem."

We waited around as Mr. Randall dismantled the remaining prints and put the mounted coins into evidence bags that the lieutenant sealed. I said, "There's a highly respected numismatist in Boston named Simons. George Simons. I would suggest we give him the collection along with a catalog for verification."

"To verify that this is the collection?"

"Yes, and to verify that they're real."

"You think . . . ?"

"Once burned."

"Okay. I'll leave that in your hands. Take a couple of dozen coins from Randall. He'll make you sign for them. And send them to your man."

Up on the sunny deck, the lieutenant looked around at the taut lines, brass fittings, and other nautical paraphernalia of a large and expensive sailboat. He said, "The rich are different, aren't they?"

"Some are. Not Heinie. Not a lot of them. They are as ordinary as dirt."

We said good-bye to Mr. Randall and, though it was getting late, dropped into a nearby coffee shop to go over what we had found. We took our coffees to a booth at a window overlooking the boatyard. The lieutenant had one of those involved latte things, which surprised me, but, then, he is considerably younger than I.

"Well, I think we can eliminate this as a motive implicating Shofar."

He nodded. "And you get your real coins."

I smiled most ruefully. "The merry widow Merissa will be able to claim them. He gave us the fakes." And, I thought, another public relations disaster when this story broke.

We sat there for twenty minutes following our new discovery through a rat maze of motives, implications, and hypotheses. We decided it made more sense for Heinie to murder someone to keep the forgery a secret than to be murdered. Disclosure would be more than an embarrassment: He would have faced criminal charges for defrauding the IRS.

We were getting ready to leave when the lieutenant said, "Tell me, Norman, why do you keep this . . . chimp around?"

I explained in general terms what Alphus was. "He is both more and less than human. If you got to know him, you would find it impossible to put him back in a cage."

"Yeah, but that doesn't mean taking him to restaurants."

"True." I decided then to mention to my friend and colleague Alphus's gifts regarding truth telling.

"You might be interested to know that this chimp, Alphus, is a living, breathing lie detector."

"How can he do that? He doesn't speak."

"No. But he understands most of what's said. We communicate in sign language."

"Whole sentences?"

"Whole paragraphs."

"All right."

"I was thinking that we could arrange to interrogate our suspects with Alphus behind the one-way glass signaling yea or nay to their responses."

The lieutenant shook his head. "That sounds great. Trouble is, most of them would show up with lawyers who would tell them to say nothing. And, besides, none of it would stand up in court.

Think about it. Your Honor, our infallible ape has indicated . . ."

"I see what you mean."

"But what you might do is get the prime suspects as you call them to come into your office for an informal updating. And in the course of that you ask them a few pointed questions. You have your chimp there. Sitting to one side. He indicates when they're telling the truth and when they're lying."

"Yes," I said, enthused now. "I could covertly tape Alphus's reactions, his hand signals as they answered questions."

"It wouldn't stand up in court, but we would know where to dig."

We decided on the questions I would casually ask along the way. Did you murder Heinie von Grümh? Did you want to murder him? Do you know who did murder him? Do you know where the murder weapon is? Did you see anyone else around the victim that night?

"Who do you include among the suspects?" he asked.

"Well, there's Feidhlimidh de Buitliér. But a long shot."

"Okay."

I checked my watch. I still had a long drive to the cottage. "Anyway, the others would include Merissa Bonne, Max Shofar, Col Saunders, and . . . well, myself."

His eyebrows went up. "Really?"

"Lieutenant, I want to clear my name . . ."

"But you know you didn't do it?"

"That's what I'd like to think. But I think I could have. I certainly wanted to."

We stood and got ready to leave. He said, "I'll pretend I didn't hear that. And, by the way, if you need any help in those interrogations, let me know."

. . .

I had a feeling the weekend with Diantha and Elsie would not go well. I blame myself. Seeing firsthand, indeed, ransacking their snug love nest on the boat reopened the old wound as though I suffered from a kind of emotional scurvy. I sat in traffic and told myself again it wasn't that Diantha slept with someone else, but the person she chose. Which didn't make a whole lot of sense. Might I have been less wrought had she bedded down with a distinguished professor, with someone of charm and wit, with someone, more tellingly, younger than I?

Not only had the search and talk with the lieutenant taken longer than I'd planned, but the traffic proved treacherous. It being a fine weekend, hordes from the south clogged the coastal interstate heading north. It truly became life in the breakdown lane when bridge work on one of the smaller roads kept me and the old car fuming for nearly half an hour as some piece of equipment, which looked like a giant orange toy, got maneuvered into position.

"What took you so long?" was the aggrieved greeting from my beloved, who appeared frazzled by the heat, by loneliness, and now, quite clearly, by me. She wore a skimpy halter top, light shorts, and the look of a besieged single mother.

"I went with Lieutenant Tracy to search the *Albatross*. We found the original coins."

"Really? Where?"

"In the framed prints in the master stateroom."

"Oh" was the best she could manage. Perhaps because she sensed that the visit had revived my old demons. Not that she didn't have demons of her own, in particular a large, hairy fellow primate. There was no kiss, no offer of a drink. Instead, "Could you watch El for a while. I need some personal time."

Isn't time with me personal time? I wanted to ask. But I knew what she meant. Besides, right then, Elsie and Decker made the best of companions. She sat on one of my bony knees and made very convincing talk with her hands. "Mommy sad." Then, her little fists striking her chest, "ape," followed by her right-hand fingers together down into the open palm of her other hand, "at," followed by the bunched fingers of her right hand from edge of her mouth up to her cheek, "home."

"Yes," I said aloud as, like Alphus, she comprehends spoken words.

Then a new and favorite project — teaching Decker to respond to sign language. I found some dog biscuits for bribes along with a rough martini for me on the side. To my amazement, the animal already knew "come" — both hands held in front, the index fingers extended, the right in a beckoning circular motion around the other toward the speaker in what amounts, as in a lot of sign language, to the gestural equivalent of onomatopoeia.

We moved on to "sit," a command he understood perfectly when vocalized. Elsie, wearing a light summer frock, perched beside me on the wickerware couch. Decker, eyes and ears alert, sat on his haunches facing us, tongue out panting in the residual heat. The problem in teaching him to respond to "sit" was to get him to stand. Which he did eventually. Elsie signed the word, the middle and index fingers of the right hand in a downward motion onto the middle finger of the left. Then I would say "sit."

Incredibly enough, after at least half a dozen repetitions, the dear beast got it. Elsie high-fived me after her fashion and then indicated it was her turn for a treat.

Diantha returned presently having had her personal time, and I asked her if she would like a drink. I could tell something was afoot from her averted manner that somehow managed to combine defiance and beseechment. The drinks, white wine for her and a larger and better-built martini for me, sustained the truce that held through a quite delicious if cold dinner of lobster salad, green salad, and pasta. We remained civil, even friendly, until we had cleared the ring by putting Elsie to bed.

Even then, I detected something contrived in her opening volley, a predictable, nearly *pro forma,* "Norman, really, when am I going to be able to come home again?"

I sighed audibly and repeated what I had said before, how I was doing everything in my power to rectify the situation, et cetera, et cetera.

We were on the porch, the humid, cricket-loud night all around us. I had showered before dinner and put on slacks and short-sleeved shirt. She said, "Someone told me you were seen at The Edge with him."

I didn't answer her. "You should know, Diantha, if you were to spend ten minutes with Alphus it would change your opinion of him completely."

She also ignored what I said. And then lobbed her little bomb-shell. "You should know," she said, echoing my diction, "that I have been invited by Sixy to a concert in Foxborough next week-end." Sixy, Sixpack Shakur, to be exact, is King of the Redneck Rappers and her former swain.

"Where exactly is Foxborough?" I asked calmly. Perhaps I would make her ex-boyfriend into an ex-person by holding my instrument of death against his shaven skull and . . .

"South of Boston. It's where the Patriots play," she said, her *duh* in the tone of her voice. "He's opening for the Stones."

The gallstones? I nearly said. "And you plan to go?"

"Merissa and I would drive down together. Bella'll take care of Elsie. I would have invited you, but I don't see it as your scene."

True. *What is my scene?* I wondered. "You'll be staying over-night down there?"

"I have to. The concert's in the late afternoon. It would be stupid to drive back then."

What rankles in a situation like this apart from the threatened breach in our marital arrangements is the reduction to smallness implicit in any spousal objection on my part. And, really, how could I object? As sophisticated, upper-middle-class Americans, we don't start throwing dinnerware against the wall. We conceal our clenching hands and murderous thoughts and say things, as I did, like, "Do you think that is a good idea?"

To which she responded with the maddening catchall, "What do you mean by that?"

"I mean, given your history with Sixy . . ."

"Oh, Norman, you really are being tedious."

So that I might have wrecked the place with my bare hands. Instead, I poured more gin over ice and pretended it was a martini. "Tedious," I repeated. "That's a big word for you."

"Then try 'f*ck you' on for size."

"Di . . ."

But the floodgates of invective had been breached. Did I know what people were saying about me? Did I know I was the laughing stock of Seaboard? Did I know . . .

Nadirs are never trustworthy. You can and will sink lower. But in the fire and ice of our exchanges, I forbade my imagination from including Diantha in any execution scene I might conjure for her paramour. We tried to back off, but it turned into an evening of too many drinks, too many words, and very little love.

I slept by myself in a bedroom said to be haunted by a local crone who died under suspicious circumstances. I woke from a dream about Heinie the night he was murdered. We spoke to each other in flawless French about Merissa, who was hovering nearby and terrifying me even though I was watching the whole thing on a television screen with the name Anna Gramma scrolling beneath the scene. "Gnats," I said aloud, waking to the buzz of a mosquito in my ear.

I took a sunrise walk around the mist-shrouded lake to calm myself. I heard the haunting, mocking call of a loon. I should have been reassured by the sight of an osprey gliding out of the sun to disappear into the brightening murk. I usually smile at the scolding chatter of chickadees. But nature availed me of nothing that day.

I managed, I think, to stay civil as I packed up for an early return. I told Diantha that I was making every effort to find a place for Alphus. I told her that if she chose to consort again with her ex-lover, that I could not foresee the consequences, but that they would be dire, certainly for myself.

16

North of here, on our stern and rockbound coast, on a grassy knoll overlooking a particularly beautiful sweep of ocean, islands, and forested points, Izzy and Lotte have their weekend cottage. It was there on an azure day of sunshine and breeze that I drove for the Landeses' annual summer picnic.

Ah, to be among friends who take you for what you are or might be. No obloquy here, subtle or otherwise, as I unloaded the back of my car — some bottles of good wine, and a cornucopia of fresh fruit and berries. No shunning here. Indeed, the welcoming smiles, grips, and kisses were perhaps a little too hearty, too reassuring.

Not that I minded having Harvey Deharo's arm around my shoulder. Or the Reverend Alfie's bowing graciously and extending both hands. Or Father ("Oh, please, 'S.J.'") O'Gould, elegant even in casual attire, joking about hearing my confession. Then Izzy and Lotte, of course, their son and his family, their friends from the city, and a few summer neighbors.

"Merry enough to be a wedding," someone remarked as, already well wined, we sat around two long tables bibbed and tuckered for a surfeit of lobsters, steamed clams, fresh corn, Lotte's potato salad, and a marvelous white Graves that Izzy had found at a bargain. I nearly wanted to make a toast as I looked up and down the table at the happy people. Then I made a toast.

I stood up and rapped my glass. "To Lotte and Izzy," I said. "And to us, their lucky friends."

Afterward, while others occupied themselves in various ways, Izzy and I took a walk on a rugged path that led through an evergreen forest and then along the shore where waves crashed and seabirds called. I had told him back in town that I needed to talk to him. So now, as we made our way along a sandy beach in a cove where sailboats lay at anchor, he said, "Talk."

"Easier said than done," I quipped. Then I hesitated, not sure how to broach the subject on which I wanted his advice, namely Elgin Warwick's proposal for his mummification and all that might entail. When I finally managed to get it out, in bits and pieces, making his brow knit and smooth until he stopped and burst out laughing.

"Old Warwick as a mummy! My God, that will be worth seeing."

"Felix not only wants to accept the offer, he wants us to open up a mortuary wing. For a fee, anyone could join the permanent collection, with niches and shrines of various sizes for cremated remains. Even funerals and receptions. He said it would be a cash cow."

"A regular herd."

"But . . ."

We had stopped and were watching a small sailboat with a party of three casting off its mooring, the sound of its snapping main coming over the water.

Izzy, his abundant white hair lofted by the wind, was shaking his head in mirth. "How about a deal for me and Lotte?"

I smiled at him, suddenly relieved. The alchemy of friendship is the greatest balm. "You'll have your own temple," I said. "Right next to mine."

We paused again to catch our breath and take in cormorants on a shoaling rock looking imperial with their wings spread to dry.

"The fact is," I said, "human remains have to be old before they become interesting, at least to a museum."

"Yes. And the older the better. It's the paradox of death."

"Meaning?"

"Meaning that the past is the future for all mortal beings."

"Put that way, it doesn't seem so bad. I've always half lived in the past."

"Like most of us. What's that old saw? I don't mind being dead, it's dying I don't look forward to."

We resumed our walking. "So I take it you have doubts," he said when the path widened to allow us to amble side by side.

"I am absolutely torn, my friend. Everything Felix says is true. He says we would make a killing, no pun intended. Nor am I a disinterested party in all this. Elgin is on our Board of Governors. The board is meeting on the twenty-fourth to decide whether or not I continue to serve as director . . ."

"Given your recent contretemps?"

"Exactly. I will be putting myself in professional jeopardy if I continue to dawdle or say no."

"What do you want to do? In your heart of hearts?"

"I want the museum to prosper, even to grow, but not in that direction. I do not want it to become the Mausoleum of Man."

He laughed again. Then he stopped and took me by the arm. "Then don't do it, Norman. Because, if you do, you'll regret it the rest of your life."

He was telling me something I already knew, but his saying it gave me the courage of my convictions. I felt a weight lift as we climbed to a high bluff and followed the path along the edge of a precipice buffeted by a clean, salt-smelling breeze.

In wending our way back to the party, we spoke about what had become known as the "coin crisis." That led to observations about what is genuine and what is false. After some desultory rambling on the subject, Izzy said, "I used to think that finding and championing what's real was the most important thing a historian could do. That is, I thought that the best way to expose the fake, the exaggerated, and the meretricious was to establish the real and the valuable."

We paused to watch an eagle turning in a gyre over a sunlit headland. When we resumed our walking, Izzy went on, "Alas, Norman, relativism and fads have grown so persuasive in my discipline that it now matters more who said or wrote something than what is said or written. And if the real, in the form of truth or beauty, is no longer believed to exist, what's the point in searching for it?"

We rejoined the party for a last glass of wine. We clinked glasses. *"In vino veritas,"* he proffered.

"Sometimes," I said, "sometimes."

Now, as I try to record the events of the day, I find myself sinking into a depthless funk. Was it Izzy's pessimism, I wondered, sitting there in the growing gloom of a summer evening. It could have been the invidious comparison between my wifeless, childless state and the happy people at the party. I was in thrall to Hamlet's plaint, "How weary, flat, stale and unprofitable / seem to me all the uses of this world."

Because nothing seemed real. The face I stared at in the bathroom mirror I saw as an apparition in silvered glass. And even if I achieved everything I wanted, I knew it would not stand the acid of time. Most especially, I asked myself, how real is this that I write? Are not words themselves a kind of counterfeiting insofar as they are a substitute for the real, a secondhand reality at best, a mere shadow, a pale reflection? Except, perhaps, for great poetry, wherever it is found. In that instance words achieve, I would like to believe, the crystalline solidity of living rock. Or is that just another of the necessary fictions by which we live?

A slow, agonizing week passed. I was soon trapped in my own routines, and in my predicaments, my house like a prison with a work-release program called the office. The weekend arrived for the day of the concert. I could not escape conjuring in my fevered imagination what Diantha might be doing with her hip-hopping ex-swain. A gig. No doubt with a party afterward with lots of drugs. What had she said? I'm a normal young woman. I need a man.

I was determined not to call the cottage to see if in fact she had decided to go the concert. She scarcely answers my phone calls, anyway. And when she does, she scarcely speaks to me. Things have deteriorated between us. She's adamant about one thing: Alphus must go. Period. My appeals are in vain. If only she knew him. He wouldn't hurt a soul. He could speak to Elsie in her own language.

I was determined not to drink, not even one of the cans of beer Alphus and Ridley were having as they sat in front of the television watching the Red Sox.

Instead I made myself a cup of green tea. It's supposed to be good for you. But I don't like the taste. It gives me a sense of futility. I tried. I sipped the wretched brew. I looked at the clock on the wall. I recalled the picnic at Izzy's. But it was no good. I picked up the phone and punched in the number for the landline at the cottage.

Bella answered. "No, I am sorry, Mr. Norman, Miss Diantha is not here. She tell me she be back tomorrow. Elsie is fine. We are watching Walter Disney."

If I still had my revolver, I might have been tempted to drive several hours to their tryst, find them, and kill him. Which fantasy only depressed me further. To the point of uncorking my Cork Dry Gin and setting up to mix a near-lethal potion. I was going about this with grim resolution when Alphus came into the kitchen with a sheaf of papers, put them on the table, and signed "Memoirs. A first sketch."

Misery has its own momentum, and right then I didn't want to interrupt my own. I wanted the solipsism of gin, enough to take me down to the small death of sleep and the smaller resurrection of waking. But in the active mode of mixing the drink, I happened to glance at the first few lines. Mechanically, I poured gin over ice. I sat down. A touch of vermouth. I sipped and read.

I remember first of all birdsound and the warmth of my mother's furry breast. She was high in the hierarchy of our troop, and the members paid court to her through me, their faces big and friendly as they loomed over us, their hands reaching out to touch me under my mother's wary eye.

I remember her love and care and how she sheltered me from the pelting rains and the flashing light and thunderous noise of storms that came in from where the sun rose. I must have been about a year old, big for my age but still vulnerable, when, seemingly out of nowhere, a muscular leopard came with deadly speed up the trunk of the tree we were sitting in. In one quick motion my mother grabbed me and swung out of danger onto an overhead branch. One of my older cousins didn't act quickly enough. There was an awful scream and brief struggle before he lay limp, his head in the cruel grip of the cat's fangs.

The rest of us shrieked and hooted from a safe distance,

throwing anything to hand, including you know what, to little effect at the leopard, which calmly dismembered and ate our fellow chimp with feline efficiency.

I experienced several such adventures. I once came close to being bitten by a black mamba that we disturbed on our way through a cape fig tree toward clusters of ripe fruit. Several times marauding males from a neighboring troop of chimps came by looking to steal my mother and more than likely murder me.

But nothing compared to our dread of human hunting parties. Oh, but they were smart and brutal. They would come from one direction making noise so that we fled right into where their comrades lay in ambush. We thought of the gun as having magic powers. It's true they make a terrific noise. But from far away. The noise would sound and someone close by would grunt, lose his grip and fall, the body bouncing off limbs before it thudded to the ground. We would all try to hide in the foliage and stay as still as though we were already dead.

That's how it happened. My mother was holding me, high in a tree where she had been feeding. A group of hunters came up stealthily and stood in a small clearing just at the base of the trunk. The sound of the gun and the thud of the slug hitting the back of my mother's head came at the same time. I clung to her and, I believe, she clung to me, shielding me even in death as we fell and fell until we landed near the hunters, three black men in khaki shorts and shirts. I screamed at them, baring my small fangs. I heard them laugh and then darkness closed in as they dropped a burlap bag over me and hoisted me up, still screaming and struggling.

I paused at this point, the gin hardly touched in the melting ice. My eyes had misted over, and I wanted to go in and give him a hug. I read on as Alphus described at some length a sad litany of abuse, by turns caged and chained as he was bought and sold, ending up in a German circus at the age of ten. This began what he called the best years of his life until taking up residence at Sign House. I'll let him tell it in his words.

Our trainer, a dour, self-tortured Scot named Campbell McDonald, treated all of us kindly, but regarded me as his favorite. I think he was lonely. Some nights he would bring me to his compartment on the train, where we drank Scotch neat in small glasses. But slowly, the bottle stoppered and unstoppered for yet another one until he fell asleep. I would curl up on a blanket on the floor, but couldn't sleep very well, not with the big-cat cages just a few cars from ours.

Camp, for that was his nickname, and I did a couple of skits together. In one of them, I played a dentist and he was my patient. I wore a surgical mask and he had his jaw wrapped in a big bandage tied at the top of his head. I did a pantomime of persuasion to get him to sit down in a padded reclining chair. He would roll his eyes fearfully as I strapped him down. I then produced a gigantic needle and forced it into his mouth. Then, after a pretend injection, he would squirm in mock horror as I used a pair of pliers to take out a tooth, which I showed him. He would shake his head. I kept taking out teeth and showing them to him. He would shake his head. I would put the tooth into a cup. Until, finally, I had the right tooth. He would nod happily and pay me large handfuls of fake money before leaving and taking his cupful of teeth with him.

We brought the house or at least the tent down with our bordello scene. In that skit, Camp played an American pimp. He wore a floppy hat, a gaudy suit, and lots of fake gold chains around his neck. As his conservatively dressed "john" I would consider a series of beautiful young women all dressed like tarts that he would parade in front of me. No matter how attractive they were, and some were very attractive by human standards, I would shake my head after giving them a once-over. Until he brought out the hairy lady from the sideshow. I would put on a show of great excitement, would nod up and down, pay him great wads of fake money, take her by the hand, and walk off our improvised stage.

I was particularly moved when I read his account of the experiments performed on him by that crazed scientist Stoddard Gottling. In an attempt to create nothing less than a new human phenotype, Gottling and his associates treated Alphus and his fellow chimps as though they did not experience pain. "Trauma," Alphus writes, "scarcely describes the endless medical tortures men and women in lab coats put us through." He was, however, heavily sedated when undergoing the angioplasty in the carotid artery in an attempt to increase blood flow to his brain.

Here is Alphus's account of waking from sedation after the procedure to a level of consciousness he had only dimly intuited before.

I gradually realized as the anesthesia wore off that I had become a highly sapient being, but one trapped in an ape's body and with an ape's instincts. For weeks I lived in a state of panic. I tried to think of ways to kill myself. But, remember, I still had the predilections of a "lower" primate. And deliberate self-destruction is unknown to chimpanzees. I had all these thoughts but no way of communicating them. Worst, I knew I would be imprisoned for the rest of my life with my poor, benighted brethren.

I despaired until the day that one of the students who was studying us brought in a boom box and played, very loudly, Ravel's *Bolero*. I was dumbstruck. I was agonized with a painful joy. Not only did I find it beautiful beyond my meager collection of words, but in its slow, building, louder rhythms, it mirrored my own dawning intellectual growth. I clung to it like a psychic life preserver. Using clumsy gestures, I persuaded the student, a pretty Asian girl, to play it again and again.

She came back a few days later with other classical music. I hung there in a state of fearful aesthetic bliss as she played operatic overtures, movements from Beethoven symphonies, something by Stockhausen, which I didn't care for much, arias from Verdi, and once again *Bolero*.

My caged companions scarcely listened. They were far more interested in the chocolate-covered raisins that the researcher, whose name was Debra, rewarded them with if they wore headphones and then played with the volume.

I say "fearful aesthetic bliss" because I knew that what happened would happen. One day Debra packed up her things, gave us some extra candy, and left, never to return again. It was then that I knew I had to escape.

I put the manuscript down and went back through it making some small edits and suggestions. I took it into the living room where Alphus and Ridley were watching the game. I began to tell him how moving and well done I found his memoir.

He waved me aside and pointed to the screen. The Sox were trailing the Yankees five to four in the ninth inning with two out and a man on third.

I returned to the kitchen in a far better frame of mind. I had not only been moved by this fragment of his memoir, I was hopeful that, with help, he would be able to find a publisher, make some money, and afford a home and keeper of his own.

17

Time can wound as well as heal. In the days following the Sixpack concert, which played to such effect on the stage and backstage of my imagination, I burned in the fire of time so well set by Delmore Schwartz. Time does, finally, consume us, but slowly, so slowly, especially when we are suffering. And suffering I was, racked by jealousy, loss, and despair.

To forestall madness, I kept busy. I drafted a letter to Elgin Warwick graciously declining his generous offer. But didn't send it. I brooded endlessly. I grew gaunt, at least in spirit, walking the streets of Seaboard like a living ghost haunting its own time. I worked in the small garden we have behind the house. I researched other places Alphus could comfortably stay. I investigated the murder of Heinrich von Grümh.

To this end, I phoned Professor Colin Saunders late one afternoon and invited him over to my office for an update on the investigation. He responded with suspicion. "What do I need to come there for? Can't you just tell me over the phone?"

"It's confidential information," I said. "I'd rather do it face-to-face."

"I'm sorry, but I'm very busy. Have your girl type it up and send it to me by registered mail."

When I related this to Lieutenant Tracy, he told me not to worry. They would bring him in for questioning. Alphus and I could be on the other side of the one-way mirror.

"But he'll have a lawyer with him. He won't say anything."

"Leave that to me."

So, at an appointed time, I drove, with Alphus on a proper leash, to police headquarters on the bypass. Per usual, we raised a few eyebrows as we went through the metal detector and took the elevator to the second floor. There the lieutenant gave us two chairs in front of the window looking into the interrogation room.

Presently, an indignant-looking Saunders and Gavin Miffkin, a red-faced, middle-aged lawyer in an expensive suit, were ushered in by Lieutenant Tracy and Sergeant Lemure.

The professor did not hide the kind of disdain a lot of upper-middle-class people feel is their prerogative when it comes to the police. He scarcely acknowledged the lieutenant when the latter reintroduced himself and the sergeant.

"We want to go over your statement about your movements on the evening Heinrich von Grümh was murdered."

"We've been through this at least twice," Saunders said. "I really do have other things to do."

"We won't take long." Lieutenant Tracy spoke equably. "Some routine questions."

No one said anything for a moment. Then Sergeant Lemure started. "It is true, as you stated to Mr. Ratour and to us subsequently, that you did see H. von Grümh on the night he was murdered?"

"You don't have to answer that," the lawyer said and glanced at his watch.

Lieutenant Tracy opened a folder in front of him. "Well . . . Let's see. We have some information indirectly related to the case that you might find of interest."

The lawyer said, "Can I see that please."

The lieutenant shook his head. "It's just part of a preliminary investigation. Privileged, I think is the word." He paused. "In going over the murder victim's computers, we found that Mr. von Grümh hired a forensic IT expert to hack into Professor Saunders's hard disk files. It appears he found considerable evidence involving organizations specializing in underaged girls both here in the United States and in Thailand. He also found documents relating to trips Professor Saunders made to Bangkok over the last few years."

Mr. Miffkin asked, "Where is all this innuendo leading?"

The officers stared at Saunders in stony silence for a moment. Then, as though rehearsed, Sergeant Lemure said, "Well, first off, this evidence constitutes the basis of a powerful motive."

"How do you arrive at that?" the lawyer asked, more cautious now.

"We think it's possible that Mr. von Grümh was gathering evidence that could ruin Professor Saunders's career."

Sergeant Lemure leaned forward. "Right now, we're not sure whether we have enough evidence to pass along to the district attorney's office for charges related to statutory rape. A problem for you is that once the files leave the SPD, we can no longer guarantee their confidentiality."

The lawyer bristled visibly. "This is nothing less than prosecutorial blackmail."

Professor Saunders put an arm on the man's sleeve. "I'll answer any questions they want me to."

"As your counsel, I advise you . . ."

"Gavin, please. In the matter of Heinie's death, I have nothing to hide."

"Good, then let us proceed." Lieutenant Tracy motioned to his colleague.

Sergeant Lemure began reading from a script I had provided. "Please answer just yes or no unless otherwise directed . . ."

"Col, really . . ."

"Gavin, shut up."

I glanced significantly at Alphus. He nodded.

The sergeant began. "Did you see Heinrich von Grümh on the night he was murdered."

"Yes."

Alphus glanced at me and his thumb went up.

"Did you see H. von Grümh with a revolver on the night he was murdered?"

"Yes."

Thumb up.

"Do you know where that gun is now?"

"No."

Thumb up.

"Did you murder H. von Grümh?"

"No."

Thumb up.

"Do you know who murdered H. von Grümh?"

"No."

Thumb up.

"At approximately what time did you meet H. von Grümh on the night he was murdered? As best as you can remember."

"As I told Mr. de Ratour, it was just about eight forty."

"That's all, Professor Saunders," the lieutenant said and stood up.

Clearly chastened, Saunders spoke in a supplicating manner. "Lieutenant, regarding that other matter . . ."

"Oh, yes. We'll keep you informed as things develop."

"But . . ."

"I'm sorry, but I'm not at liberty to discuss it further. And, like you, I have other things to do."

Afterward the lieutenant, Alphus, and I met in the interrogation room. "He passed," I said. "According to Alphus, he's innocent. At least of that crime."

The officer looked at Alphus with what I would call a cop stare. "So you really can tell when someone's lying, huh?"

Alphus nodded and signed "yes."

"But what if the answer isn't a yes or no?"

Alphus gave a little pant hoot, held up his thumb, and turned it level.

"My middle name is Chester."

The thumb went up.

"I have a dentist appointment tomorrow at one o'clock."

Alphus hesitated. Then his thumb went down.

The lieutenant gave one of his rare laughs. "He's right. It's at two o'clock. Damn, I'm a believer."

He would have been more than a believer had he read the sample of Alphus's memoir that I perused that evening. On the way home, as a reward, I stopped by a small Italian take-out place and bought him his new favorite — a large pizza with extra cheese and sausage. This he manages to consume in one sitting along with one or two cans of beer.

In fact, I'm starting to notice a decided change in his personality ever since I told him he was one of the "guys." He has begun wearing a baseball cap with a red B embroidered on the front. He has forsaken wine for beer and no longer fusses about single-malt whiskeys. And, instead of reading, he spends an inordinate amount of time watching baseball on the television.

Not that it matters. In the most recent part of the memoir that he gave me to read, he writes that escaping from the pavilion was easier to dream about than to do. He bided his time and worked, as we used to say, to improve his mind. I have to confess that I am both moved and amazed by this creature's courage, tenacity, and ingenuity. His story would do any human hero proud.

I taught myself to read quite by happenstance. Like many of my brethren, I had taken part in the farce conducted by Damon Drex in which we picked at keyboards in an attempt to prove, for no good reason, that, with a finite number of monkeys (or at least of chimpanzees) and with a finite amount of time, you could produce one line of the literary canon and through that, by extrapolation, all of the world's great literature.

But that was during a part of my life I call pre-procedure. Like the others I was chiefly interested in the M&M's with which they rewarded us. More than the others, I think I had an inkling of what was going on. I had noticed people reading magazines and the prevalence of the little markings called letters on books, signs, and, of course, the computer screen.

Upon gaining sapience, I began to think of these little markings as a kind of code, though I had no word for it. And I might not have gotten very far if I hadn't come across a child's alphabet book that someone had left behind just outside my cage.

I pretended not to know what it was for. I treated it like a kind of security blanket and if any human was around, I would look at it upside down. Because if anyone had figured out what I was doing, they would apply for a grant, put me in a cage of my own, and bore me speechless with exercises designed to show results they could publish in a paper.

The alphabet book had large letters and simple words.

It didn't take me long to understand that G for GIRL could be combined with A for ANT, O for OSTRICH, and T for TREE to make the word GOAT. It took me a while to comprehend that the number of combinations was essentially endless.

I had difficulty grasping that words not only stood for things, but for actions, descriptions, and things other than things. There were simple sentences in another child's book someone left behind and, after a while, I had learned them by heart. It took me some effort to understand the words *a* and *the*. They occurred so often, I thought they must be greatly important and that I was missing something essential.

But once I mastered the basic skill of reading, I tried to read everything I could get my hands on, which wasn't much, but people do leave stuff around. Bus schedules. Pamphlets of various sorts. Even a pornographic magazine, which I took for one of those how-to manuals. I would pretend to look at the pictures in regular magazines, all the while trying to learn words from their context.

At the same time, I failed to link the complicated noises people make with their mouths to the words and sentences I was learning. Then, one day in the rec room Damon Drex had provided for his "writers," I happened to be watching a television news program. One of my fellow chimps got hold of the remote and pressed the MUTE button. Words began to scroll beneath the person who had continued to talk, but soundlessly.

The significance struck me like a bad fall out of a tree: The words on paper, these combinations of letters, matched the vocalizations people were producing in their mouths. My own species communicate with sounds and gestures, of course, but nothing like this. I realized that people live in a sea of language, in a verbal medium that is the equivalent of air or water.

I was thrown again into one of those despairs provoked by an agitation of hope, expectation, and fear of failure. Because I knew I could never imitate the human range of sound with my own vocal equipment, I scarcely knew how to go about learning to understand what was being said.

And again, I had to proceed carefully lest some graduate student or postdoc hear what I was doing and start some infernal "research" project. I still had my alphabet book with its big letters and simple words. I decided to find someone I could trust to help me. Through bad luck, I chose Yvette, a sweet, smiling Haitian woman on the cleaning crew. She had always been kind to us and especially to me.

She laughed when I showed her the black-and-white animal under the word *cow* and pointed to her lips. "*Vache,*" she said finally, still giggling. Then "*chien.*" Then "*arbre.*"

Luckily for my purposes, a different company took over the cleaning work, otherwise I would have been utterly muddled, not knowing that there is more than one human language. Luckily, too, Dr. Simone happened to witness this exchange with Yvette while reviewing one of the monitor tapes. Imagine my relief when, instead of some dumb researcher, she assigned herself and several others to teach me to understand words. It became a kind of game. I knew some research worked its way into our sessions, especially when they tested me, usually with pictures of things I would point to when they said the corresponding word, but I didn't mind.

Then came sentences. Short and simple at first. I began to appreciate the level at which humans operate. I noticed how people used words to give each other commands, to explain things, to make jokes, to vent anger, to be nice. It helped that I could sense emotions very acutely. I noticed that people often say one thing while feeling another.

How I wanted to join the conversation! How I wanted to express my . . . my chimpness, my situation, and my yearning, above all, to be free. I went in and out of despair. Exulted one moment at what I was learning, morbid the next at the thought I could not speak. The dark song of suicide sang in me as never before. But how to do it? I knew I wouldn't have the self-discipline to hang myself, as we creatures of the trees have long powerful arms with which to reach above us and keep from strangling in a noose. I would be like a fish trying to drown itself. Nor did they allow any sharp objects with which I might sever an artery. No poison pills, either.

So I determined once again to escape even if I had nowhere to escape to. There are no tropical forests at these latitudes. There are no chimp halfway houses. It didn't matter. If I had to die trying, I was bent on escaping. Not that any of this signified: There was no way of escaping.

Until the afternoon when Jacobus, a very old chimp with a bad heart, suffered either a stroke or cardiac arrest. Alarms went off and before long a couple of guys in medic-like uniforms arrived with a stretcher, put Jacobus on it, fitted an oxygen mask to his face, covered him with a blanket up to his neck, and took him away.

I heard someone say they were taking him to the hospital at the Middling County Zoo. I heard someone use the word *euthanize,* which took me a minute to figure out. Hell, I thought, I'd settle for that.

I went about my plans with all the cunning of the desperate. I pretended not to be hungry. I kept myself awake at night and easily feigned listlessness during the day. I knew I was succeeding from the comments of the staff about me. "Looks like Alphus isn't himself today." "Yeah, he hasn't been feeling so hot lately." "Hell I'd get like that if they kept me cooped up in that place."

A few days later, in the presence of some of my more excitable brethren and a couple of human beings, I fell from a low bar and clutched at my chest, faking a heart attack. I struggled to get up, but fell back again. With predictable panic, my cell mates screeched and hooted. I heard someone say, "Oh, God, it's Alphus. Get Doctor Simone."

Right on cue, the medics arrived. I, too, was given an oxygen mask and blood pressure monitor. But, critically, no restraints were put on me as I was loaded onto the stretcher and borne out to the waiting ambulance.

One of the EMTs drove while the other one, a burly fellow with a red face, tended to me. "Don't worry, pal," he said, "We'll get you there." Then, to the driver. "I don't see why they don't just give them the old needle right there."

"Yeah. But it ain't as much fun."

"What do you mean?"

"Hell, Frank didn't use a needle on the last one we brought over. You know, the old one."

"Really."

"Nah. He fed him to the leopards. I don't think it was even dead. He said the big cats went crazy."

My heart felt like it had stopped. And then began to thump painfully. I cannot even look at a picture of one of those beasts without suffering a deep, atavistic terror. Dying is one thing. Being killed and eaten by leopards quite another.

The burly guy said, "Boy, this guy's pulse just jumped off the chart. And, you know, his blood pressure's been normal. If he wasn't some kind of ape, I'd say he was faking it."

Through the slits of my eyes, I could see, up through the windows in the double back doors of the vehicle, that we had entered some kind of forest. With one abrupt movement, I ripped off my oxygen mask and pulled off the blood pressure cuff.

"Hey," my startled attendant cried, and reached to restrain me. But even strong men are weaklings compared with chimpanzees. I quickly overpowered him. The vehicle slewed to a sudden stop. I opened the door and fled on all fours to a glorious haven in the upper branches of towering, well-leafed maples.

I put it down. I felt humbled and exalted. This animal, this beast, this fellow being had confirmed the pieties of civilization in which so many of us humans put our faith. We will, regardless of circumstances, rise toward the light. We will, at whatever cost, choose freedom when we have a chance.

I planned to make a copy to send to Diantha. But, like a lot a people, she'll probably think it a fraud. She hasn't deigned to respond to any of my overtures. I have all but given up. There is something demeaning about calling and either leaving yet another message or hanging up, knowing that it's known who called. I could swallow what little pride I have left and drive out there. And do what? Surprise her consorting with her paramour? No, I am a coward when it comes to scenes. I would rather suffer my worst imaginings in private, would rather let the green-eyed monster feed on my entrails than make a spectacle.

It doesn't help that my time is running short. The Governing Board meets next week. I am still out on bail. I am still equivocating about Elgin Warwick's proposal. I don't know what to do except to go on trying to find out who murdered Heinie if only to prove that it wasn't I.

Speaking of which, I have a call in to Merissa Bonne. She is a suspect and needs to undergo the Alphus test. She might also tell me what Diantha's up to.

18

The heavy and heavily insured package came by courier service from George Simons of Park Street, Boston, directly to the top of my desk in the museum. I won't say my fingers trembled as I scissored my way through the strong tape and opened the sturdy cardboard box, but I was full of eager foreboding.

The letter on top confirmed my suspicions.

"Dear Mr. de Ratour, I regret to inform you that the pairs of coins you have sent me match each other precisely. That is to say, the coins from the boat are forgeries as well as the ones that were gifted to your museum.

"Along with close-up photos in black and white, I have attached the results of various technical tests, including several on the metallurgy of the samples. In fact, they are among the best forgeries my staff has ever come across, not that that will be of much comfort to you.

"Also, it might interest you to know that they are in all likelihood not copies of each other, but copies from the originals, whether they be real or forgeries.

"Please call if you have any questions . . ."

I sat for a while trying to sort out the significance of Mr. Simons's report, when Doreen followed her very enlarged midsection into my presence and told me that Lieutenant Tracy had just called and that I was to tune in Channel Five. She turned then and clicked on the small television set I keep handy.

Under a flashing banner stating BREAKING NEWS, a gentleman

named Ken was telling an attractive woman named Baretta, no doubt his anchor team partner, something about "dramatic news regarding the Sterl case."

Baretta turned full-on to the camera saying, "Seaboard police this morning announced a major development in the ongoing investigation into the suspicious death of businessman Martin Sterl."

Then Ken again: "Our reporter Jack Cogger is covering the story at police headquarters. Jack, what have you got?"

The camera cut to a head-and-shoulders shot of young, crew-cut Jack Cogger in front of police headquarters out on the bypass. "Hi Ken, Hi Baretta. Indeed, Seaboard police lieutenant Richard Tracy announced that arrest warrants have been issued for Blanko Dragan and Andrijana Jakovich, aka Stella Fox, in the murder of Martin Sterl, whose apparent suicide in June has been regarded suspiciously from the start."

There followed a head shot of Sterl, a quite ordinary mortal with glasses and toupee, as Mr. Cogger's narration continued. "Tracy said the police were operating on leads supplied by Norman de Ratour, the director of Wainscott University's [sic] Museum of Man."

The video taken from the diorama monitors that I had secured for Lieutenant Tracy played as Mr. Cogger, voice over, said, "The tape of Dragan and Jakovich, shown here at an exhibit at the museum, was supplied by Ratour, who himself has been implicated in the recent murder of Heinrich Grümh."

There was a file photo of me, not very flattering, just before the camera switched back and forth between the reporter in the field and the two anchorpersons thusly:

Jack: "Back to you, Ken and Baretta."

Baretta: "Jack, are the police saying anything about a possible connection between the two murders?"

Jack: "Right now police are treating the murders as separate."

Ken: "What does Ratour have to say about his role in the investigation?"

Jack: "The Wainscott News Office told us that they had no knowledge of Ratour's involvement. They referred us to the museum. We have a call in and a news crew on the way there now."

Baretta: "Thanks, Jack. This is a story we'll be keeping an eye on."

A different voice off camera intoned, "This has been a Channel Five breaking news special report. We now return to our scheduled broadcasting."

Just then my phone rang. It was Mort in Security. A news crew had indeed arrived and I was wanted in the Diorama of Paleolithic Life.

Well, I had asked for it, hadn't I? The newsperson turned out to be a petite young woman of Chinese extraction who worked her hands up and down in front of her as she talked to the camera held by a technician whose polished skull reflected whitely in the overhead lights of the exhibit.

The newsperson asked me basic, sensible questions with the "Early Kitchen" display as a backdrop. What made me realize I had seen the suspects before? My knack for remembering things. In my opinion, why did the suspects pick the museum for their meetings? A mistaken sense of privacy. Did I think there was any connection between the Sterl and von Grümh murders? Perhaps mirror images of each other. Are you working with the Seaboard police on the von Grümh murder even though charged as an accessory? Not at liberty to say.

She thanked me graciously and, following the beacon of her cameraman's skull, left.

Back in my office, I wondered if I should call Diantha to tell her I would be on the evening news. Hoping, of course, that she might see me in a different, more advantageous light. Or would it not be more impressive if I were to consider it something of a trifle, which, in fact, it was.

I got back to work. Amid the pile on my desk was a draft of a letter to Elgin Warwick. I had been gnawing at the thing for the past several days. I had run out of equivocations. Izzy's words kept coming back to me. Don't do something you will regret the rest of your life.

Following the rapid heartbeat of the pulser on my screen, I figuratively tore up the equivocating draft and wrote instead:

Dear Elgin:

I want first to thank you very much for your generous and original idea regarding the preservation of your remains here at the Museum of Man after you die. I have thought long and hard about it. Our chief counsel Felix Skinnerman has championed the idea. Indeed, he has suggested that, centered on your temple and tomb, we create a mortuary wing open to any and all who wish to join "the permanent collection." He foresees that it would become quite popular, with many subscribers, though few on the scale you envision.

That, alas, is the rub. The purpose of the museum is to find, preserve, and display the best that humanity has created through the millennia. Any enterprise that detracts from this essential mission strikes me as self-defeating.

You might argue that yours would be the only contemporary relics on the premises. But I fear there would ensue substantial and justified pressure from other benefactors to be afforded the same privileges. We might be quickly overrun and diverted from our primary responsibilities.

So I must, in all good conscience, decline your offer. We would, however, certainly welcome your outstanding collection of Egyptian art and artifacts that, with appropriate support, we would display in a temple worthy of its excellence and with suitable, eponymous tribute.

Sincerely,

Norman de Ratour

It is one thing to write a letter like that and feel noble about it. It is quite another to put it in an addressed envelope, stick on a stamp, and drop it into a mailbox. Which is precisely what I did, thereby canceling whatever small elation that the news of the Sterl case and my part in it had provided.

I wondered if I had, with a lick of the tongue, sealed my own professional doom. Perhaps. He would receive the letter just days before the meeting of the Governing Board. I could have waited. But I had acted instead. The thought gave me a kind of depressed peace of mind. I walked home in the warm gloaming of a summer evening, my integrity, if little else, intact.

Alphus, I could tell from a smell of burned food in the air when I arrived home, had been trying to cook again. He hasn't gotten the idea of different degrees of heat under a frying pan. The hot dogs he had been trying to make for himself and Ridley were charred beyond recognition, and he had an abashed look on his face. I had told him cooking without my presence was strictly forbidden.

More to placate me than anything else, he produced a third

installment of his memoirs and, under my direction, mixed me a medium-bore martini. I put the memoir aside and took some lean hamburger out of the refrigerator and some appropriate rolls out of the freezer.

They sat on stools around the counter watching the run-up to a baseball game while I sipped my martini and made a green salad. They were both wearing baseball caps and lettered T-shirts. Ridley's read, GLOBAL WARMING IS COOL. Alphus's read, SAY NO TO THE MALTHUSIASTS.

As "guys" they are both starting to permutate into something I don't particularly admire. I want to state for the record that I had no objection when Alphus became a "guy," wanted to be called "Al," and started listening to country-and-western music. I did tell him to keep it down. A lot of it consists, as far as I can tell, of grown men and women feeling sorry for themselves. I did not object in the least when he began drinking Budweiser from a can instead of sipping rare malts from a glass. And if he wants to watch the Red Sox and other teams with quaint names go through their rituals late into the night, that is his affair.

But he has started listening to someone named Rush something or other. I have listened in a few times. I must say that when Alphus starts taking this man seriously, then I confess I am vulnerable to the usual stereotypes about simian intelligence.

I also confess that I find listening to those radio communicators so diligently sharing their ignorance with their listeners exhilarating in its own way. I quite understand the appeal to indignation. It's as though there exists a great reservoir of it out there for the tapping. From which I do not exclude myself. I just like to think that my indignation is better informed, that it is more justified, higher, more worthy of being indulged.

Take for instance those public radio reporters who use exaggerated Spanish pronunciation when referring to the names of people and, especially, places south of the border. They do it, of course, at least in part, to show that they speak the language or at least know how to pronounce it. Or, as card-carrying members of the moral class, they are signaling their commitment to "diversity," a word that itself is an exercise in virtue-mongering.

When I hear them gargling some name of Iberian origins, I ask, have they not heard of Anglice? Meaning that we say *par riss* instead of *par ree, comme les français*. The same way the French say *Nouvelle Orleans* instead of New Orleans or *Les États Unis* instead of the United States of America. We say Moscow instead of *Moskva,* which, in Russian, to be used correctly, would have to be inflected according to case, that is, the way it is used in a sentence. Of course not. But *Kooba* is starting to creep in along with *Meheeko*. Which raises another point. Should not those Latin American place-names derived from indigenous populations be pronounced in the original tongue rather than in Spanish, another imperial language? Talk about inconsistencies.

Mais, comme on dit, chacun à son goût.

I had become so distracted by this inner rant that I nearly burned the patties of ground beef. And nearly forgot that I would be on the news.

I picked up the remote and changed to Channel Five. For this I received two annoyed frowns and the sign, "What's up?"

"Watch," I said. Moments later, Ken and Baretta were back on with Jack and Lisette, as my interviewer was named. I have to confess I was satisfied that I looked good, poised and authoritative. I sounded urbane. Alphus and Ridley, not to mention a few friends who called later, were suitably impressed. But I heard nothing from Diantha.

While dining on my only slightly charred burger and drinking one of Alphus's canned beers, I went over his latest literary effort. Again, I was moved and amused.

I will always be profoundly indebted to MM as I call Millicent Mulally. If there are saints, then she is one of them. I knew the moment I saw her at the bottom of the tree that I could trust her. Her sweet, pretty face and the way she moved her hands to the others told me that these people were different. I knew they didn't want to kill me, to imprison me, to study me.

So, slowly, still fearful, looking all around me, I came down the trunk of the big maple. Millicent took my hand and together, surrounded by the rest of the group, we walked out of the park and into the sanctuary of Sign House.

I don't want to sound all goody gooey about this, but people who cannot speak or hear or both strike me as "advantaged" rather than "disadvantaged." There is the peace that comes with quietness. The constant yapping of people, especially these days with everyone walking around with a device stuck to the ear, is blissfully absent.

At the same time, there is no absence of communication. Aside from and part of signing, there are smiles, frowns, jokes, arguments and much that is left unsaid for the better. It reminded me of my childhood in the wild when a glance, a gesture, and intuition meant so much more.

My signing at first was rudimentary — the kind you see in old movies when the white man meets the Natives. Under the tutelage of Millicent and Ridley and a few others, I soon wouldn't shut up. Because what an ecstatic liberation it was to use my arms, hands, and fingers as a voice! Most human beings don't realize what a blessing it is to be able to take your thoughts, turn them into words, and speak them. And, it lets you watch other people and see what they are thinking and saying.

I learned not only how to say things, but also what not to say. Millicent taught me that words can be pernicious as well as beneficent. They can be used to stir envy, anger, distrust, hatred, and falsity. Of course, they can also be used to teach, to encourage, to tell things, even to love. As someone observed, human beings use words to groom each other, to make each other feel good.

My favorite place at Sign House was the library, a room lined with books and fitted out with comfortable armchairs and a couch. That's were I spent most of my time. In the library I found what amounted to another kind of language. Signing and understanding it are one thing. But being able to read — that is the portal to the universe.

One of the first things I did was to go slowly through an old *American Heritage Dictionary* from beginning to end. Twice. What a magic invention are words. There is at least one for every imaginable thing under the sun. And if one doesn't exist, you make it up!

I have not and perhaps won't learn to write. I do not have the hand, eye, and mind coordination necessary. Ridley gave me his old computer and taught me how to use it. It seemed as new as the one with which he replaced it. Ridley has been very generous, giving me clothes, books, CDs, and good whiskey, even if he does get loopy sometimes.

I knew there were occupants of the house that were not comfortable around me. The stiff smile of toleration is one of mankind's worst and most necessary achievements. I had to resist the urge to revert — to go apeshit, as Ridley puts it — and bite off their balls and faces.

So I learned to be modest and keep my privates covered. I learned you couldn't fart anytime you wanted to, which never made much sense to me. I learned to knock on doors, or work the ringer light, because people liked their privacy, which I still find odd. We all know what people do in the bathroom or in the bedroom when they take off their clothes. The privacy thing took me a long time to learn. Perhaps because people will do things in front of animals that they wouldn't do in front of other people.

Some of them didn't take my presence very seriously at all. I had been ensconced there six months when a young man named Tim came to live in the house. He was a big handsome fellow with curly yellow hair and a normal laugh. He could even say a few words, but he couldn't hear too well.

Well, right off, he noticed Megan, who was Fred's girl. And she noticed him. For a while they kept their attraction secret, except from me. I would be in the library deep in a book when they would come in, sit on the couch, and go to all the fuss and bother people do. There was a lot of licking and mouthing, worse than bonobos if you ask me. I noticed, peering just over the rim of my book, that Tim had a sizable member that Megan, with considerable vigor, treated like a lollipop. I pretended not to notice. Just another ape reading Gibbon.

They were discovered of course. Fred burst in on them one night when he was supposed to be giving a signing class to some high school students. He didn't find them in flagrante, but mussed up and reddened enough to be suspected with plausibility.

Afterward Fred cornered me in the television room

and bought me a beer at the house bar, which is just a refrigerator full of stuff that the residents pay for on the honor system.

"Okay," he signed, "tell me what Meg and Tim were doing on the couch just before I came in."

I took a slow sip of my beer, a bottle of Bass Ale. "I didn't notice," I lied, showing him the thick tome I had been reading.

He made a face. He's one of the skeptics where I'm concerned. That is, he doesn't believe I can read a comic book, much less Herodotus. Which in this case was to his disadvantage as I could play dumb with conviction. When he made the sign for kissing and then something more suggestive, I pretended not to know what he was asking.

"Were they sitting close?" he asked with some exasperation.

"What do you mean by close?" I asked back, taking a long swallow of the Bass.

"Touching," he signed.

I again pretended to be mystified. "The couch is small," I said, "and Tim is big." Megan was kind of big, too, at least her backside, but I thought it best not to mention that.

He gave up finally, muttering with his hands something like "f*cking lying ape," before stomping off.

Not long afterward, Tim and Megan left the house together and went to live in San Francisco. Fred has never forgiven me, as though it was my fault that his woman ran off with another man. Frankly, I don't see why they couldn't have shared her. There was certainly enough to go around.

What I'm trying to say is that in reality I was little
more than a pet to some of the people there. Not to
Millicent or Ridley and one or two others who knew
what I was. The rest were kind, but in a different way.
As a pet, I became the recipient of their affectionate feelings, and that can become irksome very quickly. They
not only petted me, which I didn't appreciate in the
least, but I could tell they were making themselves feel
good by thinking they were making me feel good.

But I am not complaining. The people at Sign House
were generous, open, kind, and supportive. Without
them I would not have survived. But they were also
advanced primates. That is to say, they were complicated, contradictory, and often difficult. But what else
is new.

19

I am not good at adultery. Not because of any acquired or innate moral qualms (and God forbid one would invoke something as passé as morals in these matters). Nor do I mean the more palpable aspects of the undertaking, the enactment, in which I believe I acquitted myself quite respectably. Wherein lies the rub.

Perhaps because I find the pleasure so intense, a pleasure not unalloyed with a thrill of violation, I suffer from a surfeit of what might be called sexual gratitude. Hence the impulse to send flowers in the aftermath, if only because a thank-you note would be as inappropriate as a tip. Hence the nagging sense of obligation conflated with a persistent hankering to repeat the experience.

Or I may simply be susceptible to anyone who will indulge me, especially the way Merissa Bonne did. To paraphrase the great Yeats, in pleasure begins responsibility. *Commitment* may be an overused word these days, but commitment or something very like it is what I have begun to feel for the dear scatterbrained creature.

To begin where it began. Merissa readily agreed to come to the office when I called and told her there had been a development in the case that I'd like her to know about. She offered to take me to lunch. "Or come here, I'll make something nice for both of us."

I demurred on the latter offer and suggested that we go to lunch after meeting in my office.

She sighed facetiously. "Oh, Norman, I'll never get to seduce you, will I?"

We both laughed.

I can't say I wasn't tempted when she showed up just before noon. She might have been a streetwalker of the more expensive sort the way her short skirt rode up her shapely haunches and the way her high-heeled boots curved up her calves. Hardly a widow in mourning. She gave me a full-on kiss when I came around the desk to greet her.

"Norman," she sighed, her memorable perfume wafting over me like some pheromone signaling availability. "It is so good to see you."

"Likewise," I returned, holding on to her hand just short of blatant gallantry.

She turned to Alphus. "Oh, so this is what you've given up Di for. Well, Norman, she is cute in her way."

"It's a he," I said. "His name's Alphus.

She made a little wave. "Hi, Alphus. I hope Norman's treating you well."

He inclined his head in her direction.

She fluttered a bit more, glancing around with a twirl. "Oh, I do love this office. It's like a little museum all its own."

I resisted a self-deprecating remark about being its main exhibit. I said, "I feel at home here."

She sat and crossed her admirable gams. I twiddled a pencil and tried to look worldly.

"So what's all this about a development?"

"Well, there has been that. But first, I would like you to indulge me in a little . . ." To be honest, I had a few qualms about subjecting her to a virtual lie detector test without her knowledge or consent.

"Anything, Norman. I've always had a soft spot for you, if

you know what I mean." She tossed her abundant chestnut hair and I did know what she meant.

"You're too much, Merissa dear, too much. No, all I have are some basic yes-or-no questions. A kind of exercise."

"I'm game."

I gave Alphus a covert glance. He nodded. I surreptitiously clicked on the hidden video camera. I cleared my throat. I began. "Okay. Did you see Heinie on the night he was murdered?"

"Yeah. Before he left the house. We had a real knock-down. I already told the police."

"You didn't see him afterward?"

"Not alive."

"But dead?"

"Well, yeah, I had to identify the body."

I resisted an impulse to look at Alphus for his reaction. But it would all be on tape anyway.

"Did you see Heinie with a revolver on the night he was murdered?"

"No, I don't think so."

"But you're not sure?"

"He was always waving the damn thing around."

"Do you know where that gun is now?"

"No."

"Did you murder Heinie?"

She laughed. "No. But there were times when I wanted to."

"Do you know who murdered Heinie?"

"No. But I'd guess it was himself if the evidence wasn't the other way."

"Why?"

"Oh, Norman, the guy was a mess. You know what he couldn't stand in the end? He couldn't stand the way I felt sorry for him. I mean I tried to be sympathetic, but a woman's got to have a life."

"With Max?"

"Mostly."

"You mean there were others?"

"The world's full of trigger-happy men."

I held up my hands and brought them together. "Okay. That's all."

"That wasn't much. So what's this big development all about?" She leaned forward and I was once again enveloped in her seductive, subtle musk, which had a touch of lavender.

"Well, it seems we have found the originals of the fakes that Heinie gave to the museum."

"Really!" And she glanced away as the implications registered. "Where?"

"On the *Albatross*."

"I should have known that's where he'd put them. That thing became his little hidey-hole. Did you ever notice the pose he struck when he was at the wheel? You'd think he was Captain Cook sailing the South Seas."

"He was a sad man, wasn't he?"

"Among other things. So where are the originals now?"

"The police have them. Evidence."

"So, who do they belong to?"

"Probably to you."

"Because . . . ?"

"Because he gave the other ones to the museum."

"And kept the originals for himself . . ."

I hesitated. "Yes . . . except . . ."

"Norman, don't be so melodramatic . . ."

"The so-called originals are also fakes."

Her eyes widened and she put a hand to her lips. "No!" Then she laughed. "Oh, that is priceless. Just like Heinie."

"Merissa, don't you realize? The originals are worth more than two million dollars."

She shrugged. "Easy come, easy go. Do you have a powder room?"

"Just down the hall on the right." She was already fishing out her cell phone to make a call as she went through the door.

I turned to Alphus and signed, "Anything interesting?"

He shook his head. "I couldn't read her."

"What was it? Her perfume?"

He shrugged. "I don't know. I don't think so. Everything she said was a lie."

"That doesn't make sense."

"I think she is one of those people who lie even when they're telling the truth."

When Merissa came back, Alphus left with Angela Simone for a conjugal visit with Dalia. She's a young female with a large, hairless face, intelligent eyes, and small ears who had come into estrus.

I should have sensed I was headed for the same sort of thing when Merissa insisted on taking me to the Little Café at the Miranda Hotel. She appeared utterly unfazed by the loss of the coins. Indeed, she was in high spirits, volubly bubbling up like the bottle of champagne she ordered.

"So really, Norman, not to be mercenary, but are the coins really worth that much?"

"They are. But you might not get that on the open market. Besides . . ."

She cocked her head. "I'm listening."

"The estate would have had some real adjustments to make. Heinie's accountants probably took a whopping deduction when he gave the coins to the museum. The IRS would have come looking for its due and more."

She shrugged. "So I haven't lost that much after all."

"Enough. And who knows, maybe they'll show up."

We drank champagne and ordered. We nibbled at some fresh crudités as we waited. Merissa vacillated between chatty nonsense and frowning introspection. Then, as though interrupting her own thoughts, she said, "I've been wanting to tell you something for a while now."

"I'm listening."

She filled our glasses. "I want to tell you my real alibi for the night Heinie got shot."

I felt my eyebrows go up. "What did you tell the police?"

She made a moue of disparagement. "I told them I went shopping. Blooms had a late-night sale, and I did in fact pick up an item. I kept the receipt and showed it to them. Then I told them that Max and I went for a drive up the coast."

"Which is what he told the police."

"Yes."

"And what really did happen?"

"We went to a club in the neighborhood."

"I see."

"It's a private, quite exclusive club. Private members only." She gave her little hiccup of a laugh. "Actually, it's more like members' privates only."

"A sex club?" I asked, trying to resist a swell of titillation.

"If you want. You can keep it social, too. You and Di might want to try it."

I nodded, but dubiously. I wondered if Di and I still existed. "What happens when you go there?"

"There's a couple of reception rooms, nicely appointed. In one of them there's music and you can dance if you want to. And drinks. You mingle and talk, meet people. If you hit it off with someone or with a couple, you retire to one of the suites."

"So you and Max went there?"

"Until about midnight."

"Did you meet anyone else?"

"A very nice couple from Argentina. Gio and Marla, if those were their names."

"And you . . . ?"

"We had a foursome you wouldn't believe. Gio had this blow . . ."

"Blow?"

"Cocaine."

"I see. Can anyone else vouch for your presence on the night in question?"

"Edgar."

"Edgar?"

"Edgar's the guy who runs it. He doesn't get involved. Otherwise there are only club names."

"What's yours?"

"Puss n' Boots." She gave me a sidelong glance. "Boots are my thing."

Her seafood salad and my turkey club arrived. We ate with hungry relish, largely silent at first but not uncommunicative as our eyes caught just long enough for significance.

To break the dawning spell, I asked, "So where can I contact this Edgar?"

She looked doubtful. "I'm not sure he keeps any records."

"But he charges . . . ?"

"Four hundred. For an evening. In cash."

"Per person?"

"Per person. But it's all very posh." She used the word as though testing it on me. "And exclusive. You need a doctor's certificate. No STDs allowed." She laughed. "And it includes breakfast."

She worked on her salad. She sipped champagne. "I think you and Di might like it. Di tells me you've got the goods."

"When did she tell you that?"

"Oh, more than once. Really, Norman, don't be so modest. Di's discreet. But, you know, a girl likes to brag now and then."

Just the mention of Diantha's name set off a complex mix of anger, wistfulness, and need within my heart. I sighed. I smiled. I said, as casually as I could, "So how's Diantha doing these days?"

"You should ask her."

"She won't talk to me."

"Silly girl. I wouldn't let you out of my sight if I ever got my hooks into you."

"I take that as a compliment."

Which made her laugh.

"Tell me, Merissa, is she seeing that old boyfriend of hers?"

"Really, Norman, I've never been one to tattle on a friend."

"Is there something to tattle on?"

She didn't answer except to give me a smile of sympathy.

I got back to business. "So this Edgar. If he takes the money, then he keeps records. Somewhere."

"I hadn't thought of that."

I tried to dissemble an edge of prurience in asking, "Where are the premises?"

"Devon Street. Right next to the First Seaboard Bank."

"Really? Does it have a name?"

"Garden of Delights. GOD for short."

"So why are you telling me this?"

"I'm trying to tempt you."

"No. Seriously."

"Because, if and when things get hot and heavy, I want it on the record that I was otherwise occupied. And the cops trust you."

"So why not just tell them?"

"Well, you know, Max isn't quite divorced yet. And his wife's . . ."

"I'm listening."

"It's none of the cops' business. They ransacked the whole house trying to tie me in to this thing. They went through my things, my really personal things . . ."

"That's their job."

She tittered again. "I know, Norman, I know. But they shouldn't have enjoyed it so much."

The waiter, a blank-faced older man, came by and asked us if we would like coffee or desert.

"Both," Merissa said, looking at me.

"A regular coffee, black."

"A cappuccino, the cheese selection, and another bottle of the Taittinger. Upstairs."

"Upstairs?"

"Room three twenty-one."

The waiter left before I could change the order. "Merissa . . . Really," I protested.

"Oh, come on, Norman. I won't bite you. Unless you want me to."

So there we were, sitting in comfortable chairs at a small table within reach of a large bed. I know I should have quaffed my coffee, grabbed a piece of the aged goat cheese, stood up, given her a peck on the cheek, and left. But her booted leg had entwined itself with mine and we were both a little drunk and . . .

"Norman," she said, "it's your move."

"Stalemate," I muttered weakly.

She laughed. "No stale . . . mates allowed."

Laughter under these circumstances can be hazardous, easing as it does the tricky mechanism of complicity. And we all know that it is incumbent upon the gentleman to make the final advance, if only because the female of the species needs to be vouchsafed a scintilla of reticence, however blatant her role in the seduction.

I will not burden the reader with the details of our initial kisses and caresses, our tidy, provocative divestment, our progression into the sublimities of carnal bliss. Too often attempts to render the felicities of sexual congress result in a "copulation of clichés," as the author of *Pale Fire* so succinctly put it. On the other hand, one should eschew obfuscating polysyllabic latinates such as concupiscent erubescent tumescence and the like. Not that wordplay and foreplay are mutually exclusive.

Happily, I can report no erectile dysfunction on this occasion. Indeed, I was seized by an avidity that made me feel like the butt of that hoary old joke: What happens when you give Viagra to a lawyer? His whole body enlarges. I exaggerate, perhaps because I felt exaggerated in every fiber of my being, and, like many beings, mine is quite fibrous.

In all seriousness, and sex needs be taken seriously even as the mounting tension and the giddiness of license make one smirk inwardly . . . In all seriousness, sex might well be the most palpable if not the ultimate indulgence in earthly beauty. In this spirit, Merissa would not have the lights dimmed, and nor should she have, given the visual feast she knew herself to be. At the risk of being unchivalrous, I would like to paint if only with words such details as Merissa's finely sculpted clavicles, her darkly prominent aureoles, which were ever so slightly pebbled and pink-brown against the creamy swell of her breasts, her shapely legs, and her remarkably well-toned nether cheeks. But also the fan of her rich hair, her smiling mischievous eyes, her perfect nose and lush mouth. As one Amis or another has remarked, the most beautiful part of a naked woman is her face, the Duc d'Orleans notwithstanding. (Delacroix's oil of the Duc d'Orleans displaying his unclothed mistress to the Duc de Bourgogne has the former veiling the upper part of her body.)

Among other things, Merissa provided me with a whole new appreciation of the adjectival phrase *clean-shaven*. Her depilated state was such as to vitiate, nay, razor to the roots, the synecdochic and metaphorical links between what I describe and the eponymous small felid. Indeed, her cloven, glabrous quiddity achieved nothing less than a second order of nudity, one that had me on my knees indulging in what an eminent poet has been amused to call the oral tradition. But even then, though tongue-tied and up to my nostrils in pungent lubricity, immersed in the pleasure of giving pleasure, I thought of the young Augustine and his prayer — Oh Lord, grant me chastity. But not just yet.

In returning the favor with enthusiasm and practiced competence, Merissa persuaded me that the vulgar compound for one who fellates should be used as an endearment rather than as an epithet. Especially, as in my case, if that one is a woman.

It was perhaps inevitable that we should experience cell phone interruptus. Yet the movements necessary for Merissa to turn the damn thing off — a torsal twist and a reaching of lovely arm — presented to me her whole dorsal splendor and made me think sex was, among many things, a cleaving of symmetry. This brief relapse to the mundanity of modern electronics had the salutory effect of making us more or less start over again, intermission leading to re-intromission, so to speak.

I cannot claim that Merissa proved a "revelation," as fictionalists are wont to say. Sex ends up being sex whatever bells and whistles of the flesh precede the final tupping. But she was appreciative, eager, friendly, and, to say the least, generous in the succession of venues she offered for my unflagging delectation, the last of which I declined, much to her merriment.

"Oh, Norman, you really are an old stick in the mud."

"Yes and no," I murmured, "yes and no."

But I am not good at adultery. For all its culminatory excesses (the sound effects on Merissa's part must have carried into the hall), the encounter left me unappeased and hankering, but for what, I did not know. What I could not fathom, as the afore-mentioned gratitude took hold, was what, if anything, I owed Merissa. Respect, certainly. But it's presumptuous to assume I owe her anything. One has to assume the gratifications are mutual. In fact, she may regard me as little more than an over-ripe plum she plucked from a low branch. Or found lying on the ground. She'll surely tell Diantha, as though by mistake, scoring points, giving them something to spat about and then patch up, closer than ever. Women are a strange species.

And what about my own motives? Other than simple lust, though lust is seldom simple, how much of my sudden ardor for Merissa might have sprung from anger? Was there not an element of preemptive retribution? Because I feared that Diantha was off cavorting with her minstrel boy and his merry band of drug addicts? It wasn't any sense of conquest. I have no urge to take pelts of the kind you either hang on the wall or record in your diary. But I did worry in wondering if I had indulged the primal act of possessing the woman of a man I had murdered.

I decided not to analyze any of this too closely. Drained but not satiated, I made my way home with a noticeably subdued Alphus next to me in the front seat, both of us staring out at a steady rain through the metronomic *swish swish* of the wind-shield wipers.

20

Limbo can be hell. In three days I face the Governing Board. If they ask for my resignation, then life as I have known it for several decades will cease to exist. Even now, when I glance around my office or walk through galleries of the museum, I feel like I am walking through my past.

If fired, what will I do, I ask myself now in a steady refrain of foreboding. Vegetate? Smell the roses? On what, my own funeral wreaths? I am far too old to revive my youthful dreams of doing field archaeology. I will be financially embarrassed, as my pension will be puny and many of my securities have become insecurities. All work may be honorable, but I can't quite see myself bagging groceries at the supermarket.

I suppose I should have delayed writing to Elgin Warwick about his mummy scheme. Felix shook his head in disbelief when I showed him a copy of the letter I had sent.

"So what's his response been?"

"Nothing. A deafening silence."

"Not good. Not good. Guys like Warwick are used to getting what they want. Especially when they're willing to pay for it."

I looked out the tall windows of my office at the overcast sky and said nothing.

"You know, Norman, you don't make it easy for people trying to help you."

I apologized. But how to explain that I needed to tie up at least one loose end and that the letter to Warwick did just that, perhaps in more ways than one. Because I have still not heard from Diantha. Bella called to tell me that Elsie was doing fine. "She teach me hand talk, Mr. Norman."

"That's nice," I said, grateful for at least that tidbit. Still, I was craven enough to ask, "Is Diantha there?"

"No, Mr. Norman. She says to be back later." I did not press it. If I have not succumbed to the temptation to call Merissa and propose another lunch, to put it euphemistically, it's because my emotions are in one big mangle. Of course, I would like to roger her royally again, to use the British idiom. Nor, in desisting from making such a call, do I want her to think I am slighting her.

That's the simple part. I suspect my real reason for wanting to contact Merissa is to hear about Diantha. Has the former told the latter about our little tryst, thereby giving Diantha justification for carrying on with her slanging troubadour? Merissa, for all her feather brains, would sniff out my intentions immediately. And laugh. God, why does love reduce us, big grown-up people, to little more than adolescents?

For all that, there have been a few dim bright spots. If I wasn't in such danger of losing all that I cherish, I might have enjoyed the anomaly of being out on bail on a charge of accessory to murder while working hand-in-glove with the police on two cases, including my own. That strange state of affairs was no more evident than in my meeting with Lieutenant Tracy at police headquarters, a meeting at which we both had significant developments to relate.

Indeed, for the first time in what is becoming a history of close cooperation with the SPD, I was taken into the office of Chief Murphy. He is a busy man of my years with a pear-shaped head, stem up, the hard eyes of a lifelong cop, and a brusque, friendly voice.

He stood upon our entry, extended a hand, and shook mine

warmly. "I want to thank you personally, Mr. Ratour, for your help in the Sterl case. I am distantly related to the Sterls through marriage. I can tell you the pressure that came from all quarters has been . . . memorable."

I thanked him in turn and took a chair with the lieutenant in front of the man's big desk.

He knit his hands together. "Just so that you know, Mr. Ratour, I am pulling every string and chain I know to get Jason Duff to drop those charges against you. But Jason's like a bulldog once he gets a bone in his mouth."

"He says just because you're helping in one case doesn't mean you aren't involved in the other," the lieutenant put in.

"It would help me considerably," I said. "I appreciate very much what you're doing for me."

"Bribe me with a bottle of good bourbon when I get it done."

We settled down to business. "This is strictly off the record, Norman," the lieutenant said, "but we arrested Andrijana Jakovich yesterday. She's been singing like an opera star ever since."

"So it was murder."

"As clean a case as we've ever had," the chief said.

"What about Branko?"

The chief leaned forward. "His face is plastered in so many places, you'd think he was running for office."

"He was last sighted in Pittsburgh," the lieutenant said. "We don't expect him to get far." He paused. "We'll need affidavits from you and your people as to the authenticity of the video you sent us. Routine stuff."

I allowed as that would not be a problem. I then opened a large manila envelope I had been holding in my hand. "These are the coins from the boat that you allowed me to have tested. These are results." I spread out a couple of the photos. "It seems the coins on the boat are also fakes. In fact, identical to those given to the museum."

The two policemen inspected the samples and photographs. "Fascinating," the chief said. "Who does it point to?"

"Max Shofar," I said, but without much conviction.

They waited. I said, "He might know who does this sort of thing, but I don't think he deals in fakes. He's got too much to lose."

"All right."

"But if Heinie . . . von Grümh took the originals, the real coins . . . to a forger, then Max might know where to look. I wouldn't mind talking to him again."

The chief glanced at his lieutenant, who said, "It's okay with me. But, Norman, if you find or suspect anything incriminating, we'll take it from there."

We parted on friendly terms. I drove home with such a sense of elation that I ran an orange light before I could stop. I was pulled over and given a warning by a crew-cut woman cop who could have been a bodybuilder.

People have gotten used to me showing up at the museum with Alphus in tow. For the sake of appearances, I keep him on a leash attached to a collar around his neck. I know it makes me appear weird, but frankly, I have too many other things to worry about. Alphus understands why I need to do it.

On this particular afternoon, we had two important appointments. Just after lunch, Max Shofar dropped by for what I told him on the phone would be an important updating on the von Grümh case. He can be a gracious person when he wants to be, especially in his unfeigned and knowledgeable appreciation of the objects in my office and in the collections generally.

"I always go away renewed after I've visited here," he told me, seated in front of my desk in a blue blazer and tan trousers.

I explained the presence of Alphus who was seated off to one side as a kind of pet-sitting I had to do. He nodded at my primate friend, who nodded back very civilly.

We exchanged some small talk, mentioning Merissa, but in no particulars. I detected an enhanced level of respect in his attitude toward me. I wondered if Merissa had told him about my amorous accomplishments. More than likely it had to do with my role in the Sterl case.

"So what's this updating you mentioned on the phone?"

I leaned forward over my desk and caught a whiff of his subtle cologne. "We found the originals in Heinie's sailboat."

The man's face lit up. "Well, that gets me off the hook."

I waited a moment. "Not quite. I've learned that the so-called originals are also fakes."

His smile turned knowing and rueful. "He shouldn't have done it."

"Done what?"

He paused, glanced over at Alphus, evidently pondering what to tell me. He said, "Heinie outsmarted himself."

"How so?"

"I would say he found a forger to knock off copies of his collection to go to the museum. For that he got the kind of public applause he so desperately needed and a hefty tax break. But the guy he went to made two copies and kept the originals."

"Who might that be?"

Again he hesitated. He sighed. "Okay, for defensive purposes, I keep track of the better fakers. They're getting so good with lasers and metallurgy, it's more and more difficult to distinguish between what's real and what's a replica, to use a nice term." He looked at Alphus with surprise, as though noticing something odd.

"Who?" I repeated.

"Well, of course, there's the Lipanov establishment. Bulgaria. They make replicas, have for a long time. But I don't think they would have done business with Heinie for what he wanted."

"Okay."

He thought for a moment. "Since Heinie had a boat, he could have taken them to Levi Stein. He's an Anglo-Israeli who set up in the Bahamas some time back. He makes replicas openly and forgeries on the side. Or so I've heard."

I was taking notes. "Anyone more local?"

"There's Henry Song in Manhattan. I've heard he supplies the growing market in China with first-rate fakes."

"That doesn't sound like it would have been Heinie's cup of tea."

"You're right. He would have looked down his nose at Chinese-made fakes."

"But no one local?"

"I've heard of a Swiss guy out in the Berkshires in one of the small towns. Nothing really substantial. And more in the line of antiques, swords, old guns, even medieval armor."

A distant, dim bell rang in my memory, but more as a number than anything tangible.

"Otherwise," Max continued, "he would have had to go to Europe. And that's got problems of its own."

"Such as?"

"Taking them out. Bringing them back. It isn't like the old days."

"And you never put him in touch with anyone?"

He looked at me with rueful resignation. "Norman, I've told you. I don't deal in fakes. I go out of my way to find them because they're toxic. That's why I'm trying to stay away from this whole thing."

I believed him. I thanked him and asked, as casually as I could, "Do you mind if I ask you a couple of basic questions regarding Heinie's murder?"

He shrugged. "No, why should I?"

Still, he frowned at the bluntness of the questions, particularly when I asked him if he murdered von Grümh. But he answered them all with no hesitations.

"What was that all about?" he asked when I had finished. Again, he was aware of Alphus's intent gaze at him.

"Just something I told Lieutenant Tracy I'd do."

"That's right, you're working with him, aren't you? I mean that Sterl murder. Of course we all knew Marty Sterl wouldn't shoot himself. He might shoot someone else if they crossed him. But never himself."

I cleared my throat preparatory to a difficult matter. I said, "I happen to know, Max, that you and Merissa didn't take a drive up the coast the night of Heinie's murder."

"Oh?"

"You and she went to a club instead. The Garden of Delights."

"She told you that?"

"She did. And she didn't make that up, did she?"

When he simply stared at me, I said, "Look, I know the GOD exists. And, I can have Edgar brought in for questioning . . ."

"Okay, okay." He was clearly embarrassed, which to me, in my persona as a newly minted man of the world, I found inexplicable. The Garden of Delights wouldn't be my dry martini, but I am, despite everything, not a prude. "Okay, Norman, we did go there. I just don't want it to get around."

I nodded. "It's safe with me. But I do need to know that everything else you told me about that night is the truth."

"It is. Everything. I swear."

I looked him right in the eyes. I said, "I believe you."

We both happened to glance at Alphus. He nodded.

Max Shofar put on his fashionable summer hat, a modified Panama. He stood and shook my hand. "Merissa's something else, isn't she."

"She told you?"

"Naw. I can tell."

I was chagrined after he left to take down the small video camera from the shelf to find I hadn't turned it on.

Alphus signaled that it wasn't necessary. "He's clean," he signed.

"About everything?"

"Except the part about the forgers."

"Really?"

"Yeah, I think he left something out."

"Deliberately?"

"Deliberately."

Not long afterward, Doreen came in to announce the arrival of Ms. Esther Homard, a literary agent from New York who wanted to meet Alphus before considering him as a client.

A woman in her late middle age, hard-crusted in that New York way, she wore a business suit and an expression of skepticism bordering on suspicion. She was accompanied by an "interpreter," a tall blond woman of indeterminate age named Priscilla Watts.

We all shook hands and sat down around a small table I have under the windows facing north.

Ms. Watts looked distinctly taken aback when Alphus responded to her simple hello in sign language with an impressive display of gestural volubility.

"What did he say?" Ms. Homard wanted to know.

"He said, 'Welcome to Seaboard and the Museum of Man.' And that we had picked a nice day to travel."

"He understands spoken language," I put in.

Ms. Homard turned to him. "Do you read?" she asked.

Alphus nodded.

"What are you reading now?"

Alphus reached into a rucksack he uses, dug out a copy of Edward O. Wilson's *On Human Nature,* and handed it to her.

"What's it about?" she asked, still skeptical.

When Alphus began to sign with his usual speed, the interpreter said, "You'll need to go slower."

He nodded and began again. Ms. Watts repeated his words vocally. "It's an introduction to sociobiology as it applies to the human species . . ."

"What's sociobiology?" the agent wanted to know.

Alphus thought for a moment and then began signing. Ms. Watts, speaking for him, said, "Sociobiology is the application of evolutionary principles to behavior in everything from ants to elephants. The general theory as it relates to people explains charity, incest avoidance, and other instinctive behaviors that contribute to reproductive fitness."

Amazement showed in the faces of both women.

Alphus put up a finger and spelled something out for Ms. Watts. She said, "He says *charity* is the wrong word. *Altruism* would be more accurate."

"Who's your favorite actor?" Ms. Homard asked, much less wary but still in a test mode.

"Jack Nicholson," he spelled out for Ms. Watts.

"And your favorite movie?"

"*Chinatown.*"

"Why?"

Alphus gave it some thought. He signed and again Ms. Watts

spoke. "All of the characters are deeply flawed and yet ideal in some way."

Incredulity was giving way to awe. Ms. Homard said, "How would you count to fifteen by twos?"

Alphus thought for a moment. "Start with minus one?"

The agent looked at me. "This is no scam, is it?"

"No, he's the real deal, as you might say."

"Are you handling his affairs?"

"The museum's counsel, Mr. Skinnerman, has agreed to represent Alphus's interests in making any arrangements with an agency such as yours."

I provided her with Felix's coordinates.

"Tell him he'll be hearing from me shortly."

We all stood. "And you, Mr. Ratour, are you working on anything right now?"

"I'm neck-deep in a murder case."

"Are you writing it up?"

"I'm keeping notes."

She gave me her card. After handshakes all around, they left.

I tried to shake Alphus's hand, but he insisted on what is called a "high five." He then used my computer to text something to Ridley of which, with a shudder, I caught the word *celebration*.

21

On the morning of the meeting of the Governing Board, I woke feeling like a condemned man on the day of his execution. I expected no reprieves. There had been no last-minute phone call from Lieutenant Tracy regarding the charges against me. Elgin Warwick had not deigned to respond to my impulsive letter. Even Felix seemed to have vanished.

I was certain the board would ask for my resignation and that they would accept it with voiced regret and unvoiced relief.

While shaving I regarded the face that regarded me, the face of an adulterer, a possible murderer, a former museum director. Izzy Landes once remarked that low self-esteem can be a sign of intelligence, but on this occasion, I took it as a measure of reality. Good thing my revolver is missing. Only a slight pressure with the index finger. Quick and painless. Go out with a bang. And not much of a mess.

I dressed carefully in a well-tailored chino suit, blue button-down shirt, and tan tie with a subdued red floral design. I had a frugal breakfast of toast, two five-minute eggs, coffee, and tomato juice. I made sure Alphus had someone coming to watch over him. Knowing my situation, he gave me one of his hairy hugs just before I went out the door.

The meeting was set for eleven. I dawdled at my desk as I waited. Doreen came in long enough to make sure there was coffee and elegant little pastries on hand in the Twitchell Room. I nearly suggested she provide a blindfold for my execution.

And, indeed, it began badly. I could tell from their faces and from the look of pained sympathy on the face of my old friend Robert Remick that they were ready to pronounce sentence. We seated ourselves awkwardly around the long table in this room, which had been the scene of so many memorable events in my professional life. At ten minutes after eleven, Felix had not arrived and we agreed to start without him.

I imagined that the profound, existential loneliness that I experienced is what one feels as the blade is about to drop, as the trapdoor of the gallows is about to open, as the switch to the electric chair is about be thrown, as the pump for the injection is about to start. But I also knew I was indulging in gratuitous self-pity not to mention self-dramatization. Looked at in another way, these worthy people were about to set me free.

Robert Remick began uneasily. "At the behest of several members of the board, I have called this extraordinary meeting. We have some difficult and perhaps painful decisions ahead of us. I do not think we should move hastily or rashly regarding complaints as to the management of the museum. Norman de Ratour has served this institution long, faithfully, and with considerable success.

"Having said that, developments of late have been such that Norman's judgment has been called into question. On this matter, the Rules of Governance are unequivocal. They state that the Director of the museum may be removed for 'dereliction of duty, obvious incapacity to perform his functions as Director, public censure, criminal activity, or moral turpitude.'"

He turned to Maryanne Rossini, the university's representative. "Maryanne, I believe you wanted to go first."

Damn, I thought, *they've rehearsed this thing.* I sighed and settled back in my seat as the poison gas drifted in clouds around me.

An attractive, distracted woman in her fifties, Ms. Rossini works in Wainscott's international office. She pushed aside wisps of her abundant dark hair and, like a district attorney with an ironclad case, read the bill of indictment. This she prefaced with remarks about what she called "the lurid publicity surrounding recent events at the museum."

Then her statements began, with bullets in front of them. "First, authorities found it necessary to break up a pornographic ring within the museum that involved students, younger faculty, and dangerous animals."

"That's nonsense," I heard myself say. There's nothing like false accusations to get the blood boiling.

"You'll have your turn, Norman," old Remick said.

Ms. Rossini shuffled her papers. She continued. "The museum management, despite warnings from its own expert, accepted a significant number of coins that proved to be fakes. The incident, unfortunate in and of itself, has called into question the integrity of the entire collection."

I looked around the table at the grim faces. Where the hell was Felix? Not that his presence would change anything.

Ms. Rossini droned on. "The current administration of the museum has caused irreparable harm in its relations with the disadvantaged communities of Greater Seaboard and beyond by proposing that the models in the Stone Age exhibit be made fair-haired and white-skinned."

Harvey Deharo raised his pencil. "I'll address that one."

"In due time."

"In due time."

The next one took me by surprise. Ms. Rossini, still reading from her bill of particulars, said, "It has come to the attention of this body that the museum has turned down a proposal from a member of the board that entailed a significant and generous donation. While currently solvent, I think we would all agree that the MOM needs all the assistance it can get during these times of financial decline."

I glanced in the direction of Elgin Warwick. He pretended I wasn't there. I had my answer to the letter I sent him.

Ms. Rossini paused to frown and went on. "Under its current management, the museum has become involved in no less than two murders. It turns out, according to reliable media reports, that the planning for the murder of Martin Sterl, a prominent businessman, took place in the aforementioned Stone Age diorama. More seriously, the murder of one of the museum's own curators, the late Heinrich von Grümh, took place in the parking lot of the museum."

I didn't even bother to shake my head.

"And finally and most lamentably, Mr. de Ratour has been arrested and charged with accessory in the murder of Curator von Grümh."

Before anyone could clear their throats, Ms. Rossini went on. "I would like to add a professional note to these proceedings. Under Mr. de Ratour's administration, relations between the museum and the university have reached an all-time low. He has refused to acknowledge that Wainscott and the Museum of Man are and have been for generations part and parcel of each other. His campaign to assert the independence of the museum despite solid legal, historical, and institutional ties to the contrary have contributed not a little to the situation in which we find ourselves today."

"Thank you, Maryanne, for that sad litany," Robert Remick intoned. "Are there any comments."

Harvey spoke up. He demolished the item regarding the pale-skinned Neanderthals. "And most of the rest of these allegations are so spurious as to be ludicrous."

"Norman?" Remick turned to me. "Do you have anything to say?"

"Before you pass sentence?" I joked. I contemplated making an impassioned plea for my job, my career, my reputation. But I knew it would be to no avail. I simply shook my head.

"The chair will entertain motions."

Ms. Rossini said, "I move that we ask Mr. de Ratour for his resignation. And, failing compliance with that request, that we vote to dismiss him as Director of the Museum of Man."

Someone had seconded the motion when the door opened and Felix Skinnerman came in with a flourish worthy of the stage. I had the novel experience of hearing him apologize. A bit out of breath, he plunked a wad of folders down on the table in front of his seat but didn't sit down.

"At the risk of interrupting," he began, "I would like to present to the board some pertinent, important information before it proceeds any further."

"I believe a vote is in order," Ms. Rossini interposed.

Old Remick smiled and something of his old character asserted itself. "I am ruling that we hear all the pertinent information before we make such a vote. Proceed, Mr. Skinnerman, you have the floor."

"First, all charges against Norman . . . Mr. de Ratour . . . have been dropped." He handed out a folder to each member. "The first document should be a copy of an affidavit signed by the District Attorney Jason Duff." He glanced at me and smiled a crooked smile.

"That's all well and good," Elgin Warwick said huffily, "but the damage has been done."

There were enough assenting nods to quell the sudden hope that rose in my breast.

Felix bowed. "I'm not quite finished. In fact, I've hardly begun."

He lifted from his folder a stapled clip of e-mails originating in the Victim Studies Department from no less a personage than its chair. Several were addressed to the University Vice President for Affiliated Institutions, that is, to Malachy Morin.

Felix began with the first one, reading aloud.

Dear Mal:

I want to follow up on our conversation at lunch on Friday re the utilization of the MOM as headquarters for Victim Studies. A lot of the displays are not only offensive, but superfluidous [sic] in any event and could be dismantled to make room for offices. I'm going over there tomorrow with a therapeutic architect who designs work spaces for people working in charged atmospheres.

Also, I want to tell you that I am seriously considering backing your candidacy as numero uno at Wainscott. I am not one of those people who consider white maleness as an automatic disqualification.

Keep chugging,

Lal

"Should I read on?" Felix asked.

"By all means," said Harvey. "This is fascinating."

Robert Remick nodded. "I agree."

Felix gave me a nod. He went on,

Dear Mal:

I appreciate very much your support for my proposal

re the Museum of Man. (A ridiculous, sexist name to begin with!) I was over earlier today with Rex Rawler, the workplace therapist architect I mentioned earlier. He pointed out the enormous amount of waste space. The whole central part of the main building is nothing but air! Why they have kept that sky light and the five floors of emptiness is beyond me. I'm sure we could raise the funds to gut the whole exhibition space and modernize it like they did the Longworth Library.

I think F. de Buitliér is a good choice to take over temporarily from Ratour. We'll need a transitional figurehead. I'm sure he would be amenable to a job in your administration.

Keep plugging,
Lal

"And one more."

Dear Mal:

I know we'll have to go slowly on the museum do-over once Ratour is out of there. My think group here at the department came up with a wonderful idea. Once we take over, we change the name to the Museum of Victimization. Or the Museum of Victims. We'll keep some of the exhibits, but give them a whole new spin with new labels. We'd include all appropriate groups, of course. Fund-raising would be a cinch. And Rex thinks it would add greatly to the environment in which the department would be operating.

Keep slugging,
Lal

"And finally . . ."

Dear Mal:

I would agree upfront that income from the gen lab would accrue to the central administration. You must understand that my object in all this is to take a monument to the victimizers and turn it into a monument to the victims. I have already sounded out some contacts in the relevant foundations and I'm hearing a lot of agreement. And, of course, we'll commit all this to paper when the time comes.

> Keep hugging,
> Lal

"None of this would stand up in court," Ms. Rossini asserted.

"We're not in court," Felix said with a smile.

"These e-mails could have been faked," Elgin Warwick said. "I frankly think they have been."

Felix kept his smile in place. "Perhaps. But the next document in your folder could not have been faked. I refer to the requisition form signed by Professor Laluna Jackson for an initial assessment of the museum space by the university's facilities. It would be a preliminary step in its reduction from the wonderful space it is now to another warren of offices for academic drones."

He paused, taking them all in, one by one. Then he said, "I am not a disinterested party in this proceeding. But I believe it is clear from what I have shown you that firing Norman de Ratour at this juncture would be tantamount to destroying the museum and what it stands for."

It was Remick, a gentleman of the old school, who cleared his throat and said, "There is a motion before the committee that I for one, given these facts, move be withdrawn."

Elgin Warwick, another gentleman of the old school, did not demur. "I have changed my mind," he said with dignity. "As much as I have reason to disagree with Norman on some things, his continued service to the museum is essential. The motion should be withdrawn."

Someone began, "I move . . ."

Carmilla Golden pointed out that the motion under consideration had to be voted on before another motion could be considered.

I put up my hand at this point and said, "I actually would like to say a few words before any motion is voted on."

The room grew very quiet. I sipped some coffee and actually tasted it. I said, "For those interested in accuracy, Heinie, Heinrich von Grümh, was not murdered on museum property but on a right-of-way between the parking lots of the museum and the Center for Criminal Justice."

"Close enough," Ms. Rossini murmured.

"Also," I continued, "whether or not Martin Sterl's murder was or was not plotted in the Diorama of Paleolithic Life is immaterial. Is Ms. Rossini suggesting that we put up notices to the effect that the fomenting of conspiracies is prohibited on museum property?

"As for the pornography ring in the museum, Ms. Rossini is misconstruing the minutes of an Oversight Committee meeting in which facetiousness abounded.

"And, finally, the generous gift she refers to involved the display of the mummified remains of the donor in a special temple that would have seriously undermined the overall purpose of the museum."

"What about the coins?" Ms. Golden asked.

"I admit I should have had them tested. But in the scale of things, I believe that dereliction is scarcely grounds for a vote of no-confidence."

I carried the day. Only Golden, Rossini, and old Farquar, who didn't seem all that sentient, voted yes on the motion to ask for my resignation. The others voted no. Moments after that, I was alone in my office with Felix.

"You are a miracle worker," I began. "You pulled it right out of your hat."

"I've been flat-out on this for three days. I should have called, but I didn't get the affidavit from Duff until this morning."

"Why did he change his mind?"

"He didn't have a case after I showed him the new evidence I had gathered."

"New evidence?"

"Well, I got a sworn and notarized statement from Diantha stating that she loaned von Grümh the revolver. They could get her on some kind of firearms violation, but that would be peanuts."

"I should have thought about doing it earlier."

"It might not have signified if Diantha hadn't come up with copies of e-mails from von Grümh telling her he needed a weapon to defend stuff he had on the boat."

"How did that happen?"

"Diantha called me a couple of days ago. She told me she was dropping everything and conferring with a data-recovery honcho and working on it."

"She initiated it?"

"She sure did."

"And the e-mails from Jackson."

"That req form was the smoke. I hired a PI. It wasn't difficult. Laluna Jackson's office is a collection of self-righteous fools. And the righteous are seldom discreet."

"Felix, I love you."

He stood up to go. "Wait till you see my bill."

"It will be worth every penny."

I was alone, finally, in my office. I was still Director of the Museum of Man. And while a great relief, it was as a trifle next to what Felix had told me of Diantha's involvement in getting the charge of accessory to murder dropped. I left a message on my answering machine to the effect I was not there. I flew out of the building and, despite the warmth of the day and my leather shoes, all but ran home.

I found Alphus at the kitchen table picking at the keyboard of his laptop. I told him my good news. And that I was leaving him alone for the afternoon and possibly overnight as I had to go to the cottage.

"If you leave here, Alphus, and the police detain you, there will be nothing I can do. It will either be the zoo or the cages in the museum. Or worse."

He nodded and signed, "Ridley's coming over. We'll be working on my memoir."

"Okay. But the same applies if you burn the place down or make a lot of noise."

"Trust me, Norman, I will be responsible."

I did trust him. Since the meeting with Esther Homard, Alphus had undergone another transformation. He had become a writer, which is to say, careless of his appearance, careful about what he said, and altogether much less verbal, as though saving his words for the page. He wasn't nearly as interesting to be around as he had been.

I drove as fast as my rattling old Renault would go, wishing I had one of those sleek little things that can do 130 standing still.

Where had all the traffic suddenly come from? And what would I find when I arrived?

Diantha's hulking SUV was parked as usual in the gravel space in front of the cottage. But there was no sign of her or Elsie. I went out the back and down into the garden. There they were, working on my espaliered apple trees.

Elsie turned without a sign and ran toward me. I swept her up into my arms and held her to me. She leaned back, all smiles, her little hands moving with words. "We missed you, Daddy. Where have you been?"

With her in my arms, I approached my young wife. I said, as I had in my heart on the way there, "I want to thank you for helping Felix."

"The board didn't fire you?"

"No. I am still Director of the Museum of Man." I hesitated a moment. "But that is not important next to the fact that you helped me."

She drew closer. I could see her eyes under the brim of the sunhat she wore. "It was the least I could do."

"I love you," I said.

She came into my laden arms, tears on her cheeks and lips as she kissed me.

Hand in hand, Elsie toddling behind us, we walked through the warm summer garden to the coolness of the cottage.

"Why didn't you answer my calls?" I asked without animosity as we sat at the kitchen table still holding hands.

She shrugged as though to minimize it. "I was ashamed of myself. I thought you only wanted to rag on me."

"Dear girl, I only wanted to beg your forgiveness."

"Have you eaten?"

"No. I'm not hungry. Not for food."

She made me a thick toasted cheese and ham sandwich,

anyway, chatting, as she worked, about keeping up the cottage and the garden.

Bella came in after being dropped off by a neighbor with whom she had been earning some extra pay. A large, dignified woman, she greeted me with much evident joy. Then she took Elsie out to help her pick flowers.

I cracked open the two beers Di put on the table. I found I was ravenous. I ate the entire sandwich and an early apple from a neighbor's orchard. At length, I asked, "So what brought about your change of heart?"

She blushed and covered it by pouring beer into a glass and sipping it.

"Sixpack didn't work out?" I prompted gently.

She met my eyes. "That was never a real possibility. I knew it even before I got there."

"Tell me about it."

"Well . . . his concert." She made quotation marks with her fingers. "After five minutes I wanted to leave. You've spoiled me, Norman dear. I don't know how anyone with an IQ over forty can listen to that stuff. They barely speak an intelligible language. They celebrate their stupidity."

"It's only an act."

"I know, but it's stupid to pretend to be stupid."

She came and sat on my lap. I stroked her back as she talked. "I saw an old movie with Leslie Howard in it and all I could think of was you. You are civilization. And I need civilization."

"I've missed you horribly as well."

"Really?" Diantha, spoke with an edge to her voice I recognized with a touch of alarm. "Merissa let it slip that you and she . . . hooked up."

"That's one way of putting it," I admitted, surprised to find myself scarcely embarrassed. I wondered if my afternoon with

Merissa had helped in Diantha's change of heart.

"How was . . . it?"

I smiled. "I'm afraid she was a Joe DiMaggio."

She mock-frowned. "But we're even."

"We're even."

"Can you stay?"

I was afraid she would ask that. I grimaced. "I should go back soon."

She grimaced back. "Because of your friend?"

"No. I need to find out who murdered Heinie."

"Oh, Norman, let the police figure that out. It's their job. You've done enough for them."

"It's not just that."

"Then what else?"

"As I told you before, I'm afraid that I may have murdered Heinie."

"But, Norman, if you shot him, you would remember doing it."

"I know. But I need to make absolutely sure. I not only want to clear my name, I need to clear my conscience. If I don't, I'll be haunted by this thing the rest of my life."

22

I might not have learned about Shetland Falls had the weather not turned unseasonably chilly a few days after the meeting of the Governing Board. In dressing that morning, I put on the jacket I had worn the day I discovered Heinie's body and accompanied Lieutenant Tracy to Kestrel Meadows to tell Merissa the news. In the side pocket I came across the piece of notepaper I had lifted from the telephone pad in their kitchen.

I doubted it signified much as I lay it on a flat surface and shadowed it lightly with a soft pencil. What looked like a telephone number emerged. I noticed a crossed seven, which had been one of Heinie's smaller affectations. The area code was 413, which I quickly learned was in western Massachusetts.

I called Di at the cottage and asked her to do a reverse lookup for me. She's a whiz at that sort of thing. We chatted as she keystroked in real time. Nice phrase, that, real time.

"It's in Shetland Falls. It's registered to one Alain LeBlanc. Hold on, there's a business listing. Antique Valuables, Jewelry, Coins, Objects, Assessed, Repaired, Reproduced . . ."

"Would you fancy a drive to the Berkshires?" I asked.

"It's more like the northern Berkshires."

"Better still. I can't stand all that artsy stuff around Lenox. We'll have to take an overnight."

"Are you trying to seduce me?"

"Yes."

"Okay. When?"

"Wednesday. We leave in the morning and return Thursday afternoon."

"Good. I'll get Bella to stay with Elsie and you'll find someone to stay with your . . . friend."

The prospect filled me with a zeal and an energy I had not felt in months. I yearned for action, for resolution. Still, I did not try the number I had lifted from the pad. I wanted an excuse to get away with Diantha. I also wanted to show up unannounced. I had a broken brooch of amber and pearl set in silver and gold that my mother wore for years. I knew the pearls were worth stealing and faking, and I wanted to test this Mr. LeBlanc.

I thought of calling Lieutenant Tracy and telling him what I had found. That would have been the sensible thing to do. But I felt that this was my case. It involved personal demons that I and I alone could vanquish.

We planned originally to drive via Boston, mostly for the roads, but decided instead on a cross-country route in Diantha's APC — armored personnel carrier. I suggested she call it Bigfoot given how few miles it got to the gallon. Still, it is comfortable. Di drove and I relaxed, taking in the scenery. It was reassuring to see that much of New England appears to have escaped the sprawl of malls that have disfigured so much of America the Beautiful.

We stopped for lunch at a country inn run by a couple who had left the rat race of New York's financial world. A more harried-looking pair I have seldom seen. Karl and Nance skittered hither and yon, scarcely stopping to say hi to Diantha, who knew them when. Apparently, they have to do much of the work themselves to make ends meet.

We arrived in Shetland Falls by midafternoon. It is a

prepossessing small town, with a main street of good buildings in brick, stone, and wood. We slant-parked right and began an apparently aimless stroll. There was method in the approach. I wanted us to appear as absentminded, average tourists. We wouldn't act dotty or anything like that as I showed the damaged brooch to Mr. LeBlanc, just a bit distracted.

With Di as my accomplice, we walked along in search of number 47, third floor. We found 21, then 33, then 43, and then a large gap where a building had obviously been until recently. A chain-link fence surrounded the cellar hole where bits of charred debris were still in evidence. On the other side the numbers continued with 73.

There we entered a gift shop calling itself The Wretched Stalk. It proved to be an emporium specializing in local artisanal items with dazzling price tags. The keeper, a woman in a painter's smock, told us she had known Mr. LeBlanc only casually, but that Jed and Glad in the Donut Hole next door knew him well.

"Well, not well," Jed explained, as we ordered coffees to go. "He was a nice enough guy. Very polite. He was French . . ."

"French Swiss," Glad corrected him.

"I guess. He came in here every morning for espresso and orange juice to go."

"He really liked our maple cakes."

"But then the building burned. Just like that. We're lucky we're stone. Hard to burn granite."

"How long was he here?" I asked. "In Shetland Falls."

"Couple of years. Not long after we started."

"Did he leave a forwarding address?"

"Not with us. You could check the post office. Or the chief of police. He knows everything about that sort of thing."

"How did the fire start?"

"No one knows."

We thanked them and, sipping our brews of coffee, walked a few doors down to the Shetland Falls Police Department. Chief Russell Ballard remained seated in a comfortable, worn swivel chair but seemed relieved to see us, to have something to do.

"Yeah, Mr. LeBlanc. He was a real foreigner. But a regular gentleman. He could make just about anything new again. Earl Mason took him an old samurai sword, the real thing. It was about two hundred years old but a bit tarnished. He got it back good as new."

"Tell me about the fire," I asked. "How did it happen?"

"Don't rightly know. The state fire marshal told me privately he smelled a rat, but he also couldn't prove anything. If it was arson, then they had a professional do it."

"When did it happen?"

The chief squinched his mild round face. "Let's see . . . late April? No, come to think of it, second of May. I got a call about four in the morning. When I got there they were just trying to save the building on the right side. The other one's granite with a slate roof."

"Was LeBlanc's business still there at the time?"

"No. That's why the fire marshal thinks there ought to be an investigation. Mr. LeBlanc cleared out about a week before. Told people he had to go back to Switzerland and take care of the family business." He shot me a searching look. "You know, you're the second person from Seaboard who's been here poking around about Mr. LeBlanc."

"Really?"

"Eyah . . . Not long after the fire, a fellow came through asking pretty much the same questions."

"Did he give his name?"

"He did, but I didn't write it down. Phil somebody. It sounded foreign in a fakey kind of way."

Though I had a pretty good idea he was talking about de Buitliér, I asked if he could describe him.

"I can and I will. He was on the short side, beard, and a tweed jacket and tie even though the day was hot and humid." He paused. "You know of him?"

"As a matter of fact, he works for me."

He glanced at me sharply. "Tell me, how do you spell his name?"

"It's complicated."

"I ain't simple."

So I spelled it out as best I could remember. I wondered what he had been doing here. I asked, "What was LeBlanc's shop like?"

"Never was in it. Wally Marsden did odd jobs for him. He helped him pack up. I heard around town that there was some pretty high-tech stuff in there."

"Such as?"

"Computers. Laser-guided lathes. Gas-fired smelters. Drills. Presses. All kinds of chemicals."

"Did he leave a forwarding address?"

"Not with me. You could check the post office." He rubbed his chin. Can I ask what your interest is in all of this?"

I took out my card. "I'm director of a museum up in Seaboard. I'm trying to trace the origin of some counterfeit coins."

He glanced at it. "Right. You've had a couple of murders up there. Bad business all around."

"Where could I find this Wally Marsden?"

"Wally lives over on the other side of Route Two. Go right on Bear Creek Road. First place on the left. Kind of run-down. Can't miss it."

We left Chief Ballard and ambled over to the post office playing tourist as we went. We duly took in the glacial potholes worn into beautifully patterned granite bedrock along a green-banked river. We strolled along the Bridge of Blooms, an old railroad structure, now a marvelous linear garden of color and scents. Diantha took pictures of the displays with her remarkable little camera.

I paused to read the names on a war memorial dedicated to those from the town who had perished in recent conflicts. As I went down the list, I tried to imagine their faces, where they were born, how they died, the heartache. *These are the real heroes,* I thought to myself, *the ones who gave all.* Yet how small were their names. Compared with the very wealthy who, after some ingenious swindle of one kind or another, have their names emblazoned in huge lettering in granite on the outside of some building as proof of their magnanimity. And sometimes all over the interior as well, so that one cannot escape their futile, ostentatious benefaction. Futile because, as Felix so aptly pointed out, after a while a name is only a name.

It's another reason I'm glad I turned down Elgin Warwick and his mummification scheme, even if his money is "old." (The robber barons at least made and built things, unlike the latest crop of super-rich.)

But I digress.

The interior of the post office looked much as it would in Key West or Attu in the Aleutians what with special issues advertised on the walls and the usual array of packing materials.

Yes, Mr. LeBlanc did leave a forwarding address, a box number in Zurich, but a couple of things forwarded there had come back.

In Diantha's formidable vehicle, we drove over to Route 2 and followed Chief Ballard's directions. Sure enough, we arrived at a ramshackle sort of place, two old barns, one virtually collapsed near the road and, well up from there, a porched cottage set back against a wooded hill. We drove into a clearing between them and parked beside a spanking-new pickup big enough to be a trailer truck.

I morphed into my private eye persona and made my way through a litter of junk that included an overturned ski mobile, a rusting lawn mower, old tires, what might have been a hay baler, and assorted car parts. I mounted uncertain steps to the paint-blistered porch. I knocked on the screen, though there was a man standing just a few feet away in the gloom of the interior.

"Wally Marsden," I said neutrally.

"Who wants to know?"

"A friend of Alain LeBlanc's."

I guessed the man to be in his late thirties. He had stringy light hair, dissipated eyes, bad teeth, and wore a sleeveless T-shirt tucked into oil-stained jeans. He pushed open the screen and came out far enough to stand in the doorway.

"How do I know that?"

"You don't. I'm not exactly a friend. He did some work for my company."

His eyes stayed skeptical and puzzled at the same time, as though trying to gather his wits. "He did lots of work for lots of people."

"Actually, Mr. Marsden, I owe Alain money and I'm trying to find out where to reach him."

"He left a forwarding address at the post office."

"I know, I tried."

He glanced down at the yard. "Who's that down in the four-by-four?"

"My wife."

He nodded. "Nice."

"I think so."

"You say you owe Alain money?"

"I also have a piece of jewelry I want to send him."

"How much money you owe him?"

"Depends."

A sly smile came and went. "Depends on what?"

We didn't entirely drop the pretense. I said, "I need to know a few things."

"I'm listening."

"I know that he made . . . replicas of old coins."

"Nothing wrong with that."

"True. I just want to know if he did any work for anyone up in Seaboard."

"I think you would owe him about a hundred for that."

I took out my wallet and fingered a couple of fifties. I gave him one and hung on to the other.

He nodded and glanced with longing toward our vehicle. "LeBlanc never told me much. There was a guy with a German name that dropped off a set of really old coins."

"Heinrich von Grümh?"

"Sounds about right."

I gave him the second fifty. "How many copies did you make?"

"Hey, listen, I didn't have anything to do with what he did."

"What did you do?" I still had my wallet out.

"I did odd jobs. Cleanup. Supplies. Packing and shipping. He said he'd teach me how to use his gear, but he never did."

"So how many copies of those coins did you make?"

"You'd owe another . . . fifty for that."

I took out two twenties and a ten and looked at them.

"Okay, I'm pretty sure he made two copies."

"And sent them both back?" I handed him the money.

"As far as I know."

"Nice truck."

"Yeah, ain't it."

"How did the fire start?"

His eyes turned hostile for a flash. He shrugged. "Fire marshal's been up here asking me the same thing. An insurance guy, too."

"What did you tell them?"

"The truth."

"I'm still listening."

"Look, I had nothing to do with it. Nothing at all. There was lots of chemicals left behind. Oil-soaked rags, that sort of thing. Could have been spontaneous combustion."

"And you don't know where I could reach Mr. LeBlanc?"

"He's back in Switzerland all's I know."

"Well, thank you, Mr. Marsden. You've been a great help."

"What about that money you owe him?"

"I thought I just paid that."

We drove up into the hills for some sightseeing through forest and farmland before checking in at the Inn at Mountcharles. A rambling quaint clapboarded affair, it dated from the Revolutionary War. I liked it immediately, though Diantha balked at the accommodations, which were rudimentary but comfortable. We settled in and then lingered down to the bar and restaurant. I was charmed by what might be called the inadvertent authenticity of the place, especially the framed sepia-toned photos from long ago and folk art in the reception rooms with the chintz-covered armchairs and sofas.

"It's very local," Diantha said after we had taken our drinks to a table by a window looking out over a well-wooded ski slope.

"That's exactly what I like about it." I was perusing the menu but really thinking about the case. It was clear now that de Buitliér had found something that led him to suspect the authenticity of Heinie's collection. He had a few samples tested, confirming his suspicions. Did he then try to blackmail Heinie, threaten to expose him unless . . . ? Heinie refused to pay. De Buitliér leaked the story to the *Bugle*. They met, argued. De Buitliér got the gun away from him and shot him. It didn't add up.

"I'm going to have the chicken," Diantha said to the matronly waitress, who had highly recommended the rib roast. *Local,* I thought, looking up at the work-worn, pleasant face. "The rib," I said, "medium rare."

Later, on a comfortable bed in our sparsely furnished room, I lay spent in the aftermath of lovemaking that had been truly lovemaking. In the course of our prolonged encounter, Diantha had noticed that the level of my amatory expectations had risen. Not that she objected except to say, with a rueful laugh, "It's Merissa, isn't it? She's spoiled you."

23

I must confess that I have been remiss in not investigating Feidhlimidh de Buitliér's possible role in the murder of Heinrich von Grümh. He still does not appear to me as a probable suspect. What did he have to gain? Academic spite can corrode steel. But murder? Members of the professoriat of whatever rank are seldom people of action. With the exception, perhaps, of paleontologists and other natural historians.

Perhaps I simply cannot take him seriously as a suspect in a murder when I do not take him seriously as a man. I could not believe that he would have the gumption to kill someone in cold blood. Not when I thought of what it takes to hold a revolver up against the temple of a fellow human being and pull the trigger.

But Chief Ballard's description had been smack-on. De Buitliér had been out to Shetland Falls snooping around. Or had he been in on the deal? Had LeBlanc double-crossed him? I had a moment of unease wondering about the authenticity of the other items in the Greco-Roman Collection.

The first thing I did the morning after I returned was to call the financial office and tell them I wanted to review phone records for the last couple of months.

A patient voice directed me how to access the file on my own computer. It proved childishly easy. I clicked into the subfile for Greco-Roman Collection Curatorial Office. Lots of long-distance calling. And then, there it was, the 413 number for LeBlanc's operation. It had been called three times, once in March and twice in April.

I subdued a frisson of predatory anticipation and pondered my next move. I knew I should call Lieutenant Tracy and tell him what I had found so far. But what had I found? The forger? Possibly. But I had no real proof.

In the midst of these cogitations I received a text message from Alphus containing what sounded like good news. Esther Homard, the literary agent, has a renowned and well-financed publisher interested in his memoirs. So interested, in fact, that they are chartering a plane to fly him to the great big apple for a meeting.

Alphus wants me to accompany him, but frankly, I think Felix would be far more useful. There's already been some e-mailing back and forth about establishing a trust of which I would be one of the trustees. It strikes me as strange that Alphus is not recognized as a legal entity.

I sent back a text message (I am not comfortable with *text* as a verb) congratulating him. I also asked him to stand by for a lie detector exercise in the afternoon.

I called Diantha out at the cottage. "Angel," I said, using my Humphrey Bogart voice, "could you do a background check for me on Feidhlimidh de Buitliér? There's a site called something like WhoWasWho.com."

"I could try. How do you spell that?"

I spelled it out for her and then told her about Alphus's good news.

"Fly him to New York?" She sounded skeptical.

"On a private charter. I think he would do better in a car."

"Whatever."

I heard some of her old exasperation. I said, "Diantha darling, if Alphus gets a nice fat advance, he'll be able to afford some place of his own and hire a keeper."

"If . . ."

"Yes, if."

Rather than call my latest suspect and arrange to have him come by for an interrogation, I decided to drop in unannounced at his small office on the third floor.

He wasn't in, but a young man, a veritable ephebe of Hungarian birth named Josef, asked me if he could be of any help. I told him who I was and that I wanted to speak directly to Mr. de Buitliér.

"Doctor de Buitliér won't be back until later," he said vaguely. "Do you want that I take a message?"

"Yes, tell him to call me the moment he gets in. Tell him it's very important." Then, neutrally, I asked him what he did in the museum.

"I'm Doctor de Buitliér's assistant."

"Really? I don't think personnel knows about that."

"Actually, now I am only an intern."

In the course of this exchange, I happened to glance out the window. It was, like most of the windows at the museum, a large, generous thing. It gave out onto both the museum and Center for Criminal Justice parking lots and would have afforded de Buitliér a direct view of what happened on the night of von Grümh's murder. That is, if he had been around.

Why hadn't I thought of this before? I asked myself. I had not even checked the electronic log for him or others who might have been at the museum that night.

Cursing myself for neglecting such routine yet critical investigative tasks, I took the elevator down to the basement to see Mort. He was in his office keeping an eye on the big panel of security screens while watching a baseball game on one of those little things that fit into a drawer.

I let it slide. I had better things to talk to him about. "The records for the night of May tenth," I said, taking a seat nearby.

He nodded, pecked at a keyboard, and after several false starts brought it up with a flourish. "There," he said, giving the word two syllables.

I frowned. The record showed that de Buitliér left the building around six thirty and did not return that night.

"Mort, tell me, is there any way of getting into and out of the building without swiping your card?"

When he began to squirm and shake his head, I said, "Mort, this is very important."

"Well . . . You know the loadin' dock in the back and the two big doors that open out. Off to the side, there's a small access door. You need to swipe there to get in, but it ain't wired into the records yet. They're supposed to come look at it all summer, but you know how contractors are."

"Who knows about this?"

"Don't know. Word gets around."

"Good. Thanks. And what's the score?"

"Three to nothing Sox in the fifth. Last I knew."

Back in my office I again considered calling Lieutenant Tracy and letting him in on what I was doing. But I felt I needed to tie up a few more loose ends first. For instance, who had reported to the police the meeting between me and Heinie at the Pink Shamrock? Who but de Buitliér?

It was one o'clock and I had gotten a bit peckish. I printed out a likeness of de Buitliér I found on the museum's Web site. With this in pocket I drove over to that establishment, which I found to be busy with a mixed crowd in terms of sexual preference, at least as far as I could tell.

A large-faced genial bartender by the name of Pat asked what he could do for me. I ordered a pint of ale and glanced at the menu. "The ham on rye looks good," I told him.

"Ham on rye it is."

I sipped my ale and ate the sandwich, which I found excellent. I didn't begin my inquiries until it was time to pay the bill.

"You're Pat?" I asked, fishing several twenties out of my wallet.

"The very same. Pat Kelly." He reached a big hand across the bar. "From Ballinasloe, County Galway."

"Norman de Ratour. I work at the Museum of Man."

"Just up the road."

I nodded. I said, as casually as I could, "You don't strike me, Pat, as very much like a lot of your clientele."

"As indeed I'm not. It's a job. And they're people, you know, no less than you and me."

"Do they confide in you?"

He laughed. "Some of the more desperate ones do."

"What do you tell them?"

"I don't. I just listen." His eyes turned shrewd. "What can I do for you, Mr. de Ratour?"

I produced the folded printout of de Buitliér's likeness and showed it to him. "You could tell me if this gentleman frequents this bar."

Pat eyed me suspiciously for a moment. "You're not police, are you?"

"No."

After a glance at the picture, he leaned over the bar and, keeping his voice dramatically low, said, "That's Philly de Buitliér. He's not really a regular. He comes and goes. I would say he was from Ulster if I had to, but I don't think the man is from anywhere."

I thanked him and placed a couple of twenties on top of the few dollars I had left as a tip.

"That won't be necessary," he said, but accepted them

graciously when I insisted. "And do come back and see us."

I drove home and picked up Alphus. He was in a rare good humor, showing me the e-mail he had gotten from his agent. Then raising his hand to slap mine.

Feidhlimidh de Buitliér came in to my office and sat down, glancing at Alphus and generally acting like a cornered rat. The insolence had gone out of his eyes. He didn't exactly grovel, but his body language was that of someone very nervous.

I softened him up for my interrogation as I had before with some generalities about changes in the Greco-Roman Collection. Did it really fit into the scheme of the museum with its heavy emphasis on native arts and traditions? I asked. Especially since the coins had proven fake.

He didn't say much until I mentioned the plans the Wainscott administration had for the museum once I had been removed.

"What do you mean?"

"Your name appears prominently in the documentation," I said, fixing him with a stare of real anger.

"How's that?"

I showed him the e-mail in which his name was mentioned as my successor.

"I had nothing to do with that," he lied.

I let silence descend. I leaned back, "Tell me, Mr. de Buitliér, what was your business with Alain LeBlanc in Shetland Falls?"

"Who?"

"The Swiss gentleman who made expert copies of the coins von Grümh gave to the museum."

"I don't know what you're talking about."

I produced a printout of the phone records with his calls to the number circled in red and handed it to him.

He glanced at it. "This doesn't prove anything."

"It proves that someone from your office called the number of a forger who had set up business in a small town in western Massachusetts."

He shook his head.

I pressed on. "The chief of police in Shetland Falls is willing to testify that you were out there making inquiries about Mr. LeBlanc. It also turns out that the fire that destroyed the building where LeBlanc made his forgeries is considered of suspicious origin by the state fire marshal's office."

He said nothing.

"You've been very busy, Doctor Buitliér. You're the one who told the police, anonymously, of course, that I was with von Grümh in the Pink Shamrock on the night he was murdered."

"You can't prove that."

"I checked with the bartender. The big Irish gentleman. He says you're in there quite a bit."

"That doesn't prove anything."

"You also sent the anonymous letter implicating Col Saunders in the murder."

"Why would I do that?"

"Confuse things. Saunders doesn't think much of you. Never has."

All the while to one side, Alphus was regarding him intently and with his right hand making signals for the video camera on the shelf.

Again I said nothing for a while. Then, without preamble, I launched into the set of defining questions. "Tell me, Doctor Buitliér, did you kill Heinrich von Grümh?"

He looked at me almost with alarm. "Why do you ask me that?"

"Just yes or no."

"No. Why should I?"

"Did you want to murder Heinrich von Grümh?"

"No."

"Do you know who murdered Heinrich von Grümh?"

"No."

"Do you know where the murder weapon is?"

"No. Why should I?"

"Because you were here the night of the murder. I think you know a lot more about this than you are telling me. I think you are hiding something."

He said nothing, but a touch of the old defiance had crept back into his eyes.

Not long afterward, I thanked and dismissed him. I locked the door so that Alphus and I could review the results undisturbed. They proved very interesting. According to Alphus, de Buitliér's response to the first question was ambivalent. Was he like me in that he didn't know if he did or didn't murder the man?

De Buitliér told the truth about not wanting to murder von Grümh. Out of principle? Because his murder would not be to his advantage? Because, complementary to that, he was more valuable to de Buitliér alive than dead?

When Alphus said de Buitliér lied about knowing who killed von Grümh, my blood ran cold. Because it still could have been I. But then, if it was, why wouldn't he simply have called the police and told them?

It gave me a distinct throb of excitement to know that he lied when he said he didn't know where the murder weapon was. But what if my prints were on the weapon? What if . . .

I didn't hesitate. I put in a call to Lieutenant Tracy and left word that I needed to see him as soon as possible. I didn't want to waste much time, because de Buitliér had the keen intuition of the cunning. He knew something was afoot.

While I was waiting for the lieutenant to get back to me, Diantha called with some results from her search of de Buitliér's background.

"You were right. I'm e-mailing you his information." We chatted. She asked me if the interest in Alphus's memoirs was the real deal. I told her absolutely. I had checked into Esther Homard and found that she was not someone to waste anyone's time, especially her own.

It turned out that Feidhlimidh de Buitliér had an intriguing résumé. For starters he was born Philip Bottles in Riverbend, Missouri. While attending a small local college, he spent a semester abroad at University College Cork in Ireland.

However, it appears he didn't get his name changed until after he graduated. He worked for more than a year in a pet-grooming business in Milwaukee before becoming an "associate" at a large home-improvement chain in upstate New York.

During this time, he enrolled in a doctoral program run by an online university not known for its rigorous standards. His doctorate was in "Classical Studies." The title of his dissertation, if any, was not listed.

How he ended up in Seaboard is not recorded. Under the late Dr. Comer, he began in a curatorial training program. From there, he simply insinuated himself into the woodwork of the place, starting as an interim curator for the Greco-Roman Collections.

The lieutenant appeared in my doorway wearing a light tan jacket and open collar. "I was in the neighborhood," he said without preliminaries. "What's up?"

"Some developments, I believe." I stood and shook his hand. "We may have a break."

He looked at me quizzically as we both sat down, the tension in the room suddenly electric. "You've been busy."

"I have. And I think we will have to move quickly."

"I'm listening."

I launched into a brief account of what I had been doing, starting with the day we went out to inform Merissa Bonne of her husband's murder and the number I found on the pad near the phone.

"You should have told us about that," he said, half smiling, half rebuking.

"I forgot about it myself until a couple of days ago. Anyway, Diantha traced it to an antiques restorer in the Berkshires by the name of Alain LeBlanc. Not only was he gone when we got there, but the building where he'd had his shop had burned to the ground in what the fire marshal out there regards as a suspicious fire."

The lieutenant listened with a frown as I detailed the rest of the story. Chief Ballard's description of de Buitliér as someone else who had been out poking around. How I found and questioned a local named Wally Marsden who confirmed that LeBlanc made replicas of coins and that he had made two sets for von Grümh.

"So you think de Buitliér . . . ?"

"There's more." But I made it brief. The fact that the curator frequents the Pink Shamrock, indicating that he could have been in the neighborhood at the time. The fact that there was a back door to the museum that didn't record swipes. And, finally, the results of the Alphus test I put de Buitliér through.

It surprised me to find the lieutenant skeptical. "So what do you suggest we do?" he asked.

"At the very least we should search his office."

"What do you think you'll find there?"

"My gun."

"You'll need a warrant to do that."

"Why? It's museum property."

"Because you need a warrant these days to look in your own refrigerator."

"Then let's get one."

"On what grounds? No judge is going to grant one on the basis of what a chimpanzee thinks."

For a moment I was stymied. Then I said, fishing in the folder I had on the case, "These are the phone records for the Greco-Roman Collection. They indicate that someone in that office of one employee called LeBlanc several times in March and April."

The lieutenant glanced at it for a moment. He took out and snapped open a cell phone. I produced the documentation as he required it, exact name and location of office, Chief Ballard's name and phone number, and other details.

"Tell Lemure to get it here as quickly as possible," he said into the phone. He snapped it shut. "Let's go down and talk to Mr. de Buitliér."

24

I pushed open the door to de Buitliér's office without knocking and walked in, the lieutenant just behind me. I hadn't quite expected to find the curator so obviously covering his tracks, but there were two cardboard packing cases on his desk and files and drawers opened up.

"Are you leaving us?" I asked him. We had caught him off guard and he looked vulnerable without the carapace of his tweed jacket, which hung on the back of a chair.

"As a matter of fact, here is my letter of resignation." The man made a visible effort to muster some dignity, but I could tell he was nervous if not scared.

I took the envelope he proffered and pocketed it. I picked up the phone on his desk and dialed Security. "Mort," I said, "don't let de Buitliér or his intern leave the building with any boxes or items until I've inspected them."

De Buitliér looked aggrieved. "I am not taking anything that isn't personal property."

"Of course," I said. "This is Lieutenant Tracy of the Seaboard Police Department. He would like to ask you some questions."

"About what?"

"About the night of Heinrich von Grümh's murder," the lieutenant said. He kept his voice equable, almost friendly. "We can do it here, or we can go down to headquarters."

It may have been the sound of a distant siren that made the curator say, "I think I would like to call a lawyer."

The lieutenant inclined his head. "As you wish."

De Buitliér hemmed and hawed. "What exactly do you want to know?"

I could tell the lieutenant was stalling for time. He said, "Where were you the night von Grümh was murdered?"

"I've decided to wait until I have a lawyer before answering anything."

The lieutenant's phone buzzed. He snapped it open. "Upstairs. Third floor. The corridor right behind the Greco-Roman exhibit."

He looked at me. "That was Lemure. He's coming up with the search warrant."

De Buitliér paled visibly. The lieutenant said, "You want to talk about it."

"I'm not saying anything without a lawyer . . ."

"Then we'll just wait."

The sergeant showed up a moment later. He took in de Buitliér and nodded to me. He handed an envelope to the lieutenant, who showed it to the curator.

The lieutenant said, "Mr. de Buitliér, please wait outside with Sergeant Lemure."

"Are you arresting me?"

"Not yet. We're detaining you temporarily."

He was halfway out the door when he turned to come back. "Sorry," the lieutenant said. "Outside."

"But . . ."

"Outside."

We gave the office a thorough going-over. There were lots of nooks and crannies, though not as many as on the boat. Nothing. No gun. No incriminating documents.

"We'll have to search his home," the lieutenant said at length.

"Getting a warrant for that will be tougher. The probable cause is already weak."

We were about to go outside when I noticed the jacket hanging on the chair. I took it by the collar and lifted it, surprised by its weight. I felt along the side over the pocket and smiled. Sure enough, there it was, my Smith & Wesson .38-caliber revolver.

The lieutenant put on a pair of latex gloves. He picked up the weapon carefully and delicately and put it in a plastic bag, which he sealed.

He opened the door, "Sergeant, bring Mr. de Buitliér in."

The curator came in with a resentful, hangdog look on his face. The lieutenant launched right into a Miranda warning. Then, "You'll have to come with us to police headquarters, Mr. de Buitliér. You can phone an attorney from here if you wish."

De Buitliér shook his head. "That won't be necessary. I mean we don't have to go to police headquarters. I can explain everything."

The lieutenant glanced at the sergeant, who shrugged. He said, "Let's get some chairs in here."

We settled around a small, rectangular table that was off to one side.

"Let's start at the beginning," the lieutenant said. "The sergeant will take notes. Mr. de Ratour will be a witness."

"Fine with me," said the suspect, who seemed relieved, even jaunty.

"How did you find out about LeBlanc?" I asked to get things started.

He pondered for a moment. "When the collection first arrived here, there was something about it that made me suspicious. It had been packed and repacked, but not very professionally. There were balled-up pieces of wastepaper mixed in with plastic pellets. Anyway, I noticed a piece of billing stationery with LeBlanc's name and address on it."

"Maybe he sent them there just to get framed." the lieutenant said.

"There's a much better place in Boston. And it's closer."

"What about the night von Grümh got murdered?" Lemure said, using his voice like a hammer.

De Buitliér nodded. "On that night I was in the Pink Shamrock when I noticed Mr. de Ratour come in with Mr. von Grümh. I stayed in the background, out of sight, and watched them as they talked and drank. I noticed that Heinie, Mr. von Grümh, seemed very agitated. After a while, I left the pub by a rear entrance and came over to the museum. I let myself in the back way because, well, it's handier."

I noticed his accent had reverted to something from the Lower Midwest.

His phone rang and we ignored it.

"Go on," the lieutenant prompted.

"I happened to glance out the window just when von Grümh's car came swerving into the road between the lots. I recognized it right away. I watched it for a while. Then I noticed Mr. Ratour. He was walking toward the main entrance. He seemed to notice the car and turn toward it for a few steps. He stopped and began to walk again toward the main entrance when I heard von Grümh call to him. Then Mr. Ratour went over to the car and got in."

"How long was he there?"

"I don't know. Maybe ten, fifteen minutes."

"And you watched the car all the time?"

"Yes."

"What happened then?"

"Mr. Ratour opened the door and got out."

"And during that time you didn't hear a shot or anything?" Lieutenant Tracy asked.

"No."

My heart lifted. It wasn't me. Unless . . .

"Then what happened?"

"The car just stayed there. I watched it, wondering what was happening. Or what had happened. A little while later, Professor Saunders came along walking his dog."

"And during that time, no one else either got into or out of the car?"

"No."

"What did Saunders do?"

"He wasn't far from the car when the door opened and I think von Grümh called to him. Saunders went over. His dog got in the car and then Saunders himself."

"How long was Saunders there?"

"I don't really know. Ten, fifteen minutes."

I started to relax. Von Grümh had been alive when Saunders talked to him. Which meant that I had not murdered the man. Until that instant, I had not realized how much the possibility had weighed on me.

Still, we were all on the edge of our seats, waiting for the curator to continue. He appeared to be enjoying his moment in the dim limelight of our attention. After a moment he said, "I was watching the car when my phone rang. I knew it was him. He had probably seen me in the window."

"What did he say?"

"He insulted me. He said I was a creep. He told me to come down and talk to him."

"And you did?"

"I did."

"And at that time, did he know that you knew the coins were fakes or suspected them of being fakes?" I asked.

"Yes."

"Were you blackmailing him?"

"No."

I'm not sure any of us believed him, but right then it didn't make a whole lot of difference.

"Go on," the lieutenant said gently.

"I really didn't want to go down. He had been acting really strange lately. I didn't mind if he made a scene, I just didn't want any violence."

"Unless you initiated it yourself?" Lemure asked in his inimitable way.

De Buitliér kept his silence. Until, in a low voice, he said, "I can show you what happened next."

We all looked at him and at each other. Really?

"Proceed," said the lieutenant.

He got up and went over to a flat television screen hanging on the wall and turned it on. Then he took out what looked like a cell phone and plugged it into the television using a slender cable.

Standing to one side of the blank screen like someone about to give a presentation, he said, "Before I went down, I rigged up my cell phone camera. It allows me to put a small lens in my lapel and transmit the sound and video back to my computer. But I'll let the results speak for themselves." He touched a button on his phone.

There is the jerky movement of walking as he goes down the hall, down two flights of the fire escape stairs and out the back door next to the loading dock. The car comes into sight. The window rolls down. Heinie is heard saying, "Get in," just as the door opens and he comes into view. The sound is raspy but clear enough so that what's said is intelligible. Most of the time the lens, which is wide-angle, includes the driver in its field of view. Heinie says, his gloved hands on the wheel, staring straight ahead as though driving, "You've really messed things up, you know that, Butler."

"My name is de Buitliér." The voice is closer, muddied, but still distinct enough.

"Whatever. You had to go messing with my coins, didn't you. You had to make a fool of me . . ."

"They're fakes. It was my responsibility . . ."

"Bullshit. You were doing anything you could to make me look bad."

"So what? That doesn't change the facts."

"Even if it destroyed me in the process."

"I was only doing my job."

There's a silence in which von Grümh reaches down beside him and comes up with the revolver. "And I'm about to do mine, damn you."

De Buitliér's voice is shaky. Whose wouldn't be? "You should know that this whole thing is being taped. I have a setup through my cell phone."

Von Grümh laughs. "You always were a sly one. Phony as a . . ."

"You should talk."

"You little . . ."

"Heinie . . . give me the gun and we'll pretend this never happened."

"I'll give it to you if you'll shoot me in the heart with it." He lapses into a mutter. "Everyone's been screwing me. Or my wife."

There's a silence. In the distance, through the front window, a dim figure can be seen walking a small dog on a leash.

"I can't do that."

Von Grümh laughs. "Because you think I'm not worth shooting?"

De Buitliér says, reverting to his ersatz brogue, "You're right enough there . . ." He trails off.

Heinie says, "You don't think I have the balls to shoot myself, do you?"

De Buitliér is silent for what seems a long time. Then, in an accent that is neither here nor there, he speaks. "Why would I think that? All you have to do is put the gun to your head and pull the trigger. All of your misery will be ended. Nothing could be simpler."

A mad hope sounds in Heinie's voice. "I don't want it to look like a suicide."

"Why not?"

"Because people who commit suicide are losers."

"There's something to that."

"Look, if I do it . . . will you take the gun?"

"I should take it anyway. To keep someone else from getting it. It would be the responsible thing to do."

Heinie snorts at that. "God, you're a coldhearted little bastard."

"He's right there," the sergeant interjected.

There's another long silence. As though impatient, de Buitliér says, "Heinie, just give me the damn thing. You don't have what it takes to shoot me or yourself."

In the silence that follows, von Grümh nods slowly, the gun still pointing firmly at the curator. When his voice is heard again, it's as though from a distance. "You may be right." He turns to de Buitliér. "But if I kill you first, then I won't have a choice, will I? And this whole dirty nightmare will be over. I mean, I won't have a choice. Not if this is all being recorded . . . for posterity. Posterity. What the hell does that word mean?"

Von Grümh, gripping the steering wheel with his free hand, stifles a sob and keeps talking. "With my net worth, I could buy and sell this whole miserable town. Did you know there have been some very important people, I mean, A-list movers and shakers, who wanted me to run for governor. I could have done that. Then senator. And then, who knows . . . Because I know how things work. I know . . . Instead, all I did was write checks. All my life, I've been trying to make other people happy. God knows I've tried. All I've done is give, give, give. And at every turn I've been betrayed. Betrayed . . ."

He sounds like a man trying to bare his soul only to find that he doesn't have one.

He says, "So you'll take the gun after I've . . ."

"I've said I would."

In a movement that takes less than seconds but replays in the mind with slow, awful clarity, von Grümh raises the gun to his head and cocks it. He holds it there for what seems an eternity. He gives a short, strangled cry. A blinding noise is heard. The body slumps forward and a trickle of blood comes out of the wound in the right temple.

De Buitliér momentarily sounds panicked. He says, "Jesus!" Then the camera pivots around, scanning the area around the car as though to check for witnesses. There are none. No lights go on anywhere. With one last "Jesus," de Buitliér reaches over, unclutches the dead man's hand, and takes the revolver. The screen goes blank.

It was then that I remembered the detail that had been tantalizing me to the point of distraction for weeks: Heinie had been wearing gloves. He had cold hands even in warm weather. I looked at de Buitliér. "You also removed his gloves, didn't you?" I swear I could have punched him in the face, such was my anger.

"No, why would I?"

"To make it look like a murder," Lieutenant Tracy said. He stood up and disconnected the cell phone. "I'll be taking this for the time being. It obviously clears you of von Grümh's murder. But you may still be charged with tampering with evidence."

"For what crime, may I ask?" De Buitliér had some of his old confidence back. "Suicide was decriminalized in this state several years ago."

"Then why did you take the gun?"

"Someone else might have found it and used it to commit a crime."

With uncharacteristic sarcasm, the lieutenant said, "You mean you were being a public-minded citizen?"

"You could say that."

"Why didn't you just lock the car?"

"I didn't think of it."

The police officers asked him a few more questions and told him not to leave town without calling first. Turning to me, the lieutenant said, "I'll call you. Good work."

When they had left, I regarded de Buitliér for a long minute. "So why?" I asked finally.

"Why what?"

"Why not come forward when I got accused of accessory to murder?"

A red flush of anger suffused his face, but he kept his voice in check. "Why not?" He stood up and pointed his finger at me. "Because people like you . . . you look down on people like me. You get all the credit and we do all the work. But I got my own back, didn't I?"

"You did it deliberately just to get at me?"

"Don't pride yourself. I did it . . . for reasons of my own."

"You did it because Malachy Morin promised you that he would name you director of the MOM if you found a way to get me out of the way?"

He shrugged as though to say, *So what?*

"And the fake coins were only a start?"

"Yeah, that was nice. And I kept my eyes open. Then I heard about the problems with the Neanderthal exhibit."

"And you leaked that to the *Bugle?*"

"Leaked? No, I just turned on the spigot."

"And you took the gun more to discredit me than to honor your promise to Heinie?"

"I did. The fact that it was your gun was a bonus."

I turned to go. I stopped at the door. I tried to think of something utterly damning to say to him. But nothing sufficed. It would be like trying to insult a cockroach. "Keep packing" was all I said.

25

From where I lounge I can see a rubythroat preening its gossamer wings with its long, slender bill. I have read that they use spider silk to line the tiny nests in which they lay their tiny eggs. Yet what large, enchanted lives they lead, including an annual round-trip to Mexico or thereabouts. To watch in angled light one of these creatures stationary in flight over a nectarous, deep-throated flower is to know that evolution, among other things, is the wellspring of beauty.

I am rusticating. Some golden days of summer remain, and I have retreated to the cottage by the lake with Diantha, Elsie, and Decker. Here I spend hours drowsing on the porch, book or notebook in hand, undergoing something akin to isostatic rebound — the slow rising of compressed land after an ice age, when high glaciers retreat and release all beneath from their cold, heavy grip.

There are the usual loose ends to this sad case of Heinrich von Grümh. The original coins have not been found. According to Lieutenant Tracy, Interpol reports that the person known as Alain LeBlanc has lived up to his name. I picture him enjoying life in some Swiss lodge with a mountain view as he moves his loot, a few coins at a time, to private collectors not overly scrupulous about their provenance.

Which doesn't trouble me unduly. Valuable things have a way of taking care of themselves. The coins will gather in other collections. Those collections will be bought and sold and perhaps donated to museums by wealthy numismatists (provided they are honored for doing so and provided they receive an adequate tax break).

But then what is life but one big loose end that we strive mightily to keep from being tied up? In the several weeks since de Buitliér's "confession," time itself has snipped off or bundled up much that had become unraveled. And more.

Diantha and I are in love again. The beautiful people with their sleek lives little know what passion can burn in what seem the most placid, even humdrum of marriages. We are mindful of each other, gentle, considerate, and at times perhaps too careful in what we say and how we say it. In the past couple of weeks, Diantha has positively clung to me. It may be nothing more than a late-summer lassitude, but I doubt it. Or the possibility that she is pregnant again, which gives me great joy even though at my age it may look like she is having my grandchildren. All the rest is commentary, as the Talmud tells us.

Alphus has landed on his feet or on all four hands, as he likes to say. He has privately confirmed reports that the advance for book and film rights to his memoir amounts to nearly five million dollars. His new wealth has allowed him to rent a secured bungalow not far from Sign House. There he lives with his official keeper, a young graduate student in anthropology who travels with him and vocalizes his signing when necessary. Through a trust set up by Felix, he has bought a vacant lot close to the Arboretum where he hopes to build a habitation suitable to his needs, a leopard-proof tree house I am told.

The guy is suddenly everywhere — news interviews, talk shows, the cover of *People* magazine, a visit to the Oval Office. The public cannot get enough of him. With great fanfare and with Felix at his side, he has applied for "personhood," with all the rights that pertain thereto. The problem is that the requisite agencies to grant such a thing are not in place, not to mention the legal hurdles.

From the heat of the debate that has flared up — apparently another round in the culture wars — you would think the imminent fate of civilization hung in the balance. The usual arguments are trotted out: If chimpanzees are admitted as members of the human family, will dogs be next? What about cats, canaries, snakes, pet rocks? One respected theologian has asked, "Does he have a soul?"

It begs the question whether any of us have a soul, other than the one we might fashion for ourselves out of the vicissitudes of life. By that measure, Alphus may well be more soulful than a lot of people.

His friend Ridley has also landed on his feet. Though he completed only a couple of years at Vanderbilt, his flair for mathematics is such that he has been admitted to Wainscott at a graduate level. And while he still "hangs" with Alphus, I'm told he has found or been found by a young woman who takes up much of his time.

Speaking of which, Doreen has been delivered of a bouncing baby boy, which is the good news. The less than good news for me is that she wants to stay home and raise the child the old-fashioned way while helping her husband with his ministry in a small church a fair distance from Seaboard. This happy event necessitated a visit on my part to our Human Resources Department to begin the process of hiring someone to replace the dear woman. When I used the word *secretary,* the efficient person in charge informed me that the proper title for the position was *administrative assistant.* To no avail did I point out that if the nation can have a secretary of state, why could I not have a plain secretary? Surely that title carries more weight and dignity. You don't find anyone called an administrative assistant of defense.

Merissa and Max are now very much a couple. We had them over for a cookout not long ago. She remains quite irrepressible. "Max and I are getting married, aren't we, Max?" she announced as we sawed into the thick steaks I had done with lots of fresh oregano on charcoal.

Max smiled and nodded and kept chewing.

"And we're going to have lots of babies."

Max sipped wine and raised his glass. "Whatever you say, darling."

Professor Laluna Jackson remains undaunted by her failure to take over the museum to use as headquarters for the Victim Studies Department. It seems that funds are being raised for a new building to be designed by the same therapeutic architect who would have gutted our fabulous old pile. I also hear that Ms. Jackson is contemplating something called the White Male Apology Initiative. It apparently involves collecting signatures from members of that designated group on a document attesting to their remorse for all the evil they have caused through the millennia. I wonder if, as the former John J. Johnson, she will sign it herself.

Malachy Morin. The man simply will not go away. Incredible as it seems, he has been appointed President *pro tem* of Wainscott in place of George Twill, who has retired a year ahead of schedule because of failing health. But then, as Izzy Landes had remarked, chief executives of universities are not the people of substance and stature they used to be. Izzy claims that knowledgeable people can usually name more members of the Red Sox starting lineup than they can the presidents of even the premier universities.

I take some comfort in the fact that Mr. Morin will have a year in which to mess things up enough to prevent his permanent accession. That is not a remote possibility given that one of his first acts has been to appoint Feidhlimidh de Buitliér director of the Wainscott News Office despite the role he played in the suicide of Heinrich von Grümh.

Regarding Mr. de Buitliér, I do not think justice has been served however exculpated he may be in the eyes of the law. He cannot be charged with the murder of von Grümh, but he certainly abetted the man's self-slaughter. At the very least, he should have tried to stop him. Yet what makes my inner skin crawl is the theft of the dead man's gloves. To imagine him peeling them off those lifeless, limp hands just to make it look like murder . . .

But who am I to judge? I have not had a change of heart about Heinie however much I know I should regret the man's decease. I am scarcely sorry that I am not sorry. I am working on it, but I cannot pretend to have a large enough spirit to forgive. That capacity remains for me, at least in this case, the realm of saints. Or of fools. I believe it too much to ask a man to forgive someone who threatened your life, who duped you with forgeries, who not only slept with your wife but gloated about it, and who very nearly ruined your career. The best I can summon for Christian charity is to tell myself and a God I doubt is listening that Heinie is better off dead if only because his life had become such a torment. I also think it presumptuous to second-guess the judgment of suicides in cases like his.

I regret not having taken the gun from him when I had a chance to. Doing so would have avoided this whole dreadful mess and, perhaps, his untimely death. Unless, in possession of my weapon, and surely I would have recognized it as such, I might have shot the wretch myself. And while I can now deny having the wherewithal to kill any human being in cold blood, I know too well that most of us have a dark side no matter who we are. I am not speaking here of the reptile within, of the despots old and new, of the blank-faced serial killer, of the bowlegged gunslinger. No, I am referring to you and me and the guy driving by in his car. I am referring to good old, highly evolved *Homo homicidens,* a species distinguished by, among other things, a propensity to murder its own.

As for some final perspective? The question, curiously enough, has become academic, at least where I am concerned. Marvin Grimley, the Director of the Center for Criminal Justice and a friend of Harvey Deharo's, has invited me to give the annual Bernard Lecture in October. After considerable thought, I have decided the title will be something like "*Crimen Delectabile* and the Moral Problematics of Using Murder as Amusement."